A
GODDESS
AMONG
MEN

DANIEL DAVIDSOHN

Edited by Polgarus Studio
Additional editing by Michelle Hope
Revision by Deborah Dove
Additional consultation by Andy Ross
Interior design: Polgarus Studio
Cover design by Pineal Publishing
Published by Daniel Davidsohn
Original cover photographs:
Isis França / Restyler

PAPERBACK ISBN: 978-85-922784-9-6
HARDCOVER ISBN: 978-65-00-00225-6
EBOOK ISBN: 978-85-922784-8-9

"As for me, I want others to have the defects, rather than share them."

— Allan Kardec

PART 1

Julian Welch & Alan Reid
Early 20th Century

1

It wasn't just another country. It was a different planet entirely. Turning his head, Julian saw ships on one side and a myriad of foreign-looking people on the other—brown-skinned, Asian, and Caucasian. He sat up coughing, realizing he was left alone on a stone quay. There was no sight of the RMS *Amazon*.

I've made it!

The fever had gone, but he was still weak.

"American?" said a commanding voice out of nowhere.

He swung his torso back, almost lost his balance while rising, and faced an abnormally tall, 260-pound colossus standing with his hands on his waist looking down at him. The man wore boots, earth-colored pants, a dirty white shirt, and a cowboy hat. And he looked young, approximately the same age as Julian.

There were tales of excesses in the jungle. Fortunes to be made and pleasures to be had that attracted young dreamers like Julian Welch. He'd said farewell to his parents and headed to the port of

Southampton, where he'd boarded the RMS *Amazon*. By his own estimates—and after he'd paid for a second-class passenger fare to Brazil—his savings would last for two months. He hoped to find a job in the rubber industry. His father's last words were inspiring. *We'll be here for you when you fail.* Julian laughed bitterly at the memory.

The weather got warmer as the days went by, indicating that the ship was approaching its destination. He felt his body burning with fever during the nine hundred miles from the Atlantic Ocean up the Amazon River. The destination was the inland Port of Manaus, the largest city on the Amazon. It was a hot and humid trade hub that became prominent along with the rubber boom, bringing luxury to what used to be a small jungle outpost.

The sudden riches of the city were best symbolized by the tales Julian had heard of the construction of an unthinkable opera house in the middle of the forest. The wealthy people would hang Venetian chandeliers on their ceilings and order extravagant velvet-covered mahogany chairs. Laundry was sent to Europe, if you really wanted to get things done properly. Rubber was the fuel that made extravagance possible.

The trip to Brazil had been challenging. Julian had lost considerable weight, ending up skinnier and more fragile than when he'd left his middle-class house in Tottenham.

Now back on solid ground, he found steadiness once more. *Thank God.*

And an incredible mugginess. It was like being in a stew of your own perspiration—sticky and gross. He had no memory of disembarking. *Someone was kind enough to leave me here.*

"English," Julian finally said.

"Alan Reid. Texas," the giant said.

"Julian Welch."

"You leaving?"

"No … I've just arrived, actually." He glanced around at the port activity. "I mean, this is Manaus, isn't it?"

Alan nodded, sizing up Julian with his protuberant, street-trained eyes. "Let me guess. Rubber?"

"Yes. What do you know about it?" Julian said.

"Not much … You got any money?"

Julian shrugged. "A little. I'm looking to get into the business."

Alan laughed. "Forget it."

"Well, I need a job. Anything."

"That makes two of us. I'm kind of broke myself." Alan took off his hat and scratched his sweaty blond hair. "What do you know about railways?"

Julian stared at the Texan. He didn't know what to think of Alan Reid, what he wanted, or how he could be of help. At least they spoke the same language, which was a start.

"I mean construction," Alan explained.

"Nothing. Why?"

"They gonna build a railway."

"Who?"

"Some Yankee hired by the Brazilians."

"In the middle of a bloody forest? Right, then. So, what do *you* know about construction?"

"Not a damn thing. But it ain't gonna hurt to learn."

Julian spent a moment evaluating the situation. "Where do we apply for a job?"

"I know just the place."

"Good … I also need to find accommodation," Julian said as he stood up, but he was so weak he couldn't lift his bag.

"Gimme that," the Texan said helpfully.

"Wait. Why are you helping me?"

"I'm glad you asked. I ain't helping. I'm investing in you."

Alan moved fast, despite his size. Julian found it hard to keep up with him.

"Five minutes and we'll be there. Can you make it?" Alan said, looking back at Julian.

"I suppose I can. You were saying—"

"We're in a tough place, Jules."

"Julian."

"Yeah, Jules … A jungle of heartless men. It makes sense to team up with folks that speak the same language, don't you think?" Alan looked back again and waited until Julian nodded. "Thought so."

"Where are"—Julian couldn't finish; a cough interrupted him—"we going?"

"The Hotel Cassina. Best in town."

"I can't pay for it."

"Don't worry. You'll stay with me."

"I thought you were broke."

"I said *kind* of broke. But not yet."

"I'll pay you back when I can."

"You'd better ... You need to put on some weight. And deal with the damn cough."

They left the port area and reached the heavily European-influenced city center. Julian was particularly attracted to the mulattas, women with visible European and African descent who were as beautiful as an article he'd read in an English newspaper described them. A mix of rich and poor, locals and foreigners, and the bustle in the streets turned Manaus into an improbably cosmopolitan city.

"Here we are," Alan announced, warmly greeted by a porter's handshake at the entrance of the Hotel Cassina. Julian felt like an intruder when the same porter stood in his way. "He's with me," Alan yelled from inside.

Julian walked into the lobby, dragging himself as fatigue set in. Alan had apparently already arranged for his stay there. *I need to be careful with this one*, Julian thought.

"Two-story, twenty-five rooms, the meeting

point for businessmen, politicians, and intellectuals, my friend. A bohemian man's favorite place in the whole jungle!" Alan described the Cassina.

There was a ballroom designed with Oriental motifs, round tables, and chairs brought all the way from Europe, and silk curtains all around. Next to the access staircase was a stage for artistic presentations equipped with electric chandeliers and noble hardwood.

They ascended the staircase.

"The food's great. Boy, you can have anything you want—Russian caviar, champagne from France, Norwegian codfish, salmon, and sturgeon … I tell you what, if you fancy a virgin, that could be arranged too. The concierge and I are good friends," Alan said.

"Right."

"This is home, Jules," Alan went on babbling as they got into their room. "Nice Italian furniture, don't you agree? American spring mattress, goose-down pillows, and Indian satin cushions."

"I need a bath."

"Yeah. You go ahead and wash off the jinx. I'll be downstairs inquiring. Oh, and, uh, you take that bed over there. I'd appreciate it if you kept a distance from my stuff."

"Of course," Julian said.

When Alan left him alone, Julian sat on his bed and took in his immediate reality. He was in the fanciest hotel in town, for which he wouldn't need to pay a penny, and already learning about the city. Other than the unpleasant crossing of the Atlantic, things looked promising. Someone was building a railway in the forest; a job was on the horizon. It was starting to look like a plan. He would tell all of that to his parents when he got a chance to write them, determined not to be the failure they predicted he would be. A warm bath and a clean bed were all he wished for now.

*****

In a private room behind the stage of the Cassina, the soft, velvet voice of a soprano filled the air with Mozart's *The Magic Flute*. The room was poorly lit, but clear enough for anyone to observe Alan Reid's forehead showing the first signs of extreme overheating. Beads of sweat began to form, accumulate rapidly, and slide down his desperate, rectangular face. A drop of sweat fell into his glass of whiskey.

I'll be damned.

"Do you need some water?" asked the raspy voice of El Pepe Steward, the cause of Alan's perspiration. At a table cluttered with tobacco and alcohol, the offer of a glass of water was an offense.

"No thanks, Pepe." *Go to hell, Pepe. I want you to show your cards. I've got a set of queens. If you got something better than that, I'm screwed.*

"Are you sure?" El Pepe teased as he smiled with

all of his disgusting gold teeth.

Alan forced a smile. And as he did, another drop of sweat entertained the other three players who were like jackals waiting for that humongous man to faint at any moment. With them was Commander Sebastião Alcantara, the chief of the military police of Manaus, and an obstinate bribe taker; Pedro Oliveira, a notary public and dedicated husband with a weakness for prostitutes; and Gustav Keller, a European banker specializing in money laundering. Eight hungry eyes saw when the tiny drop fell into the Texan's mouth, and instinctively, he licked his lips.

Alan was in trouble, suffering his share of bad luck. No amount of muscle would help him there.

"Come on, Pepe … What've you got there? I bet you ain't got nuttin'," Alan teased with a heavy Texan accent. *For the love of God, hurry up and show me your damn cards!*

El Pepe moved slowly. He seemed to enjoy how a tough-looking guy like Alan was suffering—that loud and young Texan, always bragging about his business but never showing the fruits of it. El Pepe turned over the cards one at a time. Alan's forced smile faded in synchrony with what they revealed, and with the dying pitch of the soprano in the background. By now, Alan was close to crying. It became evident that El Pepe had better cards.

The massacre started with two aces, and then El

Pepe stopped his hands for an instant and looked at Alan. No smiles now. The Mexican wanted to make it clear what the consequences of the game were: El Pepe Steward always came to collect his gambling debts. He'd built a reputation for himself in Manaus and Belém—enchanting, rich, and violent.

The Mexican showed the third card: another ace. It was the end for Alan.

The fourth card just continued the pattern and brought the smile back to El Pepe's face. Another ace. The robust and now red-faced Texan spread his thick lips in a pathetic attempt to smile. But it was game over. He stood up, looking at each of the players, and tipped his hat. Outsmarting them, like he'd promised his mother he would do to rich foreigners, was nothing but a young man's delusion. Those men were not the teenagers of San Antonio.

"Gentlemen, I'm pretty much done," Alan said.

"See you soon," said El Pepe, the rattlesnake. Alan stepped away from the table and left that room knowing he'd made a terrible mistake.

He crossed the corridor behind the stage where the soprano was being applauded. *Hell.* He tensed up, thinking he couldn't pay El Pepe. How long would it take for the Mexican trader to figure out it was up to God and El Pepe himself? Alan was smart enough to know the forest was a big place to hide, but at times, the world seemed too small when it came to troubles.

He got back to his room, letting out a prolonged sigh, his mind running quick calculations. There was no short-term solution. He would have to retreat and find a way to get stronger. He tilted his head to the side. Julian had fallen asleep with his dirty clothes on, leaving a stink in the room. But that was the Englishman's problem. The only reason Julian was enjoying a clean bed was to make Alan's escape easier in case he lost to El Pepe.

Alan moved with the agility of a lightweight boxer and the soundlessness of a professional thief. He grabbed his stuff, put it in a bag that was half full of clothes, and turned to Julian when he was by the door. *Good luck, my friend,* he wished. Julian would need it.

Down at the lobby, the concierge saw Alan leaving with his bag on his back.

"Taxi, Mr. Reid?"

"Not tonight, Victor. Thanks. I'll just say hello to the girls, bring them some gifts. I'll come back later when my partner wakes up." Alan winked.

Victor smiled. "I'm sure they'll love it."

Alan left the Hotel Cassina on foot and disappeared into the city night.

*****

A few hours after the Texan had left, Julian heard knocks on his door and woke up. He coughed terribly, saw the sun beginning to rise through the

12

window, and realized he was alone. Alan Reid's belongings were gone.

"Just a moment," he said.

But the knocks got louder. Julian was confused, still half lying on his elbows. Next, he heard a loud bang and watched the door violently open all the way, slamming against the wall. Two rough-looking men entered, sending chills up Julian's spine.

"Alan Reid?" one man asked.

"I—I don't know where he is," Julian said.

It meant nothing. Before Julian could understand the situation, hands and fists were all over him. "Wait!" he pleaded in vain.

Julian's eyesight went dark after a punch in his face. A succession of powerful blows made breathing a struggle, sent shock waves across his entire body, and caused him a pain he'd never experienced before. He could do nothing but accept the punishment and hope that it would end soon.

It did when he passed out.

Julian was dragged all the way to the hotel kitchen. There, the two henchmen pulled him by the arms like he was a piece of rag. Next, they emptied a bucket of water on his head. When he opened one of his eyes—barely—he saw a man grinning at him with golden teeth, and another he recognized as the concierge.

"Mr. Welch, can you tell us where Mr. Reid might be?" the concierge said.

Julian shook his head no.

"I'm afraid someone needs to pay for the room."

"I understand ... but I have no money."

Julian wanted to explain his situation, but he lacked the strength to do it. He preferred dying to losing the money his father had given him, which was tightly hidden in his underwear.

The concierge and the man with gold teeth briefly exchanged a glance.

"I'll ask the police to lock him up," the concierge said.

El Pepe nodded.

2

Julian lost count of the days. The prison floor was putrid. The atmosphere was repellent, filled with cadaverous-looking inmates, making it a true catacomb of living creatures. His scabs bled when he touched them, which left no doubt he looked exactly like the others sharing his cell. It forced his true self to seek comfort in the refuge of the mind, taking turns between his immediate reality, the cozy past, and his desperate fantasies of a better future.

The geometry was oppressively square, made of humid stone. Freedom lay beyond long, rusty bars running from floor to ceiling. When sunlight illuminated his cell, he preferred to keep his eyes closed, as with light came truth: this was the dirtiest, shittiest place he'd ever been.

So far, so good, he thought, poisoning himself with pessimism.

Since he'd been incarcerated, Julian had been visited by several of nature's more vile creatures, from cockroaches to mice, but none had been as hard on

Julian as the fleas that were consuming his skin.

Lord, have some mercy.

Outside his cell, the monotony of the past days—or was it weeks?—was broken by a sudden intermittent symphony of cursing. He couldn't comprehend Portuguese, but the intensity of it sounded like hell. He heard the groaning and howling, the smacks and punches which reverberated in his own body, reminding him of the severe beating he'd suffered and the generalized pain he felt.

Julian turned his broken body toward the cell bars when the sounds of a brawl intensified. *It's getting closer*, he feared, and waited. But the fighting didn't last long. The prison got quiet an instant later, and steps approached his cell. Keys touched iron. From the corner of his eye, he captured the silhouette of a large man standing outside his cell. Only one of Julian's eyes was functioning—the other severely swollen—but it was enough to recognize the massive human opening the padlock and entering his cell.

"Can you walk?" Alan said.

"No."

Alan grabbed him below his armpits, lifted him in the air like he was a bag of feathers, and put him on his shoulders. "Hang on," Alan said.

"They'll arrest you too!" Julian said, part-relieved, part-panicked.

"This ain't my first rodeo."

Before he had time to complain about Alan's

shoulders pressing into his broken ribs, Julian felt the rain wash over his body. *The fleas must be drowning*, he hoped. They were outside, entering a cul-de-sac, getting to a clump of bushes safe from the view of passersby. Julian still couldn't decide whether the arrival of the Texan was a blessing or a curse. Whenever he was around, Alan brought pain.

He placed Julian on the grass and sat down next to him.

"Damn cowards!" Alan said while inspecting Julian.

"They're looking for you."

"I know."

"Apparently, *you* should have been the one who took the beating."

"We'll see . . . Who did that to you?"

Julian took a couple of breaths. "A man with shining teeth and two associates."

Alan nodded to himself and glanced away. When he looked back at Julian, he had an unshakable resolution in his eyes. "They'll pay us back."

"What did you do to them?"

"Nothing. It's just that some folks want it all for themselves."

"Forget it, mate . . . I just need that job."

"Yeah … First, you need to heal."

"What if they find us? You owe money, and I'm a fugitive."

Alan spat on the ground. "Then you're gonna have to heal as we go."

"That's just brilliant," Julian said.

"It's our only option … We'd better leave town."

*****

The steamboat took twenty days to reach an old port seven hundred and fifty miles from Manaus down the Madeira River. Julian and Alan slept in hammocks, taking half the journey to get used to it. Julian recovered well from his beating, but not completely. The food onboard was surprisingly healthy and nourishing, which helped. They tried local fruits like acai and cupuaçu, and fresh pirarucu, a four-hundred-pound fish enjoyed by the small riverside communities along the Madeira.

To further cheer themselves up, they shared tales about an American businessman, Percival Farquhar, who was the founder of the Madeira-Mamoré Railway Company, and the stories ranged from stimulating to legendary.

"The man's building an El Dorado, hiring folks from all over the world. I mean, putting two hundred and fifty miles of rails in the middle of a damn forest?" Alan reported to Julian.

Julian gleamed at the account. "This is our chance!"

"You take your time. Get all the rest you can, Jules. Word is, only the strongest will make it. It's like the Wild West out there, except you have the gunmen plus the wild beasts of the Amazon."

Just when Julian showed clear signs of recovery, he and other passengers faced a silent enemy: bites from infected anopheles mosquitos. It didn't take a specialist to figure out what they were going through. All shared, give or take, the same symptoms—shaking chills, high fevers, and terrible headaches accompanied by nausea and vomiting. One passenger fell into a coma and died the very next day, which turned the initial hope about a job at the Madeira-Mamoré Railway Company into a somber pessimism.

"You've got yourself malaria, Jules," Alan explained, which prompted Julian to wonder if his friendship still offered any advantage to Alan. Julian was either terribly unlucky or unacceptably fragile for the challenges awaiting them. Probably both.

With every new stop at community ports, they heard further information reinforcing the problematic realities ahead of them. The railway construction workers were facing many health issues. Tropical diseases were killing first and asking questions later. Working conditions were poor, especially in the face of the gargantuan challenge of cutting down centuries-old trees. Alan explained, "We got to flatten the ground, then dig, deposit the ballasts, and lay the tracks. It's as hard as it gets. But that's not all. We need to get along with people from over forty different countries—plus the natives. You know what they're calling it? The Devil's Railway!"

"Is th-that a-all?" Julian said during one of his shaking chills. He hoped he wouldn't continue to be a burden to Alan. "I'll understand if you choose to go ahead without me."

"Why would I?" Alan responded.

It had been raining for the past twenty-four hours when they arrived at one of the camps of the future city of Porto Velho. The steamboat docked at an improvised wharf that resembled a war field. There were endless piles of wood scattered around a muddy terrain occupied by precarious accommodations, and all sorts of equipment. Men bustled to put the place in order and resume construction as quickly as the weather allowed. It was chaotic.

Alan disembarked the steamboat to ask for help. Julian needed urgent medical attention.

Someone pointed in the direction of a shack at the American ward, where Alan would find a doctor. The Texan followed with his heavy feet sinking into the mud. On his way, he saw several men lined up side by side holding what looked like a dead boa constrictor.

"I hope dead snakes don't bite," he said to himself. Everywhere he turned looked disheartening.

He walked up a short staircase leading to the medical tent.

Inside, he found a middle-aged woman with a short blonde ponytail and freckles. She was busy behind a small desk filing reports and didn't bother acknowledging his presence. Farther down in the tent, amid two rows of five beds divided from each other by dirty mosquito nets, he saw a nurse helping a man onto a bed. Alan looked downward and glanced at the face of the man next to her, who was the preamble of certain death. The nurse looked at him sideways. Alan tipped his hat. "I need help for a friend. He's very ill."

"I'm Dr. Miller," the blonde at the desk answered before the nurse did. "What's he got?" she said with an American accent.

"Malaria, I think. He's got every symptom you can think of."

Dr. Miller resumed her report filing, not at all impressed. "Jandira, will you handle this?" she asked the nurse and then briefly glanced at Alan. "You're in good hands."

"Yeah. Thanks."

Jandira stood up from her chair and walked toward Alan. She was a mulatta with beautiful brown skin and long, honeyed dark hair with light hazel eyes and thick lips. The sight of her was a relief in the middle of that green hell.

"Now, let's get your friend," Jandira said in Brazilian Portuguese–accented English.

Alan took a moment to compose himself.

Jandira passed by Alan, and he followed right after. "We've just arrived. He's in the steamer."

Outside the tent, she ordered two natives in

Portuguese, "*Venham comigo*"—*come with me.* They picked up a stretcher and joined her.

On his way back to the steamboat, he saw hunched over men whose spirits appeared broken after days of strenuous work, small gatherings of foreigners with desperate looks on their faces trying to communicate with each other in odd languages, and a long line of men waiting for their payments.

"Shit," Alan uttered to himself. All those miserable men were barely making it through the day.

Alan pointed as they boarded the steamboat. "That's my friend over there." He led Jandira to the hammock. Others in a deplorable state caught her attention, but Alan didn't want to wait in line. "He's over there." He almost pushed her forward. "That's him."

Julian opened his eyes and saw Jandira filling his entire field of vision.

From his low angle, he saw more than the person who had come to help him. The nurse's head was blocking the rays of the sun that was setting in the west and piercing through the dissipating clouds of the torrential storm that had ended earlier. The light formed a shining halo around her hair. It could be that his illness was making Julian delirious, but to him, it was the most beautiful sight he'd ever seen. Those few seconds stuck with him, fascinated him, and had an immediate positive effect on his helpless state of mind.

Jandira signaled to the two men that came with her on the steamboat. They swiftly transferred Julian from the hammock to the stretcher.

During the four hundred yards' distance between the wharf and the medical tent, Jandira checked on Julian a few times. He counted three instances. Each time, their eyes would lock for a bit.

That frail Englishman had an intense gaze that emanated purity. His aura was different than that of the rude men populating the camp.

Before he realized it, Julian found himself shirtless on a clean—and steady—bed, and Jandira was gently cleaning him with a wet towel. He immediately felt at home, like he'd been magically transported back to England. Time flew faster, and in a better direction. *She has the hands of an angel,* he was sure.

He tilted his head sideways, searching for the Texan, but Alan wasn't there. When he got better, Julian thought, he would find a way to show how grateful he was for Alan's help.

He asked the nurse, "What's your name?"

"Jandira."

The sound of her name was like a balm. "What does it mean?"

"Why?"

"Names matter," he said and gasped for air.

"Don't speak," she ordered. "You have a serious condition."

"I thought so."

"I'll do my best to help you."

Julian nodded, and when the hand holding the towel reached his chest, he made an effort and clutched it delicately. Looking into her eyes, he whispered, "I know you will."

3

"Your friend has made a remarkable recovery," Dr. Miller said at the first opportunity while inspecting the row of patients in the tent.

"He's a fighter," Jandira said.

"Just don't forget why you're here. People are dying. Only God knows when the quinine pills will get here—more people will die in the meantime. Patients come and go; better not get too attached to them."

The unsolicited advice had no resonance to Jandira. Every day since patient Julian Welch was admitted in that precarious infirmary, Jandira would methodically prepare local medicines given to those under the curse of malaria by cooking bark, boiling teas, macerating leaves and seeds, and even burning plants to produce ashes for vapor baths. Three times a day, under the close supervision of Dr. Miller,

Jandira would offer Julian a glass of the bitter tea produced from the guts of the forest.

One hot afternoon, when Julian was eagerly waiting for his daily bath, Jandira brought him bittersweet news. "You're better. The baths are no longer required."

"But they're helping me," he said.

"You understand I can't babysit you all the time."

"I do . . . but it's a shame. I'm missing it."

"Missing what, exactly, Mr. Welch?"

"It's Julian, please . . . I'm missing your company."

Jandira stared at him. "I know. I noticed an erection during your last bath."

Julian was caught off guard by her bluntness. "I— I couldn't help it."

At sunset, when she brought one of her special soups—knowing that Dr. Miller was away—Jandira sat next to Julian and they ate together.

"You're much better," she said.

"Thanks to you."

"We're going to let you go soon. You can now apply for a job at the railway construction. Isn't that why you're here?"

"I'm here to get rich."

"You'll be lucky if you survive the job."

When they finished eating, she collected his soup bowl and eyed him. "If you want to make money, you need to produce rubber. That's the reason many are risking their lives."

"I know. But I don't have the money to start my own business yet."

"You don't need much."

Somehow, her confidence gave Julian the impression that Jandira knew what she was talking about. After all, she was a local. "Please go on," he said, eyes and ears sharply focused on what she had to say.

"I hear things. Prospectors come and go, and they're worse than fishermen telling their tales," she hedged.

"I have a friend," Julian said while Jandira returned to sit next to him. "You've met him. His name's Alan, the American chap? The one who saved me."

"*He* saved you? OK. Well, he doesn't look like someone with money."

"I don't know him that well. But I'll ask."

"Julian . . . How much do you trust him?"

Julian shrugged. "Why wouldn't I?"

"Because he undresses me with his eyes every time he shows up. Down here, trust is a sacred thing," she said.

"What about you? What's your story?"

"My father was an English businessman. My mother used to work for him in his house. They got involved, and I was born . . . Anyway, they abandoned me a long time ago. They're in Europe, I think. I've been on my own since I was a child. I got an opportunity here about two years ago. Dr. Miller taught me everything I practice here, except for the herbs I use. I learned that from the natives." She looked at the sky growing darker. "Well, it's getting late. I'm going home."

"Where's home?"

"My camp is a short walk from here. I'll talk to Dr. Miller about you."

"I'm not in a rush to leave." Julian gently touched her face. "You're . . . a beautiful person. I'll miss our daily talks."

Jandira placed her hand on top of his, caressed it, and got up. "I know what you're missing," she teased, then walked away, leaving Julian daydreaming about making love with her. And just when his thought of a sweet future with her heated up, he heard a man throwing up on a bed next to his. The roses in his mind gave way to the odors of the infectious patients that were his bedfellows right now.

*****

Outside the tent, Jandira crossed paths with Alan.

"How are we doing today?" he said.

"You mean Julian?"

"Yeah. Him too."

"He's likely to leave tomorrow."

"You're that good, huh?"

"Excuse me," she said and moved on.

There was lust in Alan's eyes.

"See you around." Alan stayed still, watching her leave.

Laughing like he was somehow on the top of a rude game, Alan went inside the tent and confirmed that Jandira hadn't lied. Julian's appearance was definitely better. "You're looking good. I bet those female hands played some role in your miraculous recovery."

"She's wonderful."

"Oh, boy. Sounds like you've been listening to the birds sing. In love already?"

"She's clever. And she knows things that might help us."

Alan dragged a chair over and sat next to Julian. "I'm interested."

"What about the railway company?"

"Tell you what—out there? It's brutal. Those poor men look like they'll drop dead by the end of a day's work. Not that I'm afraid of honest sweat. It's just that the payoff isn't nearly as attractive as I'd expected."

"Jandira mentioned something else. That money is in rubber."

"Not to hurt your feelings, but you ain't got to be a genius to know that."

"What I mean is, she might be able to help us. She knows people."

"Ah . . . Sounds like she wants a piece of the action."

"She's just trying to help."

"Bullshit," Alan said and glanced around. "Maybe we should go back to Manaus. I still got my connections there. Here? I don't trust anyone."

"People are looking for you in Manaus."

"For us, you mean."

As Alan talked, Julian felt dubious about him. As much as he wanted their new friendship to work, the Texan was surly and unpredictable. "I'm staying. I hope you stick around," Julian said.

The Texan clapped his palms on his knees and stood up. "I'm looking forward to those connections Jandira claims to have."

*****

That night, Jandira didn't go directly back to her camp. Instead, she followed a different track in the forest leading to a Karipuna village three miles from where she stayed with other Brazilian workers.

Weeks earlier, she had been a firsthand witness of a shooting. A Karipuna native named Moacir had been shot in the shoulder region right next to her camp. She took him to the infirmary while no white man was watching and removed the bullet. Three days after the incident, a Karipuna woman showed up at the construction camp and asked Jandira to follow her to their village. No explanations were needed. When she got there—a clustered human settlement built on simple forest assets—she found

Moacir shaking with a high fever. Their traditional medicine wasn't helping. All she could do was make sure his wound remained clean.

Jandira and Moacir knew that the greed caused by the rubber boom was the root cause of all the terrible things happening to the natives. The more they talked, the more surprised she was to see how Moacir understood the economics of the problem, planned to take advantage of the interest in rubber, and was determined to turn the tide in his favor.

On one of her last visits, a conversation had taken place that would put Moacir's plan into effect. The native told her he needed men and money to prospect rubber, and that he knew where to find a lot of it.

That night, when Jandira arrived at the village, she was on a negotiation mission.

"There's someone I want you to meet."

"Why?"

"You said you know where to find rubber. And that you needed people."

"This"—he waved his hands in the air—"is my land!"

"Yes, Moacir."

He pointed a finger at her to make it all as clear as possible with his broken English. "*My* land . . . It is *me* who help white man! *I* will pay for them. *I* control things."

"All right. He is an Englishman. His name is Julian Welch."

"A foreigner. I don't like."

"Julian's a good man. He's . . . different. You can trust him."

"I only trust *you*."

"Then trust me."

Moacir was more than ready to claim the fortunes of the forest that belonged to his people and confirmed what Jandira had already heard—that an individual wasn't required to own the land to extract latex, and all you had to do was occupy it before someone else did. That's what the foreigners did. And he knew a great deal of the territory by heart.

"My place is located deep in the forest, about three days' walk from this village. An untouched land, as you called it. It has a good concentration of the *Hevea brasiliensis* trees. The rubber tree. We need to hire tappers. We extract rubber by gouging the tree trunk with an ax. We make a big dent in the tree, and then we put a small bowl underneath to collect the latex that comes out of the trunk."

"How do you know all that?"

"I worked for an English prospector in the past."

"I'll talk to Julian then. When can we start?"

"Tapping is good until August. We need to find tappers now."

"What about your people?"

"The Karipunas are dead or scared by the white men. Your friend brings the tappers. We'll build shacks close to the river. After it's smoked, rubber goes by boat to the big city."

"Manaus?"

"Yes."

There was more than determination in his voice, Jandira felt. It was rage that drove Moacir's heart. Even as a native, he knew the power that money represented, its life-and-death nature. He'd felt the consequences of that power in his own flesh, and by witnessing losses of life among his people. In his heart and mind, a lesson had been learned. He was more than ready to make the power of money work to his own benefit and that of his people.

4

What's your plan now?" Jandira asked Julian after Dr. Miller agreed he was ready to leave.

"Find rubber. Get rich. Buy the world."

She grabbed his hand and walked with him to a pile of abandoned lumber nearby. They sat. "The man I told you about is called Moacir. He's a Karipuna Indian."

Julian arched his eyebrows. "Aren't they dangerous?"

"Everyone's dangerous, Julian. The Karipunas are not aggressive, if that's what you meant."

"Will you come with me?" he said.

Jandira shook her head, abashed by the boldness of the invitation. "I'm a nurse. I'm needed here."

"I know your job's important. It's what makes you the beautiful person you are," he said.

"I think I can help you and Moacir. That'd make me happy as well."

Julian held her hands and pulled her closer. "I'll be back when I succeed. And I'll marry you."

"Sounds like a wonderful plan."

Julian leaned forward and kissed her. Right there, in a jungle filled with beasts and fear and death, they'd found each other. Julian was fortunate to pursue a dream in a place that seemed like a cesspool of lost hope.

When their lips parted, he looked her in the eyes and saw fear.

"You're not happy. Why?"

"That's not it. I'm concerned. You seem to be a man of monumental dignity, but you're fragile. You've lost weight. Your ribs were broken by a brutal beating, and you've just recovered from malaria."

"Oh. That."

"Promise me you'll take care of yourself," she said.

"Only if you promise you'll wait for me."

Julian was smiling like a child, the portrait of new happiness. His prospects felt as high as the two-hundred-feet kapok trees around them. He saw himself as a real-life protagonist of what once had been a distant dream. In his blurred vision of love and conquest, he was about to venture into an exciting mission. He looked deeply into Jandira's eyes and played his role as he saw himself. "I'm in love with you. I'll promise you anything you ask me."

"I want to hear it, Julian."

"Yes. I'll take care of myself."

*****

Julian told Alan his story while in a line of railway workers waiting to buy a meal. "And Jandira told you all that in exchange for . . . what?" Alan said.

"If we succeed, Jandira and I will get married."

"How damn convenient. You're gonna end up giving her everything."

"That's not how I see it."

"You bust your ass, she collects the benefits?"

"Here's what you need to do, Alan. Go find a trading post. We need supplies. You still have any money?"

"Some, yeah."

"Good. Go find supplies for a team of thirty. We split the profits after your initial investment. Would that work for you?"

"Yeah . . . Thirty men, you said?"

"I was told we need scale."

Alan didn't know much about the native tribes of the Amazon and had certainly never heard of the Karipunas, but if there was someone who knew the forest—and probably where the rubber trees could be found—it was the natives. What mattered was that they finally had a blueprint, one that Alan saw as the foundation for a fruitful partnership with the Englishman. His good manners were a magnet. People trusted him almost instantly, which was a quality Alan lacked.

They shook hands and began to work.

Julian remained in the Porto Velho region getting

acquainted with Moacir. He recruited a group of rubber tappers made up of former railway workers and a few Karipunas.

While they organized, Alan traveled to the nearest trading post, which was about a day away by boat down one of the Amazon tributaries. What he found was not a trading post per se, but a rather small shack owned by a Frenchman named Jacques who got his supplies from larger sellers in Manaus or Belém. Like most trading-post owners, Alan heard, Jacques was terribly in debt to the big suppliers.

"What do you need?" Jacques asked the huge Texan standing at his counter.

"Basic supplies for rubber tappers."

The Frenchman smirked. "You know what you're doing, my friend?" Experienced tappers knew exactly what to ask for. Alan clearly didn't.

"Make it for thirty men."

The trader scratched his forehead and leaned his elbows on the counter. "I supply people on credit based on the upcoming rubber harvest. They pay me in kind. Now, I don't know you, *seigneur*—"

"Alan Reid."

"Mr. Reid. You're asking too much."

Alan nodded. "I understand cash is not seen very often around here."

"As I said, tappers pay me back after their harvest. Latex is the common currency."

Alan saw an opportunity. He didn't have much

money, but for a small trading post far away from the main cities, he bet he could impress the Frenchman if he showed him some cash. He pulled out a short stack of money from his shirt. "I have three hundred dollars with me." Jacques stood back and took in the money. Alan put his full height behind his stare. "Will you help me?"

"I suppose I can."

"I'm just at the start of what's promising to be a very profitable enterprise."

Jacques sighed. "I'll accept your money as a guarantee, but you'll still have to pay for every man's supplies at the regular rate."

Alan and the Frenchman shook hands. "I'll be back in a few days."

"Sure, *seigneur*. I'll be ready."

*****

After two weeks, Jacques saw the men arriving at his shack and smiled. He was waiting for them. Every man got his supplies, enough for three weeks of work in the jungle—flour, soap, salt, kerosene for lighting, a shotgun with ammunition, and rudimentary bowls and buckets.

They headed back to the main camp, crossed the Railway Company, and gathered at the Karipuna village. The six days of walking to the trading post and back left them exhausted. That night, they shared a meal together, restless to get to work.

Though Julian and Alan were the primary investors in the group, all recognized Moacir as their natural leader.

"We leave before the sun," the Karipuna explained with his troubled English. "It takes four days to seringal. Three in the morning we work. We make cuts on trees, place bowls below the cuts, and let them fill with rubber. We return to every tree before day ends and collect latex with the buckets. Remember, before sleep, we do the rubber smoking. Then, day ends."

"Hell, if I knew Jandira had such good connections, I could easily have fallen in love with her," Alan whispered, much to Julian's displeasure.

A few hours later, they formed a line and followed Moacir down a forest path. Julian and Alan were in the middle of the line when they reached a river crossing. Alan looked up. "The sun—"

"What about it?" Julian stared upward.

"Can you tell if it's to our north or east?"

Julian moved on. It didn't make any difference. All they had to do was follow Moacir, a reality more readily accepted by Julian. Alan didn't like not being in control. "These darn swings drive me crazy!"

"Nature's full of curves. Get used to it," Julian said, more focused than ever.

The tall canopy towers made it hard to sight landmarks. "Tell you what, if a man can navigate here, he can find himself anywhere," Alan said.

Julian didn't bother to answer.

During their second day of walking, they spotted a jaguar at a considerable distance. Julian and Alan froze, terrified by the stories they'd heard about the Amazonian beast. The others were equally frightened, which didn't help. Poorly accommodated over mud and leaves, they spent the night haunted by sounds that were at times menacing, and at others enchanting. Monkeys and birds ruled the lullabies of the night.

Time went by, hot and humid, exhausting and tedious. After five miserable days crossing a remote part of the Amazon rainforest, Alan got edgy and suspicious. The truth was, Moacir had promised they would reach the seringal in four days.

The Texan left his central position in the line and passed each of the men until he reached Moacir.

"Hey," he called, but Moacir kept his pace. "How far are we? The mosquitos are eating me alive. Do you understand?"

Moacir looked back at him without stopping. "We arrived yesterday."

"What? Where?"

"We're walking to the middle of this seringal," Moacir said.

"Where's the rubber?"

Moacir looked both ways, found a particular tree, and touched it. "That's our tree."

From that point on, their eyes got used to

identifying the *Hevea brasiliensis* and how to spot the one-hundred-feet-high species everywhere. The seringal looked promising. There was an abundance of rubber trees in whichever direction they looked.

About midafternoon, the group reached a small clearing by a river, which the Karipunas had opened on a previous trip.

"Let's eat," Moacir told the group.

The men settled the best they could. There was nothing there except for one small shack made from rotten branches. It would be their headquarters for the following weeks. The Karipunas set up a grill, went out for an hour, and when they returned, they brought back freshwater fish, reinforcing the notion that they were their supreme hosts.

"All around us," Moacir said, "many rubber trees. Each of you find one hundred trees and work. We stay for as long as you can handle. Smoked rubber follow by canoes down the river."

"I see no canoes." Alan glanced around.

"We'll build them," Moacir said.

"Right. What about the furnaces to smoke the rubber?"

"The forest has everything we need. We'll build them tomorrow."

As far as the Karipunas were concerned, everything they needed was freely available all around them.

The uninviting company of some of the rainforest's most bizarre creatures eventually broke the hard work and monotony of those days. One night, when everyone was enjoying the sleep of the righteous, screams of terrifying intensity woke up the group. A man had taken a short walk to urinate when a forest insect with the homely name of titan beetle, whose jaws were said to be strong enough to snap a pencil in half, accidentally landed on his genitals. The tortured crying that followed required no further verification. Yet, the sounds of pain were mixed with the uncontainable laughter of a few men. Of all the species on Earth, only humans were capable of laughing in the face of such an intimate tragedy.

The Karipunas also warned them about the barber bees, which had the ill-mannered habit of flying into one's mouth and ears. That was the case with Julian during a lunch break when he accidentally hit a nest near the ground and had to brush against it like crazy. Fortunately, he wasn't hurt.

What mattered to everyone was the fact that the amount of *Hevea brasiliensis* in that seringal was outstanding. Over two and a half months of intense labor, the men led by Moacir were able to produce almost twenty tons of latex.

"This is what I came here for!" Julian said while inspecting the latex.

Alan smiled. "I like the greed in your eyes, Jules."

The challenge now was to transport such a large haul back to the trading post. If it weren't for that, the group would've stayed longer.

The morning they left, Moacir saw Julian scratching one of his eyes. It was swollen. "You've been bitten?" he asked, but he already knew the answer.

"Some bug," Julian explained. The thought of getting ill again frightened him.

"Scratching is no good," Moacir said, trying not to worry Julian. If the bug in question were the barbeiro, Julian would feel its consequences—which were untreatable—in a decade or two.

Julian had no time to think about illnesses. He saw the canoes being filled up with latex, and his heart yearned. He was longing to get his share of the production. After that, he knew exactly who to look for. He'd been thinking of Jandira every day and night, missing her dearly. He forgot about the bug bite and joined the others. The sooner they left the seringal, the better.

5

Jacques's small, quasi-negligible trading post was bustling with activity. Rubber had been counted and weighted. Usually, tappers ended up only covering their expenses with Jacques, rarely collecting a profit themselves. Not this time, though.

When Alan and Julian heard the final balance of their hard work, they couldn't believe it. "You're cheating us," Alan put it bluntly.

"Rubber is being traded at eight hundred dollars per ton," Julian told the Frenchman.

"In the United States. And in Europe. Not here," Jacques said. "I have costs to consider."

"I'm sure you do." Alan stood tall, arms crossed, waiting for more clarification.

Jacques snorted. "My supplier is eighty miles down the river. He'll pay me whatever I can get, and I'll be thankful. Then he'll move the rubber to buyers in Belém and Manaus. That's where the big export houses are, OK, *mon ami*? We're at the lower end of this. We do the hard work, *le chargement de l'âne*.

The donkeys! What did you expect, huh?"

After all that had been said and done, Alan collected his three hundred dollars and an extra one hundred dollars. Julian got even less, considering his debt with Alan. Outside, as the group dispersed, Julian pulled Alan closer. "I don't think we're being cheated."

"Oh. I feel better already," Alan said with his stare fixed on the Frenchman.

"We've been stupid. That's different."

"Now, that settles it."

Julian raised his palms in the air, quieting the Texan. "What I'm saying is, we need to sell higher up in the supply chain."

"Any ideas on how to do that?"

"Yes," Julian said, leading Alan outside the post. "Try to be friends with the Frenchman. See whom he sells rubber to. Maybe we can sell directly to larger buyers at a better price."

*****

Alan had planned his own version of that approach, and it didn't include allowing that fragile Englishman to tell him what to do. From his perspective, Alan was the only one who'd taken risks so far. After all, he'd bet his last dollars. Besides, Julian was all excited about marrying Jandira. Which, Alan figured, wasn't going to help their business partnership in any way.

I wouldn't mind finding a whore for myself, Alan thought. But the timing was not appropriate.

He waited until the minuscule settlement where the trading post was located was empty, consumed with growing bitterness. The rewards he'd so dreamed of were taking longer to flourish than he'd expected. The relative safety of the forest, in the sense that El Pepe would never find him there to collect his debt, needed to be left behind. Before the night fell, when the mosquitos fed on humans and animals, he saw Jacques carrying the last cargo of smoked rubber onto a precarious convoy of horses.

I'm all for the jungle rules, he thought caustically.

Alan watched from a distance. The Frenchman locked his miserable shack, mounted a horse, and departed with the convoy. They followed a muddy track, advancing slowly. Alan followed them on foot for thirty minutes. A steamboat was waiting for the cargo at an improvised port. All Alan had in mind was to find a way to get aboard that boat without being seen, which, considering the darkness of the forest, didn't seem difficult.

One hour later, he closed in from a sidetrack. The seventy-foot steamer had two main decks and an upper storage area that was already packed with rubber.

They won't bother me up there.

When night fell deep, and while Jacques was away from the boat with the captain, he found his moment and darted toward the steamer. Getting inside and finding a spot to hide was easy. Alan accommodated his massive body between piles of the smoked rubber his group produced in the seringal. Exactly what he would do next was another story.

The rubber in here belongs to me. He touched and smelled the rubber.

Just like magic, something in his head had determined that a product he'd been paid for should now return to his possession. He found the idea of someone else's sweat being entirely in the hands of middlemen to be repulsive, but if that was the game, he'd rather be the one on the repulsive side. And if there was a jungle out there, he was *in*. The Amazon was no place for a gentleman.

*****

Jandira came out of the infirmary like one returned from war. There was a malaria outbreak in the ever-growing number of railway workers arriving at her camp. She looked drained, with shadows under her eyes and a heaviness to her step.

Julian was waiting for her outside the tent. She wiped the sweat off her forehead and walked toward him. Julian beamed at the sight of her: the shape of her breasts highlighted by the sweat on her apron, and the swinging of her firm thighs molded by the daily walks on arduous forest trails.

"You don't look so happy," he said.

"You don't look rich."

"Does it matter?"

"Yes, Julian. It means we can have a better life when we get married."

"So, you do love me."

"Do you?"

"I'm here." Julian softly clasped her face and kissed her. Then he grinned. "Not as easy as I thought it was."

"What, the rubber-tapping business?"

"That too. But getting rich . . ."

Jandira took a good look at him. "How's your health?"

"I've never been better," he said with a blaze in his eyes.

"I mean your physical health."

"Right now? Hungry."

"I bet you are."

It was a great day to return to Jandira. That night, someone in her camp had caught a nice tambaqui fish, which he'd gladly devoured around a bonfire with some of Jandira's friends. He washed the fish down with generous sips of cachaça. It was precisely the kind of warm, friendly atmosphere that he'd hoped to find. It eased the harshness of life around the Madeira-Mamoré Railway work and the rubber frenzy. Whenever the workers could remind themselves that they still had a soul, they did so with high spirits.

"Let's go to Manaus," Julian said.

"That's a big change for me."

"True money is in the city. I asked Alan to go ahead of us. We'll sell rubber for a better price there."

"That's what you believe now?"

"Have you lost your faith in me?"

"You're just a young man, Julian. But I do trust your heart."

"Then let's leave tomorrow. I have some money. It's not much, but we can get by for a while."

Jandira stood up and headed to an improvised table behind the bonfire. She picked up a bucket of water and poured some over her body with a cup. While she cooled her head, she glanced at him. He had a confident stare like he somehow knew everything had already worked out.

He approached her. "Are you ready to leave this life?"

"If I don't leave now, then when?"

6

It was just a recollection of what his mother had once said about a client.

He dresses like a gentleman and loves like a bull.

The part that worried Alan was getting dressed. He'd long accepted the fact that his mother had turned to prostitution after his father died. His casual cowboy look was no longer suitable for what lay ahead. He required a more established, formal facade.

The proper look of a businessman. It was what she said men should look like. He'd never listened to her then, but now, it made sense.

The first thing he did when he got to Manaus was learn where the rubber would be taken. Before he escaped unnoticed from the upper deck of the steamboat, he overheard Jacques mentioning the name Casa Souza Pereira. It was where the Frenchman would be selling the rubber he, Julian, and the Karipunas had extracted in exchange for flesh sacrificed to mosquitos. During the cumbersome trip sandwiched between the cargo, it became deeply set in his mind that fairness had nothing to do with making a serious profit. That rubber pressing against his body belonged to him. Getting his hands on it was a matter of when.

Find the weakness in people. Another valuable lesson from his mother.

No one would ever take advantage of him again. Jacques had underestimated Alan's drive to be fairly compensated for his hard work deep in the forest. It was Jacques's weakness.

The second thing Alan did was go to the Camisaria Old England on Municipal Street. There, he bought himself a top-of-the-line suit made of white linen, new shirts, shoes, and socks. He completed his new look with cologne and imported cigars. More than opening a new line of credit to extract rubber in the jungle, he was buying the right perception. He even let go of his Stetson hat, which he kept inside his bag from that moment on, replacing it for an elegant, local straw hat.

When he was done with his transformation, he checked into Hotel Augusto, which was much more modest than the Cassina but a safer place to stay. Alan had a reputation for being a big spender. El Pepe wasn't going to look for him there.

He left the Augusto shortly after he checked in. Except for his size, he was almost unrecognizable. He asked directions to the Casa Souza Pereira. It was a twenty-minute walk from his hotel, and he got there before Jacques did. The Frenchman was busy moving his cargo at the port. Alan waited patiently across the street under the leaves of a *Bertholletia excelsa* tree, protected from the midday sun but still dealing with the stifling moisture cooking his skin under the fancy white suit.

Today's a whole nuther thang, he thought. The days of playing by the rules were over. They had to be. He'd been watching the air of corruption since he first arrived in Manaus, but he couldn't find the entrance door until now. He left that humid street corner and headed in the direction of the military battalion just two blocks away. He had a plan of action. It involved Julian, who—he hoped—would arrive in Manaus in one or two days.

"I'd like to see Commander Sebastião Alcantara," he asked a military policeman at the battalion entrance. Alan's superlative stature had been dramatically increased by his new outfit. He looked much more prominent and mature.

"Yes, sir. Who would like to see him?"

"Alan Reid. It's an urgent matter."

"Follow me, Mr. Reid."

Alan trailed the young policeman to the commander's office. His smooth walk didn't reveal the rush of adrenaline in his veins, the same rush he experienced every time he bluffed in poker. This time, Alan was counting on his old gaming friendship with Commander Alcantara, whom he usually lost to at the poker—and whom he always paid punctually. He and the commander used to spend more time drinking than gambling. Instead of rivalry, they enjoyed a proximity that resembled friendship. Now, Alan was going all in on the grave lie he was about to tell—his most risky bet so far.

"Please wait," the policeman said. Alan stopped outside a door.

Moments later, the policeman came back out and passed by him.

"Crazy Texan. Get in here!" the commander yelled from inside his office.

Alcantara, who was a good fifteen years older than Alan, was behind his desk and didn't bother to stand up. He found it amusing that Alan was looking for him during the day, as they usually met at the Hotel Cassina at night. The fact that Alan was impeccably dressed caused some sneering.

"A bit early to drink, isn't it?" Alcantara said. They shook hands. Alcantara gestured to the chair before his desk.

"Thanks," Alan said. "I didn't come here to drink. Unfortunately, there's been a problem."

"Haven't seen you for a while. I heard Mr. Steward has some issues with you."

El Pepe's time will come, Alan promised himself.

"He's just too temperamental. I take it he prefers

to threaten his friends rather than wait to collect his debts. I've paid him, but I wouldn't be surprised if he's still defaming my name. Is he?"

"I don't care. I don't like him that much."

Good, Alan thought.

"Anyway, what can I do for you, Alan?"

"As you've noticed, I've been out of town for some time."

"Whereabouts?"

"Porto Velho and a few other places."

"Yes. The railway business. Lots of gambling, crimes, and illnesses over there."

"Actually, I've grabbed some land for myself. I put together a team of rubber tappers and set up a small trading post far north of Porto Velho. I came back to sell my harvest."

"Doing well, huh?"

"Modestly. Problem is, I got robbed."

Alcantara squinted. "Where?"

"Coming out of the trading post. They got all my latex. Twenty tons of it."

"Sorry to hear it."

"Then the sons of bitches burned down my shack. Can you believe it? They did it during the night. True professionals."

"So, you don't know who did it?"

"No. But they're going to try to sell it. It's either here or in Belém."

"That's going to be hard to crack."

"Maybe. I heard a rubber cargo has just arrived at the port. I didn't want to risk confronting them directly, but word is they're going to try to sell it at the Casa Souza Pereira. In fact, they could be heading there as we speak."

"Is that so?" Alcantara ran his fingers through his mustache.

Alan moved his large body forward and rested a hand on Alcantara's desk. It was time to up his bet. "Do you think you could have a look at it?"

"Are you sure this is happening right now?"

"Yes. I can go with you if you want."

"Oh, no, no, no. I don't want a foreigner meddling with our police business. You stay right here, or maybe go get yourself a drink. I'll send my men to the Casa. Come back later."

"A drink's not a bad idea. You wouldn't believe how hard it is to work the darn seringal. I just want what's fair, Commander."

"Leave it to me. And, boy, you look all grown up in that suit."

"Thanks. And good luck." Alan stood up, tipped his hat, and left.

He was taking a huge risk. He'd bet that the word of one man would somehow prevail over another's. Jacques had no receipt of his transactions with him, as they usually kept it in the trading posts. He'd seen the Frenchman throw it inside a box filled with old receipts. All he had was a cargo manifest. Hopefully,

Alcantara's men would be satisfied to find the exact amount of rubber Alan had reported stolen.

Alan waited outside the battalion for five hours. He watched everyone who came in and out of it. Then he saw a captain and two policemen bringing Jacques in. Alan held his breath when he walked back to his poker friend's office.

It's all or nothing now. For Alan, Jacques's weakness had been established. Now he needed to find the commander's weak spot, a much harder task.

"This is the man you've stolen the merchandise from. His name's Alan Reid," Commander Alcantara said as Alan walked in.

Jacques turned and let out his ire. "I know him. Yes! It was I who bought from him!"

The Texan said nothing. The commander stared at the suspect. "You know him, then? Or you've just repeated his name after I've mentioned it to you?"

"I said I was the one who bought his latex, not the other way around," Jacques said.

"No, sir. We've never met," Alan said, calm on the outside, pre-heart-attack on the inside. *Looks matter*, his mother told him once. *I look gratified even when I'm about to fall asleep. My clients fall for it every single time.*

"I have the transaction papers!" Jacques said.

"Let me have a look," Alcantara said.

Alan watched and tried to keep his head cool.

"I don't have them *with* me. But they're at my

trading post," Jacques explained.

"You're making it hard to believe," Alcantara said.

"Commander"—Alan stepped closer to the desk—"can't you send some men to the Porto Velho region and finish this? I really need my cargo back."

"Yes. Great idea!" the Frenchman barked. His eyes were so wide they appeared about to explode.

"Forget it," Alcantara said. "Here's the problem. You need to prove that the rubber cargo we've found belongs to you. But you can't."

"Then why doesn't *he* need to prove it?" Jacques rightly protested, staring at Alan.

"Because the amount of cargo we've found with you matches Mr. Reid's description. And I don't believe he's got psychic abilities. It can't be just a coincidence, can it?" Alcantara raised his hand and called the captain in. "Please take this man with you and lock him in." Turning back to Jacques, he said, "We're going to prosecute you."

"Wait a minute! This isn't—"

"Quiet!" the captain ordered while twisting Jacques's arm.

Alan shook his head, rightly aggrieved, playing along. His heart was still pumping fast, and he hoped he wouldn't break into a sweat in front of the commander like he'd done when he lost all his money to El Pepe Steward. Alcantara knew him well enough to tell when Alan was bluffing. He took long, silent breaths while Alcantara watched Jacques being removed from his office. When they found themselves alone in the office, Alan sat down and said, "This is revolting!"

Alan was too excited to notice that Commander Alcantara was now eyeing him with a different focus. "You know, you're too large a man to be so affected by this."

"That man stole all I've got!"

"We're done here. Your cargo's at the Casa waiting. All you have to do is go there and collect your money."

"Thank you, Alcantara. Hell, thank you!"

"You're welcome." The commander wore an astute smile that Alan hadn't noticed before. He wanted to get out of there as quickly as possible. It had all happened as he'd planned.

"I better be going," Alan said.

"Do that. And, er, why don't we meet later? I could use a drink, maybe chase those girls at the Cassina. What do you think?"

"Absolutely. Drinks and girls are on me."

Alan got up and was walking past the door when Alcantara called, "Oh, Alan?"

Alan turned. "Yes?"

"You understand we're partners now."

Alan frowned, not really following. "Sure. Looking forward to celebrating later on."

"That sounds good. But what I mean is, we're partners in this little scam of yours."

Alan's heart was in the fast lane again. Just when he was about to celebrate, he'd been caught red-handed. He began sweating profusely, and his face turned pale. "I—I didn't—"

"Yes, you did. Nicely played, by the way. Now that we're being frank with each other, you also match the description of someone who had broken into one of our stations a couple of months ago. A gentleman named Julian Welch was rescued, and one policeman is still out of work recovering from the aggression. So, to sum up, you now owe me thirty percent of whatever you get from the rubber sale at the Casa."

Alan froze and evaluated the situation. All he had to do was agree to give the commander a cut. It was a big cut, but not entirely unfair considering the alternative. He nodded, spent decisive seconds digesting it, and accepted the new situation as being even better than what he had anticipated. With Alcantara as his partner, the Frenchman would not be able to prove his innocence.

That thirty percent was starting to look like a bargain.

"See you at the hotel, my friend," Alan finally said.

7

The Cassina doorman eyed Alan Reid suspiciously after his months of absence. The once-regular customer—lately a kind of pariah—forced the doorman to squint. He almost didn't recognize Alan. That tall man in white was indeed Mr. Reid. Except he looked tanned, clean, and shining.

"Don't fall in love, Victor," Alan said.

"No, sir. Welcome back. Oh, and—"

"Don't worry, Vic. Tell everyone I'm back, especially Mr. Pepe Steward. If they look as silly as you do right now, let them know it was Commander Sebastião Alcantara who insisted I return."

Alan was back to the center of activity in Manaus. This time, he was determined to be recognized as one of them—the wealthy, influential figures he so craved to be among. There was a telegram waiting for him at the front desk sent from a police post near Porto Velho. It announced Julian and Jandira's imminent arrival.

During that week, Alcantara and Alan had

enjoyed their renewed friendship the best they could. They'd shared women, expensive drinks, and played poker religiously every night in the dark room behind the Cassina stage. They felt very much at home. More than the trivialities of life, they anticipated the future rewards of their recently formed partnership. Plans of expansion were drawn up.

The twenty tons of rubber stolen from Jacques gave Alan a sixteen-thousand-dollar profit. Less the commander's share, eleven thousand dollars remained to be split between him and Julian. The amount was far from making anyone rich, but Alan saw it as just the start. A completely new vision was in the making—one that included the guidance of Commander Alcantara. To further crown the promising future, the commander and Alan had a mutual distaste for El Pepe Steward, one of the largest exporters of rubber in Manaus. Between sips of champagne, shots of whiskey, and hands of poker, they discussed ways of teaching that arrogant merchant a lesson.

"The important thing to remember," Alcantara recapped in case the excess of booze had blurred Alan's memory, "is that you don't move a finger before letting me know. You may think of me as your private little king, but there are greater forces at play. We need to be careful and timely."

"But you're the one with the most revolvers."

"Firepower exists to be a deterrent. If we have to use it, we're in trouble."

"You're quite the philosopher."

*****

Julian checked in to the Cassina three days later. He requested a room for himself and another one for Jandira. They planned to marry very soon. "Tomorrow," he told Alan the minute they met in the hotel. When the Texan gave Julian his share of the money, everything aligned. He finally had a decent amount of money in his pocket, and marriage was in sight. It was like a dream. *Who said I was going to fail?*

Julian and Alan drank heavily to celebrate. They watched the other distinguished guests walk by the bar and almost felt like one of them. "I'm guessing you've robbed someone," Julian said.

Alan laughed.

"Seriously, you must have repurchased the rubber we harvested and sold it to someone else at a much better value," Julian insisted.

"You're a good guesser. That's exactly what I did."

"You're joking, right?"

"I promise you this, Jules. We're never gonna have to deal with the likes of Jacques again. Our place is here, where the real businessmen do business. We're one of them now. Well, we're getting there."

"I suppose we are." They toasted, but Julian wasn't entirely comfortable with the idea that Alan had actually robbed the Frenchman. "If you don't mind me asking, I have a feeling that there's something else you're not telling me."

"Again, a good guess. There is. It goes by the name of Commander Sebastião Alcantara. He's the regional chief of the military police. He's helping us. Having protection is important. And you, my friend, can stop looking behind your back every darn minute. El Pepe will never touch you or me again. Guaranteed."

Julian remembered his father's warnings about playing nice. *Whatever it takes*, he'd told his father. That was precisely what Alan was doing, Julian was sure. He didn't like the taste of it, but he wasn't going soft. "I'm relieved to know that," Julian said.

"Me too. Now, are you sure about tomorrow?"

"She's perfect, and I'm in love. What can I say?" Julian's eyes gleamed at the thought of Jandira.

"Now what? You're just gonna find a priest somewhere?"

"We don't want anything too formal, just to do the right thing. Besides, we're not rich. There's a lot to accomplish before we go out on a spending spree. We have to discuss what to do next."

"We will. For now, focus on your marriage. I'll ask Alcantara for recommendations. I'm sure he knows someone who could do some praying for you and Jandira. In a few days, we get back to business."

"I appreciate that. Right now, I feel like I'm back aboard the RMS. Everything is spinning. I've had enough to drink," Julian said and motioned to leave.

Alan held his forearm. "One more thing. We need to do this properly."

"What do you mean?"

"Our partnership."

Alan pulled out a stack of papers from his inside pocket. "Our contract. I had it drawn up by a lawyer. I'm sure we trust each other, but this is what real businessmen do."

"You're right," Julian said, but when he saw the number of pages the contract contained, he froze. There was no way he was going to be able to go through all those pages tonight. He could barely read on a good day, and at the moment he had many drinks in his system. His hesitation caught Alan's attention.

"Let me help you with the most important parts. The ones that matter. May I?"

"Sure."

Alan turned the page and showed him a paragraph on page two. "Can you read this?"

Julian cleared his throat. It took him a while to read the two lines and sum up bits of it. "It says we are equal partners. Fifty percent each."

"That's right." Alan flipped the pages until he reached the last one. "See right here? That's your name next to mine. No one else has any business with us. We're our own masters, Jules, and I'm damn proud of it."

Alan offered Julian a pen. Both signed it.

"And that's your copy."

Julian smiled. "Thanks."

"I say we celebrate."

"Oh, no, no. I'm done. I'll see you tomorrow, mate."

*****

The wedding took place in a rushed ceremony at the Igreja Matriz, a two-story building with Portuguese bells and views of the Rio Negro. The morning after Julian arrived in town, Father Cruz got a visit from a policeman who, on behalf of Commander Sebastião Alcantara, had asked for a brief wedding ceremony to be conducted later that afternoon. Father Cruz consecrated the Englishman named Julian Welch and his Brazilian wife, Jandira Welch, with the American Alan Reid as their only witness.

"God bless you," Father Cruz said.

Julian kissed the bride. She wore a beautiful pale-pink, S-shaped corset and a bodice with puffy sleeves narrowing down the forearm. The wife of the Cassina manager had offered the gift by request of Alcantara.

Julian wasn't behind in style. The new Alan—a grandstander nouveau riche to be—had taken him to the Camisaria Old England. He'd bought Julian a long, dark-navy sack suit with loose-fitting, wide lapels and a three-button closure. Despite the heat and humidity, the attire was all wool with hints of striping, checks, and plaid.

When they left the church that afternoon, Alan followed closely behind the newlyweds. While he gave them their much-desired privacy, he watched every step the bride took, the delicate sway of her bottom, and the happiness on Julian's face when he glanced at his new wife, which disturbed Alan. It was the very scene he'd told his mother would never be part of his life. As much as he tried to be happy for them, knowing that nothing about Julian and Jandira represented a menace to him, Alan couldn't find an opening in his soul for the beautiful side of life. He recognized how damaged he was, and how distant the answers to his torment were. His blood boiled in unreasonable anger and jealousy of his friend, and his mind was flooded by an almost uncontrollable sexual desire for the female parading before him.

Lucky son of a bitch, he thought of his friend.

There was no party after they left the Igreja Matriz. They headed straight back to the Hotel Cassina.

"Thank you for everything," Julian said, then he and Jandira retreated to their bedroom.

"I'll be down here if you need me," Alan said.

Alan watched Julian and Jandira moving up the stairs until the last step. He put up a great effort to root for their well-being, but the negativity began to blind him. That thing next to Julian was no longer a woman, but a piece of meat asking to be eaten alive. *He's not good enough for her*, Alan concluded without any hint of reason. *He is too gentle for a cow like her.*

*****

Julian found their bedroom beautifully decorated with a mix of delicate roses and exotic tropical flowers. There was champagne and soaps and towels exquisitely arranged over their bed. Life had changed enormously since the last time Julian had been in Manaus.

"Thank you," Jandira whispered with a soft, faltering voice.

Julian spent the next few minutes trying to open the bottle of champagne and then serving it. Then he closed the curtains and unfolded the bed linens while glancing around the room like something was missing. Jandira didn't take her eyes off him. When she had his full attention, she undressed from a comfortable distance. Her beautiful body came into Julian's view with the exuberance of an exotic flower opening. He didn't move or speak.

"I'm as new to this as you are," she said carefully. Then, she stepped forward and helped him get undressed.

"Let's go to bed," he said.

When he turned, Jandira smiled to herself. He was a true gentleman, and terribly inexperienced. She would need to give him a hand. She switched off a side lamp. The room went partially dark, sunset rays piercing through the curtain gaps.

"I love you, Julian Welch."

8

Alan counted the hours in his head, trying to expel the repulsion that Julian and Jandira's wedding night had caused him. It was as if two different people lived inside him. One was conscious and ashamed. The other was consumed by rage and blame and destructive impulses. Down at the Hotel Cassina bar, he had already gulped down several glasses of whiskey. He declined to play poker with his usual friends and failed at thinking about anything that wasn't related to what was going on in Julian's bedroom. Jandira had become an obsession. She was a woman. Like his mother. A powerful force that drove men crazy. In his twisted mind, the closer a man got to a woman, the more vulnerable he became, and the only way to deal with the female sex was by force.

"She needs a real man," he voiced like a wild beast deprived of any sense of order or decency. Blinded by another emptied glass of whiskey and an emotional tsunami, he darted upstairs.

Alan found the first-floor corridor empty, reminding him of the big house his mother owned in San Antonio, Texas. It was early evening. Guests were either outside the hotel or entertaining themselves downstairs. He slowed down as he approached the newlyweds' bedroom, leaned his back against the wall, and closed his eyes. He saw himself as the little boy with no father and a widowed mother who kept herself busy with the strangers that frequently visited the Reid house. The door of his mother's room opened, and his mother, Becky, said, *If I catch you out here, I'll teach you a lesson. Now, out!*

Alan opened his eyes when he heard moaning coming from Julian's bedroom. The effect that Jandira was having on Alan paralyzed him. "Give me more, baby," Alan whispered, an echo of what Alan had heard over and over again coming out of his mother's room in his childhood. Then, footsteps interrupted his delirium.

Alan walked away from that door. Like in old San Antonio, he had found a suitable place to hide while others savored the better side of life. Jandira's sighs faded away as Alan retreated. He waited against the wall farther down the corridor. When the coming guest got into his room, Alan dragged himself down the stairs and back to the bar. He was devastated.

"Another shot, Mr. Reid?" the bartender said.

Alan nodded. More whiskey was served and gulped down in one shot. Alan let the effect of the alcohol numb him, but the cloud of darkness engulfing him just wouldn't recede. Then, a light touch on his shoulder distracted him, and he turned. It was El Pepe.

"We missed you at the game," the serpent said in his raspy voice.

Instinctively, Alan reached into his inner pocket, pulled out a stack of money, and threw two hundred dollars against El Pepe's chest. "Eat it," Alan said, then he stood up and curved his large body toward the Mexican. Emboldened by the booze and the promises of fortune, the Texan said, "Next time you come after me or my interests, I'll crush you like an insect."

"Your drink, Mr. Steward," the bartender said as he served El Pepe.

El Pepe smiled a thank-you and stared back at Alan, showing off his golden teeth.

"I heard you've got powerful friends now."

"You bet," Alan said.

"You know how it is with friends."

"How is it, Pepe?"

The Mexican raised his eyebrows slightly and casually said, "Someone always comes up with even more powerful friends. Now I have to go. I have some girls waiting for me. You, my good friend, look kind of lonely. Care to join us?"

El Pepe finished his drink and walked away without waiting to hear Alan's response. Despite the display of arrogance, Alan had to agree with him. There was always someone more powerful, more steps to be anticipated, and movements to make. If he wanted to be on top—and better protected—he needed to be more socially involved.

"I get it," Alan told himself. "More," he said, touching his glass.

His head swirled with possibilities, each worse than the last. Attachments would have to be temporarily, only for as long as they served a purpose. After that, discarded. In a cruel world, real friendships were a thing of myth. Families were an emotional fantasy, as his mother proved. Love? A weapon used by opportunistic women, stored between their legs, with dangerous effects on a man's senses. The divagations went on and on . . .

When Alan saw Julian coming down to the bar, he frowned, surprised. Something had to have happened for a man to leave his wife's company during their first night together. But even with Julian trying to contain his happiness, his entire face shined with childish delight. By then, Alan had plans of his own. He got up and walked toward Julian with purpose.

"Bless your heart. Too hot up there?" Alan slurred.

"I just wanted to have a drink."

"Well, come with me."

Alan held Julian's arm jovially and walked with

him toward a bar table at a corner. Commander Alcantara was seated there with two other acquaintances. "Jules, this is the man who arranged for Father Cruz. Commander, this is my good friend Julian Welch," Alan said.

"Congratulations," Alcantara said. "Sit down. Have a drink with us."

"Thank you. Please, let me offer you something." Julian pulled out a chair and sat.

Alan waited until the drinks arrived. "I'm tired. See you around," he said as he got up and walked out of the bar.

He reached the staircase leading to the first floor, moving sloppily.

Once there, he struggled with the effects of the alcohol in his blood and adopted a more determined pace. He set his gaze upward, climbing with focus. The dark, noble wood of the corridor floor magically assumed lighter tones, much like his childhood house, but he was no longer the scared boy watching others pursue pleasures with his mother. He was a man of free will and desires of his own. No longer a witness to others, but the one in charge of things to come.

"No one tells me what to do," Alan reassured himself.

He was big enough to knock any man down if required. If he found someone in his mother's room, he would use his clout without hesitation, but it wasn't his mother who was there. It was Jandira. Alan entered, not bothering to look behind him or close the door.

He was blind and deaf and downright out of his mind. Jandira sat up in bed, covering her breasts, her mouth open in shock. That brutal man was coming in her direction with the appetite of a starving lion. The poor woman had no time to protest. In an instant, his strong hand was over her mouth, shutting it, and he was pulling her hair with a mind for total domination. His lips sucked on her full, teardrop breasts, and his knees spread hers apart.

Then, Alan felt a pressure on the top of his head that was followed by a spark of light, the noise of shattered porcelain, and the stiffness of the floor against his body.

Time stood still.

Alan heard the rumble of what sounded like the entertainment going on downstairs invading the room. And voices.

". . . I am. God, is he dead?" Jandira said.

"I don't know . . ." Julian said.

"This madman!"

Alan turned his heavy body. His shoulder and head rolled over the porcelain vase with which Julian had hit him.

"Get out, you bloody animal!" Julian said.

Alan sat up, legs spread like a child, head reeling with a terrible ache caused by the excess of alcohol and the blow. He looked upward at Julian and saw the Englishman holding a sharp, broken piece of the vase toward him, and turned to Jandira. Her emotional collapse came in the form of silent whimpering. "I'm sorry," he barely managed to say.

"What were you thinking?" Jandira said.

Alan lowered his head, hiding his shame, "I . . . thought you were Becky."

"Who?" Julian said.

Alan curled his lips, disgusted with himself. "My mother."

Jandira and Julian exchanged a glance.

"Jesus . . . What's wrong with you?" Julian said.

"We're leaving right now," Jandira said and began collecting her things. "C'mon, Julian. We're done here."

Alan brushed his hair out of his face and stood up. Julian raised the pointed piece of porcelain in his direction. Alan smiled sadly. "Look at you, Jules. Braver than I ever assumed you'd be. I admire you, but I could smash you right now with only one arm."

"Why don't you try?"

Alan sighed. "Because I don't have to."

"Let's go, Julian!" Jandira yelled.

Alan glanced at Jandira, bumbling and ashamed. "You two are a fine couple. Me, I'm damaged. I crossed a line, and I shouldn't have."

"Yes, you did. Don't ever look for us again," Jandira said.

Alan nodded. "I understand. But that's not how this ends."

"Come near us again, and I'll go to the police," Julian said.

"We're going to the police anyway, Julian," Jandira said.

"No, you aren't. Jules, have you read the contract you signed?"

"What contract?" Jandira said. Julian's eyes turned toward the side table, where his bag was. Jandira rushed toward it, found the contract, and held it up. "This one?"

"I didn't read it yet," Julian admitted to Jandira.

"Never mind, Jules. I'll tell you what you've signed. The contract says you get fifty percent of what we earn together, but at my discretion. It states how much money you owe me, and the conditions to be respected. You'll understand when you read it. I mean, assuming you *can* read."

"I don't care. Jandira and I are going to the police."

"Commander Alcantara is at the bar. As you know, he's our partner. He won't do anything."

"Why the hell do you need my husband?" Jandira said.

"Because I need people like you and him. It keeps the business stable."

Julian and Jandira looked lost. "My husband is a good person, and as we all now know, he can barely read. Clearly, you don't need us," Jandira said.

"I do. I need the appearance of normal. Because I'm not."

9

The wealth brought to the region by the rubber barons was obscene. By 1908, the city hosted the world's greatest consumers of diamonds and cigars lit by one-hundred-dollar notes. The excesses and temptations—the need to show off luxury and lovers—were creating a field day for the informal intelligence gathering led by Commander Sebastião Alcantara.

The Teatro Amazonas, a true renaissance revival in the middle of the jungle, was living proof of the extravagances of the city. If someone wanted to see or be seen, a special night at that theater was the perfect place. It was where Alcantara, along with Julian, Jandira, and Alan, were about to make their next move.

That night, Pedro Oliveira, the notary public and one of Alcantara's poker friends, was expected to attend the program. Pedro had carefully projected the image of being a dedicated husband, but it was just that, a vision. Everyone knew that Pedro had a severe weakness for prostitutes. In public, he was a very religious, family-oriented bureaucrat serving directly under the governor of the State of Amazonas. But being the gambler that he was, Pedro enjoyed taking some risks by occasionally showing off his favorite girls.

The Teatro Amazonas was playing a reenactment of the Italian opera *La Gioconda* by Amilcare Ponchielli, which was beautifully performed by local artists. It was a place to be seen, an event to bring a spouse to. Instead, the beacon of morality that was Pedro brought along a prostitute known by several of the Hotel Cassina guests.

"Good men don't lie to their wives," Alcantara told his partners in a second-floor theater box, his eyes firmly on Pedro's box.

Alan and Julian were not aware of what exactly Alcantara had in mind, but when they were invited to the theater, they knew some kind of breakthrough was about to take place. "Follow me," was all the commander said after the performance ended. They followed.

Two boxes away, Pedro found his way obstructed by three of his poker friends as he came out of his box. "How are you doing, Pedro?" Alcantara said. He didn't waste time. "Mr. Reid and Mr. Welch would like to request a favor. Would that be too inconvenient?" Alcantara stared at the escort holding Pedro's arm in a way that left no doubt that her presence was noted—as well as his wife's absence.

"Let's have a drink. All of us. At the Cassina?" Pedro said.

"Not tonight. I suggest that we meet tomorrow at your office. Eight o'clock?"

Pedro swallowed hard. "If you prefer."

"See, these are fine people with me."

"I know. How are you doing, Mrs. Welch? Alan . . . Julian . . . We're among friends."

"True. And fine friends, whenever required, make for wonderful and credible witnesses. And that's my point, Pedro. There's something important we need to discuss."

"I see. No need to make a fuss."

"Agreed. All we need is your public authentication. There are documents in your custody that will need to be updated."

Pedro twitched his lips. Forging private documents posed one level of difficulty, but if they were of public interest, it could be harder. "Can you tell me more about it? Maybe I can expedite things."

"The gentlemen here are buying a corporation. They're in a rush. It's the nature of businesses these days—everybody wants things done yesterday."

"I understand. I'll be ready."

"OK, then." Before they left Pedro alone, Alcantara whispered in his ear, "Not being ready is not really an option." Then he nodded at the escort and left with Alan, Julian, and Jandira.

The next day, first thing in the morning, Pedro Oliveira welcomed Alan and Julian to his office. Right there, as Alcantara and Alan handed Pedro some documents, Julian learned what he'd gotten himself involved in.

After they sat, Pedro went through the pages of a document and then placed it back on his desk. "So, Mr. Pepe Steward is selling his export company to the two of you, Mr. Reid and Mr. Welch."

"Correct," Alan said.

"Then why isn't he here?"

"Because I'm here," Alcantara said, "and I have a written authorization to act on his behalf. Here's the power of attorney. As a notary, you'll authenticate it."

The commander handed the authorization to Pedro. The bureaucrat read it and shook his head. "I'm sorry. I don't see Mr. Steward's signature."

Alcantara leaned forward. "Don't worry." The commander picked up a pen and signed the document.

Pedro shifted in his chair. "You're not Mr. Steward. As you know very well, the power of attorney needs to be signed by him. You're forging his signature!"

"I'm not him."

"Exactly."

"I know. But that whore was not your wife either, was she?"

"Of course not!"

"There we are, then. Will we have problems with you?"

Pedro looked lost. There was nothing he could do other than go along with the fraud. Anything else would mean a scandal, a terrible thing for an ambitious public servant like him, and the sure end of his marriage.

Pedro cleared his throat. "And he's selling his company to Mr. Reid and Mr. Welch for . . . ten dollars?" He tilted his gaze up from the document.

"That's correct. Mr. Steward is very fond of us," Alan said.

After a few more seconds of fake reading, Pedro authenticated the papers.

"Good. That's all we need." Alcantara stood up. Alan and Julian followed suit. "One more thing. I understand Mr. Reid needs to go to the bank to make the deposit immediately. That will confirm and seal the transaction."

"That's correct," Pedro said.

"Will I be seeing you tonight at the Cassina? I mean, if you're officially in Belém, as you told your wife, you can't simply go home."

"Probably."

"Then I'll see you later," Alcantara said like this was just another day.

*****

The offices of the Steward Export Company had been busy dealing with delays in shipments due to a problem with the vessel responsible for transporting rubber to the United States. Merchandise accumulated and affected sales in the previous months, but with the recent acquisitions, the volume shipped by the office soared. El Pepe Steward had signed for twelve hundred tons of rubber at eight hundred dollars per ton, totaling revenues of $960,000. It had been his largest shipment so far, and a day to remember.

El Pepe was immersed in work behind a pile of papers at his desk when his accountant burst into his office, followed by a small party of gentlemen. The Mexican glowered when he saw the accountant's troubled face. He hated being interrupted when he was literally counting his profits, but he had to lean back in his chair in response to what he saw next. Alan Reid, Julian Welch, a captain, and a policeman were following right after the accountant.

"What's going on?" El Pepe barked.

The accountant was holding a document that he immediately placed in front of El Pepe, who stood up and stared over his glasses—first at the accountant, then he shifted his stare to the other men who'd just invaded his office. Only then did he read the piece of paper put before him. When he finished it, he placed the paper back on his desk and took off his glasses. He was smiling on the outside but convinced that something terribly out of place was going on.

"Mr. Steward," Alan began with unnecessary politeness. "You weren't supposed to be here. We wanted a smooth and discreet transition. But look at you—all attached to this office like a dog to his bones."

"This?" El Pepe raised the document in the air. "It won't prosper."

"What are you talking about?"

"It's just a bad joke. I mean, a forged signature? My company being sold for ten dollars?" he mocked with his raspy voice, but it had no effect on the men standing around his desk.

"The bank receipt for the deposit." Alan placed it on El Pepe's desk.

"It doesn't matter. It won't succeed."

Alan nodded. "I expected you might dishonor our deal. The gentlemen in uniform are here to enforce it."

"What deal, you Texan piece of shit?"

"The one sealed in a round of poker at the Cassina. You may not remember all that clearly because you were too drunk. But I assure you, we do."

El Pepe turned to the soldier. "The men in uniform can go to hell. I'll be contacting the governor. You will pay me for this. Until then, you're welcome to leave."

"Sir, please step aside," the captain ordered. He and the policeman cornered El Pepe.

The Mexican knew better. There were no

pyrotechnics he could think of at that moment. It was best to play along and see what could be done later. A talk with the governor, or maybe some breaking of legs along the way. This swindle looked amateurish. El Pepe was convinced he could not only nullify it, but also be compensated by the state in some way.

El Pepe stood up and walked around his desk, the hard soles of his shoes tapping against the floor, and put his hands in his pockets to convey confidence. But right then, when he managed to control his anger for a strategic payback that would surely come later, another two policemen came in holding bags with samples of a dark powder.

They walked toward the captain and showed him the contents. "We found this mixed with the rubber cargo," a policeman said.

The captain grabbed the powder and smelled it. "That's coffee." Then he stared at El Pepe. "Do you have the manifest to confirm this cargo?"

"You know it's not mine," El Pepe said.

"Looks like contraband."

"I'm a rubber exporter. I don't deal with coffee," El Pepe said idly.

"That's what I thought. Contraband." The captain turned to Alan. "Mr. Reid, this will be recorded as a pre-transition crime. Your company remains clean; only Mr. Steward will be responsible for this."

"I appreciate that," Alan said.

"Please arrest Mr. Steward," the captain ordered his men.

While the policemen motioned to hold El Pepe, he managed to approach his desk, which was now grandiosely occupied by Alan Reid like a king who had claimed a throne. "You've gone too far. You wait and see."

"No, Pepe. You're going to rot in jail. That's all there is for you."

The captain nodded. El Pepe was dragged out of his office.

*****

All day long, Julian thought about what people were capable of doing for money. He'd been made a rich man by the hands of a criminal partner, and yet, the goal he'd set before his departure from London had been successfully achieved. Julian would write to his parents and proudly brag about thriving in the jungle. He would, however, omit the details that revealed he'd been part of a law-breaking scandal. The bottom line was, he hadn't failed. One year before, he'd found himself working hard at the seringal and surviving the brutal realities of that place, but he'd unwillingly formed an alliance with greedy, unscrupulous men of no morals. The kind of men his father had warned him about.

At the post office, he dictated a letter to his parents to a clerk.

These are both sad and happy times, Mother. It's true what they say about dreams. Nothing feels more rewarding, but realizing your goals doesn't even get close to the original aspiration. I'm now married to a woman of invaluable sensitivity. She is a faithful companion who will make you and Father proud. I will take her to London at the first opportunity. There are riches in the forest beyond belief, but they come at high personal costs, as you warned me. When I'm back home, it will be as a successful person.

That same night at the Cassina, the new owners of the Steward Export Company forgot about playing poker and decided to feast on excesses, Manaus style. Commander Alcantara and Alan were each accompanied by two of their favorite girls. Gustav, the money launderer, had joined them when he'd scented the joy of wealth being celebrated. Julian and Jandira were a bit uncomfortable among them. Later, Pedro found himself a place at the table. The drinking and the unavoidable social coexistence with those people made it convenient to play along. The only person hurt that day was El Pepe, who was now behind bars, paying more for his arrogance than his crimes. Nobody really missed him.

In a sort of trance caused by alcohol, Alan felt detached from the presence of everybody else at that table. Mouths laughed, but sounds were faded. Vivid memories of his childhood were once again haunting him—the horde of men that visited Becky came to his mental sight, but the anger was gone. *I am now one of you.*

Alan finally understood what drove those men to smile when they passed by him up the staircase of his San Antonio house. *The pleasure of violation.* The sanctity of a home and the purity of a child? *Degrade it.* The values of motherhood, the pain of a widow in need of money and companionship? *Exploit it.* The corridors of the church on Sundays? *The perfect place to gossip and denigrate your fellow brother.* It was all bad until you were too far gone to care.

The scents of fine food, the deadened senses caused by a mix of champagne and whiskey, the false impression of owning the world. It all liberated Alan from the annoyances of nostalgia and fear. Why bother with guilt and self-pity if one could eliminate all that from the mind and heart?

Life's good. Others better get out of my way.

"We're going to get some sleep," Julian said.

"You two have a good time," Alan said, but they didn't listen.

The Texan looked at Jandira as she walked away. Whatever Julian got, it belonged to him too. They were partners. And as Alan thought about the relevance of Julian's role in their unlawful acquisition of the Steward Export Company, he almost felt too generous. He had none. The Englishman was too kind and noble, a world apart from his old friends of the San Antonio streets. Julian was the trustworthy face of a partnership that was promising to mock the law. On top of that, Alan felt his groin burn with desire for Jandira.

"That's what friends are for," Alan thought out loud.

*****

Climbing the staircase leading to their hotel room, Jandira asked Julian, "Did he pay you?"

"Yes . . . three hundred and thirty-six thousand dollars!"

"Let's leave now, Julian."

"I wish."

"Don't just wish. Let's get our stuff and leave at once! We're rich now—we can go anywhere we want!"

At the top of the stairway, Julian glanced down at the lobby, and then he stared at Jandira in a way that left no doubt of their reality. "Our partner has committed a crime with the help of the authorities. He stole an entire company. In other words, *we* committed this crime too."

"You were forced to!"

"Was I? I don't think so. Alan and I are legitimate partners. Even if I ignore the contract I've signed with him, a crime has been committed, and the police commander is our partner. Our money is in a bank account controlled by Alan—the bank manager plays poker with him, sleeps with women he offers him. I wasn't forced into anything, Dira. Ignorance is what dragged us to where we are. My ignorance."

10

In 1916, Julian was finally ready to come home to England after being away for nine years. He'd been postponing his return for as long as his business with Alan flourished, finding himself ever more trapped by his partner's shady business activities.

I've accumulated over two million pounds, Julian wrote in his last letter to his parents.

And this was just from Steward Export Company's main operation—purchasing rubber below market prices and selling it to avid buyers in the United States and Europe. For the most part, Julian was unaware of the methods employed by the Texan, and he preferred not to know. As expected, Julian became the face of Steward with his refined manner and friendly approach to customers and partners. Behind his back, he was seen as just that— a face, and nothing more. Alan was the driving force behind it. Gossip was calculated, and it all went along with the export company's dual dynamics—Alan inflicted pain, and Julian the medicine.

But a major war broke out in the world and convinced Julian that London was the place he needed to be. It was where his family lived, and also where stock companies were created to raise capital through the London Stock Exchange. He'd dictated many letters to his parents over the years, and lately, Julian has been preparing them for his arrival with Jandira. He would buy a lovely house in central London and still have plenty of money to live comfortably with all of them for the rest of their lives. Julian would go back to London even if Alan wouldn't, and perhaps make his father a partner.

After he got this last letter from Julian, his father wrote back informing that he had to enlist under the Military Service Act. His squadron was assigned to Admiral Beatty's Battle Cruiser Fleet to intercept a sortie by the High Seas Fleet into the North Sea. Jutland was a chaotic and bloody battle involving 250 ships and around 100,000 men. Edgard Welch was shoveling coal in the bowels of his ship when a German shell hit it. Julian's father died before he could enjoy the company and the success of his son.

The letter Julian received from a navy office in London shocked him.

Locked in a battle with the German battlecruiser SMS *Von Der Tann*, the HMS *Indefatigable* was hit midship and lurched out of line to starboard, when she was struck again in her turret and ignited cordite charges. The *Indefatigable*, which was the lead ship of her class of three battlecruisers, was covered in smoke when she sunk by the stern and listed over to port. She took over one thousand members of her crew with her.

When the navy tried to notify Julian's mother of her husband's death, they found their house in Tottenham locked. There was a pungent, rotten smell outside their door, and the police were called. Margaret Welch was found dead on her kitchen floor. Apparently, she had died of a heart attack before she received the news of her husband's fate. In Tottenham, word spread that Margaret had somehow sensed her husband's passing and just couldn't cope with it. The episode became the talk of the streets. Conclusions ranged from her death representing the ultimate proof that love had no boundaries and could be felt from a distance, to the idea that the Welches were cursed for letting their only son face the dangers of a remote forest, with the single purpose of becoming rich themselves. Subsequent letters from a neighbor friend arrived, and Jandira read them to Julian with a heavy heart.

Nothing of that rubbish mattered to Julian.

He now had no one left in England, no reason to return. The loss of his parents after all Julian had been through took away his most cherished and anticipated moment: his glorious return home. And home—that thing made of little conversations, routine visits to the markets, and the occasional laugh that made it all bearable—had hit him like a flash of light made of vivid memories that broke his heart into pieces. There would be no sharing with his family, no celebration of the achieved dream. Julian Welch was a devastated man and only had Jandira now. He hoped she would help him cope, as he needed her now more than ever.

Alan and Julian met for dinner at the Hotel Cassina restaurant, something they did at least once a week after each had moved to a fancy house when money started pouring in. The hotel had seen its better days and was beginning to look decrepit, which helped bring up the subject they'd been avoiding for some time: the need to move to a different country.

Asian rubber production was starting to pick up, and Alan and Julian didn't want to be late in their strategic decisions. Besides, both had been on the right side of the business and making money the old-fashioned way—by exploiting other people's sweat. But Manaus wasn't a financial center. It was going to have to be New York or London.

The Texan looked around the Cassina. It was cabaret time, and they were alone at the table. Alan gulped down his whiskey and waited for Julian's take about leaving Manaus.

"I suppose we could go anywhere we want," Julian said.

"Yeah, lad," Alan said playfully. "We're in that

category, you know, where people kind of have all the money in the world."

"More than we could spend in our lifetime."

"Hell, no! I definitely could spend it!"

They were in their early twenties when they met at the Port of Manaus almost a decade ago, and now they were over thirty. Life expectancy was a little beyond fifty. It didn't seem so distant anymore.

"New York seems right for us," Julian said.

"Different kind of jungle. We made it down here. We can make it anywhere. Including New York." Alan glanced away in no particular direction. "So, it's New York, huh?"

"Why not? Think about all the beautiful women up there. Maybe a wife can steer you in the right direction."

"Look at you, the matchmaker," Alan sneered.

"You know what's the difference between New York and Manaus?"

"Five million souls, last time I checked."

"The insects."

"They ain't got no titan beetle over there. You know, the one with an appetite for testicles."

The truth was, Julian wanted to leave Manaus as soon as possible. That city had always been part of a dream that included returning home to savor his conquests with his parents. Julian wanted to rid himself of the feeling that life had betrayed him somehow, in spite of all his success in the rubber business.

"Yes, but in New York, insects shake your hand, take you out for dinner, smile, and cleverly patronize you. They can be likable, unfathomable beasts. You fall in love with them, dream with them, and learn to trust them no matter how smart you think you are. And when you least expect it, they'll not only go for your testicles, but they'll pointedly aim at your jugular. They may not use spears like our tribal friends, but their pens are mighty and tempting."

"Yeah . . . Sounds like a challenge." Alan raised his glass of whiskey, and Julian toasted with him. A decision had been made.

"To cold winters."

Alan squinted purposively. "You know who's in town? The American counselor. He's a kind of second-ranking officer at the embassy."

"The elusive counselor . . ." Julian said.

"He's Alcantara's friend."

"You should invite him for lunch. *If* you ever get to meet him."

"Dinner. I heard he's more like me, if you know what I mean."

"You're incorrigible. I'll be home with my wife."

*****

Over the years, Alan had learned to respect Julian's high moral ground, though it still annoyed him. He had a conflicting understanding of where his relationship with Julian stood, accepting the fact that he was closer to Julian than anyone else in his life. On more than one occasion, Alan apologized for his appalling behavior during Julian and Jandira's wedding night, though he was unwilling to admit that Julian's forgiveness actually made a difference. Now, business needed to move forward.

Alan was told that no one got to meet the counselor. It was he who decided whom he met. Commander Alcantara, who was approaching retirement, had been known for his close relationship with the American Embassy. The counselor was the go-to man for a range of problems concerning the State of Amazonas, and Alcantara could help connect Alan with the counselor.

"Because I'm an American," Alan said, as if this was enough to meet the man. He was in a bathtub. The commander was in another bathtub next to his.

Alcantara shook his head. "I'm afraid that's not nearly enough. You need a reason."

A naked Polish woman showed up behind them. She emptied a bucket of cold water over Alcantara's head and shoulders, the most refreshing thing a man could ask for after a long night in Manaus's newest brothel. "Thank you, Gosia."

Alan glanced sideways at that tall, gorgeous woman. "I'm gonna marry you someday. I'm gonna marry all of you."

Gosia leaned forward and whispered in Alan's ear, "Apolline's ready for you." Then she left.

Alan sighed and got out of the bathtub, showing off his naked body. Alcantara turned his head to the other side, avoiding the sight. "Well, I'm ready for Apolline," the Texan said boyishly.

Jungle Apotheosis was a brothel built on money supplied by a mysterious foreign investor. It hosted a team of carefully selected European and Brazilian prostitutes. It was a miniature version of Teatro Amazonas, not in taste but in its excesses. It had all the marble and crystal and velvet one could wish for. Food and drink were of international quality—and ridiculously expensive. Clients knew they were being ripped off, but they didn't care. Ostentation was part of the appeal.

Apolline, the jewel of the crown, was a French woman whose sex appeal was legendary, and who was said to cure even the most impotent of men. Her résumé included dating a Brazilian president, ambassadors from a broad range of nations, renowned artists, and bishops. What excited men the most about Apolline was the fact that she was the only one who could choose her clients. When she chose them, they felt like they'd received some great honor.

Alan Reid had been chosen.

An hour later, Alan met Alcantara at the brothel's restaurant. He ordered veal with tomato, basil, and onions for both of them. Clients usually spent one hour inside the luxury suites of the Jungle

Apotheosis. Alcantara was marking it.

"Very timely," the commander said. Alan sat down, happy as a kid. "She's something, isn't she?" Alcantara said.

"Yeah! Fiery and talkative. Never thought she'd be so interested in my business affairs. No dissimulation at all. What she wanted to know, she asked."

"Seriously?"

Alan leaned forward and spoke carefully. "I was all over her, hard and mean. Instead of begging me to slow down, what did she do? She got the stamina to ask what my favorite government bonds were, what a gentleman like me was worth in dollars, and if rubber prices were going up or down. All while moaning like a queen!"

"That's Apolline, Alan. She's not of this world."

Alan tried the veal and gulped down a glass of red wine. "Three women in one night. Great women, I must say. All of them a bit chatty, but not a problem . . ." He glanced around, his mouth full. "By far, my favorite spot in the jungle!"

"If you're glad, I'm glad," Alcantara said.

"How come I've never heard of this place before?"

"I told you. It's invitation only."

"Thanks for inviting me."

Behind Alan's back, Apolline, freshly dressed like the night had just started, was ready to leave the brothel. She and Alcantara exchanged a brief glance on her way out.

The bottle of Château Latour was finished, and so was the dinner.

They moved to a terrace and lit Por Larrañaga cigars. Alan bragged about Gosia, Apolline, and the Italian girl whose name he'd forgotten. Alcantara patiently listened to him until the Texan got tired of hearing his own voice.

"About the counselor—what's his play? Why is he so darn hard to get? Maybe he's some kind of a diva. Nothing that money can't buy."

"There are things money can't buy, Alan. You know it. The counselor is a discreet man. So, again, what do you want from him?"

Alan stared at Alcantara with a frowning face. "My time here has ended. I'm going back to the United States. I need someone with influence there. Julian and I will keep the Steward Company and start a business in New York. I wonder if you'd be interested in running things for us here when you retire."

"I would certainly be interested."

"Good. Can you retire immediately?"

Alcantara laughed. "You know I'm about to leave the military. Yes, Alan. I think this is a great idea. We'll be on both ends of the trade."

"Fantastic!"

They finished their cigars in the next hour while they redesigned their partnership.

Apolline was back in the house, attracting stares.

She went straight to Alcantara and handed him a note. Then she looked at Alan as she walked away and said sensually, "*Au revoir*, Hercule."

"*Au revoir* yourself," he said and glanced at Alcantara. "Love letters?"

The commander showed him the note: *WAITING AT THE RIVER HOUSE. HARPER.*

"Harper?" Alan said.

"Harper Taylor. That's our man, the counselor."

"And he knows we're here?"

"That's his business. To know things." Alcantara smirked. "Apparently, you've been deemed someone worth seeing. There's a taxi outside. Harper doesn't like to wait. Shall we?"

*****

It was one of the most impressive properties in that wealthy Manaus neighborhood, an eclectic mansion of the golden age of rubber with two magnificent cast-iron sculptures crowning the access guardrail. The taxi dropped them off, and Alan and Alcantara knocked on the door. It was Harper Taylor himself who opened it. He was a thirtysomething man of medium height. The mansion's living room was dark, with only a pair of lampshades at the entrance hall. Harper was dressed in a slim-fitting, four-button suit that would do well in London or Paris, and certainly did in Manaus. His eyes were the darkest that Alan had ever seen, and they were piercing into Alan from behind wire-rimmed glasses. And while the eyes criticized, Harper's thin lips curved up, expressing a restrained welcome.

"This way, please," Harper said.

The counselor took them to what he called his library bar. Guests were transported to an Edwardian atmosphere. Harper showed them where to sit—on two red leather couches—and then sat behind a mahogany desk. While Alcantara knew Harper, he found it amusing to watch how unusually quiet Alan had been since meeting him.

The counselor's eyes were still aimed at Alan when he said, "I understand you wanted to see me. How can I help you?"

Alan cleared his throat. "I thought that maybe we, er, could help each other."

Harper kept his eyes fixed on Alan like they were glued to his very soul. He arched his brows. "When people help each other, no one gets hurt. The same with countries, I should add. Now that the world is burning, help has become a valuable asset."

"Can't say much about the world. I know my world is doing well, thank you very much. I've been in this hell for a decade. And I've had it. I'll be going back to the United States soon. I'm looking forward to meeting people with a mind for business. Forward-thinking people."

Harper finally turned his stare away from Alan, much to the Texan's relief. He glanced at Alcantara now. "You were right. He's just the man we're looking for."

"I told you," Alcantara said.

That brief exchange aroused Alan's curiosity. "Feeling a little lost here. I'm the right man for what? I thought I was the one looking for the right man," he said playfully, but he was bothered by the fact that he was not the one leading the conversation.

"The right man for big things," Harper said.

"And how would you know that? We've just met."

"I know enough about you."

Alan shifted uncomfortably in his chair. "Is that so?"

"Here's what I know. You're a man primarily driven by the impulses of the stomach and the pelvis. You're loud—and loquacious. Your brain functions at an alert level. Your survival instincts? Remarkable. They prevent you from letting out sensitive information about yourself even in extremely emotional situations."

"Sounds like horseshit, if you ask me."

Harper went on, unaffected. "You're very self-conscious. You miss your father, but, for reasons I ignore, you also hate him. And you definitely hate your mother. You think women exist to be used. You're sadistic. Nothing gives you more pleasure than inflicting pain on a woman. And even at the most rapturous moments of that sadism, your reflexes protect you from revealing things you consider sensitive."

Alan was baffled. "Was that meant to impress me?"

"No. It's simply ... a test. What you've experienced with Apolline? That is what I call impressive. Your ability to say a lot without actually saying anything."

The Texan sat up straight, realizing the man had deeply invaded his privacy and showed no respect for the reputation Alan believed he enjoyed. In the next instant, Harper felt two strong hands putting pressure on his neck. Chairs tipped over, and the room reverberated with the tension. "Some game you're playing here ... I'm not sure I like it. And what was it that impressed you the most?" Alan said.

Alcantara stood up, drew his concealed revolver, and aimed it at Alan. "Let him go. Now, Alan!"

The Texan released Harper's neck.

The counselor straightened up his suit, glanced briefly at Alcantara, and went on. "The fact that Apolline, even when she offered everything that you wanted, couldn't get the juice out of you. That's what impressed me the most. Sure, you told her you're rich, but not where your wealth sits. You bragged about your ambitious plans without revealing what they were and when they would take place. You're cautious, even at the apex of your pre-orgasmic moments. In short, you're a man for the world ahead of us. A world of majestic transformations."

Alan sat down, processing Harper's psychological

dissection. "I'm already in it. The Industrial Revolution depends on rubber to keep its wheels spinning."

"Sure," Harper said, sitting with his eyes fixed on Alan, his expression unaltered. "But I'm really talking about the other revolution. The one happening in the mind. If you control a man's head—if you understand how he behaves at the gut level—you control the direction of nations."

Alan looked at Alcantara. He was putting his revolver back in its holster.

"It's more than just profit," Harper continued. "It's about control—taking control before someone else controls *you*."

"Tell you what, no one's controlling me. You've said so yourself. I'm not easy prey."

Harper nodded. "If you have any ambition beyond Brazilian borders, and I now know you do, you need to listen to a little story."

"I'm not in the mood."

"Listen to him. You'll get it," Alcantara urged.

Harper moved on. "Let me give you an example of what vision means. Before the turn of the last century, seeds from the *Hevea brasiliensis* trees were illegally collected and sent to England. That was forty years ago, Alan. The seeds were planted in seedbeds. Many germinated. Then they were sent to the British colonies of Ceylon and Malaya, which have lower labor costs, and now they're thriving. The decline of rubber production everyone is whispering about these days started a long time ago. The monopoly Brazil has been enjoying for quite some time is about to come to an end."

"I know," Alan said unconvincingly.

"Now, one must wonder how that many seeds could be smuggled without the interference of the Brazilian authorities," Harper said as Alcantara shifted in his chair. "Those responsible for this smuggling were part of a coordinated effort that involved the control and connivance of authorities. Key people were identified, along with their weaknesses. They've been bought with money, and when they couldn't be bribed, they were blackmailed. Because, Alan, *everyone* has weaknesses. My job is to exploit them. And once you're in control, you're actually capable of changing the course of nations. The kingdom of rubber production is changing hands. That's no small feat. All you have to do is identify an opening—"

"And corrupt the hell out of men," Alan said. He couldn't believe what he'd just heard from Harper. The man sounded like his mother.

"Precisely. Are you in? I bet you'd be interested in being on the controlling side of this. You're not a man to be controlled, are you?"

"I'll be controlled when I'm dead."

"Is that a yes?"

"Where are we going with this?"

"Everywhere. But for now, there's a need for

expansion of our domestic intelligence capabilities. The US Department of Justice is hiring agents for all sorts of needs—internal security, smuggling activities on the Mexican border, and things of that nature."

"So you're with the Department of Justice?"

Harper arched his eyebrow. "I'm with something entirely different."

"So what exactly do you need me for?"

"I need you to handle the girls, and much more."

"Oh, well. I'll give it a go then."

The men shook hands.

PART 2

Christel Reid Welch
1948

11

In 1948, the Great Depression was as distant a memory as the Second World War that had ended three years earlier was beginning to feel. There was a collective sigh of relief in the air, and the future looked brilliant. Julian would never forget that day, a cold, windy late afternoon in December, seasoned by snow and precocious darkness. It was as if all the stars of hell perfectly aligned over his head, and the angels of luck went missing.

Julian arrived at his doctor's clinic, a Brazilian named Dorival Bragantino who had become a general practitioner in the United States after marrying an American woman. The doctor was an acquaintance of Julian's wife, Jandira.

He waited patiently on the ground floor of the clinic. Until his time came. Then Bragantino started a series of questions that forced Julian's memory to revive events that had taken place over three decades before.

"Do you recall being bitten by insects when you were younger?" the doctor began after carefully examining Julian's chest.

"Several times. I've survived malaria. I'm sure Jandira must have told you."

"Yes, Mr. Welch. But I'm talking about a particular bug."

In another life, in the Amazon rainforest when Julian was prospecting latex, he remembered a brief exchange he'd had with Moacir, the Karipuna tribesman. "Vaguely. It was ages ago," Julian said.

"Do you remember being bitten on the face?"

"Yes, I do. Around my left eye. It got swollen, but then it went away."

Bragantino pursed his lips. "Your description and symptoms suggest that you might have been bitten by a kissing bug."

"Can't be that bad. I'm still here."

"It's common where I come from. The bug usually shows up at night while people are sleeping. It feeds on their faces and ingests their blood. Then, it defecates on the person. Their feces carry the *Trypanosoma cruzi* parasites. Ironically, it contaminates people only when they scratch the bites."

"So, what are we talking about?"

The doctor sighed. "You have Chagas disease. I'm afraid it cannot be cured in this phase. Your heart is damaged. The irregular heartbeats will only worsen. You have a terminal illness."

"Jesus . . . Would it be appropriate to ask you how long I have?"

Dr. Bragantino shrugged. "Months—maybe a year. I'm sorry. Enjoy your time the best you can."

Julian wasn't a young man anymore. Death had been a subject of concern in recent years when he'd thoroughly discussed his will with his lawyers. Jandira was sterile. They didn't have children to inherit the fortune that had grown exponentially over the past decades as an equal partner of the Reid & Welch Company. Death was never a pleasant subject.

Julian had become a philanthropist and warmhearted businessman, a man of the arts, and a champion of humanitarian causes. He was a sensitive person who still remembered the effect of his parents' premature death during the First World War. Now death wasn't a bitter subject of a distant future anymore. It became a primary issue. Unavoidable. Imminent.

He thanked Dr. Bragantino and left the clinic in a state of disbelief.

He decided to leave his Jaguar parked outside the clinic and walk the twenty-block distance to his Park Avenue home.

What will I tell Jandira? he forced himself to think.

She was his only love and lifetime companion. He lived and breathed for her. Making Jandira happy was his most cherished cause. She was a simple woman born in a forest region. In all those years, not once had he seen her dazzled by the fortune they'd accumulated. All the expensive things she owned were bought by Julian as gifts. She rarely asked him to spend on luxury, and—he suspected—the few times she did was to make *him* happy, not herself.

Julian got home by nightfall with a plan drawn in his head. *I'm going to lie.*

If death was inevitable, then it was only fair that he chose to live happily for whatever time he had left. He would spend the rest of his days giving his heart to that humble, noble woman, and not once would he mention his illness. Jandira had saved him once, treating him the best she could in the harsh conditions of the Amazon forest. She'd done her part. Sacrificed.

The house felt oddly quiet as soon as he entered.

Julian called Jandira a few times but heard no answer. He went upstairs, calling to her like a happy kid. His plan to escape from the inevitable reality felt so right that he'd even forgotten about the Chagas disease. He was determined to die a happy man no matter what. But of all the plans he'd made in his life, none was so short-lived as this one. As soon as he walked into his bedroom, he found Jandira's body on the floor.

The image before him painted a landscape of horror. She wasn't moving. Blood was everywhere around her head, and it trailed from the sharp edge of a side table. It appeared that she must have gotten up from the bed, fallen for some reason, and knocked her head.

Her eyes were open but lifeless.

Jandira was dead.

Julian fell on his knees, desperate to escape his tortured thoughts, immediately distancing himself from that reality. Anywhere was better than being in that room. Preferably, a refuge beyond this world his mind was now fiercely creating for him—where pain magically ceased to exist, an instinctive mental bubble shielding him.

It took him two hours to gather the strength to call the police.

And two weeks to determine it had indeed been an accident.

An angel knocked on heaven's door.

12

Chicago was covered by snow.

Harper Taylor had just come out of a dinner at The Berghoff with his usual crowd—congressmen and big business. He was heading back to his hotel when he asked his driver to stop. He noticed something out of place: a woman showing her legs in a short overcoat, despite the uninviting cold.

In Chicago, prostitutes circulated mainly in nightclubs of the South Side Black Belt, the streets on the Near North Side, and some intersections in commercial districts on the South Side. This woman was alone trying to find clients in Lincoln Park, a nice, family-friendly neighborhood. And she was in front of a church, which seemed like an unnecessary provocation.

For ten minutes, Harper waited and watched.

Five cars had either slowed down or stopped to talk to her. The woman—a young, slim blonde with the face of a doll—behaved like she owned the world, performing a small ritual every time someone stopped. She would lean cockily over the window, smile, and then quickly turn into a ferocious beast after whatever she'd heard from the men stopping to address her.

Having worked his whole life servicing intelligence agencies and an assortment of interests, Harper had become a keen observer of people. There was something about that woman, at that particular location, in that weather, and with that attitude, that evoked thought-provoking notions. It was possible that she was drunk or drugged, but it could also be that she was putting her womanhood to the test, trying to offend someone in particular. It was a thin speculation, and her body language was tricky. In any case, Harper would bet he was watching a young woman searching for an opportunity, and perhaps brave enough to embrace one when she saw it.

"Pull over next to her," Harper told his driver.

The woman saw the gray Pontiac Streamliner stopping and, as expected, began her little ritual. Harper rolled down his window three inches, stared at her, and said nothing. Instead of leaning her elbows on the windowsill like she did with the other cars, she placed her hand on the top of the car and rested the other hand on her waist. And, for as long as that man inside the vehicle wanted, she would maintain her stare.

"How're you doing?" Harper finally said.

"I'm cold, thank you for asking." She was neither

drunk nor drugged. Another silence followed. Harper wanted to see how she reacted if she wasn't provoked. "I don't go out with weird people. You look weird, mister."

"I'm simply admiring your beauty," he said.

She knocked on the window twice with her fingers. Harper rolled down the window all the way. The woman leaned over like she'd done with the others. Their eyes grew very close. Both, in their own ways, carried depth and purpose. "You know . . ." she began in a mellow way. "You don't have to fear me. I'm friendly." Her smile was now broad and beautiful.

"You looked angry just a while ago."

"You've been watching me?"

"I confess I have. No second thoughts here, just was attracted by you."

"I tend to get angry when I'm cold and hungry."

"Let me ask you one question."

The woman rested her hands in her overcoat pockets. "You have to make up your mind. I see potential clients slowing down behind your car. What's it going to be?"

Indeed, two other cars were waiting in an improvised line, Harper saw. "What do you want?" he said.

The woman was one step from blowing up. "I'm cold and hungry," she said again and backed off a couple of steps, looking at the two cars waiting to pull over next to her the moment Harper gave up.

"I can warm you. And feed you. And I can do that for life."

She reassessed the man. He spoke in a fatherly way, appearing to be sincere. But she knew better. "You are that much in love already, are you?"

"No, I'm not. I'm simply offering you the opportunity to meet someone who might change your life. A businessman."

"Uh-huh."

"Are you willing to try? And what is your name?"

She walked back toward the Pontiac. "Are you trying to fool me? I've seen creepy people before. You're starting to remind me of one of them."

Harper reached into his pocket and pulled out a hefty sum of cash. "This is for the patience you've shown so far," he said.

The woman could not believe her eyes. "My name's Denise."

"I'm Harper. Let's meet tomorrow and talk. The restaurant down the corner would be fine?"

She raised her eyebrows. "Yep! Food for the rich."

"Meet me at noon. Let's have lunch."

"Sure."

"Just to appease my curiosity, why here?"

"You mean, in front of a church?" She smiled.

"Exactly. I have a feeling there's a statement somewhere in that choice."

"My father preached here. Didn't work for him, did it?"

Harper smiled back in sympathy. "Don't be late."

When Denise showed up the next day, Harper barely recognized her. She was wearing wide-legged, high-waisted pants of a neutral color, a white blouse, and walking elegantly in peep-toe heels. Her hair was perfectly combed, which had not been possible in the windy streets the previous night. Most importantly, she could pass as a family woman or someone who worked for the Reid & Welch Company.

"Do I even know you?" Harper joked when she stopped by his table.

"Can't say you do."

A waiter pulled out a chair, and she sat. "Thank you."

"I'm having a glass of wine. Would you like one?" He raised the bottle.

"No. I really would like to know what this is about."

"Very well. First, I need to learn more about you."

"Right. This is the thing. Believe me or not, yesterday was my first time on the streets. What happened was, my father caught me sleeping with a friend of his, a gentleman more than twice my age. Daddy also found out I'd accepted a gift, which, he presumed, was a thing a whore would do. Well, it just happens that I enjoyed his friend, and to be honest, I also enjoyed the gift. Yesterday? It was meant to embarrass him."

"I believe you."

"Good. I can't stand lies."

"How about your mother?"

"My mother is a lonely housewife. She has no voice. It's about my father, you know."

"Fair enough. Crimes?"

"Really?"

"I have to ask. Life-changing opportunity, remember?"

"I'm not a criminal, and I don't do drugs. I enjoy drinking every now and then. And taking sincere gifts in exchange for some loving. Does that make me a prostitute? Maybe. If it does, I don't care. Now, will you reveal your magical offer to me?"

"I'm at the board of a major corporation. Reid & Welch."

"Never heard of it."

"Our CEO—Alan Reid—employs women like you for special tasks." Harper saw the waiter approaching with their lunch. "I'm sorry, Denise. I went ahead and ordered us some steaks."

Denise smiled. "About time. I wasn't joking about being hungry."

"You would be working for a fixed income."

"How much?"

"Five thousand dollars a year."

"That's . . . a good salary," she said. Harper was starting to like her juvenile sincerity.

"And that's just to make you financially comfortable. The real money will come from those gifts you're such a fan of. You will, under our express guidance, date someone of our interest—lunches, dinners, nights out. You will sleep with him if he is interested, and only if you choose to do so. You'll never ask for money."

Denise nodded. "You're very direct, aren't you?"

"I guarantee you, the gifts will be generous if you're generous. I'm talking about an important man. Rich. Influential."

Denise rested her silverware on her plate and looked at Harper. "I get it. What about risks?"

"He is a well-educated man. But a man nevertheless. You'll be under my protection."

"I accept."

"Clever girl."

"So, am I hired?"

"It's up to Alan Reid. If you're ready, you can pick up your things and meet me at the hotel. I'm at the Palmer House. I'll be driving back to New York this afternoon."

"All I need is right here. You won't get rid of me now, mister."

She concentrated on her steak. After lunch, Harper brought Denise to his hotel. She waited in the lobby while he packed. Before leaving, Harper called Alan and told him about his finding.

"I'm dying to meet her," Alan said over the phone.

"She's a perfect fit for Julian," Harper said.

13

In 1950, Julian celebrated his sixty-second birthday.

Nothing excited him, enticed his curiosity, or brought him joy. He'd been in a permanent state of alienation since Jandira died, waiting for his turn to leave this unfair world. His five-story limestone town house rarely saw that many people. It had been Alan's idea to throw a party. He wanted to cheer him up somehow, and make sure people saw his effort to do so. Over time, whenever Alan had to show a public presence, it usually involved Julian. He was the *Welch* in the Reid & Welch building they owned, an architectural landmark of New York. Julian was the soft, trustworthy face of their company.

Dr. Bragantino was present at Julian's party, amazed that he was still alive. After Jandira's tragic death, he had diagnosed Julian with reactive depression and given him a tuberculosis medication called isoniazid, which proved helpful. Like the other guests, he would glance at Julian seated in his favorite corner and pity him.

In total, fifty people were present, including the inner circle of the Reid & Welch Company, a mix of wealthy entrepreneurs and government officials. Commander Alcantara, who was now a veteran military attaché at the Brazilian Embassy, was there. Harper Taylor, former counselor and current member of the board of directors at Reid & Welch, was there too, directly from the subterranean of the civilized world.

While a staff of formally dressed waiters served cocktails, a jovial woman with blonde hair grabbed two glasses of champagne and brought one to Julian. She had a candid smile, sure of her place at that party.

"Thank you, Denise," Julian said.

"C'mon, darling. Everyone's so happy. Why don't you join us?"

Julian shook his head no.

Denise Welch had been married to Julian for almost a year. She had established herself as one of Alan's many high-level assets. When Alan had first introduced Denise to Julian with a long speech about living in the present and letting the past go, Julian considered the idea of getting married again. *What is a man without a woman?* It was Alan's stroke of mercy. Alan himself had many women, but none he would call Mrs. Reid.

Alan didn't know about Julian's terminal disease, as Julian had told no one, but he knew that his friend wouldn't survive living alone in his house. Julian said yes to Denise, married in a discreet ceremony, and things returned to relative normalcy.

Julian's new wife walked back to entertain the guests, and they all saw when Julian stood up and went upstairs to his bedroom, looking moribund. But the pity they showed only lasted until their curious glances returned to the party on the ground floor.

"Meet me in the basement," Alan whispered to Denise and walked away first. She followed him a minute later, heading toward the kitchen. From there, she went out and reached their rendezvous point through a lateral door.

Alan was waiting with his pants down and his penis in his hand. Denise kneeled and performed her usual oral sex. Before he reached orgasm, she stood up, turned her back to him, and let Alan finish in his favorite way. When they were done, Denise lit a cigarette, leaned her back against the cold basement wall, and stared at Alan.

"What?" he asked.

"I'm pregnant."

Alan smirked. "Congratulations. How did that happen?"

"It just happened, OK?"

"I don't need you pregnant. And don't look at me like I have something to do with it."

"It's Julian's."

"Oh, boy . . . Do what you have to do."

"I'm keeping it," she said.

It was a blatant defiance of Alan's unquestionable authority, but Denise was not the simple, innocent woman that Jandira was. When she left the basement and returned to her guests, Alan knew he had a problem. Denise had friends. As much as he controlled her with contracts and a hefty allowance behind Julian's back, she was not someone he could quickly dispose of. And he saw how disgusted she felt every time they had sex. The fact was, a baby would require substantial changes in Alan and Julian's will. It was an unexpected event. Denise, like everybody else, knew how much Alan hated not being in control of things to come.

After all of the guests left, Denise headed to her bedroom, ready to tell Julian the news. Despite their age difference, she liked him, even though their marriage had been arranged and contracted. Her level of ambition wasn't beyond reasonable. Marriage had been a convenience, but she was genuinely excited about becoming a mother and had been anxiously waiting to tell Julian about their baby. Now that Alan hadn't objected—at least not in a clear way—she was looking forward to bringing the news to her husband.

Julian was already sleeping when she switched on the lights of the bedroom.

"What is it?" Julian said.

"There's something I need to tell you."

"Now?"

"Uh-huh."

Julian sat up. Denise sat next to him and held both his hands with tears in her eyes. "Darling, you're going to be a father!"

14

The upper floors of the Reid & Welch building were busy that morning. An influx of government money was lurking on the horizon and making the top executives edgy. Not that the company relied on public money, which represented only a fraction of the hundreds of millions in annual revenues, but being close to power meant that licensing and permits and official approvals of all sorts flew rapidly and without much pain whenever they were needed. Reid & Welch had interests in consulting, pharmaceutical, engineering, and the aerospace industries.

To keep the engine moving, Alan accepted specific projects in his portfolio that were sure money losers but gave him valuable political clout. He'd given up explaining the intricacies of his company culture to his younger executives. Whenever a bizarre, obscure project came up, they had a tendency to discourage Alan. To deal with them, he had hired Harper Taylor. Besides being a board member, he was the vice president of corporate relations. He merely did what he'd always done, which was act as a bridge between the business and government, the surface and the deep.

After the Second World War, more than sixteen hundred Nazi scientists and engineers were brought to America for government employment, including the notorious Wernher von Braun, who served as a NASA director and years later received the association's highest award, the NASA Distinguished Service Medal. Siegfried Knemeyer, one of the heads of the Reich Ministry of Aviation, was awarded the Department of Defense Distinguished Civilian Service Award. And Hans von Ohain, designer of the first operational jet engine, received the Goddard Astronautics Award. The purpose of bringing Nazis to America was to maintain a military advantage over the Soviets. In that spirit, eyes were turned away from Nazi atrocities and focused on the pragmatism that competition required.

Just like the US government, Harper associated with Nazi scientists, particularly those planning to use mosquitos as a biological weapon. He obtained protocols from the Dachau entomological institute and learned they were interested in continuing their research. A panel of scientists hired by Harper concluded that the German project was a mere eccentricity with no foreseeable value. However, the idea of developing an entomological weapon sounded promising, and Harper began operating on his own terms. He took the initiative of showing his concept to the government. His plan was seen in a good light. When government representatives contacted Alan Reid to develop it, he consulted Harper, who was more than ready to give it a green light.

"Say that word again, will you?" Alan asked Harper during a closed meeting.

"Entomological," Harper repeated.

"So, we train insects to attack people?"

"Insects are perfect vectors to deliver plagues."

"Sounds like horseshit. The plague part I get, but the rest, I'm not sure."

"The government is interested, and that's what matters. They're paying for it. And they're asking us to develop it."

"Governments can be idiotic."

"Let's not be the judges of that. They want a lab built outside our borders."

"Why?"

"It's a precaution—in case something goes wrong."

"How much are they putting into this?"

"Budget's around six million dollars."

"Not exactly a fortune."

"It could be if it works."

Alan combed his ducktail of white hair with his fingers and eyed Harper. "When you make up your mind, not even I can change it, can I?"

"When have I ever misled you?"

"OK . . . there's a place I own in the Amazon. It's just a large chunk of land covered by forest and nothing surrounding it but trees and rivers. You talk to Alcantara at the Brazilian Embassy. If he can find a way to get people and hardware down there without their government questioning us, then we might have a suitable spot."

Harper left looking satisfied.

Alan glanced outside the window where Manhattan was painted in gray beneath him. He recalled when he'd first met Harper in Manaus three decades earlier in a time of change. He felt that change was showing its face again, with fangs hidden behind smiling lips and eyes settled heavily on him. This time around, he wasn't sure if it meant attention or disdain for his current interests. Reid & Welch had grown more significant than he'd ever dreamed. He managed convoluted deals, intertwined corporate relationships, and lately, the fate of a little creature that threatened his absolute influence over the future of his company.

A damn baby.

There was a risk that the thing growing inside Denise's belly could disrupt the stability that Alan enjoyed in the company. He didn't want Julian dictating new paths for their partnership triggered by the arrival of a son. Things should, and *would*, remain as they always had—under his unbounded domination.

He heard a knock on his door and returned to his desk.

Edith McAllister came in wearing a full skirt, a blouse, and high heels. Alan's secretary was a dedicated employee who handled his official agenda and acted as a shield. She had no idea who Alan Reid really was besides being an influential and discreet businessman. Edith was a lonely churchgoer, not particularly attractive by her boss's standards. She'd been selected ten years before precisely because of those attributes. A true corporate woman with a perfect reputation.

"The Brown firm called. They're asking for an updated property list for your new will," she said.

"Thanks," Alan said, and Edith left.

The prospect of a baby got Alan obsessed with the will. Which, inevitably, got him thinking about his own mortality and the things and the money he'd accumulated. Alan was sixty-five years old. All versions of his will so far had been designed to make sure Julian's share and his private fortune came back to Alan's hands after his death, assuming Julian died first. If it were Alan who left this world first, his assets would go to Julian.

*****

Alan left the Reid & Welch building and drove his Bentley toward a property he owned on Amsterdam Avenue, a place that housed over five hundred children. It was a progressive institution where orphans could eat, attend school, and learn a trade. Boys and girls were strictly observed by the management. And while the Romans formed their first orphanages around 400 AD, the Jews prescribed care for the widow and the orphan, and the Athenian law supported all children of those killed in military service, Alan Reid had a vision of his own.

Thanks to Harper Taylor's excellent contacts in the government, he got Alan involved in a shady project organized by the Office of Scientific Intelligence of the CIA and the US Army Biological Warfare Laboratories. The property on Amsterdam Avenue was owned and run by one of Alan's overseas organizations called Maturity, a charity that wasn't part of his will.

The redbrick Victorian building of the late nineteenth century looked poorly built from the outside, and dauntingly depressing on the inside.

Alan parked two blocks away and walked until he'd reached a side entrance. He had his own key and avoided being seen around the building. After walking down a poorly illuminated corridor of walls full of mold, he reached an office door and used his keys again to get inside. He sat behind an old metal desk and made a call.

"I'm in the building. I'd like to see the subject."

Minutes later, steps reverberated out in the corridor. Two people approached the office and came in. Lory del Potro, a middle-aged Hispanic woman wearing a white apron and a Maturity orphanage badge walked in first. "Please come in," she instructed the subject outside. A shy teenage boy stepped inside. His gray outfit made him resemble a prison inmate more than an orphan.

"Please sit," Alan told the subject.

The young man nodded as he sat. Lory stood behind him.

"So, how are we doing?" Alan glanced at Lory.

"Very well. You can check for yourself," she said.

Alan turned his attention to the young man sitting before him. "Do you know who I am?"

The subject—his hair perfectly combed and with pimples on his face—smiled politely. His eyes were fixed on Alan when he said, "No, sir."

"Aren't you curious?"

"Yes. But—"

"But what?"

"I'm not supposed to be," the subject said, confident that he'd given the right answer.

"How are you feeling?"

"I'm feeling very well. I'm ready to serve."

"And how would you serve me?"

"In any way I'm required."

"Thank you. Please wait outside and close the door."

Lory sat down where the subject had just been interviewed. She looked satisfied by the brief exchange. "I told you he was ready."

Alan squinted. "I don't know."

"He behaved as expected. He was perfect."

"Almost *too* perfect . . . Have you noticed his eyes? They draw attention, Lory."

"We can change the dosage."

"You do that. But until we find out what's affecting his personality structure, the subject ain't ready—something about the way he sounds. He needs to look right."

"I'll talk to Dr. Lentz. Will you need me for anything else?"

"No. I'll walk around."

When he took his walk, Alan caught himself thinking about Denise's pregnancy. *Something needs to be done.* A few steps later, he reached a heavy metal door that almost looked like the door of a safe. He had a key for that door too. Beyond was the visible part of the Maturity orphanage, clean and warm.

It was lunchtime. The cafeteria was crowded. Alan sat, completely anonymous, and watched those human beings in need. Each had a drama, a breaking point, and hopes of a better future. Alan was aware of the influence he had over each of the souls being fed in that large room surrounded by tarnished windows. He felt like God. In his hands, he held the destiny of those he and his doctors called subjects.

But for the first time, he felt that his best days belonged to the past. He'd always been a man who lived every day like his last, not at all concerned with the future, but even he couldn't change the natural course of a force called life. He loved it for all he could take from it, and hated it for all he knew life was going to take from him in the end.

Not me, he cockily and irrationally denied. *Ain't gonna be no reckoning with life. Or death.* Existence was Alan's playground, and he could only cope with it when he was the one setting the rules.

"Mr. Reid!" a voice called and took him away from his existential wonderings. "Lory told me you were on the premises." A short, chubby man with thick glasses and a stethoscope around his neck shook Alan's hand.

"Raymond," Alan said. In private or in Harper's company, he would call that doctor "my Nazi."

"Do you have a minute?"

"Let's head back to the cage."

Raymond Lentz, the medical director of Maturity, followed his boss. The cage was everything behind the heavy door from which Alan had entered earlier.

On their way between the cafeteria and the second floor, Alan passed by the special dormitories. The subject he'd talked with moments before was voluntarily entering a small room with no furniture and no windows. Though the temperature was freezing cold, the boy took off his clothes under the supervision of a male nurse. "How long can you handle?" the nurse said.

"For as long as you need me to," the teenager said.

"What do you say we try for a day?"

Alan and Dr. Lentz slowed down and watched as the teenager entered that room, no larger than a cubicle, naked and in good spirits.

"Progress!" Dr. Lentz bragged as they continued on and up the stairs that led to the office floor of that human laboratory.

"About the subject's eyes . . . Dilated pupils are a side effect of the drug we're testing. I'm afraid the only way to overcome this problem is to do more testing," Dr. Lentz explained when they closed the door.

"What do you need?"

"Nothing. I've got plenty of material from what you've seen downstairs."

"Can you speed up things?"

Dr. Lentz tilted his head slightly to the side and chuckled. "I'd like to test younger subjects."

"How young?"

"The younger, the better."

"Young as . . .?"

"About ten seconds old. Young as the first breath."

"I see."

"Think about the benefits. To control human emotions—more than that, to mold them toward a specific goal. I mean, if that could be arranged . . ."

"What you're asking me is delicate."

"I know, I know . . . We had that, you know, back in Germany. It was easier then, but I understand these are different times. See, Mr. Reid, everyone accepted in Maturity has a record, either from distant relatives or the authorities. We would require babies without mothers, the ones abandoned in trash bins, near railways and the sorts."

"Let me think about it," Alan said.

Dr. Lentz saw the hesitation and went for the jugular. "Consider this. Get me newborns, and I'll get you the first psychologically programmable human being."

"There are boundaries, you know," Alan reminded him.

"Science, Mr. Reid, knows no borders."

15

In the eighth month of her pregnancy, Denise started to feel headaches, nausea, and pains that she believed were simply part of being pregnant. When Julian asked her how she felt whenever his new wife acted strangely, she lied. Denise didn't want to upset him now that their baby's arrival was only two months away. At the same time, the Chagas disease made Julian weaker by the day. He refused to tell her about his problem, and refuted any attempts by Denise to go with him to see a doctor.

Julian was napping after lunch and planning for when his son would be born—for the hundredth time. Denise stood firm and made it look like she was feeling great and excited, which was partially true, but she omitted the part where she was being pounded by a terrible headache. Instead, she called Alan at the office.

"I can't find Dr. Bernstein. I really need him. Can you help?"

"What's wrong?"

"Oh, where do I start? Just send him to see me, will you?"

"He doesn't work for us anymore."

Denise blinked a couple of times. Dr. Bernstein had been her emotional bedrock for years. "What happened?"

"Company problems. I didn't wanna bother you, Denise."

There was a prolonged silence on the other side of the line as if Alan was talking to someone else or thinking. "Alan, are you there?"

"Sorry. I'm right here."

"I called him at home. He's not answering me."

"There's a contractual thing. Once you're out, you're out for good. He can't see anyone related to Reid & Welch."

"Never mind, I'm going to the hospital."

"You don't have to. I'm sending someone to see you. He's the best doctor around. Can you wait a while? Say, a couple of hours?"

"I guess. I'll be waiting."

Denise hung up and walked from the kitchen directly to her bedroom. She lay down next to Julian and waited.

Raymond Lentz, Alan's Nazi, arrived three hours later.

The medical director of Maturity rang the town house bell and saw the door being opened by a panicking maid. "Quick! She's upstairs. I think she's having convulsions!" Kiara said. She was a robust African-American teenager capable of imposing great respect from whoever crossed her path, despite her young age. Her eyes were determinedly fixed on Dr. Lentz while she escorted him to the couple's bedroom.

Dr. Lentz found Julian holding Denise's head, trying to contain a seizure. Julian looked like a homeless man in his old pajamas, with his long beard and hopeless eyes.

"I'm Raymond Lentz. Please step aside, Mr. Welch."

"Where's Dr. Bernstein?"

"I don't know. Mr. Reid asked me to come."

Julian had more questions, but there was no time.

Dr. Lentz sat next to Denise and turned her gently to one side. Her breathing slowly returned to normal, and eventually, the convulsion stopped. He opened his medical bag and pulled out a sphygmomanometer to measure her blood pressure.

"She's not been well lately," Julian said.

"What are her symptoms?"

"She's been vomiting a lot ... Shortness of breath. Convulsions."

"How often?"

"A few times."

He frowned when he checked the sphygmomanometer. "Her blood pressure is high. I'm going to give her an intravenous injection with magnesium sulfate." He set the right dose. "This should help her with the convulsions."

Dr. Lentz gave her the dose and waited. Denise calmed down.

"What do you think the problem is?" Julian said.

"It's looking like preeclampsia. Has she always had high blood pressure?"

"Not that I know. Is it bad? I mean, for the baby."

"It's a serious condition, yes, Mr. Welch. For both her and the baby. It's a pregnancy complication."

Julian looked downward and took in the doctor's diagnosis. "Well, what can we do about it? Are there any treatments?" His hopelessness had now infiltrated his voice too.

"The best thing she can do is to deliver the baby. The sooner, the better."

*****

Decisions were made expeditiously in the following days.

Julian was a cherished figure among the best hospitals of the United States, being honorably described as one of America's top twenty most generous benefactors. He could choose any hospital in New York for Denise, but Alan had a different vision of what was best for her. Besides being the medical director of Maturity, Raymond Lentz ran one of the most exclusive clinics in the country, which was well equipped for small operations and could certainly handle the delivery of a baby.

Two weeks after Dr. Lentz diagnosed Denise with preeclampsia, she was taken to his private clinic, which was located just a few blocks away from the Presbyterian hospital. The place could only handle a dozen patients at a time, usually traditional families seeking privacy and the safety associated with being treated by Dr. Lentz. He was one of the first to perceive a shifting view on female beauty standards and was delighted to reinforce the trending idea that small breasts should be seen as a medical problem. His heavy accent and soft-spoken, trustworthy demeanor were skillfully aimed at making women unhappy by highlighting this new "problem." Almost all of Dr. Lentz's clients were women in search of breast-related contentment.

Alan joined Julian and Denise on their way to the clinic. He felt sorry for Julian, believing his extreme sensitivity somehow attracted the misfortunes of life. Alan stayed with him in the waiting room of the clinic, which was a challenge. Julian barely spoke or looked at him. Alan began to wonder if depression was contagious.

Dr. Lentz showed up before the delivery and stopped halfway into the waiting room. Alan turned to Julian, who was looking out the window, appearing lost and disconnected. He touched his shoulder warmly and got up, following in Dr. Lentz's direction. They had a quick exchange outside the operating room.

"We're ready," the doctor said.

"The baby's our priority. Our *only* priority, Raymond," Alan said.

"Denise . . . Well, she's not in good shape. Severe preeclampsia is delicate and can be fatal."

"Right. So, how're you gonna proceed?"

"The only thing that can help is magnesium sulfate. But no matter how careful we are, it's hard to be completely familiar with safe dosage ranges. An inadvertent infusion of a large dose in a pregnant woman can lead to death."

"And the baby?"

"We'll do our best."

16

Kiara, at nineteen years of age, was proving more mature than someone twice her age. Jandira had chosen her to work for the Welches right before Jandira's death, upon the recommendation by a friend. The young housekeeper brought the baby to the living room where Julian had been waiting dressed in black, untying his tie, looking at no particular spot in his majestic town house living room, which now seemed emptier than ever. He knew his time was almost up. Everything that he'd fought for, dreamed of, and accumulated—the artwork hanging on his walls, the architectural purpose behind the beauty that his home conveyed—would soon be meaningless. He'd been in that dangerous frame of mind before. It led to self-abandonment.

Denise Welch's funeral was carried out discreetly, just like their marriage.

No questions were asked. She'd been the unfortunate victim of preeclampsia, even though everyone had done their best to save her and the baby. The only ones present at the cemetery were Julian, Alan, Dr. Raymond Lentz, Harper Taylor, and Denise's mother, the one responsible for the most ear-piercing crying. Denise's father, the priest, performed a brief ceremony. He looked drunk, but nobody really paid attention to what came out of his mouth. Everyone had different worries. Mainly, the Reid & Welch Company's future in light of its new heiress.

Now, with the funeral over and Julian home again, the silent vortex of bitter thoughts storming his head was broken by a scream louder than anything he had ever remembered hearing. It was so loud that it could be heard even when the baby was still upstairs. And it was just getting rolling. That baby had no ability to restrain herself.

Yet when Kiara brought Julian's daughter downstairs and he laid his eyes on her for the first time, the baby miraculously calmed down. His grief had been so strong that he simply refused to see his baby earlier.

"Jesus Christ, my Lord! What is that? You two have magic together!" Kiara looked astonished. She handed the baby to Julian, who took her in his arms carefully and analytically. "That's an intense little human you've got yourself, Mr. Welch."

The baby was wearing a long pink gown and making cute, funny faces. Seconds before, she was on the verge of making everyone insane. Now the father and daughter's instant connection was growing stronger by the minute. Kiara leaned closer to her boss's ear and whispered, "We need a name, sir."

Julian kept staring at his daughter, the most beautiful thing he'd ever seen, touched, or gazed upon. Her light-brown eyes were almost green, which was evidence that she was her mother's daughter. Denise would continue through her.

"She's a thing of the gods," Julian gasped.

After prolonged staring, the little girl did something that almost sent Julian to heaven: she smiled. It was just a slight twitch at the corner of her lips, reflexive, but meaningful in Julian's eyes.

Kiara saw it and turned to Julian, who kept the same stern, fascinated face.

"I'm calling her Christel," Julian said.

"I like it. Baby Christel!"

"I want you to call Alan. Invite him for dinner with me tonight."

"But . . . you look so tired."

Julian glanced at Kiara. "Tonight, please."

"Yes, Mr. Welch."

It was like Julian had found a new source of vitality.

Baby Christel gave him a spiritual perspective he'd long forgotten, and an almost restorative hope. Yet his body felt too weak to walk to the nearest telephone, which was in his study. He returned

Christel to Kiara's arms and lay down on the sofa with a million thoughts going through his mind. It was time to face destiny with no more subterfuges. Suddenly, Julian felt useful again. He had a purpose: to ensure Christel's future, her rightful life among men and businesses with questionable scruples.

While Kiara prepared dinner, Julian stayed with Christel in her bedroom. She didn't cry once she sensed her father was around. The baby's future looked cloudy. Her only grandparents—Denise's parents—were maddening people, capable of driving their only daughter to find refuge on the streets. Julian didn't want them to do to Christel what they'd done to Denise. His daughter would be better off on his side of things. She would have plenty of money to grow up safe and comfortable and have the best education and good chances of finding a suitable husband. The only question mark on that long-term plan—and a considerable risk—was Alan.

Christel's bedroom door opened. "Mr. Reid is downstairs," Kiara said.

Julian kissed the girl on her forehead. "Wish me luck," he whispered.

Julian had requested that Kiara prepare Alan's favorite food, a spread of guacamole, chile con queso, tacos, enchiladas, fajitas, and quesadillas. And for Julian, she'd prepared a dish his mother, Margaret, had made for his birthdays: mulligatawny, a mildly spicy soup introduced to British households by southern Indian cooks. There were red wines, whiskeys, and beers in a bucket of ice.

Earlier, Julian had asked Kiara to leave everything on the dining table and stay away until she was called.

Julian saw the confusion in Alan's eyes when he saw the elaborate dinner served on the day they'd buried Denise, but there he was. The days where Alan was nothing but a rude Texan with compulsive attitudes were in the distant past now. He'd become a strategist, someone who'd mastered the art of being patient. Julian was dying before him. Soon, Alan would be the sole owner of everything that they'd built together. The baby was the only threat.

But Julian had one move to make before he left this world.

It was risky but necessary. To provide for Christel, Julian knew she needed to be part of the Reid & Welch environment from that day on. People would need to know about her, and get used to the idea that their business now had a legitimate heiress. The more public that knowledge became, the more Christel was guaranteed to be fairly treated and protected. Julian was well aware that Alan had no paternal instincts whatsoever, and how, over the years, he'd gained a veiled notoriety for being rough. Though the card Julian was about to play was chancy, it would be worse not to do it. Christel needed to be kept visible in plain daylight, not hidden in the darkness of Alan's business as an invisible, unheard-of heiress.

"You're my only true friend," Julian lied in the middle of the quiet dinner.

"Nonsense. You're a beloved member of New York society."

Julian ignored him. "And as my only true friend, I want to ask you something."

He raised his eyes to look at Alan.

"Anything, Jules."

"I want you to adopt Christel as your own daughter."

Alan froze, holding a fork full of guacamole in midair. "I'll take care of her."

"No. Be her father. On paper. And in life."

Alan nodded, lowered his fork, and said, "It's, er, an honor."

"I want you to keep her away from Reid & Welch until she's twenty-one."

"Wise decision."

"And I want all my shares to be transmitted to Christel when she reaches that age. The same agreement we have between ourselves stands with her."

"Absolutely. She's your heiress, and will be mine as well."

Julian poured wine into Alan's glass and served himself some as well, which felt very symbolic. He'd quit drinking since he'd fallen ill. "You know, we made a terrible mistake," Julian said.

"Did we?"

"Oh, yes . . . We've become hostages to money. We've missed what life is truly about."

"Well, everyone who's anyone sort of makes the same mistake."

"What everybody else does is their problem. I want you to swear you'll make Christel happy. I want you to swear, Alan, that you will allow yourself to be happy and humane. What's the point of beating them all? What do you stand to gain, really? Despite everything I've seen you do, I've never once forgotten our story. How we've built this company from nothing. See, there's value in the intangible things of life. What is friendship, after all? What is family? Everything. Don't you ever forget that."

Julian raised his glass of wine. Alan toasted him and promised, "It's been a privilege to have you as my friend and partner. Christel will get everything she deserves."

Julian sighed, and then he made an effort and yelled, "Kiara!"

"What do you need? I'm right here," Alan said after the unexpected loud call.

Kiara came into the dining room. "Yes, Mr. Welch?"

"Go get Christel."

"But . . . she's sleeping. You don't want to wake up that furious little—"

"Bring her down with all her things!" Julian ordered while staring at Alan.

"Jules, I think Kiara here has a point. Let the baby rest. We can talk about her tomorrow," Alan said.

"I don't know if I'll be here tomorrow. Or the day after tomorrow. Why waste time? You'll take her home with you tonight."

There were few times when Julian remembered winning an argument with Alan. That night, Julian cornered him. There was a determination in his voice.

Alan Reid was a skillful lawbreaker, born for business and shady deals. If it weren't for the substantial financial interests they shared and Alan's need to be discreet in the way he conducted his businesses, Julian doubted that Alan would have any genuine interest in his daughter.

Kiara brought the baby to the dining room.

Christel's peaceful sleep had been disturbed, and she was now crying like a powerhouse. Alan forced a smile when he saw the little girl, and struggled to cope with the noise coming out of her lungs. Julian was secretly enjoying the panic on Alan's face. Kiara held the baby in her arms and glanced at Julian. He nodded, and she handed Christel to Alan.

He held her clumsily, rocked her a little, and faked a smile with a telling frowning forehead.

"There's something else, Alan."

"Anything, Jules."

"You'll adopt her as Christel Reid Welch."

"If that's what you want. Christel Reid Welch . . ."

Alan repeated while he tried to calm the wild little creature.

Kiara looked at her boss with inquiring eyes.

Christel would only find peace in Julian's arms. She was a Welch, not a Reid. But the baby would have a better chance when the word spread that Alan had a daughter. The eyes of society would be all over her. There would be light.

After Alan left with Christel, Kiara returned to the living room looking appalled. Julian was getting up on his own, but he couldn't walk by himself anymore. She helped him to his bedroom, but instead of getting into bed, he moved toward his writing desk.

"Thank you, Kiara. You can leave me alone now."

"I'm sorry. I've got to ask you. Why did you give Christel to that man?"

Julian opened a drawer and pulled out a sheet of paper. He grabbed a pen, sighed, and closed his eyes. "Sometimes, you need to take the more dangerous course."

"Mr. Reid doesn't have a good reputation, sir."

Julian opened his eyes and gazed down at the blank sheet before him. "You're wrong. Alan Reid doesn't have a *shred* of good reputation. But he does have a name, and people will pay attention to the fact that he has a daughter."

"They sure will," Kiara said. "I mean, the ways of the rich . . ."

"It's good that you see it. You're a witness to my choice. Now, I need to write."

17

When Alan held Christel in his arms for the first time at Julian's town house, he had felt mixed emotions. Julian was dying, leaving his only daughter alone in the world, and Alan was considering Julian's advice, which emphasized the value of the intangible things. The value of life.

Alan took Christel to Arles, where he owned a nineteenth-century stone farmhouse comprised of several reception rooms, a family-size kitchen, and two staircases leading to the six bedrooms on the first floor. He flew with a nanny who joined the estate's permanent staff, which included a cook, two chambermaids, and a gardener. If any comfort was needed, Alan was covered.

For a whole week, Alan experienced everything people said babies did that brought joy. Acts that were supposed to melt anyone's heart, no matter how cold and insensitive a person was. From a distance, Alan heard the sweetest of giggles, but they weren't directed at him. Christel liked being around

Monsieur Lacroix, the gardener.

One morning, the nanny called to Alan, and he rushed upstairs. "You need to see this, Mr. Reid." They stopped by the cradle and watched. Christel stretched and yawned adorably, like she belonged to Arles and was part of such inspiring scenery. The nanny adored watching Mr. Reid's adopted baby. She hoped Christel would melt his heart too.

"So, the baby's waking up? Is that why you had me run upstairs?" he said.

The nanny leaned over and whispered, "She smiled."

"I'm sure it's some sort of involuntary muscular contraction. What would a baby smile about?"

The following day, when Alan was savoring his lunch outside in his garden—a celebration of Provençal and Moroccan delicacies and perfumed tomatoes—the nanny interrupted him and pointed at the cradle. "Look, Mr. Reid!"

Alan turned to see whatever was happening inside that box. "I'm looking. What am I supposed to see?"

"She's playing with her feet!"

Alan sighed.

And one night, while Alan discussed business with Harper over a transatlantic telephone call, he heard the nanny burst into laughter for no reason and became curious. "Is everything all right?" he said, covering the mouthpiece of the telephone.

"More than all right, sir. You should've seen her."

"Seen what, for Christ's sake?"

"She just sneezed. The cutest thing!"

After a few days in Arles, the nanny mostly stopped approaching Alan to tell him things about Christel, but she couldn't resist when Monsieur Lacroix brought his own baby one morning and the two children lay on the grass holding hands.

"You must come outside, Mr. Reid!" the nanny said.

Alan dropped his newspaper and followed her outside. He watched his gardener glancing down at the two babies and thought about how lazy that Frenchman was—there was so much garden to be tended. The nanny approached, smiled like she'd just won the lottery, and looked back at Alan, hoping that he saw what every human being would.

"Look . . . they can't really see each other, but they're holding hands!"

Alan spent about three seconds looking down at the babies. He felt nothing but disgust for the fact that people could be so dramatic when it came to pain or joy. Instead, he turned to Monsieur Lacroix and said, "Get the boat ready. I wanna see if the flamingos are around."

The night before his return to New York, the nanny took a leap that could have cost her job. She brought Christel to Alan's bedroom for a good-night kiss.

"Come in," Alan said when he heard the knock on his door.

"She's taken a bath. She wants to say good night to Daddy," the nanny said and froze.

Alan groaned. "Give her to me."

He took Christel in his arms. She indeed smelled nice and was surprisingly calm. "Huh," Alan expressed timidly. The nanny saw what looked like the shadow of a smile stretching her boss's lips. And when she was about to celebrate the fact that he was a human being after all, she saw his expression turn to disgust. He raised Christel up in the air and handed her back to the nanny.

"Oh . . . little baby just pooped," the nanny said.

When they left, Alan thought about the purpose of his week out in Arles. It was meant to honor his friend's request. A dying man's request. But the truth was that living with Christel for a few days did nothing to change how he felt about her, Julian, or even about himself. He regretted being so soft about the whole subject. Bonding with another human being who didn't offer him instant benefits wasn't really his thing.

When he was alone in his bedroom, he focused on the papers before him, which described the details of the project Harper was leading down in the Amazon—the entomological laboratory. Distractions on the personal side, such as the arrival of Christel, and the imminent death of Julian, wouldn't keep him from doing what he did best.

Damn Arles.

*****

In New York, Julian waited until the man wearing a gray overcoat got into a cab and left. His name was Everett Johnson. He was a young lawyer of strong ethics who had been recommended by someone outside the Reid & Welch domain, which was the reason why he'd left the town house holding a heavy box of files and a power of attorney in his suitcase.

Julian knew that Christel's future couldn't depend solely on Alan's commitment to honor his promise. He needed a hedge, someone to keep an eye on Alan. Everett was now in charge of overseeing all of Christel's interests, including her personal safety. Julian had paid the young lawyer half a million dollars to keep an unblinking eye over his daughter until she reached twenty-one years of age.

"I'm going to my bedroom," Julian said when Kiara called him for dinner.

He got into bed and pulled the blanket up to his chin.

While his body was deteriorating, his mind was remarkably active, with Christel dominating all spheres of concern. "It's done," he told himself.

With Alan committed to registering her in his name, she would stand a good chance of inheriting what was hers by right. And if something went wrong, Alan Reid would face an aggressive guardian named Everett Johnson. There was nothing else Julian could do but hope he'd made the right choices.

He'd warned Everett during their afternoon

conversation that Alan was a psychopath. Julian had been forced to accept him for his whole life. He was manipulative and dangerous. And he suspected that Denise's death could've been avoided. He even suspected that Jandira's domestic accident might not have been one.

The cold penetrated Julian's bones that night.

I'll talk to Kiara in the morning. She needs to ask someone to fix the heater. He pulled the blanket farther up, covered his nose, and left only his eyes out. They were wide open, staring at the blank ceiling.

Have you seen how well I did, Father?

He remembered his parents, Edgard and Margaret, in his old house in Tottenham. He imagined the conversation he'd dreamed about having had with them. *You were right all along. Everything that you warned me about, every word of caution, every piece of advice . . . But I've kept my guard up. I thought you were too stern and old-fashioned. I thought many things about you, but I was wrong.*

"Mother?" Julian called. "I'm coming . . . What've you cooked for me tonight?"

The cold was gone.

Julian felt warm under his blanket.

Christel came back to his mind and heart. "I love you, my tiny goddess." Then, he gasped for air. "The world is a j-jungle, my princess. I—"

Words failed him and he couldn't breathe.

Christel had been assured a name and a right to a

fortune, but it depended on Everett's ability to make that happen. The little time Julian had spent at her side told him Christel had all the hallmarks of being a Welch at heart in a world dominated by Reids.

Christel was now on her own.

18

Julian's death, though expected, came sooner than Alan had anticipated and affected him emotionally. He had not yet registered Christel as his own daughter, nor had he had the time to take care of the changes that would make Christel the heir of the Reid & Welch Company. Alan returned from France the following morning with the clear idea that he wasn't built to take care of a baby. But at the same time, he couldn't avoid feeling isolated and even lonely. A major part of his life had died with Julian. The best way to deal with it was by immersing himself in his work and ignoring any intrusive feelings that dared him to think and act differently. He was too old to change.

At the office, the older employees mourned, and the younger ones couldn't care less about the old man by the name of Julian Welch who'd never showed up at the building but was often seen in newspapers, revered for his philanthropic acts.

"Call Raymond Lentz. And call the Brown firm.

Ask Simon to come immediately," Alan told Edith. By the end of that morning, Alan was meeting with Dr. Lentz and Simon Brown, the company's principal lawyer, to decide Christel's future.

"I want you to appoint Raymond as Christel's legal guardian," Alan said.

"Are you the father?" Simon asked Alan.

"No. Julian is."

"I understand he's just passed away."

"Correct."

"Then it's complicated."

"Well, uncomplicate it," Alan said.

With Alan, it was never about clarifying how the law worked. He demanded his lawyers to always find a way around it and not get caught. "The simplest way is for Dr. Lentz to register Christel as his daughter," Simon suggested.

"What about Reid & Welch?" Alan said.

Simon turned to Dr. Lentz. "Raymond, are you a partner of the company? Do you own shares?"

"No," the doctor said.

"Then his daughter would have no right whatsoever to Reid & Welch."

"What have I been telling you over and over, Simon? Always go for the simple solution."

"Are you OK with that?" Simon asked Raymond. They were discussing the future of a child.

"Yes. No problem," Raymond said.

In any case, it was all settled. Raymond Lentz was

a reputable doctor and Alan's close friend. Simon was not aware of the activities of the Maturity clinic. Alan knew his lawyer wouldn't agree with it.

Raymond registered Christel that morning before Julian had even been buried. The doctor had listed her name as Christel Reid Lentz. In the future, if the situation required, Raymond Lentz could use Christel to protect himself against Alan Reid's impulsive decisions.

The following day, Alan went to Julian's burial.

Julian had been a reclusive man for most of his life, and a dedicated philanthropist. The splendid beauty of the Green-Wood Cemetery saw a crowd of about three hundred people who came to pay homage to a name closely associated with some of the leading cultural and academic institutions in the world. Julian Welch had wings and temporary exhibits at the best museums in the United States and Europe. Sometimes, he'd also contributed anonymously.

His goodwill had been appreciated on countless occasions. He'd been the sponsor of art centers all over the world and donated to dozens of institutions that were trying to do some good for the planet and for the people. He had funded scores of educational programs, professorships, and medical research programs.

None of them had ever seen or heard of Alan Reid.

Julian Welch, on the contrary, would be missed.

*****

Raymond Lentz arrived at the Maturity clinic carrying the baby in his arms. Christel Reid Lentz had been registered as his daughter, but she got yet another name in the clinic: Subject C. Throughout this process, Everett Johnson was nowhere to be found

Julian's precautions didn't last long. Alan had outsmarted him, just as he had his entire life. The staff at Maturity, bound by top secret security clearances granted by the government, would do their best to turn Christel into a useable asset. There was a Cold War out there. All their work was done in the name of national security, shielded from the public eye by the Reid & Welch network of companies serving as government contractors.

Lory del Potro and Ulrich Kohl were summed to the medical director's office on the second floor of Maturity. They were Dr. Lentz's most trusted employees, and the only ones to have authorized involvement with Subject C.

"You'll take care of her like a mother. I want her to have the best nutrition, sleep, and affection," Raymond Lentz said to Lory.

"Where did she come from?" Lory said.

"That's no one's concern."

Lory picked the baby up from a metal crib. "Hi there . . ."

Dr. Lentz glanced at Ulrich. He was a man in his early forties, with short dark hair and blue eyes filled with anticipation. As the director's right-hand man, the psychiatrist knew exactly what the presence of that baby girl with no origin meant.

"She's the subject we've been waiting for," Dr. Lentz said.

"I thought she was," Ulrich said.

"At the right age, you'll introduce her to men's desires," Dr. Lentz said.

Lory frowned. "Excuse me?"

Dr. Lentz eyed her briefly, enough to remind Lory not to step out of line. "The Soviets are way ahead of us in this field. Nobody said it was going to be easy, Lory. It's reassuring to have someone like you caring for her. Just don't lose the broader perspective."

Ulrich approached Lory and glanced at the baby. "My directives?"

"She'll live with Lory at one of our houses. Get Subject C used to your presence, until she reaches a certain age," Alan told Ulrich. "Then she'll live with you and be gently introduced to the world of men. You'll test it carefully as she develops. You're not to hurt her beyond the necessary conditioning procedures we've tested here."

"Jesus," Lory whispered, loud enough to draw Dr. Lentz's attention again.

"Understood," Ulrich said.

"Ultimately, Subject C belongs to the inventory of the United States. And, Lory, we don't do what we do because we like it; we do it out of necessity. We serve a higher cause. Needless to say, this is under the strictest classification."

"I'm ready for the challenge," Ulrich said.

"I'm sure you are," Lory said, absolutely disgusted.

*****

Everett learned of Julian's death and expected Christel to be registered as Alan Reid's daughter. Days later, when Everett decided to check on the baby's well-being, he paid a visit to the Reid & Welch building and couldn't get past reception. He demanded to see the CEO, Mr. Alan Reid, but the receptionist told him he wasn't available. Everett promised he would call the police, sue them, and make a lot of noise.

"Mr. Reid will see you," the woman said after his little show.

The young lawyer stormed into Alan's office and was pointed to a chair. He refused to sit. "I demand to see Christel Reid Welch."

"Who?" Alan said.

"What do you mean *who*? Julian's biological daughter. *Your* legal daughter."

Alan watched Everett. His straight-hanging corduroy blazer, modern and smart, and the dander on his face reminded Alan of Julian. "Young man, you're confused. I have no daughter."

"I have documents that prove otherwise."

Alan arched his eyebrows, trying to convey surprise. "Do you? Well, I have documents myself. Julian and Denise's request that their baby be confidentially adopted."

"You what?"

"A closed adoption. It means the parents chose to keep their identities private and exchange no contact with the adoptive family during or after the adoption process," Alan said, like he had memorized it. Like he was expecting it.

"I know what it means," Everett said in bewilderment.

It struck Alan that Everett was a younger version of Julian, all righteous and certain that the world owed him a fair outcome. "If you'd ask me—which I suppose you just did—I wouldn't know where the baby is, what her legal name is, or who her legal parents are. I'm sorry, but you're wasting your time. And mine."

"May I see Julian's request?"

"Sure." Alan placed two fingers over an envelope sitting on his desk and pushed it gently toward Everett. "I knew you'd want to see it."

Everett read Julian's alleged request. It had a notary public State of New York stamp on it and looked legitimate.

"Where was the baby taken to?"

"You want me to break the confidentiality of the process?"

*****

Julian Welch had been clear in his letter to Christel, which Everett had read countless times. *Alan Reid is not just a man one cannot trust. He is dangerous.* Everett glanced around the office. The majestic view of New York out the window made the twenty-five-year-old lawyer think twice about challenging Alan.

Everett thought it best to leave the Reid & Welch building. Julian Welch had entrusted him with his life's legacy, which included ensuring that his only daughter would get what was hers by right. Maybe he had underestimated Alan's mischievousness and taken too long to act. The feeling of defeat was unbearable.

19

As 1953 started, Harper pressed Alan to be more involved with the entomological lab being built at the Amazon property. Aboard a Convair CV-240 flying to Brazil, they had champagne and lobster for dinner like they were in a New York restaurant. Reaching the forest had become a breeze compared to the first time Alan had arrived in the region.

"Explain to me again why we accepted it," Alan said, questioning the intrinsic relationship between helping the government build a lab in the Amazon and being favored for other more profitable contracts.

"Because we had to. Because they promised us computer-related contracts. A project like this puts us high on our friend's list."

"Mainframe computers will change everything," Alan agreed. His frowning face adopted a lighter expression at the prospect of more lucrative deals.

"Companies are spending more and more on computers," Harper said.

"It's the application programs developed on a custom basis that are driving our consultants crazy. FORTRAN is a huge success."

"Isn't that an IBM language?"

"It is, but they haven't copyrighted it. It's what everyone's using."

The Convair made a stopover in Manaus and finished the flight in the city of Rio Branco, in the northeast region of Brazil. A Land Rover was waiting for them at the airport.

They drove for ninety miles until they reached the northern part of the city of Sena Madureira, and another three miles inside the Fazenda Reid & Welch on a bumpy, muddy track cutting through forest trees leading to nowhere. It was the same old forest that Alan had gotten used to in his early years— humid and hot and full of sounds he didn't necessarily miss.

"We've arrived," the driver said.

They saw a clearance, then a long and narrow structure made of wood and glass sitting perfectly hidden below the canopies.

"Is that all there is?" Alan said.

"The lab's underground," Harper said.

Kevin Steel, the lab's chief entomologist, took them for a tour. He was a short man wearing a carefully tailored suit under a white apron. He strolled, trying to leave them with the best impression of the little lab in the forest.

"So, this is our main section . . . And that's our beast," Kevin said.

Alan and Harper stopped near a glass compartment populated by a tiny insect.

"What kind of ant is that?" Alan asked.

"These are termites, Mr. Reid."

"Right. Walk us through what you're doing here."

"Sure. What you're looking at is perhaps one of the most abundant groups of insects on Earth. They colonize practically the whole planet. Now, we're talking about huge societies with literally millions of individuals."

"They like to reproduce. Got it."

Kevin pulled a smile. "A termite queen has the longest life span of any insect. They can live up to fifty years. They're superorganisms with self-regulating colonies."

"And we're attempting to turn them into a weapon by doing exactly what?"

Harper jumped in. "We're trying to change their diet."

"They're detritivores," Kevin continued. "They feed on dead material like wood, feces, and plants. The species we're looking at eats cellulose. They have a powerful midgut that breaks down the fibers."

"The idea is to make them feed not on cellulose but on soy, wheat, and corn," Harper said.

"That's what *we* eat," Alan said.

"Then you see where we're going with this."

Alan turned to Kevin. "How soon can we make them do that?"

"Hard to say... This small colony here? We've brought them from the United States. We've been working on them for some time. We'll do some tests soon, but the truth is, the expected results may never happen."

Alan turned to Harper, who pulled Alan away from the entomologist. "First, it's not our money. Second, we please the government and—"

"Yeah. We'll be selling a lot of computer programs. I get it." Alan glanced at Kevin. "I've seen enough. Where does a man get to eat here?"

"We're having a barbecue, Mr. Reid."

"Nice. I'm ready when you're ready. What's on the menu?"

"Local meat."

Outside, a firepit was already cooking a crocodilian alligatorid of the caiman species. There was beer, and the mood was light. The one thing that concerned Alan was the risks he couldn't see, and the fact the lab had been built on a property carrying the name Reid & Welch.

"When you say you're testing, how exactly do you plan to do that?" Alan asked Kevin.

"There have been experiments conducted in sealed greenhouses and labs, but not yet in the open. Eventually, we'll disperse the termites into corn fields," Kevin said.

"Let's make sure they don't go beyond that."

"Absolutely." Kevin raised his beer bottle and walked away.

"It's a one-of-a-kind project," Harper said.

"I hope the government won't actually use this to destroy crops."

Harper squinted. "Tell me, would you be bothered?"

"Not if it doesn't affect my meals."

"Thought so. And no. The government wants a deployable countermeasure against engineered threats to our own food supply. Threats posed by state and non-state actors."

"Horseshit. They just want a new weapon."

Alan tasted the caiman meat and made no effort in hiding his dislike. He was getting tired. And, in a twisted way, the forest reminded him of Julian. He smashed a mosquito on his neck and checked its blood in between mouthfuls of roasted meat.

"I'll make sure our partners know how hard this has been," Harper said.

Alan nodded, but he wasn't listening. The truth was, there was no substitute for Julian. Reid & Welch had been a marriage. Alan was the impulsive one, stepping on everyone's feet and crossing every limit. Julian represented the prudent, humane side of their partnership. How much he knew about how far Alan had gone, or how dirty he'd been, Alan couldn't tell.

"What's going on, my friend? You seem somewhere else," Harper said.

"I don't know if this is working."

"Of course it is."

"For me, Harper. I'm not . . . enjoying this."

"Oh. You're probably getting old, that's all. Is there anything I can do for you?"

"Nope. Unless you can fix jealousy—of my younger self."

"We can't."

"It's all becoming a darn repetition."

"Why don't you go take a nap before we go back?" Harper tapped Alan's shoulder and walked in Kevin's direction as large raindrops began to fall.

"Where can I rest my body?" Alan asked on his way to the lab.

"All the way to the back, sir," a young engineer said.

I've gone too far, Alan's quietest inner voice mused.

A current of unexplainable thoughts struck him. And just when he was about to recognize all the wrong things he'd done in his life, the younger Alan came back to save him from repenting. He lay down in the small lab bedroom, thinking of how untimely those thoughts were. It wasn't hard for him to make them go away.

Gone. Screw them all.

There was a flight back to New York the next day. He wouldn't miss it for anything.

20

When Christel was thirteen years old, a gynecologist from Maturity examined her and informed Dr. Raymond Lentz that she was physically ready for sexual intercourse. Dr. Lentz called Ulrich, authorizing him to move forward with the next phase of the project.

"You're to move Subject C from Lory's house and operate from the City of Frederick."

"And Lory? She's developed an attachment to Subject C."

"We were expecting this, but all ties must be cut. I'll talk to her."

"Any special recommendations at this point?"

"She needs to get used to our target's appetites. Be rough but don't hurt her. She needs to have a place to come back to. A place she feels safe."

The City of Frederick was located less than an hour from Washington, DC, between the Civil War battlegrounds of Monocacy, Antietam, and Gettysburg. It had impressive architecture and a host of art centers and private galleries. Maturity had a four-thousand-square-foot Victorian home near Baker Park with four acoustically sealed bedrooms and three full bathrooms.

The day he moved in with Christel, Ulrich took her straight to her bedroom, undressed her, and saw no fear in the teenager's eyes.

"We're going to make love. Are you comfortable?" he said.

She nodded.

Ulrich penetrated her with caution, saw a slight reaction in her facial muscles, and waited until she got used to the new game. When Christel closed her eyes, Ulrich unleashed years of repressed lust for the girl. His movements were furious. She moaned a few times, but he didn't know if it was from pleasure or pain. There was no "love" in that mechanical act. His job was to get her used to it. Her future targets wouldn't care about what she felt.

Throughout the following years, Ulrich had an insatiable routine with Christel. During the day, he was a respected psychiatrist with a clinic in the city and a daughter being homeschooled by selected teachers who taught her how the world was in a constant state of war, and why personal sacrifices were needed. That rationale became the norm.

Ulrich was frequently seen parading with Christel in downtown Frederick and Baker Park enjoying summer concerts, gallery walks, and theater performances. She was gorgeous, attracting attention wherever she went. The idea was for Christel to develop a taste for art and an aptitude to lie about her private life.

At night, Ulrich was a psychiatrist with a license to abuse.

When she was sixteen, Dr. Lentz authorized Ulrich to test Christel with real targets. "We're upping the game now, Christel. You'll be transmitting short messages and collecting answers. They'll be expecting it," Ulrich explained.

"You mean like a carrier pigeon?"

"Attagirl."

Soon government officials, diplomats, businessmen, black budget contractors, governors, and congressmen were leaving their marks on Christel's psyche and on her body. When she reached eighteen, she was considered a seasoned and reliable asset, and the stakes got higher.

Now, her psychological conditioning and her endurance for pain would be put to the test.

*****

A Middle Eastern prince was about to start a huge engineering project in his beloved nation. A construction bidding process took place. It secretly included the acquisition of surface-to-air missiles, a deal that couldn't be done officially due to an embargo posed by Washington. A few American corporations didn't want to stay out, though. Strings were pulled, and the government decided that they would supply that nation with older versions of the missiles, which were still superior to the competition's.

In exchange for winning the construction bid, Subject C was sent to meet the prince and deliver that decision. Fortunately for her, the target took pleasure in watching her masturbate and didn't even touch her.

"They're open for talks," she whispered to the prince before she left to return to the United States. That was her message. The United States would be supplying the missiles, but Christel had no idea what the communication implied.

"I'll be visiting you soon in your country," the prince said. It was his message back. He'd be buying the missiles. The deal was done without any unwilling noise. It had all worked flawlessly. Subject C was not a person of interest. At best, she was just a prostitute.

On another occasion, Christel had been assigned to meet a congressman and deliver sensitive information for the leader of the opposition party. "There will be a change in the State Department. They're welcoming suggestions," she told him.

"We have a name," the congressman replied. And that was all.

Her work was carried on confidently over the years. Christel had no discernment of right or wrong; she just did as she was asked. That was part of her programming.

She had no idea what true lovemaking was until she turned nineteen and was assigned another mission that would begin to change her perception. The target was the son of a traditional private banker instead of another creepy old man. She was taken to a small cottage surrounded by private guards in Lake Geneva in Switzerland and introduced to a sweet boy of fourteen. His name was Denizard Haener. His father had heard rumors concerning the beauty and the talents of an American operative named Subject C. He wanted his son to experience the best.

Christel considered that mission the most noble so far, as she was going to be his first lover. The boy's nervousness contrasted sharply with all previous relationships she'd had. The ever-present tension wasn't there. All went smoothly. There were no unpleasant surprises and no threats. His innocence made her feel an intense connection with that boy, which allowed her to pay attention to her own feelings. Christel experienced something she never had before: an orgasm. In that sense, it was her first time too, and she never forgot Denizard. For the remaining twenty minutes of the time stipulated by the contract, both gazed at each other, enchanted, and exchanged gentle caresses.

By the time she was twenty years old, Christel had another memorable experience, but one she preferred to forget.

Ulrich sent her to a farm where a man called Mason Williams was waiting for her. He was the CEO of the Mason Williams Oil Company of Texas. When she arrived, the target had five friends with him. Christel was the only woman. Her assignment was to simply make that man sexually happy. Ulrich explained that her mission was to provide a favor requested by an undisclosed name.

That group of beasts surrounded Christel, the stink of alcohol unbearable. No words of courtesy were exchanged. Other than their disgusting breath, she remembered being punched in the face and falling over a bear rug. The hours that followed, during which the men took turns raping her, passed painfully and confusingly. She thought of that boy, Denizard, and kept thinking of him for as long as the savagery lasted. That young Swiss symbolized the possibility of an entirely different life. Maybe, she thought, life was not restricted to what she'd been taught to believe.

By morning, she had bruising all over her body. Her vagina and anus bled, which made walking almost impossible. Since that day she'd experienced post-traumatic stress disorder that included nightmares, severe anxiety, and uncontrollable thoughts of revenge. For months, she'd had suicidal thoughts.

And she missed Lory, the closest thing she'd had to a mother. Why they had to take her away from Lory became an ever-present question. She also wondered if there was a limit for pain. Maybe Ulrich would find her too weak if she talked to him about how vulnerable and lonely she felt. God forbid if she disappointed him, but something wasn't right. There was an urge to break through that sacred barrier she knew existed between her and those not involved in this silent, cold war. She'd seen or heard, here and there, that soldiers had a time to serve and a time to retire.

I'm young, but I feel old.

21

In 1971, while the Vietnam anti-war movement was trying to disrupt government business in Washington, Everett Johnson was running against the clock to save himself from the burden of failing miserably.

Twenty-one years before, he'd been assigned a task.

Julian Welch, a dying philanthropist, had paid him half a million dollars to take care of his only daughter and make sure his will was respected. Christel, wherever she was, had turned twenty-one and was now entitled to receive half the shares of the Reid & Welch Company, and much more.

But Everett had lost track of Christel after Julian died.

For the following two decades, he'd tried whatever he could to locate the missing baby. He'd hired private investigators who'd found nothing and had extensive discussions with his peers about taking legal action against Alan Reid. It was going to be his documents against Alan's, who had been Julian's partner for decades. An almost insurmountable challenge.

A master manipulator. Forged document enthusiast, the letter and the extensive files that Julian gave showed.

All the while, Everett had been considering leaving his law practice. The half a million dollars given to him by Julian was a small fortune. He finally quit practicing law five years after his meeting with Julian, but he promised himself he would never give up looking for Christel. He just couldn't. As the years went by, his concern about her fate became an obsession. He tried a meeting with Alan years later, but he was warned that Reid & Welch would consider suing him for harassment and false accusations. It was pointless.

Before NGOs had become a common thing, Everett started an organization that would focus on defending the environment wherever it was being threatened. Playing a positive role in the world, even a small one, had always been his true passion. Case by case, he started to regain his lost confidence in the law. That liberty to choose where and when to act was only possible because of Julian Welch and his generous payment.

Now, after twenty-one long years had gone by, he didn't believe he would ever find Christel. Still, Everett was feeling good about himself. His failed marriage was behind him, and he was at peace. The

NGO he'd created was doing well. His work was gratifying. He got to travel all over the world. He got to meet different people with unique and enriching values. And his financial life was better than ever. The first half a million dollars of two decades earlier had turned into almost two million. He'd bought a Brooklyn brownstone town house, a smaller version of Julian's house, where he enjoyed having dinner with some of his female friends.

One night, after he returned from a trip to California, he served himself a glass of red wine and heard the phone ring. Everett ran to pick it up. He had a particular woman in his mind, a potential sponsor for his NGO.

"Mr. Johnson? Everett Johnson?" the female voice said on the phone.

"Yes. Who is this?"

"My name's Lory del Potro. You don't know me, but I have a file on you. We need to talk."

Everett raised his eyebrows. "A file on me? What's this about?"

"Christel Lentz Reid."

Christel "Lentz" Reid? Everett's heart almost came to a stop. "Julian and Denise's daughter?" he asked.

The voice on the other side went silent for a bit. When it continued speaking, it sounded more nervous than before. "It's complicated, Mr. Johnson. But, yes. It's the same person."

Now it was Everett who spent a bit digesting that

information. Someone was contacting him about Christel. *Could this be true?*

"How is she doing?" he said.

"I think it's best we meet."

"Give me an address and I'll meet you right now."

"No. I'm sorry. You can't just come. They're watching me, you understand?"

Everett massaged his eyes. "When would it be all right?"

"Tomorrow? After four p.m. But you can't stay long."

"Will I be seeing Christel?"

"I have her phone number. Seeing you is up to her."

*****

Lory gave him an address in Altamont, a small village located in the town of Guilderland, New York. Everett arrived almost two hours early. He parked his Pontiac Firebird one hundred yards from the address, an old brick Cape Cod house. There was a detached garage with an open door showing a Ford Fairlane inside it, and a large backyard covered in snow. Why anyone would be watching that house was something Everett couldn't understand.

But he saw a man leaving the house at three thirty. It looked like a government official wearing a black overcoat and a gray suit. At precisely one minute to the appointed time, Everett got out of the car and headed to the house.

Lory looked out the window and saw him approaching. She opened the door. "Mr. Johnson?" she said while turning her head to look down both sides of the street.

"Yes. Lory?"

She nodded. "Please, come in."

Lory was about seventy years old, with profound marks of aging on her face. As Everett stepped into the living room, he was immediately struck by the number of portraits of a gorgeous brunette girl at various ages—some of them with Lory and a little dog—from a baby picture that didn't indicate much up to a teenage picture that promised an adult who would drive men crazy.

"She was thirteen in that picture."

"Any recent ones?"

"No. I'm not allowed to have any. Please sit."

Not allowed?

They sat near a fireplace facing each other. "You said you have a file on me. Why? Who are you?" Everett said.

"I'm a nurse. I'm retired now. I worked for an orphanage in New York."

"Is that where Christel was taken?"

Another nod. "I know you've been looking for her since she was a little girl. As I said, there's a file on you with the specific recommendation that we deny Christel's presence in the orphanage in case you showed up looking for her."

"How would you know about me?"

"Because the orphanage is owned by Alan Reid. He was the one who warned us. We were told to refute Christel's existence."

"Why?"

"It's a long story, Mr. Johnson. I'm afraid I'm not at liberty to tell you about it."

"Why did you call me, then? And why now?"

"I no longer work for them."

"You mean for Alan Reid."

"Yes and no. Christel was in a government-sponsored program managed by the Maturity orphanage. She's twenty-one now. She's got the Reid name. Maybe there's a different life waiting for her. Whether you believe me or not, it was Mr. Reid who asked me to contact you, as long as the government doesn't find out."

The questions were adding up fast. "Alan Reid denied Christel her right to the Reid & Welch Company."

"I'm the last person to say anything positive about that man, but he's old now. I've given up trying to understand the ways of the world."

"What's your relation to Christel?"

"I raised her. She's like a daughter to me."

"That explains the pictures. She grew up here."

Lory stood with a vacant stare. "Look, I know you have a lot of questions. All I ask you is to let Christel answer them. I mean, if she wants to. You shouldn't be here, you know. I shouldn't be talking to you, but Mr. Reid suggested I see you in person and to avoid phones."

"Fair enough. You said you have her number?"

"I lied. I had to. I didn't know if you would come."

"I understand."

Lory walked Everett to the front door. He turned when he was outside. "You need to put her in contact with me."

"A word of caution, Mr. Johnson. Christel's no longer the sweet teenager you saw in those pictures. And she doesn't remember this house."

"What happened?"

Lory sighed. "Let's say she had a different upbringing . . . I tried to show Christel how beautiful life can be. But others in the orphanage messed with her head. Be ready to be rejected or jerked around."

22

Since she became an effective operative, Christel grew more aware of her role and felt a sense of duty for her assignments. Along the way, she collected a host of small marks around her skin and bones. Cigarette burns, cuts, and bruises. But nothing changed the hypnotic effect that the five-foot-eight young woman had on men and women.

She was alluring enough to be their wives or daughters. When she talked, she looked straight into people's eyes with confidence and interest. Her voice was of an older, more experienced woman, which, when combined with her young, fit body, silken skin, and glossy dark hair, had a captivating effect when they listened to her. The marks on her body ended up being jewels on the crown for those who enjoyed seeing pain expressed on the skin of another human being.

Men, Christel learned, were selfish and sadistic. The only exception she'd known was that boy, Denizard, but he was like a ghost. After the traumatic experience with Mason Williams, Christel asked Ulrich to allow her some time without seeing anyone. During that period, she began to recall flashes of her early life with Lory del Potro.

Memory was a problematic thing. She was the most capable person when it came to short-term, mission-related assignments, but there was a truckload of items stored away somewhere in her mind. "Stored" was the term Ulrich used when Christel talked about them with him, but at times, her mind would overflow, like a reservoir of water asking for the floodgates to be opened. Images and voices appeared here and there. She had no control over these memories or when they would occur.

She was making dinner one night after Ulrich had sex with her. She cut the tomato and left it on a plate on the granite countertop next to the sink. She glanced outside the window and then closed her eyes. Her mind was no longer there. A floodgate had just opened.

A snow-covered yard. The house where she had lived with Lory. Behind it, a wide piece of land. There was a dog. An ugly but cute Pekinese. The house was full of people she didn't recognize, except for Ulrich and Dr. Lentz. They circled the young Christel like she was a circus attraction, drinking and eating. Lorry offered her arroz con leche, *her favorite Mexican dessert. She was dressed in a white cotton dress with flowers on the shoulders and a pair of white sandals to match, despite the freezing cold. Her hair was neatly combed and secured with a hair tie—also white—that made her look like a doll. The sense of ridicule and discomfort increased with the weight of all those eyes on her—and the laughter. Lory took her hand and led her inside the house. The Pekinese ran after them, but Lory closed the back door before he could come in with them. He was left outside with the wild beasts in the yard.*

When the flashback ended, she found herself sitting alone, eating the salad she had begun to prepare earlier. It left her with a nasty, empty vault inside her chest. Each time the flashes occurred, Christel took mental notes so she would never forget them. Gradually, memory fragments began to match, to make sense. There was life beyond the world of Maturity, Ulrich, and Dr. Lentz. She started to have more questions than answers.

Where are you? The memory of the Pekinese dog made her heart ache.

Steps reverberated between the living room and the entrance hall.

Ulrich was wearing shoes. It meant he was dressed for work, even though it was nighttime and Christel was tired. She saw Ulrich go into the kitchen. She shrunk back against the chair, instantly adjusting to the posture required when she was about to be briefed for a mission. Years of trauma had given Ulrich the power to control Christel through fear.

He rested a hand on her shoulder as if to take

possession of a product that he thought was his. Calmly but firmly, he raised Christel's head by the chin and forced her to look into his eyes. Then he touched Christel's forehead with his thumb. That simple touch, symbolic and without the need of any additional words, was intended to activate one of Christel's mental compartments—a short ritual that had been exhaustively repeated over the years. She'd been conditioned, just like one would do to an animal.

Christel offered him her full attention, exactly as expected. Ulrich spent the next minute watching her pupils, evaluating her reactions. There was always the possibility that Christel was pretending to be in a given condition.

"Put this on," he said, handing her a bag.

She took out the contents: a long-sleeved, V-neck, black dress, high-heeled shoes, a black bag, delicate lingerie, a necklace of black South Sea pearls, French perfume, and a full set of makeup. Her tools of work helped set the right frame of mind. Every time he brought her new things, she knew what to do. It was an insult to the female condition, but her upbringing had stripped Christel of that awareness. She had no rights or dignity to worry about.

She undressed right there. He loved seeing the scars and marks on her body. They were like trophies on a shelf.

"Did you eat well?"

"I'm not hungry."

Ulrich shook his head. "You should." Then he gave her a note. Christel opened and scanned it. He didn't have to explain much. "José Steward is the Mexican honorary ambassador. He's known as El Pepe. You'll meet him tomorrow night after he returns from a reception in Washington. In his hotel room."

She looked into Ulrich's eyes, furrowed her brow slightly, and nodded. Ulrich explained: "The ambassador likes to drink whiskey." Then, he handed her a small plastic box containing white pills. "Put one or two of these in his glass. Leave the remaining pills on display. It'll be El Pepe's choice if he wants to take one or a dozen. He knows what this is and is waiting for someone to deliver it."

"What are they?"

"The CIA's favorite drug. The ambassador is entirely at the mercy of the agency. There are no other suppliers for this, so he does what they want him to do."

"I understand."

"Mind you, one extra pill can be fatal. El Pepe's medical records say his body is accustomed to taking a maximum of two pills at a time, every five days. Now, usually, it's his private physician who gives them to him. Sometimes they use couriers like you."

"You promised me less troubled people," she protested carefully.

"Men love you, Christel. The ambassador is an old man. Do you realize what I'm doing for you?"

"What?"

"I'm sparing you. Because I care. I'm making it easier for you."

"How so?" She was curious but docile.

"The pills will likely put our target to sleep. With a little luck and skill, you'll be able to transmit the information to El Pepe without having to sleep with him."

"I'm grateful to you," she quickly conceded.

Ulrich looked Christel up and down as she rose from the chair. "It's good to be grateful," he said.

"I'll never let you down," she said confidently.

The memories of Lory and the house with the Pekinese dog were giving Christel a sort of lucidity that she'd long lost. It was refreshing to accept that Ulrich wasn't as frightening as she'd believed. *There's life beyond the rules of my world*, she thought. And if she kept following these rules and avoided getting hurt, she'd be able to find a way to the other life that her memory told her existed.

Those thoughts brought clarity to her mind. She was baffled to learn she was no longer under Ulrich's control.

Who am I? she asked herself for the first time.

"There's a plane waiting for us," Ulrich said.

"I'll do my makeup in the car."

She sounded oddly excited about her mission.

23

Harper Taylor drove a hundred miles from New York City until he reached a mansion nestled between the western backdrop of the Catskill Mountains and the Hudson River. The property was located on fifty acres of riverfront land in the historic village of Saugerties. It was served by nine full-time employees whose sole mission was to preserve the owner's privacy and attend to his every need. At eighty-seven years old, hardly anything or anyone made Alan Reid leave his hideaway.

Ten years earlier, the entomological lab in the Amazon had been abandoned. Alan wanted more money from the government to keep it running. They'd said no. Harper was sent to the Amazon to decommission the lab and bring back the people working for him. It was the beginning of a transformation in the Reid & Welch group, which had become one of the largest investment trusts in the country. It went from thousands of employees to a staff of just over two hundred Ivy League executives. Alan Reid had never made so much easy money.

Still, there was a cloud of uncertainty hovering over everyone's head.

Alan met Harper outside. They went for a walk, followed at a distance by two security agents that worked on the property.

"You know what's on everyone's mind," Harper said after five minutes of walking.

"They're well-paid young men. I'm not worried about their concerns."

"You hardly show up at the building anymore. I'm the one being asked questions."

"What about Walter Doles? He's the damn CEO."

"Alan, I'm on the board, but I don't call the shots."

Alan smirked. "Let me guess. They wanna know how much time I have left."

"Wouldn't you? What's in stock, Alan?"

The two friends exchanged a long glance. "Simon Brown will handle the transition when I'm gone."

"You'll let me know your decision through your lawyer?"

Alan stopped, stared at the beautiful landscape, and breathed in its fresh air. "I'm still making up my mind," he said.

"It's your life."

"Thanks for reminding me. But there's something else bothering me."

"Christel. I know," Harper said.

"How did that Mexican find out about her?"

"You lost control of the program the moment you cut your business ties with the government. El Pepe must've found out Subject C's real name. Playing with your Christel is his way of paying you back for what you did to him."

Alan spat. "What, decades ago? He's a sick man."

"Aren't we all?"

Alan stared at Harper. "It's the audacity of that decrepit man. He wants to mess with me. Now, I asked you for a favor. Did you do it?"

Harper nodded. "Raymond proved himself a good friend. I called him. He promised he would talk to Ulrich. El Pepe won't even have time to regret asking for Christel."

"Good…" Alan sighed. "Good."

*****

El Pepe left a United States Army Conference at the Convention Center in Washington, DC. His country, Mexico, was praising the Cuban Revolution and refusing to cut ties with Fidel Castro. President Kennedy pressured the Mexican government into joining the anti-Castro crusade, but Mexico's defense of Cuba remained central to the country's domestic stability. The invitation to meet with Pepe Steward, Mexico's honorary ambassador, was an attempt to better the United States' relationship with its neighbor.

But none of that really mattered to El Pepe.

His body had not had the agency's drug for four days. Symptoms of anxiety and irritability were already plaguing him. Another twenty-four hours without the drug would render him unable to work. Three more days, and he would probably be dead.

He had called his physician—an operative of the CIA, who confirmed that the drug would be provided by the special courier that El Pepe requested. The meeting was scheduled for that night at a hotel near the National Mall.

El Pepe was already waiting when Christel entered his hotel room.

Christel passed by a young embassy security guard, leaving a trail of perfume, and was pointed to the bedroom door where Ambassador Steward was waiting. She knocked and entered. "Good evening, Mr. Ambassador."

El Pepe's shirt and tie were loose. His skin was pale white, and he had a protruding belly. Though his old body looked fragile, his eyes were on fire. It was obvious that the ambassador needed the drug.

"You are under my command now, do you understand?" El Pepe said in a rough and slightly tipsy voice.

That's what you think, you filthy bastard, Christel thought.

Christel placed her purse on a side table. She was mentally stronger than ever. The verbal and physical commands that once worked on her seemed like a thing of the past. She scanned the room. She saw a bottle of whiskey that was almost empty.

"Can I get you some of that?"

El Pepe raised the glass he was holding. It was full. "Sit on the bed."

Christel sat down and smiled.

"I love pearls," he continued. Christel touched the necklace, fingering it delicately. "You're as beautiful as I was told you would be," he said, and then took his eyes off her. She sensed that there were other concerns in the ambassador's head.

Christel approached him and knelt down. El Pepe offered his glass of whiskey to her. "No, thanks. I'm not allowed to drink alcohol."

"You're with me. If you want, you can drink." He sounded controlling and friendly at the same time, but it didn't have any effect on her.

"Then I'll take a little sip." She took a hearty swig instead.

"Thirsty girl . . ."

She handed the glass back to him. El Pepe looked at the ceiling, wrapped up in his problems. Christel celebrated silently, her confidence growing.

El Pepe took several gulps as if the strong drink no longer had any effect on him. She got up and filled it with another shot. When she handed the glass back to El Pepe, he didn't even look at it. The ceiling seemed more interesting. He would ask for the drug at any time, Christel imagined.

"The US won't buy us out . . . You know why?" he said, still in his own world.

"No." *And I'm really not interested.*

"Because it takes more than money. It takes treating us as equals." He glanced at his slave. "They have a problem with Cuba. We don't."

Christel should have knelt down next to El Pepe like she'd done minutes before, but she remained leaning against the wall. The ambassador wanted to hear himself talk, not to have a conversation. "The young diplomats . . . They're stupid. Unprepared. And I'm too old."

Christel watched him. His body begged for the drug, but there was a protocol that involved the exchange of information. "What have you brought for me?"

"Nothing. I'm here because you've requested me."

"I don't believe you. There's always something." He closed his eyes and swallowed another massive shot of whiskey. "The agency offers no free lunch, my little dove . . ."

Christel opened her purse and took out a handful of pills. It was time.

She approached El Pepe and knelt down just like before, appearing submissive. The ambassador lowered his glass of whiskey and watched Christel put three pills inside it. He frowned.

"I usually take two," he said, but Christel pretended she didn't hear.

El Pepe leaned his bulky torso forward and swallowed the pills. When he finished, he stared at her hand. She still had some pills available, which was tricky. The ambassador might interpret that she had maliciously left them in sight, Christel thought. But she was willing to risk it.

"Being generous?" he said.

She glanced downward at her hand. "This? They said it's a backup, Mr. Ambassador."

"Call me Pepe."

Meanwhile, the pills that descended into his body a minute earlier were already taking effect.

"Pepe," he said, his eyes closing. "I want you to call me Pepe."

"I was instructed to give you no more than three or four pills at a time."

"Doesn't sound right . . ."

The chemicals were calming him, but the impulse to desire more was almost irresistible. He had drunk a lot, and looked tired. And as the minutes passed, the effects of the drug were in full throttle. Christel watched him and waited for the moment his discernment became blinded.

It didn't take much time. He turned his head to Christel and stretched out the hand that held the glass.

"More whiskey?" she said.

"No . . . Give me a couple more."

El Pepe swallowed two extra pills. More than anyone could handle.

She couldn't tell if he had consciously asked for a lethal dose or if he had lost control. In any case, it was now she, and not the ambassador, who was in control. There was an invigorating sensation taking over Christel. The taste of freedom.

"I know your father . . . Alan Reid. That bastard thief."

Christel froze. No one had ever talked about who her father was. Not even Lory. Alan Reid wasn't her father, but a name.

She looked into El Pepe's eyes and didn't have to ask him. "Subject C . . . Everyone wants a piece of you, my little dove," he said.

El Pepe produced a scared smile and relaxed on the couch. He spent the next moments inhaling and exhaling. His body was already facing the consequences of the high dosage. "You've got bad blood, Christel."

No target had ever called her by her real name.

"Tell me about my father," she said.

"Long story . . ." El Pepe was at the limit of his resistance. He closed his eyes and exhaled heavily.

"Do you know where he is?"

"I do," he whispered.

"Where, Ambassador?"

José Steward couldn't say another word. His

breathing was slow, and he loosened his grip around the glass. It fell onto the floor. His head lolled forward, forming a pile of skin under his chin. The air slowly left his lungs with a low and ominous whistle. His chest looked like it was sinking.

The next breath didn't come.

The honorary ambassador of Mexico had just died of an overdose.

Christel felt a chill. The body that now lay slouched on that couch represented a sorry excuse for a man, but still, a human being. There would be legal consequences. Shaking, she ran for the telephone next to the bed and called Ulrich.

"He's dead!" she said bluntly.

"Calm down. Tell me what happened?"

"I think he overdosed."

"It's not your fault. Stay there. I'll send someone to help you."

No way!

It was clear that she'd been used to kill the ambassador, a man who'd claimed to know her father and certainly knew her name. Christel made the only decision she could: to get out of that suite and disappear.

She opened the door and pulled it shut without closing it completely.

"Hey," she whispered to a young security guard in the suite's living room. He couldn't resist Christel's girlish grin. He got up and went to see what the woman wanted.

"Who can sleep next to something like that?" she whispered close to his face. Christel saw the hairs on the nape of his neck bristle. "Just look at him . . ." she teased.

The guard peeked his head into the room and saw the ambassador slouched on a couch, inert. As naturally as she could, she took the young man's arm as if she were about to pinch him and closed the bedroom door. She shook her head and pasted on a smile. The guard smiled along.

"Do you have a cigarette?" she asked, even though she didn't smoke.

"Sorry," he said, returning to the sofa.

"I'd die for one . . . If all of my clients were as easy as Mr. Steward, my life would be much better."

"I guess you got lucky today," he agreed, evaluating her from head to toe.

"I know, right? I don't even need to take another shower," she said, sitting on the arm of the sofa and playing with the guard's shoulder like they were the best of friends.

"There's a tobacco shop downstairs," he said. Christel already knew about the shop and had hoped that the agent would suggest it.

"I'll be right back." She slid her hand gently along his shoulder as she got up. She entered the bedroom on tiptoes to pick up her purse.

Christel walked down to the hotel lobby as slowly and naturally as she could muster. She passed by the front desk. Shortly after that, she was in a taxi heading to the airport. There was only one place she could go.

One she wished she had never left.

24

A little after three in the morning, a phone call Everett Johnson had been waiting twenty-one years for woke him.

"Mr. Johnson, I'm sorry to call you this late," Lory said.

"Yeah . . . Lory?"

"Christel contacted me a while ago."

Everett sat up. "How's she doing?"

"She's coming to Altamont to meet me. I think she's in trouble."

"Can I see her?"

"I suppose . . . Whatever she's gotten herself into, I can't help her. I'm not officially allowed to see her. That's by contract, you know."

Everett rubbed his eyes. "I'm leaving now. See you at your house."

"No, not here. She asked me to meet her at the old train station."

Everett had lots of questions. The vital thing to do was to meet Christel. He got dressed and left.

*****

It took him three hours to get to Altamont. After a decades-long search, he would finally lay eyes on Julian Welch's daughter. The late-night call full of urgency was no imposition at all. Everett would do whatever he could to mend his failure with Christel.

He saw Lory standing by herself at the Altamont Planning Association, where the train station used to be. She waved, and he lowered his car window to wave back at her. He parked nearby and walked toward her.

"Thanks so much for coming," Lory said.

"Where is she?"

"Any time now."

His eyes squeezed shut. "Why here?"

Lory glanced around with a bit of nostalgia, then with a sad smile, she said, "She loved the train. The year Dr. Lentz sent Ulrich to take her away from me was 1963. That's when the last passenger train passed through Altamont. She's coming back to me."

"I'm happy to assist her in any way I can."

"God bless you."

Lory walked toward the abandoned rails by herself.

After two hours of waiting, Everett saw Lory cover her mouth with both hands, dart down the railway, and disappear behind what used to be a depot. Everett went after her. When he saw Lory again, she was hugging Christel and sobbing.

He slowed down. The two needed room.

Christel Reid was a bit taller than Lory. Everett revised his own first impression of Julian Welch's daughter. She was quite a grown-up woman, and she was dressed like someone who'd just left a fancy dinner. The pictures he'd seen in Lory's house didn't do her justice. Even from fifty yards away, he could feel an aura about her that made his heart pound faster.

The wind softly blew her hair as her fingers ran across Lory's face, drying it. Then Lory turned, located Everett, and nodded in his direction. "That's the man I told you about." Christel turned and looked directly at him.

Everett waved.

Both women walked back down the rails. When they were closer, he walked toward them.

"Mr. Johnson, this is Christel," Lory said with a poignant smile.

Christel glanced at him. The effect of her haunted eyes was paralyzing. Everett extended his hand. Christel shook it. The touch sent waves of heat through his body. *What am I thinking?* he reprimanded himself.

"Lory told me you've been looking for me," Christel said. She sounded older than she looked.

"Only since you were born."

She nodded, and Everett wondered if she, too, felt what he'd just experienced.

"Let's go home, Chris. You look tired," Lory said.

"That's not a good idea. They'll probably come looking for both of us," Christel said.

"Tell us what happened. Mr. Johnson's here to help."

Christel had nowhere else to run. She turned to Everett. "A man died. They can blame me if they want," Christel said.

"Jesus! How did he die?" Lory said.

"Overdose."

"Then it's not your fault," Everett assured her.

"I was with him in a hotel room. I gave him the pills," she said.

"Look, Christel. We have a lot to talk about. There are things you need to know about your father," Everett said in a calming tone.

"I want nothing to do with Alan Reid," she said. Lory held her warmly.

Everett chose his words carefully. "I think you've been misinformed, Christel. Your father was a man called Julian Welch."

Lory's jaw dropped. "Alan Reid's partner?"

Everett nodded and turned his gaze back to Christel. "When you learn about Julian, you'll be proud to have had him as your father. He was a good man. I've been keeping a letter and an extensive file he kept for you before he died. You were just born, then."

"I'm not following you, Mr. Johnson. I have

some problems, OK? With my memory—I barely remembered how to reach Altamont. And I'm going through this other problem right now? I could be arrested for a crime I haven't committed."

Everett took a step forward. "I understand. But you're the rightful heiress of a fortune. You'll need a lawyer. That's what I am. Your father appointed me to help you get what's yours. With Lory's permission, I'd like to take you to my apartment in New York. You'll be safe there."

"Absolutely. You go with him, Chris. Go now," Lory said.

"You're welcome to come with us or visit as often as you'd like," Everett said.

"Oh, I will. I've missed her so much. I'll go home now. I'd better be ready to deny seeing Christel. Now, will you give us a moment, Mr. Johnson?"

Everett walked back to his car, and then the two women were alone. "Don't be afraid, child," Lory said.

"Yeah. Why should I? He's just a man."

Lory flashed a contrived smile. "I totally get you. But listen to me. You've never met a real man."

"I've met enough of them."

"You've met monsters . . . Now, everyone adored your father, Julian. If he chose Everett, that's because he trusted him. Now you go. I have your back, girl."

Christel avoided her gaze. "No . . . you've let me down, Lory."

Lory stepped back, almost in shock. "They took you from me!"

"So you say."

"I feel your pain. I never abandoned you."

Christel sighed and took a long glance at the man waiting by the Pontiac. Lory touched her shoulder and said, "Your life will change. Have a little faith, child."

25

On the way back to New York, Everett tried to engage Christel in conversation, but she kept silent. She spent the whole trip looking out the window, which got him thinking of how insecure or uncomfortable she was. It was an awkward situation for both. Maybe she needed room to breathe.

"This is home," he said while parking across the street.

Christel turned to him briefly and nodded.

Her light-brown, lost eyes reached his heart again, and that scared him. Everett had been looking for what he long considered a lost daughter. Instead, he'd found a captivating young woman.

He got out of the car and rushed to open her door. She got out, absorbed by the row of even chocolate-colored houses she'd only seen before in magazines and movies. "It's very cozy inside," Everett said.

"The outside looks OK," she said.

"Nineteenth-century stuff."

They crossed the street. "Romantic Classicism," she amended. "Art is my thing. From my years in the City of Frederick."

Inside the house, she took in every detail. Everett watched and sensed that she felt the space to be unthreatening.

"I want you to feel at home," Everett said.

Christel nodded, already on her way up the stairs. "Thanks."

She slowed down to admire a poster hanging on the wall along the staircase. It portrayed a twisted bottle. Everett waited patiently. "Do you like it?"

"You have bad taste in art," she said mockingly and continued upstairs.

"Bedrooms. Mine's down there. You can pick any of these two, Christel." She got to the nearest bedroom. "Good choice. This one has a Jacuzzi," he said.

Christel stared at him.

"Right. We need to buy some clothes for you. We can do it now, or we can talk first," he said.

"I don't want to be a burden."

He ignored her. "Do you like my house?"

"What's not to like?"

"It was bought with your father's money. Julian Welch paid me a fortune to take care of you after he died. What I'm saying is, nothing coming from me is a favor."

"Am I allowed to come and go as I wish?"

Everett narrowed his eyes. The question sounded off. "You need to understand something. You don't work for me. *I* work for you. And there's a lot to catch up on, Christel. We have a battle before us. The way I see it, Alan Reid robbed you. We're coming after him, so I need you to be emotionally ready."

Hours before, she'd been the witness—possibly the vehicle—of a potential murder. Her handlers were probably after her. Yet, here she was, Everett thought. In a house with a strange man. He wouldn't rush things. She needed more time to digest the new context she found herself in.

"Let's go shopping first," she said.

They were back to his car.

Everett was ready to suggest places, but Christel seemed to know what she wanted. "Can you take me to Abraham & Straus?"

"There are newer stores if you want."

"Abraham & Straus will do."

She spent less than thirty minutes inside the department store picking up essential toiletries and lingerie, and everything that went with jeans.

"There are fancier dresses you could—"

"That's all I need right now, thank you."

On their way back home, she saw a grocery store. "Will I be doing any cooking?"

"Only if you want."

"Who cooks for you?"

"I do."

Everett thought he glimpsed a smile on her face.

"I've never heard of a man who cooks," she said.

"Well, the world's changing."

Later in the house, Christel locked herself in her bedroom and took a long shower. Everett didn't resist the temptation to linger outside her door. For a moment, he thought he heard that young, determined woman crying. He hesitated before knocking on the door.

"Dinner's ready," he said.

"In a minute."

Christel showed up on the first floor wearing her new jeans, a T-shirt, and no shoes. Everett was waiting at the dining table like he was on a date. He made an effort to conceal his growing weakness for her as she took a seat across from him. Her wet hair had been combed straight. Her clean face was free of makeup, revealing tiny scars here and there that were oddly attractive and worrisome at the same time.

"Smells good," she said, looking at the bowl of pasta and cheese before her.

You too, he wanted to say. "Wine?"

"Please."

She drank half a glass during the entire dinner. He drank three. They barely talked. When dinner was over, Everett decided it was time to get into more serious matters.

"I want you to read this," he said. "I've been

keeping it for you since you were born."

He gave her an old letter that was part of Julian Welch's files.

She raised her eyebrows. "Julian Welch's letter to his daughter?"

Everett left her alone with the letter and went to wash the dishes to pass the time. His arms were crossed when she came to find him twenty minutes later.

"Are you all right?" she asked, leaning against a kitchen cabinet.

"Are *you*?"

"How much of this is true?" She lifted the letter in the air.

"Everything."

"The stories in the forest and all?"

"The forest, the money, and the Reid & Welch Company . . . This is your story too. It's where you come from."

Christel touched the base of her neck and lowered her head.

"I understand how you must feel. But here's what's essential, Christel—are you ready for what's yours?"

"Do I have to sleep with you?"

Everett thought she was joking. For the second time that day, that gorgeous, intelligent woman sounded like there was a screw loose in her head. "What makes you think that?"

"I've never had dinner with a man and not . . . you know."

"It's late. You'd better get some sleep."

"I see the way you look at me. No man can fool me."

"I'm sorry, but you've got it wrong."

"It's in your eyes, Mr. Johnson."

"It's Everett. And, good night."

Everett headed for his bedroom, convinced that Julian Welch's daughter was a force to be tamed. The truth was his decades-long search for her hadn't made Christel any more familiar. Whatever fondness he had about that imaginary missing baby had been confused by the complexities of this strange adult woman whose past had affected her discernment of men. The noble ideal of saving her was still there, but so were other human feelings. The first thing he would do in the morning was take her to see Alan Reid, test the waters, and prepare for battle.

He got into the shower and recapped what had happened that day. Then Christel took over his imagination, and he had to turn the knob to make the water unpleasantly cold. "This is ridiculous," he told himself.

He was ready to go to sleep.

It had been a rewarding day, he concluded. Julian's daughter had problems, yes, but she was alive and well. For the first time in years, Everett felt the weight on his shoulders fade away. He switched off the light in his bedroom, but before he got into bed, he heard a knock on the door.

"Yes?" He cocked his head.

Christel came in wearing panties only. She stopped at a hairbreadth distance from him. "No man has ever rejected me before."

"Christel . . . I'm not rejecting you."

He considered their age difference, his moral commitment to her deceased father, and the fact that she was in a vulnerable moment.

None of that worked.

They were touching tongues and lips before Everett could take into account all the reasons why he shouldn't get involved with her.

Christel pushed him toward his bed and lay down on top of him.

"You're the strangest man I've ever been with," she whispered in between sighs.

Everett didn't bother answering her, clueless as to what that meant. Right then, nothing made sense except the explosive sensations obliterating his better judgment. Christel was on top of him both physically and psychologically, Everett recognized. They both reached orgasm quickly.

Ten minutes later, at Christel's initiative, they made love again. Everett felt that she was riding her own horse, doing whatever she wanted. The second time took longer, and the emotional connection between them deepened. She clung to him afterward, making it clear she didn't want to return to her own bed. He felt an urge to protect her.

In the morning, when Everett opened his eyes, Christel was staring at him and smiling. She looked peaceful and, at the same time, intrigued. He couldn't figure out why.

"It was my first time," she said, still not making much sense.

"It didn't look like it."

"First time I felt pleased with an adult man."

That was another topic of discussion for the future. "I—"

She shushed Everett by mounting him. "This is about me. I'm simply . . . thanking you. You don't have to say anything. Maybe you're falling in love with me. That's OK."

"Let's not get ahead of things."

Christel held his gaze for a long moment before she said, "Let's see about that."

Everett could not believe how confident she was. It crossed his mind that maybe she was testing him.

"Pull my hair," she said as she turned and lay belly down.

He touched her lower back softly and moved his fingers all the way up to her neck. He kissed her skin and tried not to make the wrong move. "That's how you wanna play?" He pulled her hair gently.

"Pull it like a man," she said.

It was a long morning followed by an even longer afternoon.

They ordered pizza for lunch, just to keep them going. She took three showers throughout the day and walked around naked. She stopped at every corner of the house for short moments. Everett saw her and figured she was trying to decipher him through his art choices. He reminded himself that Christel was beginning to experience the world outside of her controllers. Everett didn't want to disappoint her. Last time he did, she went missing for twenty-one years.

26

The night came quick and cold. They were sitting on the floor in front of the fireplace with beautiful logs burning while Christel leaned against Everett's chest. She was a kid and a woman, or maybe these were all foolish concepts meant to spoil sweet things. Everett seemed more perturbed than her.

"Don't you wanna call Lory? See how she's doing?" he said.

It took some time before Christel said, "No."

"I thought she was the only person you trusted."

"There's a lot you don't know about me," she said while sitting up. "Or Lory."

Christel was turning out to be a box of surprises and incoherencies. Everett picked up the telephone and began to dial. "We need to check up on her." She kept her eyes glued on him while he waited for Lory to answer. "Hi, Lory. It's Everett. How're you doing there?"

"Raymond Lentz called me a while ago," Lory said.

"Who?"

"The man in charge of the orphanage's psychiatric department. The people I told you about. The ones who messed with my girl's head."

Everett glanced at Christel. He recalled Lory mentioning something about Christel's mental health, which explained part of her unpredictable behavior.

"And what did Raymond Lentz want?" he said. Christel turned her stare to the fireplace. He watched her for any signs that would help him understand her better.

"Dr. Lentz asked me if Christel and I are in touch."

"What did you say to Dr. Lentz?" As he mentioned that name again, Christel pulled her legs near her chest and embraced them.

"Nothing. But it didn't matter. He said they were ending the program."

"What program?"

"The one Christel has been part of since she was a baby. Dr. Lentz asked nothing else. He didn't mention anyone being murdered. And there were no instructions about Christel."

"So, no one's looking for her, then."

"Not that he mentioned. Mr. Johnson, can I talk to her?"

"Hold on—" Everett showed Christel the telephone. She shook her head no. "She's, er, resting."

"Sweet child . . . Will you do me a favor?"

"Yes, Lory."

"Tell Christel I love her. Tell her I won't die until she forgives me."

"I will."

He hung up.

Christel kept her eyes and mind focused on that flame. Everett felt his heart burn. At the moment he saw the abused child inside her, not the woman. The sort of abuse and the kind of program she'd been part of were hard to grasp. He wanted to take care of her more than ever. Christel needed a protector, the predictability of an ordinary home, and to be around regular people. A psychiatrist would possibly help, if she agreed. Everett held her in a tight embrace. He promised himself to never let her go missing again.

*****

They woke up early the following morning and had breakfast together. Christel made an effort to look happy, but Everett saw she was fighting on the inside. It lightened his heart to see that the excessive hunger for life she'd shown the previous day seemed quieted, but he was still worried about her. After breakfast, Christel went back to bed.

"I'll make some phone calls," he said.

The first was to Reid & Welch.

He demanded to talk to Alan Reid but learned that the man rarely set his foot in his building. Alan's secretary, Edith, promised to pass his message to Simon Brown, the company's senior lawyer. Then Everett asked for Raymond Lentz, whom Edith had never heard of, and finally Ulrich Kohl, who proved to be another ghost. He gently requested that the secretary give him the name and number of the person in charge of the Maturity Orphanage, for which she patiently explained he could find that information in any yellow pages, as Edith had never heard of that clinic before. Though Reid & Welch had proudly contributed to several institutions, Maturity was not one of them.

Next, Everett called Lory asking for alternative phone numbers to reach Alan Reid.

"I only have his company number," she said.

"What about Dr. Lentz and Ulrich Kohl?"

"I do have their numbers, but I can't give them to you."

"Why, Lory? It's in Christel's best interest."

"There's only so much I can do. The people involved in the program are protected by special access. So you know, that includes me. I know this is frustrating, but it's a good thing that Christel's under your protection now."

Everett hung up and walked back and forth for a good hour.

To ensure that Christel got what she deserved— by blood, by name, and as a compensation for her terrible upbringing—her right to her inheritance needed to be legally established. It mystified Everett that Christel had been registered with "Lentz" as her middle name. All the while, Alan Reid had called Lory and authorized her to contact Everett, despite an earlier file prohibiting anyone from Maturity from acknowledging Christel's existence.

The phone rang just when his head began to ache.

"Everett Johnson?"

"Yeah. Who is it?"

"Simon Brown. I'm Alan Reid's lawyer. I understand you've been looking for Mr. Reid?"

"That's right. He knows who I am and what this is about."

"I understand. Well, he won't be seeing you."

"I'm ready to fight for my client—Christel Lentz Reid, his daughter."

"Mr. Johnson, Alan Reid doesn't have a daughter. He's never had one. I believe you already know that. My client has built a business with one major partner, Julian Welch, whom he considered a friend. Mr. Welch died a widow. He left no children. Are you there, Mr. Johnson?"

"Yes . . ."

I have no case, he thought.

"Very well. If you agree not to make any further inquiries and leave Mr. Reid alone—he's an old man—then I'm authorized to see you."

"What's the point?"

"Let's say Mr. Reid recognizes the value of

persistence. Mr. Johnson, if it's convenient for you, we can meet at his house."

Everett tried to find an angle before Simon Brown gave up being nice and hung up. Why Alan Reid's lawyer wanted to meet him after making sure Christel stood no chance to inherit anything baffled him. The worse thing that could happen, he decided, was wasting his time.

"When?"

"Why not today? You'd need to drive to the village of Saugerties. Just ask for the big riverfront property. Anyone there will be able to help you find the address. Would three o'clock work for you?"

"I'll see you there, Mr. Brown."

He checked the time—almost noon—and rushed to wake Christel up.

"We have an appointment," he said as he sat on her bed.

"With whom?"

"Alan Reid's lawyer. It's a two-hour drive from here. Can you dress fast?"

"Yeah . . . give me five minutes. What does he want?"

"I don't know."

On the way to Saugerties, Everett's years of waiting reflected on the gas pedal. He risked unnecessary overtakes on a slippery road of melting snow. Simon Brown had given him an incomplete address. It would require Everett to ask around. To be seen by others. It could be that Alan's lawyer was trying to make him feel at ease, like someone who had nothing to hide.

Or, he considered, this could be a setup where potential witnesses could testify that Everett had been looking around for the Reid mansion. He felt paranoid as he speculated on the nuances of that meeting.

Alan Reid is manipulative and dangerous, Julian Welch had warned Everett decades earlier.

"Slow down!" Christel shouted before Everett approached a curve.

"Sorry."

"You said this is a meeting between lawyers. Why did you bring me?"

It was a good question. Everett shrugged. "I'm not sure."

"That's comforting."

"I can drop you at the village and pick you up after the meeting."

Christel squinted. "No . . . I'm used to this. I'll play along."

"Used to what?"

"Being shown around."

"A pretty face always help, if that's what you mean."

"Right. But don't worry. It amuses me."

"What?"

"The mediocrity of men."

Just as Simon Brown had said, it wasn't hard to find Alan Reid's property. The place was considered extravagant, even by the locals' standards, so Everett's inquiries for directions got easy answers, and he arrived at the house ten minutes ahead of time. A security guard opened the massive outside gate. It took Everett one whole minute to reach the house where another guard awaited.

"This way," the guard said after Everett and Christel stepped out of the Pontiac.

Simon Brown was standing at the entrance hall, looking older than he sounded on the phone. He had a warm smile, which helped break the tension and appease Everett's concerns about a possible setup. "Mr. Johnson." Simon shook his hand.

"Mr. Brown."

"You must be Christel."

The old lawyer eyed her with exaggerated reverence, causing her and Everett to exchange a glance as they walked toward a set of pompous leather couches in the corner of a massive living room.

The two walls on either side displayed a collection of black-and-white photographs that looked like they were from a museum exhibit. There were vintage images of Julian and Alan in the Amazon, their golden years in New York, and Alan's most recent years running the company.

Simon waited until his guests sat. His initial smile

was replaced by a furrowed, heavy expression. "How familiar are you with Reid & Welch?" he began.

"I know how Julian Welch built the company. In fact, everything I know about the company is either public or it came from Mr. Welch's perspective," Everett said.

"Julian Welch and Alan Reid came from nothing. They met in the jungles of the Amazon, where they built the foundations of what the company is today. They fought tropical diseases. Learned lessons that ripped away their naïveté. They turned themselves into respectable players in an era of great uncertainty. They were pioneers, Mr. Johnson."

"Yet, they were different. One had a taste for beauty; the other, I'm not sure."

"It's the nature of business."

"Of certain men."

"Anyway . . . Julian Welch left everything to Reid & Welch. They had a mutual agreement and a contract to enforce it. Everything went according to this understanding. Which, Mr. Johnson, leads us to the question of my client's imminent retirement," Simon said.

Everett glowered. Why would Alan Reid ask his lawyer to discuss his retirement with him? "Nothing lasts forever," Everett said, trying to gain time to think.

"Companies do. Well, some."

"And how will Reid & Welch survive without a name behind it?"

Simon nodded and proceeded carefully. He saw that Christel seemed more interested in the pictures hanging all around them. She got up, heading toward a set of portraits showing the two men in the Amazon—one with a dead *Panthera onca*, and another at a gala event in the Teatro Amazonas. Then her eyes glided toward a picture of Julian and Jandira at their wedding outside a church, with Alan Reid next to them.

"Who's this?" she asked without turning to them.

"Julian and his first wife, Jandira," Simon explained.

Alan Reid tried to rape her on their wedding night, Everett recalled from Julian's files.

Everett got up from the couch and moved to stay close to Christel. "That's your father," Everett said.

"He was just a kid," she said and moved on to the next set of portraits.

The photos were neatly organized in a timeline that told both men's stories. She passed by several portraits depicting Alan Reid but didn't bother to ask questions about him. At the end of a row, she continued past a corner where a new row of portraits showed the following decades. Christel stopped before a colorful picture of Julian and Denise, where she was dressed as a bride. Everett anticipated her next question.

"That's Denise. She died giving birth to you."

Christel maintained her serenity, the result of her

tremendous character and strength. Despite managing to avoid unpleasant drama, she couldn't prevent a stubborn tear from rolling down her cheek. That was her story on those walls. Her real parents. Her blood, Everett thought.

Simon Brown got up from his couch and approached them.

"Christel," he called, and she turned.

"My client initiated a transition period inside Reid & Welch. He's got cancer. Doctors gave him about a year. He's in France now. Resting."

Everett moved toward Simon. There was something in what that lawyer had just said that felt promising. He wasted no time. "Will Alan Reid recognize Christel as Julian's legitimate daughter and assure her place in the company?"

Simon looked down for a moment. Then he reached for a folded sheet of paper inside his jacket and walked over until he was a step away from Everett.

"When Alan Reid passes away, Reid & Welch will be solely owned by Christel."

Everett glanced back at her as she approached. Both looked incredulous.

"A dying man's regret, Mr. Brown?" Everett said. In a way, that question reflected his skepticism.

Simon swung his head sideways, looking skeptical himself. "I don't think that's the case. I've known Alan for many years. I consider him a friend, so it's fair to say I know him well. He's an old-fashioned, self-made man. Now, his moral qualities—or lack of—are irrelevant. Ultimately, he accepted he couldn't stay in the game forever. Someone needs to carry on what he began with Julian."

"At no time has Mr. Reid ever shown any consideration for Christel."

Simon Brown smirked. "You mean, affection?" The old lawyer shook his head. "I suppose you could call it whatever you want."

"What would you call it?"

"I think Christel's the person he hates the least."

Simon turned and waved the housekeeper over. She'd been waiting at the far end of the living room. She walked hastily toward Simon.

"Mr. Brown," she said.

"Louise, this is Christel Reid. She's the new owner of the property. You take good care of her."

"It's a pleasure, madam. I'm outside in case you need me." The housekeeper left.

Simon glanced at them both. "The paper you have in your hands shows a summary of how much Reid & Welch is worth, its main assets, and its top executives. An account has been opened in Christel's name with a monthly allowance that's more than enough to keep her in this house while the transition goes on. As the company's main lawyer, I'm available whenever you need me. Have a great day, Christel."

Simon nodded at Everett and left like this had been just another meeting.

Everett unfolded the paper Simon had given him and glanced at it. When he raised his eyes to Christel, he looked shocked.

"What?" she asked.

"You own an insane fortune."

27

The eight months following the transition period as the head of Reid & Welch had turned Christel into an avid apprentice. She had a tireless appetite for learning and was unashamed of asking difficult questions. She arrived earlier than anyone, worked harder, tolerated no jokes or malicious advances from anyone, and left the building late every night. Nobody knew who exactly she was. Christel had the name Reid, but rumors told a different tale, one speculating her real father was Julian Welch.

Everett was always at her side in the beginning. He taught her everything he could, but he lacked the expertise to advise her on the core business of the group—financial investments. She was a long way from being able to make strategic decisions, but she knew enough to understand what to expect from each department.

The younger males in the company—a majority— were fascinated and falling in love with her by the dozens. She found them easy to control and more predictable than the female staff. Compared to the abhorrent men she'd served in the past, they were kids. Attempts to get closer to her were severed at the root. If she weren't as young as she was, disturbingly attractive, and now the filthy rich heiress of Reid & Welch, many of the studs that had been mercilessly rejected by Christel would have quit after her harsh brush-offs.

Of the 215 employees currently working in the building, Edith—who'd been Alan Reid's secretary for decades—had special access to Christel's routine and insecurities. Christel found that the best way to relate to seventy-year-old Edith and win her friendship was to treat her like a dear aunt. She would run and tell Edith every time she dealt with a problem by applying one of Edith's wise pieces of counsel. They were getting along fine.

Simon Brown was coming to the building almost every day and became another of her elected tutors. He showed more heart than the mordant first impression he'd made at the Saugerties property. He promised to stay by Christel's side until Alan Reid died. He would retire after that.

And there was Walter Doles, the leader of the pack of studs. The snobbish former CEO—turned chief asset management officer because of Christel's arrival—was at the heart of what Reid & Welch had become. The young Ivy League creature wore a bow tie and walked the corridors of Reid & Welch with an unbearable air of superiority, but Christel needed Walter more than she would ever let him know. The problem was, she hated the investment business and was having a hard time figuring out the rules of the craft and how their company differed from their competitors.

The three formed Christel's inner circle during the transition period.

*****

At night, Everett was usually at home waiting for Christel to return. They were getting along well. He knew he was her first long-term relationship, and the first man she'd learned to trust. Their sexual appetites grew with their love, and sometimes, he couldn't keep up with her. After all, there was an age difference to consider.

But even as they grew closer, not once did Christel let Everett know the details of her past. He'd tried talking to her several times, but she always refused to open up, explaining that she'd never felt this good in her life. Why risk ruining it by bringing up the heavy stuff? There was a chance he couldn't handle the ugly truth, she justified.

On Fridays, they cooked together, talked about money and traveling, and drank rosé champagne.

"I'm planning to visit Alan Reid," she told him one night.

"Where did that come from?"

"I'm curious about the man. He's the closest thing I have to a father, at least that's still alive."

"I don't think that's a good idea."

"You said that once the papers were signed, Reid & Welch belonged to me. Well, I signed them months ago."

"Of course, he can't change anything now. But why, Christel? Let the man die in peace."

"The farmhouse in Arles looks amazing. Have you seen the pictures?"

"Pictures can be deceiving. And he still lives there."

She shrugged. "I'm changing my name."

"Now that's a good idea. Christel Welch is who you really are."

"I'm killing 'Lentz' but keeping 'Reid' as my middle name."

Everett rolled his eyes. "In God's name, why?"

Everett got the impression that she enjoyed seeing him shaken by her ideas. "There's a side of me—"

"Stop it! Really? I mean, how dark a side must one have to justify keeping that name?"

"It's good for the company image. I'll keep it. Please don't argue with me."

Everett sighed. "It's your life."

"Good. Can I have some more champagne? I need to confess something," she said and watched Everett suffer a little.

"Well?"

"I know Edith thinks I'm a talented young woman, Simon is incredibly proud of my efforts, and you believe I'm almost ready as a businesswoman."

"But?"

Christel rested her champagne on a side table and picked up an envelope. She pulled out a stack of papers and showed it to him. "You know what this is to me?"

"This is where you make money."

"It's the most boring thing I've ever come across."

"Chris, it takes time to—"

"It doesn't matter how much time I spend in the office listening to that prick Walter talking about the market. I hate it. I hate Walter. I hate the market. I'll never properly learn this business."

"But you have to. I'm sure you'll get it."

"I didn't ask for any of this."

"I'm not following you. You wanna give up?"

"No . . . nothing like that. I wanna change Reid & Welch. Send off the clients. I want it to be a family trust." She gulped down her rosé and waited for Everett's response.

He scrunched his lips. "Nothing actually prevents you from doing that."

"Are you sure?"

"Yeah. Just don't do it now. Wait for Alan Reid to—"

"Die? Does it make any difference?"

"Not on paper, but some people may find it, I

don't know, an ungrateful decision."

"Like I'm undoing everything he's built?"

"Exactly."

"I'll wait, then."

"Good for you."

*****

The next morning, Christel had a meeting with Simon Brown.

She'd asked the lawyer to prepare a detailed list of all the company's assets. The idea of getting rid of everything troublesome or hard to understand and starting over under a more straightforward organization—one she felt more comfortable managing—became a priority. Unlike Everett, Simon always acted like he didn't give a damn about things. He did what people paid him to do, and that was that.

"Reid & Welch has three thousand clients. We currently manage 4.8 billion dollars of client money," Simon read.

"How much money do we have that is not client money?"

"As of our last balance, Reid & Welch had six hundred and twenty-eight million dollars."

"Uh-huh. Well, go on, Simon."

"We currently own seven hundred properties around the world. Two percent of which are residential; the rest is made up of commercial buildings, farmlands, and forest areas."

"How much are they worth?"

"That's impossible to know. They're estimated to have a combined value of eighteen billion dollars, but that's a wild guess."

Christel nodded. "Let's sell everything except the residential properties."

Simon looked at her over his glasses. Seeing that young heiress playing around with money built over decades was something else. "It may take years. And it's not a wise decision."

"Why not?"

"Because the average annual returns in long-term real estate investments, especially commercial real estate, outperform the S&P 500 Index. Because it's good to own land. Nobody does that unless they're broke or crazy."

"But, would it be a crime if I did it?"

Simon watched the twenty-two-year-old and reminded himself that she was just that. Calmly, he said, "No."

"Well, can you sell it for me, then?"

"Christel, that's, er, way above my pay grade. It requires a bunch of people to do that. My office can certainly handle the paperwork, but not the actual selling effort."

"Can you put together a team of real estate agents for me?"

"Sure. But some properties won't be sold for many years. If ever."

"Why not?"

"Some have partners that may not be interested in selling. Others have environmental issues, and some are tied to old businesses that Alan Reid had with the government."

"Such as?"

"A forest land in Brazil that used to be a biological lab of some kind. I've never been able to access the details of what went on down there. Being a government thing, it has a military classification level."

"Oh . . . Weird stuff. Who can help us with that?"

"The person in charge of that business was a man called Harper Taylor. He used to be on Reid & Welch's board. He oversaw everything government related. He and Alan were very close." Simon handed her a slim file. "Here's what we know about the property. It isn't much."

"Let's contact Harper. Maybe he can help us."

"I'm afraid I can't. He's a spooky man. I've never contacted him directly. Don't know where to look for him."

She inspected the aerial photographs attached to the file. They depicted an intriguing vast green carpet of trees. "Who else can tell us more about this property?"

"The only other person who could offer you more details is Alan himself."

"How is he?"

"Not getting any better. Last I heard, he's taking turns between his bed and a wheelchair. Anyway, you want me to move forward with your decisions?"

"Yes, please. And do talk to Walter for me. I can't stand him. Tell him to close all client accounts and fire everyone related to them. I want only the best to remain. How many people do you think we need?"

Simon shrugged. "Ten to twenty. We'll be left with a lot of empty space in the building."

"Rent it out."

*****

Simon began to nurture a secret admiration for the young woman. She wasn't afraid to hurt other people's feelings. When she didn't understand something, she got to the bottom of it. Right or wrong, she was making a lot of decisions, small and big. Most importantly, she had a vision of what she wanted the company to be. And now that he was witnessing it, the old lawyer was having seconds thoughts about retiring. Christel had her own colorful way of running Reid & Welch. Every meeting was a surprise, and watching her was a pleasure. If only he were forty years younger.

Christel left her office an hour after Simon.

"I'll be out until Monday," she told Edith.

It was Thursday morning. An extended weekend was a first.

*****

Christel went to Everett's house, packed a light bag, and went straight to the airport where she bought a ticket to Paris and booked a car rental. She called Everett while she waited for her flight.

"I'm going to see Alan Reid in France."

"Where are you?"

"My flight leaves in two hours."

"Wait. Jesus, you're so impulsive . . . I'm coming with you."

"No need, my love." Christel knew where the conversation was heading. She changed the subject to something that actually depended on Everett's opinion. "I need you to think about something else."

"And what would that be?"

"Marry me when I come back."

Just like that, from a telephone booth at the JFK terminal, she proposed with no regard for timing or romanticism. Even though she knew Everett well, and rightfully saw herself as an expert on men, she bit her lip nervously.

"Darling, I'm honored. But don't you think we should discuss this over a bottle of rosé?"

"You-you're right."

28

From Paris to Arles, Christel followed the A6, charmingly known as the Motorway of the Sun. It was the main link between the south and the Riviera, which continued on as A9. She stopped for lunch in Chalon-sur-Saône, where she tried a red mullet. It would have been a much more enjoyable experience if Everett were with her.

But he wasn't. And he wanted to *discuss* her wedding proposal. *Who the hell does he think he is?*

They loved each other, but she expected him to have been thrilled on the phone, not indecisive. Christel was confident she could have any man she wanted, but she'd chosen Everett. Why couldn't he appreciate that?

What did I do wrong?

She continued her trip to Arles with a lot going through her head at the same time. Questions about her family mounted. Her deep and dangerous mental conditioning had impeded her from running away from all that earlier. The abuses she'd endured were coming back, strong and bitter. What kind of men would do such things to a child and to a woman? What kind of man was Alan Reid, and why did he leave his fortune to her? It didn't make sense.

Christel arrived in Arles before sunset and stopped for a quick walk in town.

She was anxious to meet the monster, but insecure. The small, winding passageways of the city were a refreshing sight, as if some of the paintings she'd seen during her teenage years growing up in the City of Frederick had popped out of her imagination and gained life. She saw ancient Roman monuments on her way to meeting the man. Maybe Alan Reid was just a ruin. But unlike stone monuments, she was sure he was perishable and forgettable.

Christel spotted the stone farmhouse listed in the file she carried with her, and checked the address and the map. This was it—a real-life canvas filled with beautiful gardens. The landscape surrounded it like a painting, engulfing Christel in a plethora of uncertainties. Time seemed distorted, the air saturated by the sweet scent of blue irises. Jazz played in the background.

She was already inside the house after being greeted by a smiling chambermaid. Was Van Gogh laughing at her?

"Mademoiselle Reid?" the woman said. *How could she have known?* Christel wondered.

"Yes. Christel Reid."

"Please, a moment, huh?"

While the chambermaid headed up a staircase, Christel followed the sunrays that led to the vast backyard garden. It looked unexplainably familiar, not that she could have remembered having spent a week there when she was a month-old baby. Still, there was some abstract sense of connection, as if she had somehow been here before.

The chambermaid showed up at a window on the first floor of the house. She yelled at a woman about Christel's age who was watering the garden. The woman rushed toward the house.

"*Bonsoir*," she said when she passed by Christel.

Christel's soul reminded her that she and that beautiful French woman had held hands when both were babies, right there in that garden.

I must be going crazy.

Moments later, the chambermaid and the other woman showed up, making a herculean effort of bringing an old man in a wheelchair down the staircase. Alan Reid. The man in the portraits hanging on the walls of the Saugerties property. The worst human being she'd ever heard of.

The women pushed the wheelchair to the terrace and left Alan alone with Christel. The word "uncomfortable" grew a new meaning. The stare they exchanged was long and nuanced, and hid their feelings, but Alan was the first one to blink. He turned his chair in the direction of the garden, away from Christel.

"I had a meeting with Simon Brown yesterday," Christel said, getting directly to the point. Alan didn't move. She went on. "I-I'm making some changes in the company, but some properties can't be sold for whatever reason. I'm concerned about one of them—a forest land in Brazil. There's some kind of issue. We can't sell it."

Alan sat quietly and appeared uninterested.

Christel decided to move on. "Simon told me there used to be a lab on the property. That the US government was involved somehow. And that the project was canceled. He told me that the lab should've been properly decommissioned, but it wasn't. Is that correct?"

Alan Reid nodded. She and the monster were talking.

"He also said," she continued, "that nobody knows what went on in the lab, and only you could explain what you did there. Simon recommended that I forget that property, but if there's a problem, I should know about it."

"Yes," Alan finally said. The huge man, beaten by cancer, looked shrunken in that wheelchair. His voice was weak, and it sounded like a child's. "The lab was built underground. There's nothing you can do about it. Just stay away."

Christel watched him speak. He wasn't the frightening, imposing man people had warned her about. That realization empowered her. She moved to stand in front of Alan, blocking his view of the sun setting in his garden. Whatever fear she'd had was gone.

"Tell me about my father," she said.

Alan looked downward, avoiding her stare. She waited. When he spoke, there was docility and truthfulness in his voice. "Julian was a saint."

"Look at me," she said, but he kept glancing at the terrace floor stones. "Tell me why you abandoned me. Why you betrayed my father."

He couldn't explain it, or look at her.

Christel felt he wasn't going to answer. Men like Alan, she knew, were only strong in the shadows, but they were cowards when exposed. His insistence on avoiding Christel made her edgy and frustrated. Desperate, she began to undress before him.

"I said look at me."

First, she took off her blouse, throwing it onto his lap. From the corner of her eye, she noticed the chambermaid and the other woman commenting from inside the house.

Next, Christel took off her skirt, her bra, and finally, her panties. She was totally naked, with only her boots on.

Alan turned, glanced up at her body, and finally looked her in the eyes. She hoped to grasp what was going on in his mind, to seize whatever emotion came out of him, and maybe identify any trace of humanity inside him. But there was only emptiness.

"You like what you see?" she said.

Alan glanced away.

"No, no, no . . . Keep looking," she demanded and waited until he looked back at her. When he did, she said, "I'm much more than this."

"Can I help, Mr. Reid?" the chambermaid said.

Alan didn't move. Neither did Christel.

"Yes. Bring the old man a napkin. I think he's drooling," Christel said as she got dressed again. This had been a waste of time. Everett was right—she shouldn't have come.

Before leaving, she leaned over and brought her face an inch from Alan's. "I know that deep inside your pathetic little soul, you left everything to me because you expected some sympathy. You're regretful, I see it in your eyes. But that's not enough."

"What is?" Alan said.

Christel shook her head. "I'm undoing everything that you've built. I'm gonna clean your dirt. The dirt men do—to women, and to the planet. You'll be my inspiration."

Christel stood up and began to leave. "When Mr. Reid dies, I want you to disinfect the house," she told the two women on her way out, but she had to stop when another old man dressed in an outdated suit stepped menacingly in front of her.

"You should be grateful for what you've got," the man said, his cold, dark eyes piercing her.

"Excuse me?" Christel said and watched Alan

approaching in his wheelchair.

"I'm Harper Taylor. And you should be grateful because Alan Reid is a generous man. And if it weren't for me, you wouldn't be here. Because I found your mother on a street, on a cold winter night, and Alan here thought she would be nice company for Julian. Things turned out very well for you. That's why. Don't ask me anything. Just move on with your life."

Christel had no doubt in her mind that Harper Taylor was the most sinister man she'd ever encountered. She took a deep breath while she processed what had been part of her life and kept her focus. "What about the property in the Amazon?"

"It's been abandoned. It's out of reach. You have plenty of wealth to indulge in. The rest belongs to a past too complicated for you to understand. You, young woman, have a golden opportunity to be happy. Most of your colleagues won't live to be thirty. Celebrate it."

Harper turned and left the house before Christel could take another breath.

Alan moved back to the terrace and fixed his gaze outward. He looked like a ghost.

I'm done here.

Christel went back to her car and stayed motionless behind the steering wheel, thinking about Alan Reid. She shook away her negativity. There was so much to be done. She took in the scenery around her, hoping that whatever beauty remained in the world could encourage her to find her place in life.

The sun finally set on that day, and she caught the last shining lights highlighting the contours of Arles's landscape. Maybe it was a sign. Nature touched her like an unexpected warm embrace. She knew that, the next day, nature would be there for her, laughing at mankind, providing. She opened the car window and inhaled the air of Arles. She felt connected, just like she did with Everett. From that moment on, Christel was determined to take care of both Everett and nature. She would find a place to sleep nearby and then fly back to Everett as soon as she could.

29

Christel arrived ten minutes after Everett when she entered Le Pavillon in the Ritz Tower hotel on Fifty-Seventh Street. She had called him before leaving Paris and agreed to talk about marriage the right way. Everett suggested they meet at the last of the grand luxe restaurants in New York. While he waited, he ordered Dom Pérignon brut rosé, Christel's favorite.

She arrived for lunch directly from the airport, embraced him warmly, kissed him briefly but meaningfully, and they had a quick exchange about her trip. The rosé and Everett's company made her feel at home.

"He's the most disappointing person I've ever met," she said about Alan Reid.

"That's not that bad of a description for a man who almost ruined your life. Anyway, you wanted to talk about marriage?"

She grinned, but half-heartedly. Everett wanted her to feel that something wasn't quite right. He wanted to fix it. To slow her down.

Everett thought that, in her fantasy, she expected him to show enthusiasm and passion. They would voice their dreams and make plans for the wedding and beyond. The reality, though, was milder. Christel was a fascinating twenty-two-year-old, but her unpredictability could be daunting for a more mature man like Everett.

"A wedding proposal requires a personal conversation. When you do it over the phone, it makes it too casual, that's all I meant," Everett said.

"And I said you were right."

"Christel, I love that you want to get married. I really do."

"But?"

"There's no *but*, I just think you have too much on your mind right now."

"You know I do. So what?"

Everett used a careful tone of voice. "When you get to be my age, you'll see things differently. Right now, you're excited about your new life. A lot has changed for you, thank God. But how can you be sure you'll still want to be with an old man like me, say, in twenty, thirty years? How can I even ask you to try to see that far into the future? It'd be unfair."

"You're probably the love of my life."

"Probably, but not *surely*."

"You've saved me, and I'm forever grateful. But I hate it when you treat me like a child."

"I'm simply saying that marriage is a lifetime

commitment. It may not go the way we expect."

She sipped her champagne, and he sipped his.

"I thought marriage was not about having a plan B. I've always had something clear in my mind. Whomever I married was going to be my forever. Is that such a bad plan?" she said.

Everett reached out and touched her cheeks. "No. It's lovely. It's the way it should be."

But the way he touched her—in a fatherly manner—brought doubts to Christel. She shrugged off his touch.

The waiter brought their entrées, and they decided not to talk about marriage while they ate. Instead, Everett chose to get an update on Reid & Welch. Christel was going to go ahead with the idea of turning the company into a private trust and sell the majority of the properties the company owned, a plan she hadn't even told him about until now.

Christel was becoming a woman on her own, maturing faster than anyone had anticipated, and revealing an untamed spirit and a natural talent to lead. Part of Everett's fantasy—of being the man who saved Christel and showed her the way—had been prematurely shattered. He'd loved that role.

And as he asked his questions and showed his usual interest in her well-being and progress, her answers became laconic. With every word he said, both of their hearts grew heavy.

"Stop it," she said when he was in the middle of

yet another comment about what she should do about the Reid & Welch Company.

"What's wrong?" he said.

"I'm not interested in discussing business."

"I'm sorry. I thought—"

"Stop talking," she said, and Everett noticed tears ready to pour down her cheeks. "I realized, Everett . . . that you don't want to marry me."

"That's not true. I love you."

"Yes . . . I believe you. I'm beginning to think that love is a very selfish thing."

She sounded bitter. Everett felt a chill. She had that look on her face, the one he got used to seeing when she was determined and would make hard decisions in a heartbeat. "Did I say anything wrong?" he said.

"Honestly? No."

She stood up and picked up her purse. "I love you, Everett. I've just realized neither of us is ready for marriage."

"You're rushing to conclusions like you always do."

"Is that what you think I do?" she said with a glazed smile.

"Sometimes. Yes."

Christel walked around the table and leaned over and kissed him on his forehead. "From now on, my love, I want us to be friends."

He held her shoulder. "Christel, please . . ."

She gently dodged his hand. "I appreciate everything that you've done for me, but we need to live our lives independently."

She turned and walked away.

Everett stood, borderline desperate. His leg bumped into a dish and knocked it to the floor. Patrons' heads turned to him, and a momentary silence took over Le Pavillon. Christel's back was still within a few steps from him, but retreating. He didn't know what to do. It was too bad he loved her like a woman, and at the same time, almost like a daughter.

*****

Christel got into a cab sobbing. If Everett wanted her as much as she wanted him, she would've stayed for dessert and told him the reason why she had rushed to ask him to marry her from a telephone booth. She would have explained how anxious she'd been before meeting with Alan Reid, and how troubled she was by all the changes going on in the company and inside her.

You fool. I'm expecting a baby.

PART 3

Maurice Welch & Denizard Haener

1978 — Present

30

It had been an entire year since Christel and Everett had last seen each other at Le Pavillon. They had regular phone conversations, but she'd never found the right moment to tell him she was expecting his son. The newly born child had a loving mother and a good father who could be included in the child's life whenever Christel found appropriate.

"We need to talk," she said during one of their phone calls.

"Chris, so you know, I'm in a relationship."

"Good for you. But you know I'll always be the love of your life."

"You're crazy."

"Whatever. There's someone you need to meet. His name's Maurice."

"Who the hell's Maurice?"

"The most beautiful little boy in the whole world."

"Little boy? Have you adopted a child?"

"No. He's our son."

"Jesus . . . You can't be serious."

"I am."

Christel thought of her son, Maurice, as a pure Welch. He was Everett's son, a man chosen by Julian to help Christel carry on her father's legacy. The Reid name was only a brand on the facade of her building. Maurice Welch wouldn't have to make hard choices in life.

There was an artist named Maurice that inspired Christel. Once, while visiting an art gallery with Ulrich Kohl, she'd fallen in love with his paintings. There was something about that artist's backstory that connected Christel with how she'd experienced life—he was a man strongly influenced by women, who never found out who his real father was. Christel was determined to make her son's existence less complicated. She planned to tell him he had no father. She would be the strong female influence. The only influence. But as her belly grew, and her temperament changed with the perspective of motherhood, she decided to keep the name Maurice but not the rest of his story.

The boy had a right to a father.

Maurice grew up living in his mother's house, just a few blocks away from Everett's town house. Maurice's weekends were spent with his father. His schooling was under Christel's jurisdiction, his hobbies under Everett's. The lines were often crossed, but both parents dealt with them reasonably and with the best interests of the child in mind. With exceptions. One day, when Maurice was five years old, the school director called Christel to report that her son had punched a female student in the nose.

"He hasn't learned that from me, my love," Christel said while recounting the incident to Everett.

"And you think I taught him that? You know what the problem is? You've picked an all-girls school. How wise do you think that is?" Everett said.

"That's not true. Most of the students happen to be girls, but not all. How else would they accept him?"

"Did the girl hit him back?"

"That'd be unlikely, don't you think?"

She heard one of his long sighs on the phone. "Can't we just give him a normal upbringing? He needs to be with boys, learn his limits, get a punch back now and then."

Christel moved Maurice to a new school suggested by Everett.

*****

The year 1978 marked the end of six years of intense transformation for Christel and the Reid & Welch Company. The young, stunning heiress had blossomed even further. At twenty-eight, she was a monument. She no longer looked like a girl in a woman's body. Her face showed an uneven skin tone from aging that was almost unnoticeable, and she was blessed by the gods with symmetrical features. Discreet lines between her eyes appeared to have been designed by painters—she was still young, but with a sexy air about her that was tempting and respectable. Looking at Christel could be harmful to a mortal man's eyes. She dazzled effortlessly.

A nightclub called Studio 54 had opened a year earlier and a friend, Eleanor Delarge, invited Christel for a night out. She was a popular journalist who'd managed to interview Christel for a fashion magazine, dedicating three pages to her in a special issue about New York's young business tycoons and leaders. The two felt at ease with each other, and a friendship grew. The article portrayed Christel in the best possible light. But it was a picture of Christel—behind her desk on the top floor of her building—that made her an instant success. Everyone became fascinated with her beauty and wealth. Christel's discreet nature only added an extra mystique about her.

"I hate dark places," Christel told Eleanor over the phone.

"There's nothing dark about it, darling. They have this theatrical set. There are lights constantly changing and all. You can actually see people's faces."

"What kind of people go there?"

"Regular folks like Diana Ross, Michael Jackson, and Andy Warhol."

"I love Warhol."

There were rocks stars present the night Christel and Eleanor went to the nightclub. The two women were seated alone drinking champagne. Christel attracted as many stares as the celebrities dancing nearby.

"Look who's falling in love with you," Eleanor said in Christel's ear.

Christel pretended to ignore a particular stare aimed at her. "I hate musicians."

"Why?"

"Because they're too obvious."

Eleanor shrugged and got up. "I'm gonna dance a little."

Christel watched Eleanor walk from their table and turned her gaze to a quiet group of men sitting across from her—where the stare came from. One of the men, about Everett's age—and stature, face, and hairstyle—drew her attention. By the time she raised her glass of champagne, the man was already on his way to meet her. They talked for five minutes. He was English, was in New York for business, and would be leaving in two days.

Perfect, Christel thought.

"Don't you think it's a bit loud in here?" she said.

"It's quieter where I'm staying. I'm just a few blocks from here."

Two mornings later, Christel called Eleanor to thank her. In a place where celebrities came en masse, she was granted the spotlight on Eleanor's gossip column. Supposedly, Christel Welch had a new mystery boyfriend.

"Everyone's asking about you. They wanna do a profile on you," Eleanor said.

"Let's talk about it over lunch. Now, whom did you go out with that night?"

"A rock singer. His band's gonna be the next Beatles."

"Nobody will ever get to be the next Beatles."

Christel and Eleanor's friendship served them mutually. The media attention was a distraction, something that projected Christel's image while she figured out what she wanted to be, or where to take Reid & Welch next.

The company had experienced profound changes since Alan Reid died six years before. Walter Doles, current president of the Reid & Welch private trust, was given full autonomy to grow Christel's money. The snobbish executive had matured and adapted to Christel's blunt management style. "If I hear of anyone making more money than us, I'll replace you," she had told Walter before he convinced her to invest heavily in a new modality called a mutual fund.

*****

In 1982, Walter came into Christel's office looking like the world belonged to him. He sat before

Christel and showed her their latest balance sheet. "Congratulations," he said. "Reid & Welch's mutual fund's position is worth over one billion dollars as of yesterday. That's double our initial investment, and fifty percent of our total assets. I suggest that we move our profits back to federal and corporate bonds."

She squinted over the numbers and looked up at him. "Walter, the conservative? So unlike you."

"It's your money. I simply think we're too exposed, that's all. It's time we get a little prudent."

"We're winning, Walter. Let's keep it bullish until it's time not to."

That was two billion dollars in Christel's bank account. Plus, the estates. Not bad for a young woman. But there was still an identity problem. Reid & Welch was not a real company anymore, just a private trust. Christel's money was growing without a purpose. She'd become a filthy rich socialite, which was fun when she was in her early twenties, but now she felt the clock ticking faster. Besides, simply being wealthy was proving to be a lousy substitute for what she still felt for Everett Johnson.

The same day Walter showed her the balance sheet, triggering her to pursue a more productive life, Christel visited Everett without prior notice. He was having dinner with his girlfriend, a fifty-six-year-old psychotherapist named Clara, who was the exact same age as Everett.

Clara saw Christel for the first time in person, entering her boyfriend's home like she lived there, showing no regard for their privacy.

"Isn't it the wrong day?" Everett said.

"I won't be long," Christel said and sat at the table with them.

"How's Moe?"

"He's fine. I'm not here because of him." Christel turned her attention to the psychotherapist, who'd been struggling to keep a friendly smile. "And how are you doing?"

"Wonderful. I see you regularly in that woman's column—Eleanor Delarge? I have to tell you, you have an impressive list of boyfriends. To be honest, I envy you," Clara said.

"What can I say, I love men. But I also hate them. Does that make any sense? I wonder what Freud would say," she said.

Clara smiled. "Never mind him. I say you're just like the rest of us."

"So, I'm normal."

"Yes, Ms. Welch."

"Oh, please. It's Christel." She looked back at Everett. "Simon Brown retired."

"About time. How old is he, a hundred?"

"More like eighty. I need you back in the company."

"What company? You own a private trust."

"It doesn't matter. It needs good people."

"Why would you require me full time? And why can't we talk Friday when you bring Moe to the house?"

Clara's eyes moved back and forth between the two. She'd become a spectator.

"I'm considering new investments. I've been thinking about doing more for the planet. That's right up your alley, isn't it? NGOs? Anyway, I wanted to give you some time to think before we talk for real."

Clara was about to roll her eyes when Christel glanced at her while standing up. "You two enjoy the night. Excuse me."

"Good night," Everett said.

When Christel left, Clara took a long swig of a whiskey and glanced at Everett with all seriousness. "Let me give you my professional perspective."

"Please, don't let Christel spoil our night."

"It's just constructive advice."

"Uh, sure."

"You, my darling, are a puppy dog. That woman? Your master."

"That's a bit harsh. Christel is the mother of my son."

"She's also a young, unswerving hot piece of ass who grabbed you by the balls and heart."

"Sounds like you feel sorry for me."

"Oh, you stand no chance."

*****

Christel left Everett's house and went home.

The Carnegie Hill house that belonged to Julian Welch was different that night. Kiara, who had served her parents thirty years before, remained on the property after her boss died. She and Everett had been good friends since those days. Kiara, who was fifty-eight years old now, took care of the house as if it was hers. She'd taken care of Julian's daughter from the moment they'd met, and they'd become the best of friends since Christel's return. It was as if Denise Welch and Kiara were the same person. The mother that replaced Lory del Potro in Christel's heart.

Still, the place felt empty. Everett Johnson was the missing part.

Maurice was eating in the kitchen when Christel came in. He was a weird and funny boy, like most ten-year-olds. He would grow inches overnight and had become scarily similar to Everett in appearance. Arguments about his diet were the thing of the moment, as it consisted mainly of pizza, cheeseburgers, and fried chicken. He would do anything other than what his mother wanted him to do. And even though he still craved her approval, Maurice was beginning to feel embarrassed when his mother picked him up at school in her fancy Mercedes.

Earlier that afternoon, Christel had called Kiara and asked her to take Maurice to his karate class. She'd briefly explained that she would be seeing

Everett. Now that she was back, Kiara wanted to know everything.

"Sit down, girl," Kiara said after Christel kissed Maurice. "I made some mulligatawny. That's what your grandmother Margaret did for your father's birthdays."

"Not too spicy, is it?"

"Just as you like."

"Mom, can I watch TV?" Maurice said. He had just finished his food when his mother arrived.

"When did you learn to be cynical? You're watching it anyway," she said.

"Thanks, Mom." He left the kitchen before Christel could change her mind.

"A gentleman. Just like his father," Kiara said. "So, where have you been?"

"I went to see Everett. I need him back in the company."

"You need *his* company. You need *him*."

"What's the difference?"

"Exactly. Time flies. One day, you'll wake up and, girl, you're gonna have regrets. Now, I know about your life. What you've been through. What men did to you. But you're clever enough to figure out that not all men are the same."

"Your point being?"

"There aren't many Everetts out there. Usually, there's only one. You keep living by your terms only? Hell, you'll make a fool of yourself."

"That's . . . encouraging."

"I just want what's best for you. How's my mulligatawny?"

"Delicious. Did Moe have some?"

"I wish. He made me order pizza again."

Christel glanced at Kiara wide-eyed. "He *made* you?"

"Don't you know your own son?"

"I do. And that's exactly why I don't like the idea of sharing a house with Everett or any man. This ten-year-old little bastard, no matter how much I love him, is a good example of what they are."

"He's just a kid."

"A miniature man. Keep watching him grow—I know the outcome, Kiki."

31

Edith stormed into Christel's office the minute she arrived at the Reid & Welch building that morning. The elderly secretary was furious. A heart attack didn't seem improbable as she walked up to Christel's desk, crossed her arms, and let out a deep breath.

"Good morning to you too, Edith," Christel said.

"Walter wants me to start using a computer," Edith announced.

"What for?"

"Exactly. He told me it would help me get organized. I swear, I'm going to punch him in his face if he ever touches my Olivetti."

"Just tell him no."

"I want your backing."

"You got it, Edith. Now, would you please calm down? I'm expecting Everett at any minute. I'm trying to, well, recruit him back."

Edith nodded, and the fuming faded away. "I hope you succeed. That's someone worth fighting for. I mean, for the company."

In the past, Everett would run to Christel's office the minute she called him. Those days were gone. It took him a week to confirm a date to visit her, which screamed volumes about how he felt about her. Everett was a mature man, and even though Christel was convinced he still loved her, there was a chance that love could lose strength one day.

There were things Christel knew about Everett, and things she didn't, like the fact that he'd visited Lory del Potro at her house. It'd been years since they'd last seen each other, more than enough time for Lory to open up about Christel's past. Everett anticipated a change in Christel as she grew older and wanted to know the missing points about her. Lory was the only one who could reveal them to him. Which, Christel found out, Lory had—albeit reluctantly.

In her only phone call to Lory since they last saw each other at that train station, Lory admitted that she'd explained Christel's defensive behavior and unpredictability to Everett. He promised Lory he would never judge her again, that he considered her recovery a miracle. She'd been abused, exploited, and tortured. Lory told him that most women who took part in the same government program were either dead or mentally ruined. The fact that Christel had found a way out, and the strength to thrive, put her in a distinct place. She was a goddess among men, a true survivor. Lory revealed to Christel that Everett felt blessed that Christel was still trying for a relationship with a man despite all the terrible things men had done to her.

*****

Everett arrived at the Reid & Welch building at ten in the morning, neatly dressed.

"Good morning, my love," he said.

Edith brought coffee and left the two alone.

"Busy schedule?" Christel said.

"Not really."

He's no longer desperate for me, she thought.

"Please, take a seat," she said.

"Sure."

"I've been curious."

"Have you? About?"

"What is it that you do at Forest Behold?"

Everett sunk back on his chair.

Forest Behold was the NGO that Everett ran. It helped local villagers from developing nations receive financial and human support. Christel herself had contributed several times to Everett's organization, but in all those years, she had never once asked him details about his work.

"I help people who need help," he simply said.

And he's being sarcastic now. God.

"I understand. Can you give me an example of what you do?"

"Chris, I've sent you reports detailing how I've used your money. Have you ever bothered to look at them?"

"No. I, er, have never been that interested, sorry. But that's not what I'm asking."

"Sure . . . As you know, demand for palm oil, soy, beef, and wood is fueling illegal destruction of tropical forests."

"I know. That's bad, obviously."

"It affects villagers in many places, and in many ways. Right now, I'm focusing on a group of Asian villagers. Naturally, nobody gives a damn about the little people who get their land destroyed. We tend to forget we're responsible for consuming all that. We're the ultimate villains."

"If there were no demand, there would be less damage. But there is."

"Yes. And someone has to do something about it."

"You. That makes me proud. Honestly."

He went on. "In my case, I provide forestry education, run workshops with local schools, and host a variety of activities to foster art and whatever useful skills the local people can learn. I pay doctors and engineers to travel to these places and train children and adults to take advantage of their resources. We help them control diseases. Teach them languages. Educate them about the value of their land. In short, I see them as people. It's the thing that makes me the happiest."

I thought it was me who made you the happiest.

"It's . . . a beautiful thing," Christel said.

"Don't tell me you've become concerned about these things."

"I was going to tell you just that."

"Well, I'm surprised. But, then, you've always been surprising."

Christel shrugged. "I'm ready to change everything. In here, and about us."

"Right . . . What do you have in mind? You know I'm always here for you."

"I do. And I recognize how unfair I've been. I wanna change that, Everett. I've been unfair to you and Moe. Please forgive me." She stood up from behind her desk, reached out for his hand, and pulled him toward a set of couches in the corner of her office. "There's so much I wanna do," she said.

"You always have a lot going on in your mind."

She raised her hands in the air, indicating *wait.* "This is what I want. First, about us. Let's move in together."

"I think Moe will love the idea."

Gosh. What about you? "I'm sure he will. He loves you," she said.

"You know, this is actually a great idea. I'd love to stay with you for the rest of my life," he finally admitted and moved to sit next to her. They kissed, laughed briefly, and held each other in a long and warm embrace.

"How foolish I've been . . . I'm sorry. You know I love you," she said.

"There's nothing to be sorry about. Let's just look to the future from now on."

She nodded and locked eyes with him with her usual intensity.

The future started right then.

"I've been thinking—actually, I've been rehearsing for this moment. You probably think I'm gonna ask you to move into my house, but—" Christel said.

"I don't care where we live. It's about the other person, Chris. Home is where you are, right? I know it sounds corny, but it's how I feel."

"Seriously. I can move into your house tonight, and that's it. No regrets. I promise you."

"Stay where you are. That's where Moe has most of his things. That's your father's house. And if I recall, you spent two crazy years refurnishing that place. I'll move in with you. Period."

"OK . . . Next subject. Let's get a civil marriage."

"Anytime you want."

"How about today? I want to spend the rest of our days doing what we love."

"Deal. But there are things we need to discuss. You're worth a billion dollars."

"Actually, several billions. How much have you got?"

"A bit less. Three million, give or take."

"I want us to marry under community of property."

"You're crazy."

"You've had thirty-two years to cheat me in one way or another. Since I was born. Will you take advantage of me now?"

"You bet," he teased.

"No, you won't. I'll see you coming. Anyway, it's been decided. Let's move on to the next subject."

"Gee . . . Have some water first."

"I wanna move out of this building. Rent the remaining space of Reid & Welch. There's plenty of room in my house."

"Oh. Right. And the people?"

"I'll fire them. Especially Walter. He's been trying to seduce me for forever."

Everett laughed. "I pity him."

"But I'll take Edith with us. You'll take care of all my investments because I'm planning on spending as much as I can. And I want you to help me spend it wisely."

"Ideas?"

"Let's talk it over. I think I'm beginning to like what you like. Maybe we can do some good in the world. I mean, not just for show. Can you help me?"

"No need to ask."

She stopped talking. Her eyes glanced away, trying to remember if anything still needed to be discussed with Everett. "Have I told you you're the love of my life?"

"In more than enough ways."

*****

In total, eighteen people still worked in the Reid &
Welch building. Walter was the first one to be called
in for a talk. Christel thanked him for his years of
service and promised a generous severance package,
but he knew he would never find a job as easy as the
one he'd just lost. There were many superfluous
positions still occupied at Reid & Welch. Experts in
mutual funds, stocks, real estate, technology,
pharmaceuticals, oil and gas, foreign investment, and
a few others. All of her assets would be under her and
Everett's direct oversight from then on. Christel fired
all the employees one by one for the rest of her day.
Only Edith remained. The secretary looked thrilled
by the idea of working at her boss's home.

Christel arrived home for dinner after a long
meeting with her accountants and the lawyers from
the Brown firm overseeing the layoffs. She was dying
to tell Maurice that his father was moving in with
them. She asked Kiara to bring her favorite rosé and
tomato juice for Maurice.

"He's just had a large burger," Kiara said.

Christel's face barely hid her joy. "It doesn't
matter. I just wanna toast with him."

"It's been a long time since I last saw you
blooming like that."

"Just bring Moe and the drinks."

"Yes, my girl."

Christel started the fireplace in the parlor and
moved to a central set of couches she only used when

she held meetings with several people. She rarely spent time there alone, but the occasion justified it. She sat facing the huge wall simulating a Marc Chagall painting called *Mother by the Oven*. Inevitably, she thought of her own convoluted relationship with the maternal figure. Lory del Potro was the closest thing to being Christel's mother, and a constant reminder of a world she wished to forget. Lory had been complicit in the making of every scar on Christel's body and soul. And there was Kiara, whom she'd been grateful to rejoin after two decades of limbo.

Kiara brought the drinks and Maurice.

"Thanks, Kiki."

Maurice picked up his glass of tomato juice and waited for his mother to fill up her glass of rosé. He looked bored. "I was in the middle of something important," he said.

Christel glanced at Kiara in the background. She smiled and shook her head.

"I'm sorry. But I have something even more important to say," Christel told Maurice and raised her glass toward him. They toasted.

He tasted his juice and waited.

"Your father and I are getting back together."

It took a moment for Maurice to understand. "You're getting married?"

"Yes, darling. And he's coming to live with us in this house. Isn't that great?"

Maurice nodded. Then he placed his drink back

on the thick glass table and walked away, head down. Christel and Kiara exchanged a glance. There was no explanation for Maurice's reaction except for the fact that he was only ten years old and the world was a confusing thing to comprehend.

"I didn't see that coming," Christel said.

"Moe's gotten used to a way of life. Parents living together will change that." Kiara was smiling from ear to ear.

"At least *you* look happy."

"You're not gonna drink all that champagne by yourself, are you?"

"C'mon. Pick up a glass."

The two sat quietly near the crackling fireplace, refilling their glasses until staring at Marc Chagall's mother painting on the wall tired them. "You know," Kiara began, turning to Christel, "who'd have guessed I'd be looking forward to washing Everett's underwear."

Christel laughed, then put her arm around Kiara's neck. "Are you?"

"Are *you*?"

"Oh, that should be fun. He's such a square guy." Christel glanced at the wall. "You know what that woman represents to me?"

Kiara followed Christel's glance. "I'll be offended if it's not me."

"Don't be. It's you, Kiki. You, Everett, and Moe. You're my family. And for the first time, we'll all be together." There was a bittersweet pitch in her voice.

"Considering all that you've been through, isn't that a blessing?"

"Yes."

"Then what's the problem?"

"To claim I have a problem would be like spitting on the plate of destiny. I guess I need to learn to live in the present."

"I'll help you." Kiara stood up. "Let me check on what's happening on the fourth floor."

"Boys always want what they want."

"Yeah, but we girls want our way too, don't we?"

"I never knew what wanting meant until I met Everett. I saw myself as a bunny in a cage. I thought running was an ailment."

"Well, you've gone the distance. Are you coming?"

Christel joined Kiara. Maurice's bedroom door was half open. He was playing PAC-MAN. The world outside was everyone else's problem.

Good for him, Christel thought.

32

The last time the town house in Carnegie Hill had seen so many people was on Julian Welch's sixty-second birthday party. In the marble gallery, guests were flanked by a floor-to-ceiling flower wall of Casablanca lilies and cherry blossoms. Before they could absorb all the scents around them, they were welcomed with smoked salmon and beluga caviar. Servers had orders to keep fingers and mouths busy at all times—and their throats wet with champagne.

The time to sit came. The feast ended with a wedding cake of sprouting sugared blooms and a message written on the dark chocolate: "Christel & Everett—25th Wedding Anniversary."

More champagne was brought. This time, only to the hosts.

Christel wore a smoke-white silk georgette dress that showed off a bit of her skin and guaranteed to keep the selected crowd of forty guests distracted when the moment to address them came. She hated public speaking. It was the only time she showed any trace of shyness. But, at fifty-four, Christel remained almost unfairly beautiful. Wherever she went, she attracted the eyes of men who were young enough to be her son, and old enough to be her father. She was the embodiment of what men thought of as a real, yet dreamlike woman. Gray had begun to replace her dark, silky hair, but it suited her. Her waist had thickened a little, which only made her curves more appealing.

"What can I say—you're the best. I love you, Everett."

They toasted, sipped the champagne, and French-kissed with no modesty.

Eleanor Delarge was the only journalist present. The crazy nights out and over-the-top parties of the seventies and early eighties were long gone. Eleanor had married the British rock singer whose band was thought to become the new Beatles. That dream hadn't lasted long. Eleanor was Christel's closest friend. The only thing that bothered Christel about her was the fact that the columnist believed she had played an essential role in making Christel what she'd become. It was a ridiculous idea, but Christel cared for Eleanor and knew that, at times, jealousy walked hand in hand with friendship.

Since Christel and Everett's marriage, Reid & Welch had become a philanthropic and humanitarian powerhouse. The two and a half decades saw the couple's wealth grow to eight billion dollars, not including the twelve billion that had been spent on humanitarian aid all over the world over the years. The couple had been fervently immersed in protecting human rights and promoting the rule of law in poor countries. They'd donated heavily to family agriculture and education, sheltering, clean water and sanitation, and environmental issues.

In December 2004, a tsunami hit the Indian Ocean, killing more than 220,000 people and leaving two million people homeless. It was an unprecedented natural disaster that shocked the world. The United Nations secretary general, Kofi Annan, alerted the public of a race against time to help the victims, and spoke against the international community for not delivering the promises of money. In previous disasters, only a third of the funds pledged had been translated into hard cash. Christel knew that private donations from individuals, trusts, and foundations would top the list and shame governments. She wanted to be part of that list but stay out of the headlines. While the combined total of private donations reached over three billion dollars, the Reid & Welch Foundation had anonymously contributed almost twice that amount. She tried to keep Eleanor in the dark. Christel wasn't doing it for notoriety.

But Eleanor had found out. There was no way to hide the huge amount of help being offered by Christel, and all Eleanor had to do was ask around.

Eleanor thought that Christel was unique and that her story needed to be shared with everyone. At her own will, she turned the already known Christel Welch into a world celebrity. Papers told the tale of a billionaire who singlehandedly gave more money than all of the other donors combined.

To make things worse, gorgeous pictures portraying Christel made people fall in love with her. TV shows requested interviews, and speculative profiles were published periodically. She'd been invited to the White House and declined. Awards were given, and she kindly refused. And the more she isolated herself from the public, the more interest she generated. Her gigantic heart, combined with her monumental beauty, had earned Christel the nickname "goddess," which Everett thought fit her perfectly.

Eleanor expected Christel to recognize her coverage, not acknowledging that her friend hated all that useless noise. Christel knew journalists had an instinct for spreading good stories when they had one, and that no other member of the press knew Christel the way Eleanor did. But that imposition had left a mark. It would stay with Christel forever. The two women remained friends, but they'd distanced themselves from each other.

"Moe?" Christel called her son. There was a young lady next to Christel with whom she exchanged conspiratorial whispers.

Maurice excused himself from a group of guests and walked up to his mother with a warm look in his eyes. The charming lady next to his mother was Trixy, one on a list of several women Christel had picked as potential candidates for a serious relationship with her son. He didn't bother. Maurice learned to have fun when introductions such as the one about to happen took place.

He was a full-grown man of thirty-five, his mother's pride and joy. And she'd been blessed by luck. He was tall and handsome, had the same square face as his father, uneven hair, and dangerously honest dark-brown eyes. Maurice had become a lawyer at Everett's insistence. He'd worked for a major law firm in New York for seven years, then he was brought to work closely with Christel and Everett, getting acquainted with the Reid & Welch history and current investment culture.

"Honey, Trixy here has a dream. I think we can help her," Christel said.

"Hi, Trixy," Maurice said.

Christel didn't let the young woman speak. She explained, "See, she's studying the arts. I mentioned our house in Arles. She'd love to visit us there sometime. What do you think?"

Maurice glanced at Trixy, all smiles. "I think you'll be bored."

"Arles screams art and history. Why would I be bored?" Trixy said.

"Oh, that," he said. Then he turned to Christel. "Maybe you two should go. I'll be busy, Mother."

"With what?"

"I'm going to the Amazon."

Christel touched his cheeks and stared at him proudly.

"I'm so happy you've made up your mind. It's the best gift I've received today."

Christel knew her son too well. He wasn't meant for the comfort and predictability of a modern city, and he thought New York was depressing. No amount of fine food, entertainment, or chatter could convince him otherwise. The excesses of the world enraged him at times. He'd done what Christel defined as homework—graduated, worked for others, and then worked for her. Maurice had proved his value. Now he wanted to find out what spoke to his heart, and spend some time away from everything and everyone.

Months before, Christel had gifted him with five million dollars. Maurice had refused it, but Christel always found a way to do what she wanted.

"Will you excuse us?" she told Trixy and walked with Maurice to the parlor on the first floor, where they sat before the Marc Chagall wall.

"We'd better not take long. Yo ur guests will miss you," Maurice said.

"What would they do without me?" she joked. "Anyway. Fifteen years ago, I sent people to look at the property. They found nothing. The forest covered everything."

"I'm not surprised. The forest always takes over, Mother."

"But then—" Christel's face transformed dramatically. She frowned, terribly concerned. "I hired a man called Harry Walker. He's a private eye, as they say. I asked him to approach Harper Taylor's daughter, Michelle. I thought, maybe there's a document he'd left somewhere. A computer file, anything that might shed some light on what that lab in the forest was about and where exactly it was located inside the property. But all my searches have failed. I've sent people there before, and they found nothing."

"Did the private eye find anything?"

"Yes. But what he found doesn't help us. The local real estate registry describes a basement larger than the ground floor. They've built the lab underground. It was meant not to be found."

"If Alan Reid were still alive, I'd punch him to death."

"Oh, Maurice . . . The dirt men do."

He took his mother's hands in his. "It's been more than fifty years. Whatever they did in that lab, it's gone. The forest swallowed it. I don't think your concern is justified anymore."

"Promise me you'll have a look at it."

"I'll fly over it at the first chance. Technology might help."

Christel closed her eyes and relaxed her shoulders. "I know it sounds crazy, but even after all these years, I still have a bad feeling about it."

Maurice smiled and squeezed his mother's hand.

They had a party going on downstairs. The idea that an entomological lab built half a century before in the middle of the forest could still be dangerous sounded unreasonable. But he wouldn't disappoint her. Even though he didn't know what had gone on in his mother's life when she was young, the people he talked to about it assured him it had been severe and traumatic. Maurice thought that his mother deserved the best.

They made a detour and reached the kitchen.

*****

Everett was leaning against a granite countertop eating yet another slice of their anniversary cake and watching Kiara give orders to the staff of waiters.

"I knew you were hiding somewhere," Christel said.

Everett had loosened his tie. He was a bit drunk, which made him more sincere than usual. "It's been a great party. Now I'm ready to sleep," he said.

"Don't you dare play the old man. Fix that tie. You're coming back to the party." Maurice and Kiara exchanged a glance and laughed. "You too, Maurice," Christel said.

Of all the people in there, no one knew Christel

better than Everett. He was seventy-eight years old. He'd known Christel since she was born. He knew her history, how every little scar on her body had come to be. Behind the excitement of their wedding anniversary, there was a veil of anxiety. She was a woman at her best. Everything she had ever attempted had thrived, but he saw a carefully hidden doubt in her soul. There was a constant noise in the back of her head asking an inconvenient question: What would she want next? What was left to conquer?

Everett knew he couldn't keep up with her.

Christel had a volcano inside her, and it was still active. She loved people, going places, and doing things for others. At times, he suspected, she had a wish for revenge, and he wondered what she would do to the men who had abused her if they ever crossed paths again. He was glad he was not one of them. All Everett wanted was to lie low, live a quieter life. But if he did that, he feared he might lose Christel.

The truth was, being by her side was proving physically challenging. He didn't know how long he could hide it from her.

You need to take it a little easier, Michael Shepard—his doctor—had told him one year ago. *You don't have a wife like mine*, Everett had explained.

He finished his cake, fixed his tie, and returned to

the party. Jazz was playing, and drinks were being passed around. "I've just had an idea," Christel whispered in his ear when he approached her.

Everett sighed. "I'm not gonna try to guess."

"The idea is as follows: What if we keep on partying?"

Everett stared at her. He had dark circles under his eyes. Right then, he wanted his bed more than anything. "You wanna stay until tomorrow? Is that it? I'll do my best, I promise."

"No . . . I want to party forever."

Everett bit his lips. He was intrigued by that concept. "How does someone go about organizing that?"

"It's in here, my love." She gently touched her chest. Then she touched his.

Everett curled his lips. "Still, that translates into actually doing stuff. What is it that you have in mind?"

"Let's travel till we drop."

"You know that the best thing about traveling is coming back home."

"Whatever. We're leaving tomorrow, if you don't mind."

"Why not. Tomorrow it is."

33

It sounded like whales chattering. Except, Christel and Everett were on the back of a Land Rover in South Africa, following a tailor-made Big Five game–viewing itinerary led by an experienced guide. The vehicle had stopped, and they were listening to an unusual, acute sound.

"Stay in the car, please. And be quiet," the guide said. He stepped out, bringing a shotgun with him.

"What do you think this is?" Everett whispered.

Christel shrugged and then squinted, trying to identify that weird sound. Before Everett could protest, she, too, stepped out of the vehicle and followed right after the armed guide.

"Holy moly." Everett went after Christel.

Soon, the three were lying low in a valley of almost impenetrable thorn thickets of Delagoa: knobthorn, scented-pod, and brack-thorn acacias. They kept silent, looking in all directions for possible threats. Before them was the origin of that sound—a scene that was shocking and revolting. A hornless two-thousand-pound rhino was on the ground, possibly dead. Next to him, a baby rhino cried.

"Poachers . . . They're still around," the guide said.

"How do you know?"

He pointed at the huge rhino. There was fresh blood coming out of a gunshot wound. The animal was still moving.

"They went for his horn, didn't they?" Everett said, voicing the obvious.

"No. This is one of our dehorned males. It helps prevent poaching."

"Why did they shoot him, then?"

"We remove about ninety percent of the horn mass, but a stub of horn remains. A horn stub has high value in the black market. They also kill them out of vengeance. You know, because we've dehorned them."

Christel stood up and began walking in the baby rhino's direction.

"Get back!" the guide ordered.

She ignored him.

Slowly, she approached the injured animal, glanced briefly at his mortal wound, and turned to the little one. She crouched, horrified. The baby rhino was begging for help. It was heartbreaking. She tried to touch the soon-to-be orphan, but it was too scared. It moved behind the giant rhino, safe from Christel's reach. There was nothing she could do to help.

"I have to report this. Let's go back," the guide said.

"Do you think they're near us?" Christel said.

"I'm sure they are."

"Well, you're armed. Let's hunt them!"

The guide thought she was joking, but she kept staring at him determinately. "Tourists are not allowed to go after poachers, madam." It was self-evident, but the guide left no margin for further discussion.

Everett said very little to comfort Christel as they drove back to their lodge.

Lately, she'd been acting impulsively, much like when she was in her twenties. Sure, they'd witnessed an unpleasant event, and Everett could easily agree with Christel wanting justice. But going after poachers herself was out of bounds.

They returned from their trip two days earlier than planned.

Subject C, a 160-meter giga yacht, was docked at the Cape Town Harbor.

The boat had been spotted at the V&A Waterfront and had sparked immediate interest as to who owned it. Word spread that it belonged to American philanthropist Christel Welch. By the time she and Everett got back to *Subject C*, a crowd of journalists and curious people were waiting. They needed help from the police to board the yacht.

"This is ridiculous," Christel said.

"The boat was your idea," Everett said.

True, the custom yacht was built in Germany by an oil tycoon who'd decided to put it up for sale. Everett had read about it in a business magazine, and Christel had contacted the German shipyard. Everett was reluctant, but she described all the perks of the yacht to convince him.

"It's a hundred and sixty meters long, which is probably among the largest in the world. That baby weights twelve thousand tons. It's got twenty-four suites, a helicopter pad, a swimming pool, an on-deck Jacuzzi, a dance floor, and an elevator. And it's ice class, Everett. A true explorer yacht. It travels eight thousand nautical miles without stopping. Don't you wanna see the world?"

"I want what you want, Chris."

"Is that a yes?"

When they bought it, Christel wanted to change its name to *Subject C*. "Now, that's a peculiar choice," Everett said.

"The letter *C* stands for 'Christel.' The word 'Subject' defines how men see women," she explained.

"I don't like it," he said. *Subject C* stood.

That night at the V&A Waterfront, with Table Mountain as the backdrop, Christel and Everett had dinner inside the boat. She was in a festive mood, considering she'd seen the stressful sight of a dying rhino just hours before. Everett knew that something was in the making. They'd been traveling around the world for six straight months, but even the impact of beautiful new places had acquired a routine flavor, especially to Christel.

They traveled at the mercy of weather and humor. They'd been to Navagio Beach in Greece, known as "Shipwreck Beach," a spectacular wreck sitting upon the white sands and limestone cliffs plunging into the sparkling turquoise water. Since the bay was only accessible by boat, the decision to buy *Subject C* had started to make perfect sense to Everett.

They'd seen the caves of Santorini dug into the rocks by the earliest occupants of the region, its landscape and architecture eye-watering. Banyuls, located off the Côte Vermeille, known for its fortified and dessert wines, was a beauty surrounded by pebbly beaches with a secret only available to those visiting it by boat: a hidden underwater trail in a protected marine area between Banyuls and Cerbère.

"We couldn't have done without *Subject C,*" Christel reminded Everett.

The loggerhead turtle reserve on Isola dei Conigli, Italy, was one of the last places the endangered loggerhead turtle went to lay eggs. Located off mainland Italy, its waters were home to dolphins, manta rays, and humpback whales. Cala Luna, Sardinia, was another place only accessible by boat and a perfect spot for diving. Besides, the local wine and cheese was a feast for any traveler. Sanary-sur-

Mer, France, just around the corner of Saint-Tropez, offered some great restaurants with a Provençal air.

No one could ask more from life.

They arrived in South Africa after a month-long trip to the Arctic. *Subject C*'s size began to feel too big for just the two of them, despite Everett's warnings that the boat's dimensions were exaggerated.

"I'll turn it into a hospital ship if we get tired of it," she promised him once.

"You look unquiet. What is it?" Everett asked Christel while they watched the nightlife at the V&A Waterfront and drank a bottle of the local sauvignon blanc.

She took a moment before answering him. "I'll see that the people in that park get all they need to hunt down the poachers," she said. Her voice wasn't laced with anger. She was smiling as if a good business decision had been made.

"I'll take care of that for you, my love. Now can you let it go?"

"I don't want to. It makes me feel good. Like I'm useful again."

"We've done our share."

"We're still around. And I've checked why they kill the rhinos."

"Traditional Chinese medicine?"

"That too. But that's not it. Men kill rhinos because *men* believe horns can be used as an aphrodisiac. That terrible, pitiful cry we heard coming out of that innocent baby rhino—it's because men believe horns are sexual stimulants. Now, how stupid do you have to be to believe in that kind of shit?"

"I agree. But you wanna cure the world?"

"I do. One miserable soul at the time. Where and when fate puts them before me."

Just when she was about to tell him how she felt about the world, a member of the crew approached their table with a satellite phone in his hands.

"Excuse me. It's your son."

Christel picked up the heavy phone. "Moe?"

"Hi, Mother. Where are you?"

"Cape Town. How're you doing?"

"Good . . . Listen, I've just found a place. Heaven on Earth, I swear to God."

"In the Amazon?"

"Yes. Eight thousand acres of private reserve. It's a hundred and fifty miles from Manaus. A bargain."

Christel glanced at Everett. She wasn't too happy. "What for, Moe?"

"Do I really have to explain? It's the right thing to do. We can build a house here. I'm a little tired of my shitty cabin on the western part of the forest."

"I got that. But why buy more land?"

"Mother, I'm buying it with my own money. You decide later what you wanna do about it, OK?"

"Can you at least wait for us? We can get there on *Subject C*."

"I'm closing the deal tomorrow. You can come later."

Christel covered the mouth of the phone and whispered to Everett, "He's buying a property in the Amazon." Christel resumed talking to her son. "Whatever makes you happy. How about the lab?"

"Nothing. It's gone. Forget it."

"Well, I'm done with it. I think we should call it quits."

"Agreed. You two have a great time there."

"Take care. I love you." Christel hung up.

Everett watched her. She got that look on her face, her eyes searching for a direction to follow. Christel was still in her prime, tanned and appearing as healthy as ever. She reminded him of the young woman he'd met decades earlier. There was a well of energy inside her, an ongoing dissatisfaction. All significant changes in her life happened when she took on that edginess. He was confident it would happen again. The mood was set, the atmosphere right. He just prayed it wouldn't be something crazy. He was exhausted.

She sipped her wine and glanced at him with her irresistible sensuality. "I've had enough wine. Why don't we go to bed?"

"A bit early, isn't it?"

"Yeah. Take a shower. Make yourself comfortable and wait for me."

"I like the sound of that."

Christel got up and walked toward the suites on the lower level of *Subject C*. Everett watched her walk. No man would ever need rhino horn mumbo-jumbo to desire that woman. He got up too, nodded good night to a stewardess, and followed to their master stateroom. He did as Christel said. There was no point in arguing with her. It was for his benefit, he had no doubt about it.

He took off his clothes and got into his bathroom tub. It relaxed him to the point of making him fall asleep. He woke up to knocks on the door.

"Are you coming, my love?" Christel said.

Everett wrapped a towel around his body and opened the bathroom door.

Christel was sitting on a chair in front of their bed. She was naked, wearing high heels and masturbating. Everett let the towel drop. He was ready for her. Before he headed toward Christel, she said in a soft voice, "Look the other way."

"Only if I'm crazy."

"Check the bed … I'm staying right on this chair tonight."

Everett turned.

When he glanced at their bed, he instinctively bent over to pull his towel back to cover himself. His face shut, and he blushed. There was a barely legal naked Italian stewardess waiting for him.

"Bianca, what are you doing?" he asked the young woman.

"Madam asked me if I wanted to have some fun."

Everett turned to Christel. "I know what men

like. It's OK, Everett," she said.

"Er . . . I don't think this is right."

"No right or wrong, Mr. Welch. I'm here because I want to be," Bianca said.

"C'mon," Christel insisted. She sounded even hornier than just a moment before. "Don't do it for you. Do it for me," she almost begged.

And while he turned his head back and forth between the two women, Bianca got up and kissed him. When his hand grabbed Bianca's buttocks, Christel moaned from the chair. "There you go."

The stewardess took Everett's hand and brought him to the bed. The thinking and hesitation were over. Everett was in bed with another woman for the first time since he and Christel got married. It was unthinkable, but it was happening.

Everett heard Christel reaching orgasm before he and Bianca did. Then he heard her opening the door and leaving him alone with the stewardess.

"I'm yours until tomorrow morning. That's what your wife asked me. You want that, don't you?" Bianca said.

*****

The following weeks were marked by an intense social schedule.

Longtime friends were happy that Christel had finally broken away from her self-imposed isolation. They were having breakfasts, lunches, and dinners all across Europe. Friends from America would fly over just to be with them for a few hours. Some slept in *Subject C*'s suites, which was considered a treat only their closest friends would enjoy. Even Eleanor Delarge was invited, and she gladly accepted with the promise that their meeting was private. During a trip to the Mediterranean, Christel shared some of the adventures she'd had with Everett, which delighted Eleanor.

"Poor Everett!" the columnist said between laughs and sips of wine.

"Push the right buttons, and men will eat from your hands, darling."

And when Bianca was revealed to be the source of some of the couple's marital adventures, Eleanor offered some friendly advice to Christel. "She's quite the temptation. If I were you, I would leave Bianca at the first port you stop by."

"You could be right. Enough playing with luck."

Eleanor stayed with Christel and Everett for two weeks, longer than they'd intended, but it was surprisingly fun. Eleanor was a wonderful companion when she wasn't on a mission to dig up dirt. They went diving in Turkey and trekking in Italy, where they said farewell to Bianca, leaving the Italian beauty with a hefty bonus.

"What did you do to Everett? He looks younger than ever," Eleanor said during one of their nights out in Europe.

"I've liberated him."

"From what?"

"Himself."

More than that, Everett had given up trying to understand Christel. It was impossible. At his age, the best thing was to go along, let Christel live the way she wanted, and be happy with what he got. Deep down, he knew that Christel was hiding her anxieties from him. The parties and the friends and the nonstop traveling were a distraction. She had a look on her face that was somber at times, remembering what men had done to her when she was younger. Everett didn't want to risk touching a wound. Christel was too unpredictable for him to try to save her soul. How long his strategy would work remained to be seen.

When they were crossing the North Atlantic, heading back to New York after ten months aboard *Subject C*, Everett spent the last two nights in their bedroom.

"I'm just tired," he told Christel every time she came in to check on him.

The night before their arrival in New York, the chef brought grilled lobster and wine. The couple had dinner in their stateroom. "I'm taking you to see Michael Shepard first thing when we get to New York."

"I don't need a doctor. I need to rest."

"I'm not asking, my love." She smoothed down

his hair. Christel's eyes gazed deep into his. She didn't need to verbally tell him how much she loved him.

"Always bossing me around."

"That's because you trust me."

Everett didn't finish his meal; he went to bed and turned on the TV. Christel didn't want to annoy him with questions about how he felt. Instead, she jumped in bed with him, and they watched a film together like teenagers in love.

They returned to New York on a cold winter day in February.

Christel was having tea with the captain and the two female shipmates. It was early morning. She went outside the cabin to check the temperature and the wind and had to cover her head with the hood of her coat. She walked around the exterior deck and took a shortcut toward the master stateroom. The last thing that Everett needed was to catch a cold or worse.

"You'd better get dressed—don't want you freezing outside," she said on her way to the bed. But when she looked at Everett, it was she who froze. Her husband lay inert. She called him, yelled, and pushed him vigorously until she realized—

Everett was serenely dead.

Christel let a long breath out, leaned forward, kissed his lips gently, and sat on a chair after pulling it closer to be next to Everett. For the following hours, she sat with her eyes on him. She mourned silently until the grieving transitioned into a collection of memories that came randomly and defied any logic.

Everett Johnson died in his mid-seventies. At that time and age, he couldn't be considered an old person. He was healthy and had everything a man needed. He loved and was loved. He was a loyal husband and an annoyingly honest man.

For years, Christel had seen Everett as her savior. She later accepted that she had played a part in saving herself even before she'd met him. She remembered her father, Julian, the one who put Everett on her path. They were the angels of her life. Now she only had Maurice, although to be fair, she also considered Kiara to be family.

Five hours after Christel found Everett dead, the captain of *Subject C* called the stateroom suite number to tell his bosses they had arrived in New York. "We'll stay for a little while," Christel said.

"Yes, madam."

"Madam" sounded strange. She wasn't one.

Everett's death felt strange. Untimely.

The question of who Christel Reid Welch was came strongly to her mind.

She'd always been someone else's something. Alan Reid's devious experiment, which translated into being Raymond Lentz's Subject C. Ulrich Kohl's sex slave and pet child. Lory del Potro's temporary daughter. When she came to see the light of the day, she was Julian and Denise Welch's heiress, which made her proud. And Everett Johnson's wife, which signified good fortune. But never a madam.

Trying not to be too hard on herself, Christel recalled the letters she'd received from people who'd benefited from her limitless generosity. A cabinet in her house held thousands of them. Refugees, victims of nature and men. The abundance of warm thanks was what reminded Christel—right there where she now mourned Everett—that she had made a name for herself. She was someone. That man, who'd been sweet and caring toward her since the day she was born, represented the last father figure in her life. It was a rupture. Men had always played a dominant role in her life, and not a pleasant one. The only exceptions, Julian and Everett, were now dead.

Christel's heart started to race after countless flashbacks. There would be no formal announcing of Everett's death, she decided. He would be buried without probing eyes around the family watching as if it were a circus act. He'd been a discreet man with an aversion to any kind of publicity. Like herself, he hated gossip—and hypocrisy even more. One day, with a clearer mind and a lighter heart, Christel would make sure that the values of her family—the real ones—left a legacy.

She got up from the chair and half leaned over Everett's body. She felt a lump in her throat followed by sheer terror. Everett had told her that Dr. Michael Shepard had asked him to take it easy. The memory consumed Christel with sudden guilt.

Have I killed him with happiness?

Tears came rolling, asking no permission to leave her soul. "Don't go, Everett!"

Staff members heard her outside the stateroom suite. Minutes later, the captain and others were standing behind Christel. She looked at Everett one last time.

"Thank you, my love."

34

Down the narrow Puturi River on an indigenous-style canoe carved from a single tree, Maurice was away from civilization but in the middle of everything that mattered to him. The Amazon Basin was home to the largest rain forest on Earth, about the size of the forty-eight contiguous United States. The Amazon River was a colossus with eleven times the volume of the mighty Mississippi. One single day of its freshwater discharge into the Atlantic was enough to supply New York City's freshwater needs for nine years. The force of its current triggered the water to continue running over one hundred miles out to sea before mixing with Atlantic salt water. Legend went that seamen were able to drink its fresh water out of the ocean. Maurice felt all that might and saw it as home.

The basin was where Maurice had chosen to live for the past twelve years since his father Everett died—in a small cabin in the middle of nowhere, home of the unknown, and six hundred miles northeast from the bungalow where he'd spent most of his time when Christel was there.

I'm being watched, he sensed, remembering his grandfather Julian's stories.

He stopped rowing and listened. The challenge was identifying a sound that only existed as a gut feeling. Gently, he pulled his paddle out of the water and glanced around.

Where are you?

He knew the Kanamari Indians north of his location, and the Kanamari knew him. As for the Kulina Indians, whose tales included the recent murder of a farmer in a ritual act of cannibalism, they could be found farther west, near the Peru border, but were never seen on that part of the Puturi, about thirty miles west of the Mapiá-Inauini National Forest.

In certain parts of the Amazon, finding a new tribe—or being found by them—was a real possibility. Maurice was alone. A forty-seven-year-old gringo with a Panama hat and a long-sleeved shirt. His face was screamingly white, despite the years spent in the Amazon. By all measures, he was an easy target. Carefully, he reached out to grab his illegal rifle at the bottom of his canoe. The last thing he wanted was to kill an innocent living being unless it was for his own survival.

What Maurice couldn't see was that the canoe wasn't drifting away from the threat. It was approaching it. Underneath the shallow waters, a seven-foot-long blowgun with a bamboo tube in the center emerged noiselessly right beside him. While he scanned both shores of the Puturi, he wasn't looking down at the water.

Then he heard—and felt it. *Damn!*

Maurice instinctively pulled it out and brought it into sight. He knew what it was—a dart carrying frog poison with powerful nerve and muscle toxins—and realized he had just been attacked.

"God . . ." he said.

His body collapsed backward in the canoe, numb, and he wondered about the other side of living in this place. As one of its many volunteer protectors, he loved his life in the Amazon. But when he considered the odds of surviving this attack, he felt foolish. He shouldn't have been out here by himself for so long.

The closest hospital was in the small city of Sena Madureira, sixty miles south of where he was now. It meant that whatever direction he chose to go—if only he could—he would be surrounded by dense, untouched rain forest and unseen risks.

I won't make it!

His head leaned to one side of the canoe.

He saw silhouettes of natives. Of which tribe, he couldn't guess. Right next to him, the blowgun showed up again, this time at touching distance. Too weak to protest, he saw the hands holding it and, finally, the individual responsible for attacking him.

A woman.

She climbed into the canoe, skillfully balancing her body. She wore only a loincloth, exposing her small breasts and the muscular physique earned from her harsh life in the forest. She was over him like a wild cat ready to feast. Their eyes locked and stayed that way for a while. Maurice heard her tribe members yelling at her, but he was clueless as to what were they saying.

"Please, don't kill me," he said.

As seconds went by and she remained on top of Maurice, relentlessly staring at him, one thing drew his attention. That woman was as scared as he was. Her dark eyes were sharp and focused, but they also showed something else. A human touch that he couldn't properly define. It was warm, though. It gave Maurice the impression that the woman didn't necessarily want to kill him.

He passed out with hope.

*****

The private reserve owned by the Welches covered eight thousand acres. It was a wildlife corridor along the Rio Negro hosting a diversity of endemic species of the Amazon, including the elusive jaguar, the exotic hyacinth, and scarlet macaws. The bungalows overlooking the river, and its surrounding infrastructure, occupied less than one acre of the reserve. The property was completely self-sufficient and only reachable by boat or helicopter. For Maurice, it was a piece of heaven. For Christel, it was a refuge from a world built by men.

By the time the property was finished—two years after Everett's death—Christel had spent her first full year there. She turned Kiara into a kind of property manager. There was also a cook, a maid, and a local young man in charge of maintenance. Maurice spent more time traveling in the Amazon cataloging new species of birds and overseeing the operations of *Subject C*, which Christel had turned into a hospital ship servicing riverside communities.

Dr. Michael Shepard was in constant contact with Christel. Besides being a family friend, he was a widow himself, which made him a good source for advice. During one of their conversations at her house in New York, she confided in him that she'd never experienced so much sadness and loneliness before.

"Everyone gets the blues."

"I'm not bouncing back, Michael."

"Is it interfering with your life? How's your sleep?"

"Bad. I've been feeling tired. I've put on some weight, you know."

Michael checked her out respectfully. "Where?"

"Well, I did."

"I don't think you're depressed. *Yet.*"

"What's that supposed to mean?"

"Try to do the things you like, Chris."

"That's all I've been doing."

He glanced at her with sympathy, and then he raised his finger in the air like he was about to tell her a secret. "Have you tried exploring yourself? I mean, for real. Reach the heart of the matter. Let's be realistic. We can't change certain things. We get older, people we love die, and politics will always be bad, right?"

"I know, I know . . ."

"Then accept it. Don't live in the past. Look forward."

"Oh, Michael, so easy to say."

"OK. What is it that intrigues you? What could you do that, you know, you've never done before? What pisses you off the most? And here's something you've never heard before—you're quite a piece of ass. People admire you. You're filthy rich. Go for it, girl! Life goes on, don't you see?"

The part that got her thinking had to do with the things that pissed her off.

But when she explored herself, as Michael suggested, she inevitably found a dark well of resentment she'd never ventured to touch. It had to do with the men she'd served as a slave, especially the sadists who'd hurt her. She'd been paying lip service to herself for too long. The exploitation she'd been through was long past, and she told herself she'd magnanimously forgotten it. But had she? And as scenes and sensations and names came vividly back to her, the past didn't seem that far away anymore. It was still there. In that well.

Where were they? What were they doing? What had they become? As she recalled them, a particular thought took her out of her blues, filling her with a rush of adrenaline. An idea that gave her purpose—a road to follow. Life was made of several things. Retribution, she carefully considered, was one of them. Not responding to the pain she'd so warily concealed over the years was what made her miserable.

Christel called Michael Shepard that same night to thank him. "You're right."

"Am I? Please explain."

"I've, er, explored myself. And it worked."

"What did you find out?"

"That my scars are still screaming, Michael."

"Can you deal with the cause?"

"I believe I can."

"Good for you. Just don't get any new scars."

After she hung up, Christel made another call. This time to Harry Walker, the private investigator who'd helped her countless times before. She gave him a long list of names over the phone. She asked him to locate each one of them and write up a dossier including everything he could find about them.

"Use every resource and contact available. I'll pay you handsomely for every name that is still alive and breathing."

The first dossier from Harry Walker came six weeks later.

Christel was on one of her long walks around her refuge when a crimson topaz with an iridescent purple-gold plumage landed on a branch nearby. She was hypnotized by its beauty and agility. It made her think about her own ability to fly, to stay ahead of the men who abused her. When she was young, she'd had no choice at all but to serve and be quiet about it. She was a prisoner of a trapped mind. But things were different now.

Those men surely knew who Christel was, and what she'd become.

Most women who'd been used like Christel were either dead or living in precarious conditions. They posed no threat to their former abusers. She was the exception. Yet, decades had passed, and Christel had never sought revenge, despite all of her money and influence. If she came to them now, she would have the element of surprise on her side. Everything, in fact, conspired in her favor.

"Chris?" Kiara yelled from inside the bungalow and waved an envelope.

The crimson topaz flew away, quick, agile, and free to dream.

Christel stood glancing at her own shadow on the grass. It distorted her profile, making her appear thinner than she was. She had lost a significant amount of weight in the past year, even though she'd told Michael Shepard she'd gained weight.

Christel walked back to the bungalow. "It came by boat while you were walking," Kiara said and gave her the envelope. It had Harry Walker's name on it.

"Thanks."

She turned and opened the envelope a few steps away from Kiara.

There were eight dossiers inside. The original list contained over one hundred references made to possible real names, nicknames, or descriptions. Attached to the files was a summary of Harry Walker's work with comments. Most of the people on that list were either dead or unreachable. He'd spent over two million dollars of Christel's money bribing contacts in the FBI, CIA, and MI-5 with whom he had close relationships. As she reviewed the dossiers, her blood boiled, her mind poisoned by the recollections that each name brought. The question was: what to do with them that would pacify her heart? And how would one go about resurrecting crimes that left no vestiges?

Three names on the list caused a tingle in the back of her neck. The others remained as a stain of the past and nothing more.

Gilles R. Jacobs, a ninety-year-old Belgian diamond merchant, had stage-five Parkinson's and was under around-the-clock nursing care, experiencing hallucinations and delusions. When Gilles was in his prime, Christel had been sent to him for a weekend in Antwerp. She carried information concerning the price of an unaccounted donation for a Senate candidate, which would be made with diamonds. Christel never forgot that February weekend. Guiles made her sleep naked in a freezing garage while he took pleasure in listening to her begging to come back inside and imploring him for a warm drink. In the height of her shivering and slurred speech, of her shallow breathing and clumsiness, and as her skin took on a bright-red color, Mr. Gilles R. Jacobs warmed her with cigarette burns around her groin. But it wasn't so much the physical pain that remained in Christel's memory. It was the mediocrity in him, the goofy smile that came along with every request Christel made to alleviate her suffering.

Luckily for Gilles, his Parkinson's made any attempt to speak with him useless.

She concentrated on the second name that had caught her attention.

Mason Williams. According to the dossier, he was seventy-eight years old and enjoyed a happy life in Houston with his wife, sons, and grandsons. He was still the CEO of the Mason Williams Oil Company of Texas. He had a host of lovers and kept his wife, Evelyn, busy with charities. The dossier stated that he and Alan Reid were close friends at the time she was gang-raped. No one had hurt Christel like Mason had.

I'm coming for you.

The third name she'd picked from the dossier made Christel's heart beat faster, but for an entirely different reason. She was nineteen years old. Her target lived in Geneva, Switzerland. Indeed, Denizard had been the best thing that had ever happened to Christel during her years of enslavement. It was the first time she'd reached orgasm with a man. And the first time she'd left the encounter with no scars in her soul or disgusting aftertastes. She'd never forgotten that young man.

The dossier stated that Denizard had inherited a bank from his father. He was the only heir. He'd sold the bank fifteen years before and had become a philanthropist. He lived a discreet life in Switzerland and had an untarnished reputation. He'd gotten married, had one daughter, and had been widowed just one year before. The picture attached to the dossier showed a slim, handsome man sailing with his daughter in a Swiss lake.

Christel's heart was still beating quickly when she closed the envelope.

35

Maurice heard someone approaching. Someone else near his remote cabin was a rare thing. He tensed up. No one came to visit him without prior radio or satellite phone contact. He had spent the last decade living in one of the most isolated places on Earth, which had given him a sensitivity to differentiate a vast array of sounds the forest produced.

A human being was walking nearby. He crouched before his rudimentary ground grill, slowly turning to check the fallen vegetation surrounding him. After he was attacked on the river months before, he acquired a permanent state of alertness.

He had no rational explanation as to why he'd chosen to spend most of his time so far from everyone. He simply felt an unwavering need to be there before the forest was destructed by soy, logging, and the cattle industries. He saw himself as a positive force, a protector of the Amazon. Twenty trillion dollars of known natural resources incited greed around the world. If it weren't for Maurice and his small cabin, the forest wouldn't survive, he was certain.

A branch cracked nearby. The intruder was getting closer.

Maurice turned in the direction of the sound. The silhouette of a woman took shape among the vegetation around his clearing. His fear was no longer justified. He knew that woman. Her name was Amana, or "Water That Comes from the Sky," as he called her in Tupi. The native who'd attacked him months before. Amana didn't speak Tupi, which was the language spoken by many tribes of the region. It was Maurice's idea to call her that. The tribe she belonged to had not yet been identified.

After the frog poisoning, Amana's people had taken him to her village, fed him, and carried on with their lives. The poisoning had been a very unusual welcoming from what he immediately established as a peaceful and pure group of natives. During his stay with them, Maurice counted no more than forty individuals. They didn't appear to have relationships with any other tribe. The tribe's decision to remain isolated was probably the result of different encounters and the ongoing assault on and devastation of their forest.

Amana came out from the green leaves around her and showed herself.

She was familiar with the cabin. She and other members of her tribe had brought Maurice back to it after he'd recovered. Even so, her presence there was unusual. Amana had never looked for him after they'd first met. It was always Maurice who took the initiative to visit them and establish his friendly intentions. Until that day, it wasn't clear what Amana's role in the tribe was, except that she appeared to be special—a master of the forest ways, a healer, and an undecipherable human being.

Come, Amana signaled while staring at Maurice.

That puzzled him. Something was wrong. Though Amana was smart and a fast learner, Maurice had only been able to teach her a very rudimentary English.

"What happened, Amana?" he said, gesticulating along.

The forest woman took three quick steps toward him and grabbed his hand. She pulled him in her direction. They moved quickly down the half mile of forest track leading from Maurice's cabin to the Puturi River. There, Amana boarded her canoe and looked back at him. She gestured for him to get in too.

"Where are we going?" he said.

She pointed south.

This intrigued Maurice. Amana knew he had no useful knowledge to help her or her tribe. The only thing he could do was call *Subject C* on his radio if they wanted medical help, which Amana would never allow him to do. Their trust was primarily based on her reliance that Maurice would never tell the authorities about her tribe. He had witnessed a member of their tribe grow mortally ill, and they'd still refused to receive help.

Maurice boarded the canoe, and they started paddling south. Five minutes later, he already felt exhausted. He just couldn't keep up with Amana's frantic pace. She kept paddling steadily for thirty straight minutes and would only look back at Maurice to reprimand him for being so weak.

When they reached the extremity of the Puturi River, they pulled the canoe up on the shore and Amana darted away. Maurice followed after her. Asking questions at that point seemed impractical. They could barely communicate.

She inched forward in the dense vegetation using her skills and an acute sense of direction. Maurice, a good thirty feet behind her, was fighting the jungle with a machete and pouring sweat.

"Amana . . . slow down," he yelled. She ignored him.

Nearly at the point of giving up, Maurice realized he had only been listening to his own noise. He stopped and looked up. He almost bumped into Amana—she stood still, looking ahead.

"Are we there yet?"

She said nothing.

Maurice squinted and tried to see whatever it was that Amana was looking at.

Then he finally spotted it. Fifty feet from them, a

massive *Hevea brasiliensis* tree had fallen with no tracks nearby. It was the tree responsible for the Amazon rubber boom his grandfather Julian had taken part in. When Amana noticed that Julian was staring at the fallen tree, she moved on.

"The tree got old," he tried to explain.

But soon, what seemed to be a single tree that had died of old age took the shape of a widening path of fallen trees. Pallas, walking palms, and a whole range of smaller trees hit by the bigger ones had fallen in a domino effect.

"Trees!" Amana said.

The path kept widening to an unbelievable distance, almost beyond what their eyes could see. Now, it was Maurice who was walking ahead of Amana, confused and daunted at the sight before him. He searched for signs of fire, machines, or anything man-made that could possibly justify such a pattern of destruction.

"How far does it go?" he asked.

"Far. Far. Far . . ."

Julian glanced back at Amana. Her eyes showed fear and moisture.

The only thing that crossed his mind, and could explain that pattern of fallen trees, was a wildly speculative scenario reminiscent of the Tunguska event, a large explosion near the Tunguska River in Russia that had flattened over seven hundred miles of forest in 1908. The supposed blast was attributed to the airburst of a meteoroid. And if that was the case here, no matter how impressive it looked, it was likely to be a local, one-time event.

Amana approached Maurice, crouched near a fallen tree, and called him with a stare. Next, she stuck her hand inside the hollow tree trunk and glanced over her shoulder at him again. When she pulled back her arm, insects of all kinds covered it. She glanced downward at her hand, inconsolable. Maurice crouched next to her and tried to comfort her with a smile, but it wasn't working.

He had to calm himself down first.

*****

In Belém, in northern Brazil, the people at the Amazon Regional Center of Brazil's National Institute for Space Research were the ones in charge of a real-time deforestation detection system called DETER. Its advanced satellite monitoring, coupled with increased law enforcement, was responsible for the sharp drop in deforestation. Every day, analysts would acquire a satellite image and work on it to identify threats to the forest.

Armando Silva was one of these analysts. With eyes glued to a computer screen, the forty-five-year-old biologist's job was to interpret the information and detect not just newly deforested areas but the exact cause of it. Knowing what was going on, and where, was vital. The system was well equipped to differentiate between the various cruelties perpetrated against the forest. He could tell if a specific area was affected by clear-cut deforestation, deforestation with vegetation, mining operations, moderate to severe degradation, burn scars, or logging activities.

He was about to enjoy his third cup of coffee that morning when the system showed an unusual image. The cup froze in midair the moment he saw what was on the screen, and he rushed to assess the situation.

"How's the satellite link?" Armando asked Marcos, an analyst who sat across from him.

Marcos, a younger man with short hair with cropped fringe, saw Armando's frowning face. "What about it?"

"Anything unusual?"

The analyst checked. "Nope."

Armando massaged his eyes with both hands. He stared back at his screen and nodded. Marcos kept watching him from his workstation. Detecting deforestation was routine for them. Reacting emotionally to it wasn't.

Marcos got up from his chair and approached Armando.

"Feeling uneasy today?" Marcos said. But after he leaned forward, he felt uneasy himself. "This can't be right."

"No. It can't," Armando said.

"Linda, will you check the system for us?" Marcos yelled to another analyst.

"No problems here. Why?" Linda said. Both men stared at Armando's screen with their jaws dropped. Linda glided sideways in her chair to join them. In an instant, her jaw dropped too. "Shit."

"Run an estimate on the affected area," Marcos said.

Armando zoomed in on a specific part of the screen. "It starts in Sena Madureira. Triangular pattern opening west past the city of Elvira, and east all the way to Pauini," he said.

"That's . . . a lot. Gone in five days?" Armando said.

"That's an area the size of Florida," Marcos added in terror. But it was real.

"No way," Linda said.

Other analysts and technicians sensed the commotion and approached from all corners of the room. They formed a dense circle around Armando's workstation. Unless there'd been an undetected malfunction, what the computers were showing seemed to be correct.

Armando stood up. "Call IBAMA. We need people on the ground right now."

IBAMA was Brazil's environmental protection agency, the group responsible for taking quick action against illegal forest clearing.

"I have them on the phone," someone yelled in the background.

"What does it look like?" Marcos said. As much

as everyone tried to keep their cool, heavy breathing could be heard all around Armando's screen.

"Trees on the ground," Armando confirmed.

"That's impossible," Marcos said.

"That's data, Marcos."

"Then turn on the TV," Marcos said.

"Why?"

"Maybe Brazil is at war with somebody, and we're not aware of it."

"Yeah. A nuclear bomb must have exploded over the Amazon, or something like that," Marcos said.

"IBAMA is on their way," the analyst on the phone said. "And I'm calling NASA too."

"That's not a bad idea," Marcos said.

The DETER control room fell into a cold silence.

While they waited for NASA to confirm the data, all they could hear was the sound of the air-conditioning and the static in the air. Computer, satellite, and other systems were checked over and over. They all hoped that sooner or later someone would find a glitch or a computer virus. When the phone rang and Marcos answered it, all eyes turned to him. He mouthed, "NASA."

"I appreciate that . . . We'll keep in touch," Marcos said and hung up. Armando and Linda walked up to him. "They see what we see. And no, we're not at war with anybody."

Linda got a text message. She read it out loud. "The seismological center had no events. It's not an earthquake. And no meteorites hit us."

Armando returned to his station and put on his leather jacket. "Someone please call the night shift. Tell them to arrive early."

"Where are you going?" Linda said.

"Out."

"It's not your role to—"

"I don't care. I need to see this for myself."

On his way to the airport, Armando verified possible locations around the deforested area to land a helicopter. IBAMA agents informed him that an American had a sleepover place nearby. They were planning to depart by helicopter early next morning and let Armando follow on foot to the edge of the devastated area. If he arrived on time, they informed him, he could join them.

36

It was the beginning of Christel's healing process. Dr. Michael Shepard prescribed finding those who had violated her body when she was young, the men who had arrogantly abducted her mind and adulterated her soul, and then deal with them without incurring new scars. As hard as it was to translate that into practical action, a plan was already underway.

She met with Harry Walker at the airport in Houston. The rectangular-faced, fortysomething private eye was waiting in a smart tuxedo. He saw Christel arriving in a sleeveless one-shouldered black dress, with pearls around her neck. She looked as dazzling as ever. He and everyone in the airport turned their eyes toward her.

But while her outsides shone, Christel's insides were poisoned.

A false story had come out in the press, stating that Christel Welch had been living in hiding because she was afraid people would find out she'd been a prostitute when she was younger. She had no idea who would say that, but Christel felt infuriated that Eleanor had said nothing in her defense when asked by fellow journalists about their friendship. That story had come out of nowhere. It was senseless, futile, and downright unfair.

It had originally been published in a major national paper but spread to hundreds of local newspapers and websites across the country, and even abroad. It sold papers, so it was good for business. Of all the people she'd helped over the past decades, only those without a voice had the courage to defend Christel. Her powerful friends remained quiet. They gained nothing by aligning themselves with certain inconvenient words.

Billionaire. Prostitute. Hiding.

Christel was in a bitter mood when she followed Harry toward a rented Lincoln Navigator and drove for two hours to Mason Williams' farm. They had invitations in the name of Mr. and Mrs. Walker bought for ten thousand dollars per person, which was the ticket price for the Williams' annual charity event. On their way, Harry had plenty of time to update Christel on Mason's weaknesses.

"He's under tremendous pressure by the board of directors of Mason Williams Oil Company of Texas. They want him out," Harry explained.

"Why? The company has his name. He's the founder."

"Apparently, they've gotten tired of him. He's been

CEO for too long. What he has in salesmanship, he lacks in corporate management. And he's no longer holding the majority of stocks. Mason Williams has a strong facade but weak foundations."

"Tell me about his wife. I bet she's unhappy."

"Oh, yeah. She's more like an employee than a wife. No kids. All she does is work to keep that facade intact. I found police files—Mason loves to beat her. The board knows about it, and that's one of the reasons why they're tired of him."

Christel looked out the window. "What else, Harry?"

"Mason's heavily in debt. All the company stock he owns is being used as collateral to secure private loans. That includes the property we're heading to, which has a pledged-asset mortgage. He gets a one-and-a-half-million-dollar salary, which he's completely dependent on."

"Let's assume the board fires him," Christel speculated.

"Then he's done. He'd basically lose everything." Harry glanced at Christel. He knew where she was going. She glanced back at him with a cold smile. She was trying to get a kick out of this little plot of hers, but that, too, was a facade. Even after all she'd been through, life kept beating her. Maybe, she considered, destroying someone else's life could help appease her soul. Or maybe not.

Mason's property was located on a secluded,

seven-acre, wooded property.

When they arrived, Harry waited for Christel to leave the car. She offered her arm to him, and they walked toward the reception pretending to be the couple listed on their invitations. "It's hard not to fall in love with you," he said.

"That's on you, Harry."

The château style reminded Christel of her farmhouse in Arles, except this estate was probably ten times bigger. There were olive trees, rose gardens, and fountains. Through the house, they could see an extravagant pool flanked by coconut trees.

"We're going straight to the Williamses," Christel said as soon as they got inside.

"No foreplay?"

"What did you have in mind?"

"The twenty-one-year-old Macallan."

"Later."

Christel felt eyes turning to her as she walked. In that respect, nothing had changed since she'd decided to spend more time living in the Amazon. She hoped Mason noticed her before she neared him, wondering if he would remember her. They strolled along the fine hardwood floor, passed by a huge marble fireplace and many antiques, and walked under chandeliers that must have come straight out of the Hermitage Museum.

"The facade," Harry whispered. The thin line between wealth and bankruptcy.

Christel couldn't care less. She knew money couldn't buy character.

Outside, under a rotunda near the pool, she saw Mason Williams. Next to him, smiling with effort, was his wife, Evelyn. The hosts were surrounded by at least twelve guests. *Perfect*, Christel thought. But as she approached the group, it wasn't Mason who recognized her first.

"Oh my God, Christel Welch!" Evelyn's smile turned into an effortless, genuine one. "It's such an honor," Mason's wife said.

"My pleasure," Christel said.

"Mason, that's—" Evelyn was about to introduce her to Mason. Christel interrupted her and turned to him in time to see the fear enter his eyes.

"Mason Williams. We've met before," Christel said.

Mason smiled but said nothing.

It was not only Christel who could see the embarrassment in his eyes. Everyone around them took note of his awkward facial contortions. Slowly, Evelyn lost her smile.

"Darling, you two know each other?" Evelyn said.

Mason wasn't smiling anymore, nor showing the expected courtesy.

"Well?" Evelyn insisted.

Mason, the ever-sure, all-knowing founder of Mason Williams Oil Company, remained silent. He stared at Christel, appearing overwhelmed by extreme and conflicting feelings. She suspected that he wanted to kill her for daring to show up at his house after all these years. She felt delightfully powerful. Men like Mason only had power when they operated in the shadows. In plain daylight, they were nothing but scared rats. That coward didn't resemble the man she'd met in her youth. She almost felt pity for him.

"Long story... I wonder if we could talk," Christel said to Evelyn.

Mason's wife still had the presence of mind to put on a friendly face. "Any time."

"Right now would be perfect."

The silence around them was full of embarrassment. That stunning woman knew her husband, but he hadn't clarified the circumstances. In fact, he'd been mute since she'd showed up. Her simple presence there had already been damaging.

"Please come with me," Evelyn said.

Harry stepped forward when Mason was about to grab Evelyn's hand. "Do you wanna talk about pledged-asset mortgages? That's a bitch when it goes south. How's yours doing, Mr. Williams?"

"I don't think we've been introduced," was Mason's only response. The small audience of friends remained, listening to every exchange involving Mason.

"Harry Walker."

"You're in oil?"

"Not really. I'm a private investigator. I love what you and your wife do to protect women and children."

"We do what we can," Mason said.

Inevitably, both turned to glance toward the library. Christel and Evelyn were already immersed in a highly intense conversation. Mason's wife lifted her hand to cover her mouth. She was in shock, which prompted Mason to excuse himself.

"Y'all have a good time. I have to catch up with Evelyn."

"I think that's a great idea," Harry said, moving along with him.

"I sure don't like the idea of my wife alone with that woman."

"*That woman* is my client."

Christel had spent no more than a minute alone with Evelyn when Harry and Mason entered the library. Mason closed the sliding wood door and walked up to Christel, fuming with anger. Harry stayed behind, but close enough.

"What do you think you're doing?" Mason said.

Christel kept her eyes on Evelyn. A bond had been established between the two women. A strong, instinctive bond that abused women develop the moment they get to know each other's stories.

It was Evelyn who turned to Mason. She was disgusted.

"You sickening son of a bitch."

"I don't know what she told you, but know this. Before people knew her name, she was a whore, OK? You've read the papers. I only met her once. You and I didn't even know each other then."

"It doesn't matter. I've known about your dark side for too long. I just didn't know how dark it was. Now I do." Evelyn stepped back.

Mason eyed Christel. "You think you can come to my house and destroy my marriage?"

"I just did," Christel said. "You don't deserve Evelyn. I just told her how you and your friends raped me . . . in this house. You still have that hidden cave behind your pool?"

Mason closed his fists, prompting Harry to move in closer. Then he turned his gaze to Evelyn. "You know what happens if you eat the crap she's selling you? We lose everything. And by that, I mean every little thing we've built. Including the house."

"I don't care," Evelyn said.

"Actually, Mason, *you* lose everything," Christel said. "I'm setting up a ten-million-dollar fund to support your wife. We'll turn your pathetic show— your fake foundation—into a real organization that protects women like Evelyn." Christel turned to Evelyn. "Are you ready to break away from all of this?"

"Yes," Evelyn said.

"Then now's the best time to do it."

Christel opened the library door, making sure it made a noise when it hit the frame. The guests in the rotunda heard and turned their heads toward the library.

"What do you think you're doing?" Mason said, his face a mix of panic and embarrassment.

"Simple. We're going to—how should I say this—gang-rape your reputation. Stand and watch." Christel glanced at the guests. "Please, join us."

Christel extended her hand to Evelyn and offered her a smile of encouragement. Mason's wife accepted fullheartedly. The two women stood hand in hand facing the small crowd. "Do you want me to start?" Christel said.

Evelyn shook her head no. She took a deep breath, wiped away a tear that had rolled down her cheek, and faced her guests. "I, er, there's something I'd like to say."

"Evelyn . . . don't do it," Mason begged.

She ignored him, gathering the final strength to address the guests. "Due to irreconcilable differences, Mason and I are going to divorce." She heard the murmur she knew would come and glanced at Christel. The smile was still there. Evelyn's confidence grew. "Actually, this, er, divorce is not about *differences*. It's more than that."

"Shut up, Evelyn!" Mason said. The guests heard him loud and clear.

"The truth is, Mason's a terrible husband. He has assaulted me several times during our marriage. The pig belongs in prison!"

DANIEL DAVIDSOHN

The faint murmur turned into a loud one.

Some guests began to leave, fazed by the scandal they didn't want to witness at such close proximity. But others walked into the library, horrified—members of the board of directors of Mason Williams Oil Company. Christel watched Mason shrink. He didn't know where to look, where his eyes would find a safe place away from the disgrace that was materializing before him.

Three of the board members exchanged glances. No words were needed. One of them—a young, cocky-looking man—stepped forward with both hands on his waist. "I always knew you were a liability to us," the young executive said to Mason.

"It's my name on your business card, don't you forget that," Mason said.

"There's no need. We're firing you."

"Now, wait a minute. Let's talk this over." Mason attempted to sound humble, but all he managed was to look desperate.

The young executive glanced at Evelyn. "We have your back, Mrs. Williams."

Christel and Evelyn were still holding hands. "I'm sorry . . . you are?" Christel asked the young man.

"Noah Garcia. I'm the chairman of the board."

"The Garcias are a wealthy family," Evelyn clarified to Christel.

"I'm Christel Welch."

"I know who you are. I'm honored to meet you.

And I don't believe the papers," Noah said.

"I'm so glad to see young men doing what's right. I'll be more than happy to provide funds for a new organization Evelyn and I are creating."

"You can count on me, Mrs. Welch. Whatever your contribution might be, I'll match it."

Christel nodded and looked back at Harry.

She was ready to go. But an image seen from the corner of her eye gave her chills. Mason was seated behind a desk, pulling a pistol from a drawer. The others turned when they saw Christel turning pale. Everything was happening too fast. Mason waved the gun randomly in the air and then positioned the gun right under his chin. He closed his eyes, and the shot came in the next instant. His hair bristled up as his head bent backward, and blood painted an ugly stain on the wall behind him.

"Oh my God!" Evelyn shouted.

The rest of them watched, at a loss for words.

Harry walked to Christel and placed both hands over her shoulders. "You're not responsible for this," he was quick to say.

Seconds before, Christel had felt she was doing good. She had always wished she'd had someone to help her when she most needed it. When she was in Evelyn's place. Everett came to her mind. He'd helped her. She'd been lucky. But the truth was, the effect of Christel's presence in this house had proved devastating. How Evelyn was going to cope with it remained to be seen. The damage was done, and it was irreversible.

Revenge felt and tasted different than what Christel had fantasized. It didn't feel a bit rewarding. Right then, the idea that she could change her past proved foolish. It vanished in a cloud of drama she would rather avoid.

Don't get new scars, Michael Shepard had told her. She'd failed.

37

Amana and Maurice returned to his cabin after she'd shown him the deforested area. Instead of going back to her village, she pulled the canoe to shore, and they both gave it a little push onto the mud. While they walked back to his cabin, Amana glanced at Maurice incessantly. Maurice didn't know why and was afraid to ask. It was likely that she blamed the white men for whatever had brought down those trees. It was her territory. Her world.

It soon became clear she was going to spend the night there. When Maurice turned his back to her, Amana pulled on his shoulder and forced him to look at her.

"Help?" she said.

"Yes. I'll ask for help, Amana."

"You." She picked up a tree branch kept dry inside the cabin for his pit fires and broke it in the middle. She was definitely blaming him. To make it clearer, she sat on his bed. She was going nowhere until he did something.

But Maurice was as shocked as Amana was. The scene he'd witnessed earlier was like doomsday. An unprecedented genocide of trees that must have occurred over a matter of days. What Amana had shown him was the area she knew had been affected, but she couldn't possibly know the extent of the devastation.

Maurice watched her on his bed. Amana was a pure human being, incapable of masking her feelings, and a beautiful woman in her own way. Seeing her mostly naked on his bed was a constant reminder of how primitive his thoughts could be. He was determined not to be the bad guy. It had taken him a while to earn the trust of Amana's tribe.

"Listen," she said and sat up straight.

"What?" Maurice said.

"Listen!"

Maurice squinted, trying to capture whatever Amana was hearing. It came shortly after. A vague, distant roar.

"Yeah . . . I hear it," he said.

The sound reminded Maurice of something, but he couldn't place what. It was unusual enough to make Amana worry. She got up and picked up the broken branch. She lifted it to Maurice and broke it in half again.

"You think so?"

Amana shook her head.

The sounds kept coming every few seconds.

Maurice fine-tuned his ears until he was able to distinguish the roar as a combination of different things taking place in a chain reaction: the fall of a big tree dragging down smaller trees and then crashing to the ground.

"How far from here? How distant, Amana?" Maurice got up with his heart beating faster, hoping that his dialogue would improve. His cabin would not remain standing if trees around his clearing began to fall.

"Near," Amana said.

"A day?"

"Near. Near!"

Maurice started to pace. "The trees weren't falling when you showed them to me earlier. But they're falling *now*. Why would they fall at night?"

His confusion left Amana with a stunned look on her face. She got up, pulled aside a small piece of cloth attached to her loincloth, and opened it in front of Maurice, gently placing her hand into an inside pocket. When she pulled her hand out, it was covered in different insects, just as it had been when she'd investigated the fallen tree earlier. She'd collected samples of the insects.

"What are you trying to say?" he said.

Maurice leaned forward as she separated the insects from each other, stretching his hand up and pulling a hanging lamp toward Amana's hand. At the center of her palm, only one insect remained visible.

"I see it. It's a termite, if I'm not mistaken," he said.

Amana nodded. "Termite." She'd just learned a new word.

"You think this is causing the trees to fall?" He pointed at the insect and then outside, struggling to find the right word from her limited vocabulary. "Hungry?"

Maurice smiled cautiously, trying not to offend Amana. He found it unlikely that termites were doing that much damage to the forest.

"So, you think this little hungry termite is doing all the damage?" He waved his hand, pointing outside again. However careful his tone was, Amana glanced away and returned the termite to the piece of cloth.

The roars and crashes seemed to be getting louder when they heard the radio.

"Maurice Welch, Maurice Welch. This is IBAMA calling. Come in, over."

He sat down by the radio. "IBAMA, this is Maurice. Go ahead, over."

"A helicopter is heading to your location. It'll get there in the morning. An INPE analyst named Armando requests to stay in your cabin. Over."

"Copy. Where is it coming from? Over."

"The Fourth Jungle Infantry Battalion in Acre. Over."

"IBAMA, what's the purpose of Armando's visit? Over."

"There's an abnormal forest event near the Puturi River. Over."

"Copy . . . I've seen it with my own eyes. You can't land a helicopter anywhere near the cabin. Over."

"We're aware of that. He'll be fast-roping near you. Over."

"I will be waiting. Over and out."

The moment Maurice ended his radio communication, Amana walked up to him.

"Help?"

"Yes, Amana. Help."

*****

Early in the morning, Armando followed to the 4th Jungle Infantry Battalion. After fifteen minutes of paperwork and interviews, he was escorted toward an AS532 Cougar helicopter. The rotor blades were already spinning when he got inside and sat next to a soldier. They greeted him with nods, and he was given headphones. The helicopter took off.

At cruise altitude, Armando looked outside and ahead. The forest occupied both extremities of his vision, but the city seemed to extend toward the forest through an abnormally narrow pattern that widened at a distance.

"How long until we get there?" Armando said.

"About an hour," the soldier said.

"Where do we land?"

"We don't." He pointed up at the forty-millimeter rope and the gear that would be taking Armando to the ground.

"Are you kidding me?"

The soldier ignored him and looked outside. "Can you believe that?" It was all he could say. Armando followed his glance. It was a vision of pure despair. The forest clearing had an incalculable magnitude. Trees had fallen in a random pattern, extending beyond what their eyes could see.

"Jesus," Armando mumbled.

A grave wound had been inflicted on the planet. Armando wanted to be on the ground as soon as possible, checking which species were most affected, where they would migrate to, and above all, what the hell was causing it.

"Get ready for some rough winds," the pilot warned over the intercom. The helicopter was approaching dark clouds.

"There's a storm coming," the soldier said.

"I hope the pilot knows what he's doing."

The soldier sneered. "Same here."

The helicopter bumped and swayed through the turbulent air. Seconds later, they heard the rain hitting it hard.

"So, what's going on down there?" the soldier yelled on his microphone.

"I have no idea. That's why I'm here," Armando said.

"I hope *you* know what you're doing."

The tropical storm kept pounding the helicopter.

After fifty hellish minutes, the weather gave them a break. The rain stopped, and the winds dropped considerably.

"Get ready," Armando heard over the intercom.

He glanced outside. They were nearing the green carpet that the Amazon was known for, and they stretched their necks to locate the cabin.

"Do you know the guy who lives here?" Armando said.

"A millionaire gringo, they say."

"What is he doing?"

"Protecting the forest."

The helicopter made a sharp turn, stopped in midair, and started to descend.

The soldier got up, signaled Armando to do the same, and began to attach the rope gear around him.

"It's still bumpy," Armando reminded him.

"It's within acceptable limits. Don't worry."

"Easy to say."

"Look . . . Our man," the soldier said. Maurice was waving outside his cabin. Next to him, they saw the naked native.

"Ready?" the soldier said.

"No," Armando said.

But he was going anyway. The soldier opened the lateral door and positioned himself behind Armando.

"Let's go."

Armando's descent was clumsy, but he managed to reach the ground safely. The soldier released him from the gear and signaled to the helicopter to bring him back up. "Good luck," he yelled to Armando.

Armando shook hands with Maurice. "Thanks for having me."

The native woman remained behind the man. The three of them looked up at the helicopter as it flew away.

"So, who's she?" Armando asked Maurice when the helicopter was distant enough, and they could hear each other without shouting.

"Amana. She's a local."

"I can see that . . . But what tribe?"

"That's our little secret. We don't need to ruin their lives, do we?"

"Good call."

38

It had taken a while for Christel to contact Harry
Walker again. She called to ask him details about the
third name on that dossier, which he reluctantly gave
her. After Mason Williams shot himself in front of
everyone, Christel had adopted the Amazon refuge as
her permanent home. She'd lost interest in all things
money related, including the extended catalog of
friends who'd orbited around her prior to the gossip
that suggested she had been a prostitute. Eleanor was
her number-one suspect for the story, but Christel
had no proof, and not even Harry could establish
that.

Christel needed to reinvent herself. Again.

She had Kiara, who was in her eighties but strong
as a rock, and Maurice. Everyone and everything else
was disposable. Still, there was a missing piece in her
life. Someone to share a bed, dreams, and laughs. At
the very least, the thrill of a new friendship, or maybe
the colors of a new soul melding with hers.

Christel was still alive.

"This time is different," she promised Harry on the phone. "He's someone I like."

Harry called her back weeks later with all the details he could provide about that name. For Christel, the most crucial information came at the end of that phone call. "He dates women sporadically, but nothing serious. So, yes, he's still single."

*****

It was a harsh winter night in Switzerland.

She'd been waiting inside a small rented car in front of Denizard Haener's house, the sweet fourteen-year-old boy she'd never forgotten. Collonge-Bellerive was a tiny village on the shores of Lake Geneva, on a street at the end of a beautiful path lined by old trees. It was a chic family neighborhood surrounded by opulent vegetation, a few shops, and gourmet eateries, no more than ten minutes from the center of Geneva.

Denizard's property was a relatively modest three-bedroom house costing around five million dollars, which wasn't much for someone with a couple of billion dollars. Most of the homes nearby were worth three or four times that much.

Christel checked the time on her cell phone. She'd been doing so every five minutes for the past hour. It was freezing inside the car, but Denizard would be home at any minute.

According to Harry's dossier, Denizard usually

got home at eight every night after having dinner out with his fourteen-year-old daughter, Aurora. The teenager studied at Le Rosey in the town of Rolle, about forty minutes away. It was where the children of royals, celebrities, and Russian oligarchs studied. There was not a single blemish on her résumé. Both father and daughter appeared to have an almost perfect life, and that was what made Christel worried. Nobody had a perfect life.

A Land Rover Evoque passed by Christel.

The car she'd been expecting. The house gate opened, and the car entered the property. Her heart accelerated. Though she couldn't see the person in the car, she knew that her new gamble was inside it. She counted off three minutes, got out of her car, and rang the doorbell on the gate.

What am I doing? She hesitated for a brief moment.

She heard steps rushing forward behind the wood door. They were light and fast.

Before she had time to change her mind and get out of there, Aurora opened the door. The teenager saw a stunning American woman dressed like a Ralph Lauren ad in old blue jeans, a white sweater, and a dark-walnut leather jacket. The woman had loose, wavy chocolate hair, was about her father's age, and had a commanding presence.

After giving the woman a once-over, Aurora smiled and finally said, "*Oui, bonsoir?*"

Christel looked at Aurora with great care and smiled back. "Hello. *Est-ce que vous parlez anglais?*"

"Sure," Aurora said. Christel widened her smile. The teenager before her was short but elegant, polite, and warm. Like a typical Le Rosey girl, she had tidy hair; no visible tattoos, piercings, or valuable jewelry; and her makeup was barely noticeable. "May I help you?"

"Yes. I'd like to speak to your father."

"You are?"

"An old friend. My name's Christel Welch. Tell him I came to Switzerland to see him."

Aurora turned almost instantly and yelled, "Papa?"

Denizard Haener came out of the house and walked down the stone pathway leading to the street door. He and Christel locked eyes the moment they saw each other. He frowned and tried to identify who she was. She looked familiar.

"*Elle s'appelle* Christel Welch . . . *Américaine,*" Aurora said as she passed her father on her way back inside the house. She didn't see the look of surprise on his face.

Christel displayed the friendliest face she could pull out.

She didn't want to look like a freak by showing up at his door half a century after their one-night stand, but here she was. The man was about her height, shorter than Everett and most men she'd dated. His hair was white, French cropped. His face was jovial, with a narrow forehead and sharp cheekbones. The eyes were hooded and light blue. Nothing about him physically reminded her of the shy teenager of the past. Yet, there was something memorable about him that sent shock waves through her body.

"Hi," he said in a silvery voice.

"Denizard . . . Remember me?"

"I know who you are. The environmentalist. Philanthropist . . . I've seen you in the media. I also think I've seen you personally . . . in a different situation," he said in a strong but pleasant French accent.

He remembers me, Christel learned.

"Yes. We've met before, Denis." There was an awkward silence as they studied each other. Someone would have to break the ice. "I'm after your money," she said.

Denizard laughed.

He crossed his arms and shook his head. Both knew she was richer than him. "You've done very well. I'm not worried," he said.

What he didn't say was that she looked as gorgeous as ever. That he'd always suspected that the Christel that appeared in the media over the years was the same woman with whom he'd lost his virginity. He'd never forgotten her.

"Please, come inside. It's so cold tonight."

Christel stepped in his direction. She surprised him with a greeting kiss on his cheek, purposely close to his lips. There was a powerful attraction, a magnet impelling her mouth to glue to his. When she distanced her face, she noticed that Denizard kept his eyes closed for a fraction of a moment.

He felt it too.

"Thanks," she said while he shut the door behind them.

Hopefully, this encounter would not end up like the one she'd had with Mason Williams. Christel was stepping into the past once more, but this time, she was walking into a fantasy—into a dream of finding love with Denizard. There was no one else besides him in her plans. It was time to bring her wishful imagination into reality. The sooner she found out who he was, the better.

The house's facade had horizontal cedar slats. The siding provided an eye-catching appeal with no splice joints. It felt uncomplicated. She entered to a straightforward layout with lots of space and warm, minimalistic décor. She stood still for a moment, waiting for Denizard to close the entrance door behind them. She glanced around the open floor between the kitchen and the living room. There was an abundance of glass covering the central part of the ceiling. The skylights were covered in snow now, but during the summer, she'd bet there was plenty of sun.

"It's so nice in here. Was it all your idea?" she said.

"Yes. I like it simple."

He pointed to a set of white sofas, and both sat.

"I read somewhere you're no longer in banking," she said bluntly.

He smiled. "As I said, I like it simple."

"Got it. There's nothing simple about banking, is there?"

Denizard twisted his lips. The question didn't bother him, but the answer was complicated. "Let's just say I didn't inherit my father's taste for laundering other people's money."

Another awkward silence followed.

"Can I offer you something to drink?" he said.

"Whiskey?"

Denizard got up and returned moments later with a small round bottle. "Swiss single malt. Have you tried it?"

"It will be my first time," she said, implying a second meaning.

Denizard flushed. He served two glasses and glanced at Christel. "First times can be memorable. You know . . . I've never forgotten you."

"And I remember it as if it were yesterday."

They toasted. He drank the whiskey in one shot and felt the alcohol burning his throat. "*Mon Dieu!* I'm usually a moderate drinker."

Christel did the same. She, too, had a hard time swallowing it. "Me too." Before they got quiet again, she decided to move a step further. "I'm curious.

How was it that I was sent to you? At the time, I mean."

"My father wanted to gift me, understand?"

"I do."

"So he found the most beautiful, you know, working girl he could find." Denizard could not believe he'd just said that. It embarrassed him, but Christel kept her cool, not showing any resentment. "I think my father was right. You were the most beautiful woman I've been with. I fell in love with you then, but who wouldn't?"

"Boys fall in love. But your father got something wrong."

"Did he?"

"I was never a working girl."

Denizard nodded. He'd probably made the most indelicate comment of his entire life. He filled up their glasses and tried to gain some time to fix it, but Christel stepped in. "It's not his fault. Or yours. There are things you're probably asking yourself right now, like why I am here. See, Denis, by the time you met me, I was part of a government program managed by private contractors. Actually, I was raised inside it. I was fortunate enough to meet my late husband when I was twenty-one. He helped me get out."

"I'm so sorry to hear it."

"Don't be . . . It feels like all of that happened in another life," she lied.

"So, that was it. You were one of them," Denizard said, and Christel squinted in confusion. "Christel, I'm familiar with these programs. I know that children are sometimes offered to clients. Sometimes boys. These things happen wherever money is big. One other reason why I hated owning a bank. In this business, the fewer scruples you have, the more profitable it gets."

Christel saw Aurora entering the living room and got up. "Thank you for seeing me, Denis. It's late. I'm going back to my hotel."

"Where are you staying?"

"The Four Seasons."

Denizard got up and walked Christel out. "How long are you staying in Switzerland?"

She shrugged. "What are you planning to tell your daughter when she asks you about me?"

"Aurora rarely asks questions about my friends."

"Trust me, she will."

"Then I'll tell her you were my first girlfriend."

"Sounds like a wonderful lie. I like it."

At the door, Christel and Denizard held hands and exchanged warm smiles. Neither could hide the gleam in their eyes. Christel turned and walked to her rented car. He waited for her to leave.

On her way back to the hotel, Christel was overwhelmed by an odd feeling. Denizard Haener—the real one, not the imagined one—was everything she'd hoped for him to be and more.

39

Amana showed the termite to Armando while Maurice fixed some coffee on an iron stove heated by wood. The biologist held the dead insect on his palm, carefully studying it with a magnifying glass.

"How's the clearing looking up from the skies?" Maurice said.

"Unreal," Armando replied.

"Is it heading our way?"

"No. It's heading north." Armando grabbed a cup of coffee. "The devastation, it's unbelievable," he said. Then, he showed the termite to Amana. "Can I keep it?"

She said nothing.

Armando put the termite in a plastic bag and kept it in his backpack. Maurice sat on a stool next to the oven and glanced at Armando. "So, what do you think's going on? I thought termites were a forest's best friend. The earthworms of tropical soils."

"They are. But they're powerful little insects. Mounds have been photographed from space covering over eighty thousand square miles—eight-foot-tall, thirty-foot-wide mounds made of waste material brought to the surface by the termites. They can carve out lots of underground tunnels."

"Can we blame them for what we've seen so far? Don't they eat dead wood only?"

"I think we're dealing with a variation of the *Rhinotermitidae* species. It's a subterranean termite capable of constructing elaborated galleries, which makes them hard to locate. The rain forest offers everything they need to thrive—food, water, and warmth. And they're the longest living insect. Some can live to be over fifty years old. Not counting the hundreds of unknown species right here in the Amazon. So, we don't know exactly what we're dealing with."

Maurice checked on Amana. She was impatient, looking out the cabin window. When he looked back at Armando, it was as if the biologist was somewhere else, silent and thoughtful. "So," Maurice said, "does this look like a natural phenomenon to you?"

Armando chose his next words slowly. "It could be climatic."

"But that doesn't help us deal with the problem."

"No. Not right now. It could also be something else. Something man-made."

It was Maurice who got quiet now.

A thought came to his mind that was ominous and chilling. The lab built by Alan Reid under a US government contract. His mother's nightmare for ages. It was a faint possibility, but the devastated area started in the city of Sena Madureira, near the property Christel and Maurice had inherited from Alan and Julian.

"What do your people know so far?" Maurice said.

"A huge chunk of the forest is gone. An area about the size of Florida."

Maurice paled. "And termites can do that?"

"Termites account for three times as much biomass as all human beings combined. Something of that scale is unseen, but not impossible. I need to see the area."

"Not to be dramatic here, but trees could fall on our heads."

Maurice knew the DETER biologist hadn't come to his cabin just to talk. IBAMA agents and other scientists were on the ground at several of the affected locations. Amana glanced at the two men picking up their backpacks. They stood and watched her. She understood they wanted to see the devastated area.

Amana took them to a location two hours from the cabin where the sounds of the previous night indicated trees were falling. When they left the canoe, she continued down the Puturi River alone. Seeing her on her own broke Maurice's heart. She was profoundly sad and concerned. There was nowhere Amana and her people could go. Unlike

Maurice, who could choose to live anywhere in the world.

After only fifteen minutes of walking, Armando saw the devastation from the ground for the first time. It was a vision of destruction backed by the distant roar of trees that continued to fall. He'd brought a satellite phone with him. He kneeled down by a fallen tree and began exchanging information with Marcos at the DETER headquarters.

"You'll like to hear this. A biologist with the IBAMA team just found a new species of termite," Marcos said over the radio.

"Right. Did he mention if this species is the one causing the trees to fall?" Armando was inspecting a giant tree as he talked over the radio. The termites weren't feeding on the tree trunks, but on roots.

"Are you serious?" his DETER colleague said.

"What do you have on the triangular pattern starting in the city of Sena Madureira? Is it government land?"

"It's private. American owned. And it's kind of shady—listen to this. There used to be a nonprofit organization associated with it, but there's no registry of activity. All we know so far is that the owners repurchased the land in the 1950s as a private reserve."

"Yeah. Shady."

*****

The first terrifying air footage of the Amazon devastation was seen around the world the next day. News spread faster than the termites could eat up the forest.

While Brazilian and American government agencies exchanged backdoor-channel accusations, members of major environmental organizations were holding emergency meetings at the United Nations Environment Assembly, the world's highest-level decision-making body on the environment. They ran against the clock to provide answers before the world learned more details about what was going on in the Amazon.

They had none.

All they knew was that a new species of termites was feeding on the forest at an unprecedented rate. The phenomenon was unexplainable and disheartening. Stopping it was their number-one priority. By what means remained to be decided. Several approaches were discussed, all bearing the hallmarks of desperation and a tint of the bizarre.

One suggestion was blitzing the affected area with fire-setting bombs, which prompted someone to remind them that post-fire forest regeneration was not an exact science. Fires would send insane amounts of carbon into the air, devastate healthy vegetation, and kill thousands—if not millions—of species of insects, endemic animals, and birds. Some insisted that the targeted area would recover after just a few years, until someone suggested that pesticides be considered. The amount required, and the impact of the large-scale use of chemicals over a rain forest, was quickly dismissed as implausible.

The bottom line was: they couldn't think of a solution for the unthinkable.

*****

Detached from the tragedy that was sending shock waves across the world, Christel remained in Switzerland. She and Denizard were seeing each other as frequently as they could. Neither could effectively hide their game from the other. Both were single, mature, and nurturing a sexual attraction and a mutual interest for the stories they told. If a romantic relationship was in their plans, which it clearly was, it had better happen soon, and it had better last.

They were involved in a sort of damage-prevention act, searching for terminal character flaws or anything that would be a cause of later regret. They could have sex with anyone they wanted, but neither wished to invest their hearts and time in someone who could potentially let them down. It was a romantic exercise of futurology. But no matter how careful they were, at some point, they would have to take their chances.

Denizard had bought tickets for an eight-people cable car between Innertkirchen and the Susten Pass, into the remote reaches of the Trift Gorge. They arrived at the upper station and descended 180 steps to the path leading to a suspension bridge high in the mountains of the Bernese Oberland, which offered breathtaking views of a glacier.

The height and the wind terrified Christel.

"No wonder this only opens during summer. Who did you bribe?"

"You're doing very well," Denizard said.

"I know I'm not."

He's an adrenaline freak, she thought. Not necessarily a flaw.

In between small steps forward, her cell phone rang. Christel crouched and sat.

They were about halfway across a bridge being dangerously hit by a draft. Denizard sat in front of her and pulled out a small bottle of single malt from his coat. She saw the name showing on her cell phone screen and arched her eyebrows. It showed five calls in the past hour. All from the same person.

"An old friend," she explained.

"Take your time," he said.

"Hello, Eleanor."

"Where are you?" Eleanor said brusquely. It was odd. They hadn't spoken in years.

"Well, I'm on a swinging suspension bridge over a gorge. How about you?"

"Christel, darling. Something is happening in the Amazon."

"I'm in Switzerland. No need to worry about me."

Denizard's and Christel's legs touched. He played with his foot, tapping her leg and waving his finger up to the clouds forming up above. Being caught in the middle of a snowstorm up there wasn't part of the plan, not even for Denizard.

"Haven't you watched the news? There's been an event. A huge area in the Amazon has been flattened by termites or something like that."

Christel shook her head. Maybe it was the loud winds blowing past her ears.

Amazon? Termites? It didn't seem relevant at that precise moment. "That sounds bad. But right now, it's not a good time to be talking. Why don't you call me tonight?"

"Oh, no, no. I'm talking to you right now. It's kind of a favor I'm doing you."

Christel frowned. "How exactly is this a favor?"

"Because I'm letting you know before it goes public."

"Didn't you just say it was all over the place?"

"The event, Chris. I'm talking about your name. A source told me that—"

"A source? Since when do we have secrets from each other?"

"Since you last called me, what, five years ago? Because you only call me when it's convenient. And then you continue on with your oh-so-glamorous life."

"You're being unfair."

Denizard stood up, glanced down at Christel, and helped her to get up. "Let's keep moving," he whispered.

"I'm actually fair with you," Eleanor continued. "Calling you before anyone else. The source told me that the devastation started on a property owned by your family."

Denizard watched Christel lose her balance. He thought it was the bridge's natural instability that was causing it, but then he started paying attention to her conversation. Her face showed panic.

Christel stopped walking. "Are you sure?" she said over the phone.

"It's been confirmed. And it matches the story you told me about Alan Reid's property in the Amazon. The one nobody seems to know anything about."

"Jesus … What's the damage? What are we talking about?"

"To you or the forest?"

"The forest, Eleanor!"

"Well, they say the affected area is as large as a small country of Europe and growing. Now, it has your name associated with it. You know it's gonna hit you. And it's unavoidable."

"I have no idea what's going on, and I've got nothing to do with it."

"Oh, you do. It's your property."

"Are you blaming me or just informing me?"

"You'll be blamed, like it or not."

"So, who's your source?"

"There is no source. I saw it on the news. I thought, considering our friendship, that I should call you before the shit hits the fan. Before your name comes up. When it does, you may need to say something. What would that be?"

"Wait. Are you interviewing me?"

"Have you become too important to say a few words to us mere mortals?"

"Go to hell, Eleanor."

"Going defensive is not your thing."

"See, right there is why I only call you when it's *convenient*. You're always looking for a good story. A scandal. You'll not find one with me. Thanks for calling."

Christel was barely breathing when she hung up.

"Are you OK?" Denizard said.

She shook her head no. "Let's go back."

40

Everything west of Maurice's cabin had been devastated by a termite hell made of fallen trees and displaced animals. Christel called and updated her son about the possible repercussions, which prompted him to return to their property. Maurice knew they had to prepare for the accusations that would inevitably fall on their shoulders. In any case, he was trapped. The only way out and back to the family's private reserve was through a northeast route. He packed light and walked with Armando to the shores of the Puturi, where they boarded a small motorboat and headed sixteen miles northwest where the river ended.

From there, they traveled thirty-five miles on foot through the jungle until they reached the Pauini River. They left the small boat behind and began the difficult walk through dense forest and dry riverbeds. It was another seventy miles until they reached the Juruá River, and when they did, they were exhausted. Not even the relief at the sight of *Subject C* waiting on the shore lasted very long. There was another issue.

A dozen canoes surrounded the hospital ship.

It could be his tired eyes, but Maurice swore he was looking at Amana and her people. The only explanation was that they must have been forced to leave their village and traveled northwest just as Maurice and Armando had, but on a shorter, smarter route than the one chosen by Maurice and his fancy GPS.

Amana was standing on her canoe. She'd seen Maurice arrive.

Vegard Rasmussen, *Subject C*'s captain, was a sizable Norwegian man fifty years of age. He stood smoking a cigarette at the bow of the ship, looking out at the tribe surrounding it. He waved at Maurice and leaned on the ship's railing, making it clear he could do nothing about the situation.

"They don't look as nice as you've described them," Armando said.

"You go ahead and board," Maurice said.

Amana brought her canoe to shore and walked in Maurice's direction.

That young, incredibly fit native woman looked vulnerable and scared, not at all the indomitable warrior he'd come to know. Her eyes supplicated him for some kind of help. Before he attempted to communicate with her, she hugged Maurice, disarming his fears about the tribe on their canoes. It was the embrace of a child, and when she turned to glance at her people, she made sure he understood any kind of help would need to include all of them.

She looked back at Maurice and said, "No home . . . Trees die."

Maurice nodded and tried to calm her down by gently holding her shoulders. "You're coming with me. On that boat." He pointed at *Subject C*.

"Family," she said in a conditional tone.

"Yes, Amana. All of you."

"No white man. Danger!" she said, her requirements growing. She wanted her tribe to remain hidden from the white man.

Maurice nodded. "Let's go, then."

He and Amana boarded the ship.

Captain Rasmussen met him with a warm handshake. "Welcome, Mr. Welch. As you can see, we're kind of stuck."

"How many patients do we have aboard?"

"None at the moment. We've postponed our visit to the villages per Mrs. Welch's request."

Maurice moved to the railings and counted the number of natives on the canoes. "Do we have enough food for thirty-six souls?"

"River," Amana said, closing her fingers and touching her lips.

Maurice smiled. "Yes. There's plenty of food in the river. Call them."

Amana signaled her tribe to come aboard.

A mumbling started, and the tribe members exchanged glances to assess the situation. Amana acted before their fear grew into a mutiny. She stood next to Maurice and yelled energetic words. Immediately, they began to pull their canoes ashore. Then a line was formed, and the natives began to board.

Captain Rasmussen's welcoming hand was ignored. They gathered around Amana. Clearly, hers was the only voice they heard.

"Do we know what we're doing?" Rasmussen said as he approached Maurice.

"No, Vegard. We'll find out as we go."

"Sounds like a plan."

After the last tribe member came aboard, Maurice pulled his captain further aside. "This is an uncontacted tribe. We must guarantee they remain invisible. Is that clear?" Maurice said with a firm stare.

"Understood. I'll take them inside. Oh, and, er, are they dangerous?"

"Just don't touch them or do anything that might be perceived as aggressive."

"Good point. I'll go ahead, then."

Rasmussen squeezed himself between the tribesmen, putting on his best smile. The stares he got back were a mix of curiosity and caution. Some touched his soft blond hair and made comments. Some laughed. And as the tension diminished, the tribe's curiosity extended to the ship's surfaces, which were made of materials they'd never encountered before and had weird textures. The mood quickly changed to one of excitement and bewilderment.

Amana stroked Maurice's face in gratitude and moved to control the tribe. Soon, she was yelling again. They formed a line after Rasmussen and stepped inside the ship in perfect order.

Armando approached Maurice when they were left alone at the bow. "I'm not sure you're not breaking the law here."

"You mean *we*."

"How are you gonna hide them?"

"My property has eight thousand acres of untouched forest by the Rio Negro."

"That should be enough."

Subject C departed soon after.

Neither Maurice nor Rasmussen wanted to be seen next to the empty canoes. The Juruá River was a southern artery of the Amazon River, full of curves and with a sluggishness about it that made navigation slow while it traversed that half-flooded forest area.

By night, the hospital ship's cafeteria saw the natives arrive calmly and in an orderly fashion. Grilled fish was served fresh from a previous day's catch, accompanied by potatoes. Soft drinks and alcohol were avoided, but Vegard instructed the cook to test one of his specialties on them: chocolate cake. Each member of Amana's big family got a generous slice. They smelled it, took small bites at first, and then finished their portions with full mouths. In the end, all of the tribe showed smiles. Some even raised their plates in a universal sign of wanting more.

While the tribe was in the cafeteria, Maurice noticed Amana's eyes on him. They displayed gratitude. When he retired to his cabin, she came after him as if it were the most natural thing to do. He looked back a few times, playfully, and wondered what her intentions were. He entered his cabin, keeping the door half open, not wanting to close it before Amana's plans became clear. He didn't want to be rude. Maurice saw her passing next to him toward the interior of his cabin. She took off her loincloth, leaving no doubt as to why she'd followed him. Then she turned and glanced at him, her eyes full of lust.

Maurice closed the door.

Her raw sexuality was tempting. Still, thoughts went through his head. Maybe this was her way of thanking Maurice for sheltering her people. Not for a second did it cross his mind that she needed to repay him in any way for doing what any decent person would. But explaining that to her would be complicated. While he stood still, considering what to do, she came closer and began to pull off his shirt.

"You don't have to do this," he said.

Amana ignored him.

She kissed his lips, his neck, and swiftly pulled

him by the arm toward the bed, where she finished undressing him. He felt her gasping, ready for him, and let her mount him when he was naked. He grabbed her buttocks, and her cries became more intense. Ethics were forgotten. He allowed himself to feel the soft skin covering her firm musculature, and he penetrated Amana with unbounded desire. She lay on him with her face slightly tilted up, eyes closed, groaning softly. Amana wasn't concerned about him. She was just . . . feeling. As soon as Maurice realized this, he closed his eyes as well and allowed himself to make love without guilt.

She came first, he felt, and he came right after her. It was quick. Amana opened her eyes, smiled joyfully, and gave him a short kiss on his lips. Then she lay on his chest, laughed a couple of times, and stayed there for the rest of the night.

The morning sunrays arrived with the vivid songs of the Amazon birds. There was the promise of heavy showers as *Subject C* left the Juruá River behind. They were now on the mighty Amazon, heading west toward Manaus.

When Maurice woke up, Amana wasn't there. He rushed out of his cabin and found her in the cafeteria having breakfast. She turned when he entered, smiled innocently, whispered something to a group of tribesmen sharing the table with her, and they all laughed.

"Good morning to you too," he said and moved

on to sit with Captain Rasmussen.

"They're quite a happy bunch," the captain said, still uncomfortable with the presence of the natives.

"Cheer up, Vegard."

"I will when we disembark them at the bungalows."

"Suit yourself."

"By the way, Mrs. Welch called. She's on the property waiting."

"Did you tell her about our guests?"

"She's your mother, sir. I avoid meddling in family affairs."

"Nah, she'll understand. But you're right. Leave it to me."

*****

Christel searched the web for hours. Almost every newspaper in the western hemisphere published a photograph posted by NASA showing what the devastated area looked like from space. It sparked fear of unknown consequences of such a large-scale disaster, and wild speculations of what may have caused it. There were angry reactions from environmentalists, and painstakingly long scientific debates reinforcing the knowledge that rain forests were regulators of climate, hosted an extraordinary range of species, and were intermediaries of global water supplies.

The Amazon rainforest was under attack.

This time, it had nothing to do with mechanized agriculture, soy farms, logging, or the clearing of trees for cattle. It was something else, the media explained without actually explaining. Nobody knew what had triggered termites to do what they were doing. Possibly, the guesswork continued, it was climate change that caused some kind of mutation in the starving little insect. For the first time, there was a risk of total deforestation of the Amazon. Predictions included a drastically reduced rain and snowfall in the United States, plus water and food shortages.

Not a single paper talked about Christel, like Eleanor Delarge had said they would. Locked in her bungalow with a laptop computer, Christel felt relieved. It was bad enough that the forest was hurting. She couldn't imagine how it would be to have her name associated with that catastrophe.

Christel heard *Subject C*'s horn and closed the laptop.

She got up from her golden straw chaise longue, went over to the window, and pulled back the curtain. Maurice was back. Christel rushed down the spiral wood staircase to meet him. She crossed the catwalk linking to the deck and glanced up at the stern of the ship. There seemed to be a lot of people inside the boat's main deck saloon. She squinted, trying to identify the silhouettes that formed a line. Then Maurice came out, glanced at Christel, and waved.

She waved back. And her jaw dropped.

The line of natives came out shortly after Maurice and began to disembark, led by a short naked woman. It looked like her son had brought an entire tribe to their private refuge. Christel lifted both palms in the air, trying to figure out why.

"Hello, Mother," Maurice said, half-smiling, half-frowning.

"Maurice?"

He kissed his mother on the cheek, hugged her with one arm, and turned to introduce the crowd. "That's Amana. She's a friend. And that one is Armando. He's a biologist."

Amana glanced at Christel. That woman was tall, exquisitely beautiful, and was dressed in a cotton gypsy dress. She had tiny scars on her face and legs and was probably a white warrior of some kind. Instinctively, Amana leaned both hands against Maurice's available shoulder, marking her territory.

"Hello," Christel said.

Amana glanced up at Maurice. He touched Christel's belly and pointed back at himself. "She's my mother."

Behind Amana, the thirty-six members of the tribe remained waiting in a disciplined line. Most of them were men carrying hammocks, small tools, food, spears, bows, and indigenous cudgels. Some wore loincloths; others were naked. All looked at Christel with the same inquisitiveness with which she looked at them. "Moe?"

"They lost their village," he said.

"I don't think we have enough rooms."

"We have enough forest. They'll settle with us. Temporarily."

"How did you meet them?"

"They, er, attacked me a while ago. Now we're friends."

Christel shook her head. "When you're done accommodating them, let's talk."

It was a lot to take in. Just when she was about to question Maurice's decision to bring an uncontacted tribe home, Christel heard Kiara yelling her name and turned to watch her running awkwardly in her direction.

"What, Kiki?"

Kiara froze for a beat, glanced at the line of naked tribesmen, and then said breathlessly, "You need to come inside."

"I'm kinda busy."

Things got busier still when the tribesmen broke the line and decided to circle the tall white woman and the equally tall African-American woman who'd just shown up on the dock. Christel stared at Maurice. *Do something.*

He looked at Amana, who yelled at her people until they stepped back to a comfortable distance. They were talking to each other and quickly losing their initial shyness.

"Your name's on the TV," Kiara said.

Christel blinked. She was expecting it.

"What are they saying?"

"Crazy stuff . . . Darling, they're accusing you of being responsible for what's going on in the forest. A supposed CIA document surfaced. The property you own on the other side of the forest used to be an entomological secret government lab or some shit like that. There are profiles of you!"

She nodded. "Not nice, I'd guess."

"No, sweetie. They're calling you a hypocrite. A criminal. And, er, a former prostitute."

All the noise produced by the tribe faded into a muted, distant hum. Christel's mouth opened, but words wouldn't come out.

Thank you so much, Alan Reid, she thought bitterly. And: *What will Denizard think?*

41

In about a week, the tribe had built a seventy-foot-long structure. The hollowed dwelling sat half a mile from the main bungalows, two hundred yards inside the thick native forest of the reserve. They were completely hidden from land and sky. The collective windowless structure was built from nearby taquaras and the trunks of trees, and covered by palm leaves. It was large enough to house their thirty-six members, with hammocks mounted inside it for sleeping.

Christel stayed in her bedroom for all that time.

There was an uncontacted tribe on her property, which was a delicate issue for Brazilians, who treated them as treasures. They would only be assimilated if they wanted to be. Sheltering them might be considered illegal.

Neither Maurice nor Kiara had ever seen Christel in such an isolated, dejected condition. She'd refused Kiara's meals, which were replaced by late-night visits to the kitchen when everybody was asleep. Her bedroom TV was kept off.

The thought of Denizard was tightening her heart. She felt that the time spent with him had not been well used. The short trips in and out of Geneva, the fancy meals and delightful conversations had all been a waste of time. She should've been more incisive, gone a step further. At her age, resolution was a necessity. Now, they were calling her a prostitute.

Christel had no doubts that Denizard was a clever man. He wasn't going to throw himself into a serious relationship unless he was convinced it was the right thing for him. Which, in Christel's mind, meant she'd failed as a woman. Her long list of relationships, the many experiences with men, were useless. Sitting on the edge of the bed with her head resting against her palms, Christel felt like a lost teenager. It was ridiculous.

I came to him first. It's his turn.

Outside was hot, and a drizzle wetted the windows. All the lights inside the bungalows were off. Christel was naked, even though the air-conditioning was on—the only perceivable sound in her bedroom until she heard the doorknob moving. She turned, but no one entered.

That was odd. Maurice and Kiara usually knocked before entering, and they were the only ones at the property who ever came to her bedroom. But never late at night.

"Who's there?"

She heard one footstep and no answer. Annoyed, she got up and walked toward the now half-opened door. It was dark, but the contours of objects were clear. She was about fifty inches from the door when Amana showed up with two quick steps, stopping at nose distance from her. They both stood still, equally alarmed.

"Can I help you?"

"Christel?" the native said.

Amana's eyes tilted down from Christel's face to about the height of her chest. She looked fascinated. Without ceremony, the young woman raised a hand up to Christel's breasts, which prompted her to block the invasive touch that was about to occur. But at the last instant, she comprehended what had caught Amana's attention and let her go on with it.

Soon, her fingers were delicately touching a scar on the lower outer part of her breast. With her digits still on the thin pink line, Amana looked at Christel with a question in her eyes that needn't be asked.

A freak politician did it, Christel wanted to say. But in what language?

When it became clear what Amana was doing, the discomfort of the situation lessened. The native seemed more at ease studying Christel—the white woman who welcomed her tribe to stay at the property while the forest bled. Her sharp eyes ran from one side of Christel's body to the other. Christel assumed she was trying to decide which mark was the most significant. When she found another, her fingers respectfully slid to it. A burn scar next to

Christel's belly button. Amana's finger circled its surface.

Cigarette burns, courtesy of a sheik.

Down her inner thighs, more scars ranged from small and superficial to large and protuberant. *Men's teeth . . . countless occasions.*

Amana's eyes were wide open when she mumbled words in her language that sounded to Christel like empathy. She knew these weren't the types of scars she was familiar with. Whenever someone of her tribe got a mark on their body, it was usually the result of hunting or fishing.

Amana looked up at Christel again, clearly craving an explanation. She opened her mouth and pointed at her teeth. *Bites.* And more unrecognizable words followed. She looked like a doctor inspecting a patient, turning Christel around with both hands. Her back was even worse. There were so many scars that Amana simply gave up trying to figure out who had done that to her, and why. Even in the darkness, Christel saw her eyes shine.

A spontaneous, warm embrace followed. Christel was so enchanted by her innocence that she found herself wanting her to stay a little while.

"Men," was all she could say.

*****

Christel checked the analog clock on the wall: two in the morning. She heard the TV being turned on down on the ground level. She put on a gown and slippers and left her bedroom. There was a small, intimate room right below her bedroom with the lights on, which partially illuminated the spiral stairs. She glimpsed Kiara and Maurice drinking coffee, eating corn cake, and watching the news. Both glanced at Christel as she approached and sat next to them.

Christel immediately saw what was on TV. "Another profile?"

The report on a twenty-four-hour news network showed Christel at the height of her social life. Pictures of a young, ridiculously sexy Christel in Studio 54. A collage of countless meetings with heads of state, business people, and artists. Praise for her immense contribution to the 2004 tsunami victims, and the awards and titles that followed. The tradition she'd kept from her father, philanthropist Julian Welch. Her perfect marriage with Everett Johnson came next. Then, the TV host began to talk about the most recent speculations of Christel being a high-class prostitute in her youth, and finally, they talked about Alan Reid, her father's partner.

"A man veiled in mystery. The former rubber baron's ties with the Nazis and his US government contracts earned him a controversial place in the annals of the business world. Maybe it's not much of an accident that ground zero of the devastation going down

in the Amazon started on a property bought by the late Alan Reid. We tried to contact Christel Welch for a comment, but so far we've had no success."

"Let me get you something to eat," Kiara said.

"Thanks," Christel said.

"How do you feel?" Maurice asked.

She shrugged. "I don't feel guilty, if that's what you wanna know."

"And you shouldn't. But it's time we do something. Someone's going to have to pay for this. Right now, it's you, Mother."

She glanced at Maurice, at a loss as to what to say. "Some things are bigger than us."

"What does that even mean? We sit and watch?"

Christel closed her eyes. Maurice was right. Now, of all times, she needed to be who she was. An outpouring of anger and determination took over. "We do things differently."

She got up and accepted a cup of coffee from Kiara on her way back to her bedroom. As much as she loved Maurice, he lacked the malice required to thrive in the world revolving around the name Welch. Though he shared his grandfather Julian's taste for adventure, Maurice was too pure for the times they were living in. She wondered what Everett would have said or done, but he wasn't around anymore. He was dead.

Denizard Haener was alive.

Businesswise, Denis was a giant compared to Everett. The Swiss man had swum with sharks dressed in suits and found a way to avoid the radioactivity of wealth. In that respect, both were wise.

In the morning, Christel checked the news. Maybe, by some miracle, the media had forgotten her. They hadn't. She was still heavily under attack. Now that they'd told all possible stories about Christel, they were asking where she was and why an arrest warrant hadn't been issued yet.

Where are you, Denis?

She needed help. Her plan of waiting, and her hope that he would call her at any moment, had failed. She used to be good at reading men, but not even that remained from her prime. Walking back and forth inside her bungalow bedroom wasn't doing any good. She glanced at the satellite phone on her desk, swallowed her pride, and finally called him.

"You think I'm a business deal?" was the first thing she said when he answered the phone.

There was a loud chopping noise in the background. He yelled, but his voice still sounded muffled. "Say that again?"

"Denis, are you flying?"

"Yes."

"Can't you land somewhere? There are plenty of nice little roads in Switzerland. We need to talk."

"We will. Soon."

"They're slaughtering me."

"What was that?"

"I said, the media is blaming me for what's happening in the Amazon."

"Yes . . . I know."

The conversation wasn't helping. Denizard could barely hear her. The helicopter pulsing over the phone was getting on her nerves. "Is that all you have to say?" she said.

"I'm sorry. Say that again?"

Christel moved the phone away from her ear and rolled her eyes.

It was weird. The chopping noise seemed to be coming from all directions now. She listened for a moment and then glanced out the window. There was a helicopter approaching her property.

"Denis?"

"I see a blue Eurocopter EC175 parked in your helipad. Is that yours, Chris?"

Her mouth opened, and she burst into tearful laughter. "Yes . . . land on the grass."

"See you in a minute," he said.

Outside the bungalow, Amana's tribe was getting ready for war.

Spears and arrows were aimed at the man-made bird approaching the helipad. They had seen Christel's Eurocopter and had spent hours studying it, but it was the first time they'd witnessed a helicopter flying. The approaching bird was white, unlike the one they'd become familiar with. It made a loud, overpowering noise, displacing air like the storms of the gods. This was not their property, but they would defend it as if it were.

Christel, Maurice, and Kiara came out of the bungalow, saw the tribe circling Denizard's helicopter, and ran toward the tribe, waving their hands.

"Move away!" Maurice yelled.

Amana knew that the white metal bird was not a threat, signaling to her people to back off. The helicopter waited until Christel signaled it was OK to land. She stood at a minimum safe distance.

The moment Denizard got out, the pilot closed the chartered helicopter's door and took off. Gradually, the pandemonium cooled down.

Christel rushed to meet Denizard. He held her in his arms.

"Why didn't you call?" she said.

All questions and insecurities she had dissipated when he kissed her.

42

Kiara was inspired when she cooked lunch. The man Christel called Denis, whoever he was, released her boss from a week of self-enclosure in the bedroom and returned the occasional smile to her face.

"Are you hungry today?" Kiara said.

"More than usual," Christel said.

Grilled tambaqui fish over charcoal was served with manioc and a fine bottle of chardonnay. Kiara joined them at the table, and the mood was light during the first half of lunch. Denizard asked Maurice about the situation in the affected region, and about the relationship between him and the tribe he'd seen earlier when he'd arrived by helicopter.

Part of the explanation was offered by Armando, who'd been staying in one of the two small guest bungalows and was scheduled to leave that afternoon. After the informal briefing, Denizard eyed Christel and said, "They're going to hit you hard."

"They already are," Christel said.

"I mean, financially. Even if they can't prove

you're responsible, and I know you're not, it still is your property."

"That's exactly what our lawyer said, Mother," Maurice said.

"You should move your money," Denizard said between sips of wine. But before he could explain what he meant by that, Amana came into the dining room.

"What is it, Amana?" Maurice said.

She grabbed his hand. "Come." And, glancing at the others, she repeated, "Come!"

Maurice stood. "Let's see what she wants."

Ten minutes after they left the bungalow, Amana reached the tribe's quarters.

All the natives waited inside their collective structure. Some lay on hammocks, others around a pit fire that served as their improvised kitchen. They were heating an old metal pan Kiara had offered them the day they'd arrived. There was water and leaves inside it.

An old male native crouched, picked up the pan, and waited until another tribesman handed over metal cups to their visitors. The content of the pan was served to each of them.

Kiara smelled it. "That's some kind of tea."

Amana sipped her cup first. Armando, Maurice, Christel, and Denizard followed.

"I prefer Earl Grey. And it's cold," Christel whispered to Kiara after her first sip.

Amana called a tribesman who had been watching from a hammock. He stood, picked up a bag made with the skin of some animal, and joined them around the fire. "See," Amana told Maurice's group. Then she nodded at the man holding the bag. He crouched, opened the bag, and released the contents.

It was full of termites.

"Jesus. Why would she bring them here?" Christel said.

"Did you see any fallen trees during your flight?" Maurice asked Denizard.

"No."

The eyes turned to Amana as she kneeled down with her cup of tea. When she was sure everyone was looking, she poured the tea over the termites.

"What do you think she's doing?" Christel said to Maurice.

The insects changed their behavior to a slow-motion pattern.

Within seconds, they were all dead.

"Has she poisoned us?" Christel stared at her cup of tea.

It required no translation. Amana stood up and grabbed Christel's cup, drinking the remainder of the tea in one long sip. To leave no doubt, she took Maurice's cup as well and drank it. When it was Armando's turn, Amana saw that he'd been smelling the tea like he was studying it.

"It has a citrus scent," Armando said.

"So?" Maurice wanted to know.

"Some orange rinds have an active ingredient called D-limonene. It's been known to kill termites. Some oils break down their exoskeletons and destroy their eggs. But I've never seen it happen so fast," Armando said.

Maurice dipped his fingers into his cup and pulled out some of the leaves. "Where did you find this?" he asked Amana.

"Come," she said.

Soon, they were all following Amana again. Christel watched the young native and started to find similarities with her younger self. Amana was determined and always in control.

They walked for twenty minutes down a track cleared by Amana's tribe inside the reserve until they arrived at the shores of the Rio Negro. Amana pointed in the direction of a shrub tree and glanced at Armando. She knew he was the only one familiar with the native plants. He approached and took a sample of its small fruit in his hand.

"Looks like a variation of camu camu," he said.

"What's that?" Maurice said.

"A fruit. I've never seen it before, but it resembles the *Myrciaria dubia*, a species that can be found all over the Amazon. No other fruit in the world has this much vitamin C. A hundred times more than a lemon."

"So, it kills termites. But how much tea would it

take to control vast areas?" Christel said.

"Not tea. Pesticides," Denizard said, stepping forward.

"Exactly," Armando said. "Think how efficient a pesticide can be if you change the active ingredient of an existing pesticide to make it work specifically for the species we're dealing with here. A low-risk formula that would bear the word 'caution' on its label, which is way safer than 'warning' or 'danger.'"

"How long would it take to make?" Christel said.

"A chemical company wouldn't have to invent a new formula. They could take an existing one and simply change the ingredients."

"But the termites are eating up the forest as we speak," Christel said.

"I contacted DETER this morning. The satellites are showing that trees are not falling beyond rivers. The termites are being contained by water," Armando said.

"How do we even start?" Christel said.

"I have an idea," Denizard said.

Maurice glanced at Denizard, the man with a French accent he'd just met.

The stranger he knew nothing about was already having ideas, which made him worried about his mother's vulnerabilities. Who this man was, and what his story was, remained to be clarified. On their way back to the bungalow, Denizard started delegating tasks.

"Do you mind?" Denizard pointed to his cell phone and took pictures of the *Myrciaria dubia* species in Armando's hands. "When can we know more about it?"

"I'll do some lab tests as soon as I arrive in Belém. It may take a few days."

"Will you keep us updated?"

"Sure."

They walked back on the forest track and returned to the bungalows. Denizard turned to Maurice. "It'd help if your friend brought us more samples."

"I'll ask Amana," Maurice said.

Amana and her people went back into the forest.

Alone with his mother in the bungalow terrace, Maurice didn't need to ask. Christel saw in his face that he felt troubled, and she knew it had to do with Denizard.

"Here's the deal, Moe. In another life, Denis and I dated. That was long before I met your father. He was a banker. He's a widower now, just like me. We've got things in common. Right now, he's trying to help."

Maurice nodded. "I'm gonna have to trust you, then."

A moment later, Denizard showed up on the terrace. "Can we talk about my idea?" he said.

"I'm skeptical of any easy way out. But yes. Let's talk," Christel said.

Denizard glanced at Maurice. "I'd be happy if you joined us."

"I wasn't going anywhere."

They stayed on the terrace, and Kiara brought out glasses of fresh orange juice. She placed them on a low round table circled by four chairs and sat with them. Denizard glanced at Christel.

"We're all family. There are no secrets between us," she said.

"Right . . . So, this is what I believe will happen. There will be money seized as reparation for environmental damages. And more money seized to compensate potential victims in cities and villages," Denizard said.

"Great. How much are we talking about?" Christel said.

"More than you have, Chris."

"You know I have a lot of money. And I'm willing to pay."

"I'm estimating several billion dollars," Denizard said and then turned to Maurice. The Swiss man wanted Maurice's take.

"Remember Vale's dam collapse a couple of years ago? Brazilian state courts confiscated billions. The scale of devastation we're dealing now is shockingly higher," Maurice said.

"He's right. Chris, they're coming after somebody. You," Denizard said.

Christel sighed. "What do we do, then?"

"This is what I think you should do. You'll need to keep your mind open because trust is the most important thing right now. First, move all your liquid assets to an offshore account. Let authorities seize real estate, jewelry, and your nice helicopter."

"Just like that," Christel said.

"Yes. Because you know they will. Now, once you move your money offshore, it needs to be moved again."

"It will look like we're hiding it," she said.

"It doesn't matter. You'll be using legal channels, the rule of law."

"Where, then?"

"To an investment company I own," he said. Maurice's lips twisted, but Denizard carried on. "No matter how much money we're talking about here, you'll only own ten percent of my company. I know it sounds ridiculous, but if they ever come after the money, they'll only be able to get their hands on the ten percent that belongs to you. Currently, ten percent of that particular company accounts for roughly thirty million dollars."

"Denis, are you suggesting I pay billions for a thirty-million-dollar stake?" Christel said.

"That's the idea."

Maurice shifted in his chair. "What are the risks for you?"

Denizard smiled. "I know what you're thinking. But I'm not in the business of taking risks anymore. That's why I said trust is the most important thing in this. They're going to hurt you anyway. Financially."

Mother and son exchanged a long glance, and even Kiara set her eyes on that charming European man. "Second," Denizard continued, "once the money is in my hands, I'll buy a controlling stake in a pesticide company. I'm not speaking about Dow Chemical or Bayer AG. It needs to be a smaller business we can control. This will be the company we'll be sending the samples that your friend Amana showed us. And, finally—once we have a seat on the board with controlling shareholder power—we'll appoint someone we trust to lead the company."

Maurice looked the other way, digesting Denizard's plan. He was astonished. The plan did make sense but would put his mother and him entirely in Denizard's hands.

"Maurice, I want you to consider something else—the opportunity," Denizard said.

"Oh, sure. That part I get. It's likely that the amount of pesticide needed to deal with the termites will exceed government fines," Maurice said.

Christel stood and walked a few steps away from her chair. Asking Maurice if she could trust Denizard was useless. In her gut, she knew he was a man of his word. But still a man. A human being. She could be wrong about him and lose everything. Yet, she had no choice. It was a matter of simply doing the math. All that she owned wouldn't be enough to compensate for the damages. That perspective made her decision an easy one.

"I'll do it," she said.

"Let's think about it, Mother," Maurice said.

She walked back over. "Moe, if you can't think of any other path to follow, then I say we take action now."

"The sooner, the better," Denizard pushed. "They could be preparing to seize your assets as we speak."

"What company do you have in mind?" Maurice said.

"Alpha Alp Chemical. It's Swiss. I know them very well, and the board knows me. I already have a significant stake invested there," Denizard said.

"Who's gonna run the company once we take control?" Maurice said.

"Obviously, it can't be you or your mother."

"I know someone," Christel said. "He knows nothing about chemicals, but he's someone I trust."

"Fantastic," Denizard said. "Another thing, Chris. You need to throw a press conference. Let everyone know you have a solution."

"But we don't! All we have is a plan."

"A plan is the beginning and end of everything. We can't anticipate the future."

Christel wasn't sure she liked that idea. She'd been out of the public eye for years, running from business gossip magazines, now more than ever. If she started looking for them, it could be seen as an admittance of guilt, and it would cause a humiliation that would only serve to sell more papers. Christel wanted to make it seem like she was offering the press a chance to meet her. She was confident they would all come to her, thirsty for a scandal and hungry for blood.

"OK, then. I'll invite the media here," she said.

"I don't like it, Mother. It's not appropriate."

"I know. But I don't want to make it easy for them. If they want a piece of me, they'll come. First, Denis, I need to know if we can turn that sample into a mass-scale production."

"I know we can," Denizard said.

43

The appointment of Harry Walker as the new CEO of Alpha Alp Chemical came as a shock. The board members knew nothing about him, and what they did know revealed nothing in terms of qualifications. Before that, he'd been the owner of an investigation firm, and that was it. The thought of having an American private eye at the helm of a centenarian Swiss company was the last thing the board had expected. In a lightning-fast deal that came out of nowhere, Denizard Haener, the new controlling shareholder with 60 percent of the common stock, came up with enough resources to pay off all the company's debts and now occupied the position of chairman of the board. His sudden interest in the company, and the origin of the money used to invest in it, remained a mystery. But the only true questioning came from Denizard himself, who'd asked Christel about naming Harry as CEO.

"He loves a challenge. And he's completely trustworthy," she'd replied a week earlier when

Denizard had bought up the control of Alpha Alp.

"But, Chris, you honestly think this is enough?" he said.

"Let's just say he's agreed to run everything by us."

Denizard accepted her suggestion with no further questions. Putting someone Christel trusted in power was a way to make her feel more comfortable with Denizard's bold plan.

The night before Harry began working as CEO, he brought a team of technicians that bugged almost every room of the Alpha Alp headquarters in Basel, Switzerland. It was a large rectangular cement building resembling the Grisons Museum of Fine Arts in Chur, a three-floor structural oxymoron with much of the working space safely nested underground. All was completed in one night. The security team and the receptionists were replaced by yet more Americans working for Harry, brought in from his investigation company. He turned Alpha Alp into an invisible war theater.

On his third day as CEO, Harry had gathered enough information on the top eight executives. Five of them were fired. "They have loose tongues, that's why," he said to Denizard and Christel during their daily conferences over the internet. The executives would be replaced in due time.

All attention was being directed to a pesticide formula kept in a vault of Alpha Alp that stored hundreds of suspended projects and patents. The pesticide in question had been tested before and had been deemed too light for the most common termites. But there was a component in the formula that had drawn the attention of Denizard and had been key in his decision to purchase the controlling shares of Alpha Alp—information that had been provided by one of its managers, who'd been duly compensated when the acquisition period was concluded. Two other companies had similar formulas in their inventories, but they weren't considered feasible for a takeover.

The component in question had a citrus quality that resembled the active ingredient that killed and repelled the termite species eating up the Amazon. All they had to do was test it on the samples brought from Brazil. If it worked, the *Myrciaria dubia* species found by Amana wouldn't even need to be researched. In the forest, before everyone's eyes, it had worked in its most basic form, as a tea. Expectations were high.

A small colony of termites was taken to the Alpha Alp lab to face its only test.

The results showed that a pesticide named AAC ExTermite, once a flawed, money-wasting formula, was indeed effective against the new species of termite. Alpha Alp had the perfect product for the perfect storm.

"It works," Harry told Denizard by the end of his second week as head of the company.

"Start making it," Denizard said.

Then, Denizard called Christel and told her the good news. She sounded skeptical. "Just like that, huh?" she said.

"Yes, Chris. It's not like we've created something from scratch. We just had to add some salt; the food was ready."

"And you just happened to know where? That's mind-boggling, Denis."

"Not really. Listen, I've been maintaining good relationships with middle management all around. I don't waste time with company leaders; they're usually competing against each other. The people with boots on the ground—scientists and technicians—are the ones who really understand the products being made or stored. So, I'm in contact with several of them. Whenever some new drug or chemical is removed from the shelf to hit the market, they call me. It's been helping my investment decisions for quite some time. I usually thank them generously, if you know what I mean. This time, all I had to do was ask around. I found a company that had what we needed. I made a move. Not that scientific, is it?"

"No. Sounds like good homework, actually," Christel said.

"What about the press conference?"

Denizard glanced at his computer screen and saw Christel arching her eyebrows. He heard a long sigh.

There was no way she could avoid facing the ire of the world.

"I guess it's time," she said.

*****

Christel Welch, the heiress to the Reid & Welch Company, had summoned the media to the Amazon. The small dock leading to the bungalows was packed with journalists. From inside her bungalow, Christel watched them arrive.

She tilted her eyes up and checked the skies, taking her time.

The daily shower would come at any minute, and what a glorious sight that would be. Christel wondered if the wooden structure was as strong as her shoulders were, capable of handling the weight of that many people. Though the dock had been designed as a disembarking platform, she wanted to make their visit to her property as uncomfortable as possible.

Let them feel trapped.

Usually, for the simple gatherings of the past, she would have hosted cocktails at the Waldorf Astoria. But if the media was expecting the cheese board of the Peacock Alley bar, or a horde of waiters standing by like when she threw some of her more memorable receptions, they were in for a sure disappointment. Those days were gone. She'd brought them to a different palace, one inhabited by over three thousand different species of mosquitos that were part of the menu, along with the coming rain.

Christel counted forty souls. A collapse would be quite the scene—a media uproar turned into a feeding frenzy for the piranhas.

Not yet, Christel thought.

The Reid & Welch Building in New York, which had been constructed by Alan and Julian decades earlier, would have been a much more suitable—and more convenient—place for a press conference. It was the obvious setting everyone was expecting for Christel to use when she was ready to talk. The journalists wanted the usual catering with the fabulous vision and style of Christel's most notorious occasions.

You haven't just betrayed me. You've butchered me.

In the past years, she'd been almost forgotten. But they'd been chasing her madly for the past weeks since the Amazon devastation was linked to her family, and since other offensive rumors were irresponsibly spread. Questions ranged from being unfair—implying Christel's culpability from the beginning—to aggressive beyond what was reasonable. They didn't address the problem, but the Reid & Welch legacy and Christel's personal reputation. A blow to the heart of the family with the sole intention of destroying them.

As much as it hurt Christel, she wouldn't let them see her wounds. A woman like her had thick skin.

And now that things were clearing up, she would do everything she could to enjoy her retribution against those who attempted to obliterate her. Today was only an aperitif.

She would present herself as proud and blameless.

Getting into the Welches' private reserve included a ninety-minute fast boat ride followed by a two-hour drive, then another sixty minutes of fast boat riding down the Rio Negro until they reached the dock of her floating palace. They could come by helicopter, but she'd booked all available flights, forcing the press to go by river.

The short notice contributed to their plight in getting there. Now that they all had come—as she knew they would—Christel planned to address them for no more than a minute. She would take no questions, excuse herself, and let everyone know that they had to return to Manaus while there was still daylight. Her refuge only had three bungalows. She had no intention of sharing her land with any more people; her privacy had already been shattered by the recent unfortunate events.

At sixty-nine, Christel still had the erect stature and curves of a model. Even in the middle of a humid rain forest, her hair was perfectly done. Her silky, tanned skin had no regard whatsoever for the mosquitos that dared bother her. She had had her share of bites from men, which was immeasurably worse.

I'm stronger than all of you.

Christel had endured abuses of indescribable magnitude. Her inner strength had taught her to move on. For most of her life, she'd had no second thoughts about business decisions or romantic problems. Relationships were meant to feel meaningful and make you happy. If they made you suffer, to hell with them. Life was too short. Whining was a terrible waste of time, and it made you uglier.

She took a glimpse at her Cartier Ballon Bleu watch. She was ten minutes late when she glanced up at the sky for the last time that morning. The rain started to pour at last.

Perfect. She moved away from the window.

It was time to face the journalists. Some of them were highly respected by Christel, but others she saw as part of a swarm of insects eagerly waiting to feed on her blood. The only thing more revolting was the thought that many on that dock used to be Christel's friends and confidants.

How foolish of me.

She exhaled, picked up the umbrella hanging on a wall, and turned decidedly toward the door. She opened it, still out of sight from everyone, and spent a moment listening to the buzz outside. It didn't sound much different than the hums of the natural fauna around her floating palace. People were capable of that. In her resentful state of mind, they seemed to her like beasts waiting for their next meal.

Nothing more than fangs and claws and venom capable of killing a person the moment you stopped feeding them.

Christel stepped down the slippery spiral wood staircase with the grace of an empress. The noise outside ceased. All she could hear now was the sound of the intense tropical shower gaining momentum.

Good. They're aware of my presence.

First, they saw her legs, still graceful and toned as in her prime. Her light-green linen dress hit just above her knees and was the right thing to wear under the circumstances, elegant despite the threats of the jungle. Usually—when there was nobody to impress—she preferred to wear jeans and an old T-shirt.

Her lean body emerged from behind one of the support columns of the main bungalow, confident and dignified, not at all the demeanor of a guilty person.

You will not destroy me.

She was about to address them. The queen bee that provided the sweet honey that helped sustain some of the carriers standing on that dock. The sugar made of gossip and business rumors. They watched Christel, and the envy and hunger ceased to exist for a moment. Her gait was as feminine as ever. The walk of someone strong enough to have survived the appetite of presidents, corporate leaders, and royalty, and all of that before she was even a grown woman.

Nothing really scared her, except the mediocrity of others, which irked her more than she would admit.

After crossing the shaky catwalk linking the main bungalow to the dock, she was finally among them. She was the only one holding an umbrella.

Christel first made eye contact with Eleanor Delarge, her friend of decades. Eleanor was the one person on that dock she'd have expected to take it easy on her. She'd lost count of how many dinners and gifts and holidays both had shared around the world or in her Arles farmhouse. They were competitive but loyal to each other. But the chief editor of New York's favorite fashion magazine had disregarded all of that when times of trouble arose. Eleanor's magazine had written in bold headlines that Christel had *"LET THE WORLD DOWN."* More than a weight on anyone's shoulders, it was a sharp knife to her back, considering the number of orgasms and the countless little sins they'd confided about to one another.

Other familiar faces on that dock brought back bitter associations in the form of cruel, unfair, and disgustingly opportunistic headlines.

"A FAKE PRINCESS DIANA: A wolf in sheep's clothing?"

"AN ENVIRONMENT PATRON FRAUD: Who else would dump an entomological lab in the middle of a forest?"

"JET-SETTER CON ARTIST: Reputation built

on billions, prostitution, and frivolity."

"A CRIMINAL WITHOUT A HINT OF DOUBT: Christel Welch should be convicted and put behind bars."

"NOTHING BUT A RICH HEIRESS: What to do when you inherit a fortune? Pretend to be concerned about the environment and throw a party."

"Chris, it's good to see you," Eleanor said, practically shouting.

The heavy rain produced an uproar against the wooden dock and the Rio Negro waters. Eleanor was soaking wet, like all the others, and she bet that Christel had been waiting for the rain to start just to humiliate them. They knew each other too well. The heat had begun to melt Eleanor's makeup an hour earlier, and by now, the rain had washed it away, turning her face into an abstract painting of bitterness.

"It's 'Miss Welch,'" Christel corrected her. Eleanor should've known better.

Christel's voice was loud enough to be heard by everyone. She waited for the last whispers to silence. "I wish I could thank you for your presence, but that's not going to happen. You came of your own will. I'm not here to entertain you."

"Are you going to tell us about the solution everyone's speculating about?" a man wearing a Panama hat asked.

It was Michael Bird, the one who'd accused her of being "a criminal without a hint of doubt." He was a veteran TV anchor, highly respected, impeccably arrogant, and there were some rumors of sexual harassment accusations against him that had yet to be investigated. A charming man who'd seen better days, but precisely the kind of guy Christel despised the most—men in a position of power abusing those who lacked it, usually the young, the beautiful, and the naive. Right now, his question had a lot of relevance. Christel couldn't afford to deny him an answer.

A chunk of the Amazon forest had been devastated at an unprecedented rate. The cause of it baffled the international community: genetically modified termites hidden for years in an underground lab inside her property.

When the story had first broken, it was the closest thing to a world war in terms of repercussions. It had been established, not entirely incorrectly, that Christel's family was responsible for it. All the while, the world had been watching and waiting for someone to be beheaded. Climatologists were predicting something like the end of the planet. New computer simulations were being done in all corners of the globe, attempting to measure the damage on the climate. They nicknamed it "the Welch Effect." It was a scandalous event of monumental proportions, a wound in the heart of the Amazon— the pain of it so severe that people could almost hear the giant forest crying out for help.

Christel turned to Michael Bird and struck him down with a stare. "I'm not taking questions."

A murmur followed and mixed with the sound of showers and thunder.

The media had traveled by plane, car, and boat to be there. They were ridiculously wet, confined on a tight dock that was swinging dangerously with the pull of the river and the wind. If that was a joke, it had been lamely told. She could very well have shuttled them there on the fancy helicopter parked just a few hundred yards from the dock.

It was unthinkable that the immensity of the accusations against her family could be taken so lightly. The response "I'm not taking questions" sounded as if the pope himself were accused of pedophilia, or a sitting president was under suspicion of murdering the first lady at the White House. Questions would have to be taken. Christel and Maurice were indisputably the most prominent names in the global scene of charities, the blue bloods of environmental causes. Now, they were the number-one suspects for the Amazon's most destructive event.

"Give us a break," Eleanor yelled.

Christel eyed her briefly, anticipating the avalanche of questions that would follow. "I want to address the rumors," Christel said and paused. "The claims that I have found a solution? They're true."

"What exactly is—" Michael Bird began to ask.

She shushed him by raising her palm in the air. He wiped his face with his forearm, but it was useless under the constant pouring of water. Christel remained dry and lofty.

"The forest will be saved," she continued. "That's all I can say right now. Oh, and make sure you write this down—I'm making a promise."

She turned before they had a chance to ask anything else.

Instants later, they saw her vanish up the staircase and inside the bungalow. That was it. After hours of traveling, all they could get was the confirmation of a rumor. No new information other than a vague promise that sounded like it was written by a second-rate PR firm.

"Bitch," Eleanor said.

"A major one," Michael Bird agreed.

44

Reality took some time to sink in. From Chicago to Edinburgh, from Osaka to São Paulo, people on the streets asked how insects could have caused such a large amount of damage to the environment. Scientists reminded the skeptics that, in the past, ground searches and satellite images had shown an immense group of large termite mounds in northeastern Brazil, a gigantic array obscured by trees covering an area of 230,000 square kilometers—about the size of Great Britain. The amount of soil processed by the termites was estimated to have a volume equal to four thousand Great Pyramids of Giza.

News coming out of the Brazilian Ministry of the Environment shed light on the origins of the destruction going on in the Amazon. With the help of a platoon of the Amazon Military Command, they painstakingly searched the piece of land where the termites had initiated their restless feast, scouring every square inch of it.

At the center of the property, sensors revealed an elongated underground concrete structure and a metal door covered by ten feet of dirt at one of its extremities. After digging and exploding their way in, the platoon found what was being considered ground zero. The structure was half filled with termite nests made of soil, feces, and chewed-up wood. The colony, comprised of millions of individuals, was a messy sight illuminated by soldiers' flashlights.

Here and there, there were remains of metal tables, chairs, and cabinets. Old files and shredded papers with indistinguishable content. And an Item Unique Identification Marking on the corroded furniture. The best thing that could've happened to Christel in the past weeks.

"They know you're not responsible," Harry informed Christel during one of their internet calls.

"Who is, then?"

"The United States Department of Defense. Obviously, they don't want fingers pointing at some shady secret government project of the past."

"Now what? They need to clear my name!"

"That's not the way this is going to play out. You're not going to be legally charged, and that's the good news. There's a bizarre debate going on right now between Brazilian and US officials. Brazil's blaming the United States for conducting secret activities in the Amazon, which our government won't officially recognize. And the US is accusing

Brazil of not properly taking care of their land."

"That's their problem."

"Absolutely. My source told me they'll blame climate change for influencing the mutation of the termite species. They'll turn this into an educational case."

"Whatever. Jesus . . . Will they retract? I got my name trashed, Harry."

"No government ever accused you of anything. It was the press that did it. So, take a deep breath, Chris. This is no longer on you."

"Millions of trees and animals have been destroyed, but, hey, I'm good. My head's pounding."

"I need you in Basel. Can you come?"

"Why?"

"Things are looking promising for Alpha Alp."

"It's not me you need. Call Denis."

"I can't find him. Do come, please."

"But I've just talked to him."

"Oh, yeah? How did he sound?"

"Confident. He didn't tell me anything—that's why I called you."

"Interesting. If I may ask, what did he say? You've trusted him with all you've got."

"I don't need you to remind me of that. Yes, I do trust him. He told me to be positive. We have a meeting in three days."

"Where's that?"

"It's a couple's secret, Harry. It's in Switzerland, OK?"

"One more reason for you to fly here. I think Maurice should come with you."

"I doubt it. My son's in love."

*****

Armed with a spear, Amana lead Maurice deep into the virgin forest located inside their reserve. She looked back constantly at him and laughed, like he was too old or too slow to keep up with her. More at ease, a stray dog that lived around the bungalows took turns ahead and behind them, checking the narrow path recently cleared by Amana.

"I'm right here." Maurice followed along with no sign of being offended.

Constantly, she would stop, wait for him, grab his hand, and pull him until he matched her frantic pace. "Come!" she said.

Maurice was curious. Every time Amana called, there was something meaningful behind it.

Soon, she was a few steps ahead of him and gaining distance again. Walking through the woods on that dark path in the forest had its risks. An hour after they'd entered the path, the dog began acting strangely. His ears flattened, and the hair on the back of his neck rose along with a growl.

Amana stopped and raised her spear at about head height. Maurice reached her and looked around, squinting through the darkness.

"What is it?" he said.

"Quiet," Amana said.

He heard something and tensed up, clueless as to what it was or where it was coming from. As Amana firmed her grip around her spear, Maurice remembered the notes written by his father, specifically the tales about the elusive jaguar—how its victims faced dramatic, deep lacerations that could be fatal.

"Quiet . . ." Amana whispered this time. She pointed the spear somewhere in the darkness, turning it slowly at the invisible animal lurking off the trail. They stood still.

The broad-headed cat with powerful jaws was avoiding confrontation, but when the dog disappeared into the woods, horrible growling sounds were heard just moments after. Amana and Maurice knew they were in trouble.

A silence followed. All they wanted to hear was the dog coming back. Minutes passed. They heard nothing.

Maurice's eyes followed Amana's. When she turned left, he turned. When she looked behind, he looked behind. Then her eyes slowly tilted up and squinted. She pointed the spear up. Her trained eyes definitely caught something distressingly close to them, and above. The jaguar was somewhere up in the trees. Maurice squinted at one spot on a branch right above him and froze.

The jaguar jumped on him.

Before Maurice could do anything, he was struck

by the compact power of the cat. He felt like he'd been hit by a locomotive. In the short seconds that followed, he realized the jaguar had bitten him on the arm, left painful and deep claw cuts on his chest, and was now mouthing his leg. His shock paralyzed him.

He tried in vain to punch the jaguar's eyes, but his blows had no effect. He was losing strength fast, and the world started to spin. He somehow made out Amana leaping past him, around the jaguar, and then wounding the animal with her spear. When the animal turned toward Amana, Maurice was sure it was going to be her end too, but the animal fell sideways with the spear deep inside its chest.

"Walk?" Amana said.

Maurice was bleeding terribly. She helped him get up. He couldn't move his left leg. Supported by Amana, they began to move away from the dead jaguar.

"Why are we here? What is it that you wanted to show me?" Maurice asked.

It needed no translation. Amana carefully leaned him against a tree and removed his shirt, tore off a piece of cloth, and tied it around his leg. "Wait," she said.

She walked into the woods, disappearing for a couple of minutes. Maurice sat down. He reached for the bottle of water he kept in his backpack. Alone in the forest, he absorbed his pain as best he could. Maybe Amana went for some medicinal plant that would help until they got back to the bungalows. Whatever she did, he wasn't going to wait for proper care. He got his satellite phone and called Captain Rasmussen.

"Vegard . . . Where are you?"

"I'm in Manaus," the captain said.

"I need you and a surgeon."

"Something wrong?"

"Yes. I've been attacked by a jaguar. I may need some blood."

"Oh, my! I'll leave as soon as I can."

Maurice hung up.

He checked the state of his wounds and frowned. *What am I doing here?* There was a time when he'd almost felt like he was running away from real life, the one that had been built by his grandfather and his mother, but those thoughts weren't fair to him. There was always a reason to be in the forest. Julian Welch survived it, and extracted a fortune from it. Now the forest served as a much-deserved refuge for Christel. Why Maurice was there, and for so long now, remained a question. There had to be an answer. Bleeding in the darkness of the Amazon forest impelled him to believe he wasn't just a lucky heir.

The attack had been painful and terrifying, but seeing Amana kill that beautiful animal had been equally distressing. He looked upward. The night was cloudless. The stars were looking down on

Maurice, mocking him with their all-knowing, unshakable presence.

He heard steps approaching and saw Amana returning with something in her arms. By now, his vision was blurred. Possibly, he was dehydrated. He forced the rest of the water down his throat. When he finished it, Amana was crouching in front of him. In her arms was the most beautiful thing he'd ever seen.

A jaguar cub.

Why would she delay helping him get back to the bungalows when he was bleeding dangerously, and why would she bring that cub to him? It was illogical by a white man's standard, but not if one trusted Amana. She never wasted time, and she was clever enough to see Maurice was in need of medical care.

"It's beautiful," he said to her and began to pet the cub. Maurice let go of his ego. Before him was a fearless woman who'd killed a wild jaguar. He trusted her, despite the pain in his flesh constantly reminding him of the existence of powerful painkillers and antibiotics.

"The mother will be looking for him," Maurice said.

Amana shook her head and gestured to remind Maurice that the cub's mother had been killed. He closed his eyes. The jaguar had simply been protecting her cub. It broke Maurice's heart.

He felt Amana's hand lifting his chin and opened

his eyes. She took his hand and pulled it toward her belly. She placed his palm against her skin, glanced at the cub she held in her arms, said something in her language, and waited for Maurice's reaction. In the forest, simple things—like communication—could easily turn into a life-and-death situation.

She was telling him she wanted a baby.

Or expecting one.

45

Warmly dressed in a trench coat and a wool hat, nobody recognized Christel while she flew from Manaus to Switzerland. When she reached her favorite suite at the Four Seasons with a view of Lake Geneva, she ordered a tomato soup and opened a bottle of her favorite rosé. It had been some time since she'd last drunk champagne by herself. The powers that be had found her not guilty. It had taken a military operation to find the underground lab in the forest. Breathing in the air of justice felt good.

The next day, Christel met Harry for lunch at the Izumi, the hotel's rooftop restaurant. It was a pleasant winter day, clear and reinvigorating.

"News from Denizard?" Harry asked right after their first sip of wine.

"I don't know where Denis is."

"Huh."

"What?"

"Is there a problem between the two of you?"

"No, Harry. No . . . He's been meeting former

bank clients across Europe. People he still keeps, I don't know, on an advisory status of some sort. Mostly friendly family people. I'm not worried."

"Right. I've got more good news."

"Well?"

"About AAC ExTermite. I've just left the meeting we all have been waiting for. The government has chosen us, Chris. They're gonna use our pesticide."

"Good Lord! I never thought I'd be celebrating the sale of a pesticide."

"It's gonna take three years to deal with the termites."

"You're kidding me."

"Production requirements demand time. They'll start flying to the borders of the affected area. That's what stops the problem from spreading. It's gonna take months and a fifty-airplane joint effort between Brazil and the US. If all goes well, they'll start attacking the affected inner areas and kill the remaining colonies."

"Sounds like war."

"The scale of it, yes. But you haven't asked me about money."

"Oh. That."

"Glad you asked. The money you put in to acquire Alpha Alp Chemical? Well, think of a fivefold return if our estimates are correct."

Christel raised her glass of wine. "Well done, Harry."

"That was Denizard's plan from the start. His vision."

And the one controlling all my money, Christel thought. "He's something. The discreet and efficient type."

She glanced out at the Geneva landscape, smiling. Yet, her eyes weren't.

Harry looked at her. "You want me to find out where he is?"

"No. Not this time."

"Sure. What is your gut telling you?"

"That he is kind and honest."

"That's your heart speaking."

Christel eyed him. "Are you trying to say something?"

"I'm here for you. As always."

"I know. You suddenly don't trust Denis?"

"I don't know him enough. In my business, I've learned not to trust other human beings. Except you. And perhaps my mother. Chris, there's a lot of money on the table."

"So?"

"It changes people. It breaks the honor of even the most honorable of men. Anyway, I'm just saying. I don't mean to be a spoiler."

"You'll have to wait until tomorrow."

And so will I.

Lunch came. Roasted sea bass for Harry, shrimp for Christel. The perfect diversion for the silence that followed.

"You know you're my friend." Harry patted his lips with a napkin until she looked at him. "Do you have an off-the-record contract between you and Denis?"

She shook her head.

"Right," he said and nodded.

"Stop. You're making me nervous."

He stared at her. "You too. Frankly, a woman of your experience?"

"It's done, OK? He's a rich man, for Christ's sake. If things are working out for me right now, it's because of him."

"Still . . . would you like to have a look around?"

Christel thought for a bit and stood. "It wouldn't hurt. Can you skip work?"

"I guess."

Harry made two phone calls on their way from the rooftop to the lobby. He asked someone from the Alpha Alp office to call Denizard and his daughter, Aurora. A minute later, he learned that neither had answered their phones.

"Wanna try?" he said.

Christel called Denizard and frowned. "First time he hasn't answered me."

"I don't like it."

"He told me this could happen."

"Maybe his clients live in the Sahara, or in the Arctic," Harry said, upping his skepticism a notch.

Harry made another phone call while the staff

brought his Lexus to the hotel entrance. "I need you knocking on doors. Yeah ... I know. Check all addresses in Switzerland first, then Europe. I'll be looking around Geneva. Track his phone too. Thanks."

They got in the car and left.

"Where are we going?" Christel said.

"His home. First things first."

"He's not there."

"His daughter should be in school, right? When she's back, we'll talk to her."

Christel checked the time. "She'll be back in three hours."

"I'm sure there's a nice little place for coffee somewhere."

They arrived in the village of Collonge-Bellerive, passing in front of Denizard's house just to see if there was life inside it, and moved on to Route d'Hermance, where Christel and Denizard had lunched once during her previous stay in Geneva. The Café des Marronniers was nearly empty by the time they arrived. They ordered drinks and promised the waitress they would stay for dinner.

"Your dossier says Denis has an untarnished reputation," she said while avoiding looking at Harry. There was a hint of embarrassment in her question.

"I remember."

"Any chance that you might've missed something?"

"No."

"Then why are you suddenly full of thoughts?"

"Chris, there's no chance I've overlooked something traceable."

"Not the Harry I know."

"And Denizard Haener is not your average billionaire. He comes from a three-generation banking family. He has contacts all over the world. Long-term, almost unbreakable ties. He handles secrets from wealthy families. Their most sacred assets. The very blood that makes them what they are."

"You're not telling me anything new. What's that supposed to mean?"

"All I'm saying is that he's smarter than us. He's cautious. Meticulous. Brilliant, really. Think about how fast he came up with a solution to your problem in the Amazon. He turned it into a hell of an opportunity to make money. He had it all figured out. A solutions kind of guy. And he made it happen swiftly and flawlessly."

Christel massaged her face and exhaled. "There's no way he could've planned the acquisition of Alpha Alp. He only found out about the tea that Amana gave us when he got there."

"That only reinforces what I've just said—smarter than both of us."

In the phone calls that followed, Harry got only negative results from his team. Denizard couldn't be located.

Christel and Harry shared a pizza and a bottle of red wine. By seven at night, they left the restaurant and went back to Denizard's house. The lights were off. Harry rang the doorbell, glanced back at Christel in the car, and returned after five minutes of waiting.

"Maybe Aurora is with friends," Christel said.

"Or maybe it's time you tell me where your favorite secret meeting place is."

"There's nothing secret about it. It's a private thing."

"I don't care if it's kinky, Chris."

"Don't be silly. I'm supposed to meet him there tomorrow. There's nothing to see there now."

"And where would that be?" he insisted.

Christel shook her head. "Parc Bertrand. Near a statue."

"Why?"

"Does it make any difference?"

"It could. Everything helps."

In the car, facing Denizard's empty house, Christel thought of reasons. "I don't know . . . We like the simplicity of the place. The statue conveys a sense of belonging, a healthy childhood, and joy. We felt good being there, that's all. We joked when we asked a tourist to take a picture of us next to the *Les Petites Amies* sculpture. It is our favorite place so far, meaning we haven't spent enough time together to actually have one," she said, turning to Harry. "Happy?"

"Thanks for sharing."

"Please take me back to the hotel."

Harry stopped by the Four Seasons and escorted Christel to the lobby. He couldn't help feeling guilty for meddling in the romanticism of her meeting with Denizard, but it was with her best interests in mind that he did so.

Before he left, his phone rang. Christel was ready to go to her suite but waited.

"Where to?" He paused. "Thanks," he said and then hung up.

"What?" Christel said.

"Denizard left Switzerland with Aurora. Three days ago. He used his private jet. He could be anywhere, Chris."

"Or returning to Switzerland as we speak," she said. "We're supposed to meet tomorrow."

"You're right . . . Good night."

46

Maurice was taken to *Subject C* in bad shape. Physical examination showed that the jaguar's fangs had fractured his left arm and left profound scratches on his chest and several perforations to his body. The surgeons brought by Captain Rasmussen removed bone fragments and devitalized skin, sutured skin lesions, and were relieved to find no affected vessels. If there had been any, consensus was Maurice wouldn't have survived another day.

Maurice was recovering from his surgery, waking up and falling asleep soon after. He knew Amana was waiting in the infirmary with him and refusing to leave when asked by the doctor and nurses. With the spear that killed the jaguar still displaying the animal blood, and perfectly leaned against the wall as a reminder of that battle, no one dared challenge her.

Every time Maurice opened his eyes, Amana said something in an authoritative tone. He had no idea what she was telling him and preferred to keep his eyes closed. He was sure that whatever she said was in his best interest. There was no ego involved, no references to the outside world. She acted in a purely defensive way, as a fierce protector. Thinking of the women in his family, starting with what Maurice knew about Jandira, then his experience being Christel's son, got him thinking about how well-served the Welches had been by strong women.

Even in his fragile condition, several things became immediately clear. Settling in the Amazon for good was the clearest of all.

He'd come years before in an attempt to grasp what his grandfather Julian had felt a century before, but in the back of his mind, he'd always known he would eventually return to New York.

Not anymore.

It'd be unfair to Amana. She had a perfectly balanced life in the Amazon. Her people were the epitome of what a sustainable society should be. They killed no human beings unless critically threatened in their own territory, emitted zero pollution, consumed no mass-produced products, left no garbage, needed no money, and cared for the forest better than anyone else. They were truthful, joyful, and loyal. To remove her from that solid, enviable environment would be criminal.

And she was expecting his baby.

The forest is my home for good, Maurice realized.

When a nurse came in to check on him, Amana appeared jealous. Maurice would love to know what the poor nurse heard as Amana yelled at her and stood right next to the bed supervising whatever the white woman was doing to him.

Someone needs to learn a language.

Minutes later, Captain Rasmussen walked into the infirmary with a satellite phone in hand and stopped before reaching Maurice's bed. Amana blocked his way.

"Quiet!" she told him.

"Let him pass, Amana," Maurice said.

"Mr. Welch . . . It's your mother. She refused to talk to me," the captain said and handed the phone to Maurice.

"Hello, Mother."

*****

Christel's son had just been attacked by a jaguar. He'd barely escaped alive. What was he doing walking in the forest at night? It was the way Amana found to communicate with him, she was told. The coming of Maurice's baby. When he could, Christel inevitably thought, choose any of the gorgeous women waiting for a chance with him back in the USA.

I'll be the grandmother of a child born to an undiscovered tribe.

Christel sighed and shook away the thoughts of how that was going to play out for the family. She had other things occupying her mind.

Of all the dossiers supplied by Harry Walker, she'd studied none so thoroughly as the first one she'd commissioned him to make almost two decades earlier. A large pile of papers that put together all the information Harry could find on Julian Welch and Alan Reid. Pictures, testimonies of old friends, employees, and partners. Lawsuits, awards, rumors, and flaws. It pacified Christel to remember she was Julian's daughter, and it baffled her that those two different personalities could ever find common ground for such an enduring partnership.

Alan Reid was loathsome, hardworking, dominant, and choleric. Julian was the opposite. An analytical introvert, warmhearted and fair. Who Denizard Haener really was turned out to be an impossible thing to determine at that point. Two days before, the sum of all that he represented could be summarized in one word.

Hope.

For all the hellish childhood had she endured, her emotionally empty early adulthood, and the lonely mature phase, she'd always dreamed of a later life cemented by serenity, one that would taste like dessert. But she believed that inner peace could only be achieved by sharing her life with someone. Now, that hope was hanging by a thread.

Christel looked out the window of her suite for the umpteenth time. At eleven thirty in the morning, she glanced outside again. It was snowing heavily, a day painted in white and gray.

The hotel phone rang. Harry was waiting down at the lobby.

"You look like you haven't slept at all," he said when they met.

"Any sign of Denis?"

Harry shrugged.

They left the hotel and drove across Lake Geneva on the Pont du Mont-Blanc. It took less than eight minutes to arrive at Parc Bertrand. She rubbed her hands constantly during the short ride, which signaled to Harry that he had better leave her alone.

The area around the *Les Petites Amies* sculpture, Christel and Denizard's secret rendezvous spot, was empty. At midday—the scheduled meeting time—and for almost half an hour after that, not even the tourists showed up. The place was desolated and cold.

Harry stepped forward. "Let's find a warm café and grab something to eat. We need to discuss how we're going to handle this."

Christel didn't listen.

She kept staring at the sculpture, heartbroken like a young girl, blaming herself for being so naive, upset at no longer maintaining the sharp instincts that had kept her on top of the game for so many years. Her head tilted down, defeated. She felt Harry's friendly hands on her shoulders. Whatever he was about to say would symbolize and confirm her defeat.

"Look, Christel—" he began saying when her cell

phone vibrated inside her coat. She swiftly and clumsily took off her gloves and picked it up. The screen showed "Home." Someone was calling her from the bungalow's satellite phone.

"Hello?" Christel said.

"Where are you, my girl?" Kiara said.

"I, er—"

"Someone's very angry at you. Hold on—"

Christel glanced at Harry. Her heart stopped for a bit. It began pounding fiercely when she heard Denizard's voice over the phone. "I miss you."

"But I'm here!" she said.

"Where? Weren't we supposed to meet today?"

"I'm standing at our favorite place."

"Well, me too..." He sounded lost and heard Christel laugh nervously. "Chris, did something happen?"

"No, no. I thought... Never mind. I don't think we're in perfect synchrony yet."

"I thought the Amazon was our favorite place. Well, at least yours. Isn't it?"

"Never mind, Denis."

"Is Harry with you?"

"Yes."

"Ask him to check his email."

She glanced at Harry. "Denis sent you something."

Denizard continued, "I understand you're no longer being investigated for what happened in the Amazon. You've nothing to fear, and you owe nothing to anyone."

"Yes. I know."

"Good, then. I've just moved my Alpha Alp shares to your name. I sent the stock transfer form to the registry agent. The original amount, to the cent."

Christel watched Harry open his email. Seconds later, he nodded. "You're good."

She walked a few steps away from Harry. "Thanks, Denis. I love you for everything you've done."

"God, I wish you were here."

She closed her eyes. "I am."

*****

Christel returned to her hotel in time to pack and catch the night flight to Brazil. After she got her things ready, she had a quick lunch and lay down to try to get some rest. The uncertainty of the previous weeks had taken a toll, leaving her exhausted. She set the alarm clock to go off in one hour, but just when she'd begun to relax, there were knocks on her door, though she wasn't expecting anyone.

She walked to the door and opened it to find Harry waiting outside.

"Sorry to bother you. We need to talk," he said.

"Sure." She let him come in. "You could've called."

"I think we're being monitored."

"Are you sure? By whom?"

Christel opened the curtains, and they sat in the

suite's living room. "I don't know, and it doesn't matter. The government is calling off the deal," he said.

"Why? What's going on, Harry?"

"It's too big a deal. We're not deemed big enough—which we aren't. They want a piece of the pie. The big guys. They pressured the US government."

Christel shook her head, trying to figure out the implications of that information. "But you said the government chose us."

"Chris, if someone wants to create an obstacle, they'll do it. Regulation infringement, requirement of unreasonable guarantees, and even questioning our product, even though everyone knows it's the best."

"So, which is it?"

"It's all of that if the big guys and the government so choose."

Christel let out a long sigh. "They want a piece of the pie, you said? We've developed the AAC ExTermite. We used our money to make it. *We* took the risks!"

Harry raised his palms in the air. "Calm down, will you? I know, Chris."

"Then do something. We can't just let them steal from us."

"Understand something. This is not about fairness, OK? They'll delay the final decision for as long as they want."

"Harry, the forest is being devoured as we speak."

"I know that too. Big businesses and the bureaucrats don't give a damn about the environment. This is a once-in-a-lifetime, emergency fund money grab opportunity."

"Oh, Harry . . . You said everything had been decided. Now this?"

"And it was. Until they changed it. It stinks, but it's the way it is."

Christel frowned. "Have you called Denis yet?"

"No. I wanted to see you first."

"Don't you go doubting him again. He did everything he promised he would. We're past that now."

"That's not what I'm thinking. I just wonder how a former banker would react to hearing the news that he won't exactly be making a profit. By my estimates, Alpha Alp will merely recoup the money. Unfair? Absolutely. But not tragic. The forest would be taken care of, and life would go on for you and him."

"What if he says no?"

"He can't, really. Your money would be completely lost."

Christel stood up, hands on her waist, pacing for a moment. Then she turned to Harry. "Do you know if Denis has any participation in our competitors' businesses?"

"Wow, Chris. That's borderline paranoia, even by my standards. No, he doesn't. Not as far as I'm aware of. Just call him, will you?"

Christel grabbed her cell phone in the bedroom and returned to the living room. She called and waited for Denis to answer.

"How much is enough for you?" she said when he picked up.

"What are you talking about?" Denis said.

"Money. When is it enough?"

"Is there anything wrong?"

"Answer me. Please."

"All right . . . My personal number? The moment I realized I had more than enough? That was when I sold my bank. I believe I've told you that already, haven't I?"

Harry signaled to her to calm down, but she ignored him.

"Yes, you did. The thing is, Denis, the government just pulled the plug on us."

"Are you sure?"

"Apparently, the big folks want a piece of our business, I'm told. Harry is here with me. He'd just brought me the news."

Denizard quieted for a bit. "Chris, turn the speaker on. I want to talk to him too."

"Sure . . . we hear you."

"Harry, what's going on?" Denizard said.

"Well, you heard Christel. That's pretty much all there is. They're either in or else we have no deal whatsoever."

"Oh. Well, I'm surprised," Denizard said.

Christel crossed her arms. "Couldn't you have anticipated it? You knew there would be competition one way or another."

"I did. But I was wrong about the timing. I thought we would have more problems when we started. Not now. In fact, I bet half of all I've got on our company stock futures. I bet *in favor* of Alpha Alp, Chris. It seems I've lost twice."

"Er . . . I don't know what to say."

"This has nothing to do with you. It was a little side bet, an echo of my greedy days. I suppose I've just got the lesson I needed. Money is poison."

"Are you going to be OK?"

"Financially? Sure. It just hurts my ego. Big time, as you say it. But all I really care about is you. I'm waiting . . . Harry, are you still there?"

"Yes."

"I guess there's not much I can say to you . . . Slice the cake. Let us all go home."

"I thought you would say so," Harry said.

"Denis? How's Maurice doing?" Christel said.

"Fine. They moved him to the bungalow. I think I'll have a drink with him. We're both wounded and need you here."

Christel hung up and Harry stood. "Well, you heard the man. I'm going home," Harry said.

"Thanks, Harry. I would hate doing what you do for a living. The suspicion and all, it would kill me."

"Whenever you need me, Chris."

47

Eight months after the Amazon rainforest began being bombarded by the AAC ExTermite, signs of natural regeneration could be seen from above. Christel and Denizard were only making a fraction of what they've envisioned, but it didn't matter. The scientific community had selected passive restoration as their primary strategy, and it was working. The flooded forest would restore itself. The majority of endemic species began to return. Four years later, new trees had grown twenty-five feet on average. The dominant ones reached over sixty feet. It was remarkable. Animals and insects proliferated as well. Experts were confident that in twenty years, the ecosystem would go back to normal. Left alone, nature proved to be a brutal force conspiring in favor of life.

"Nana," the toddler yelled when Christel returned from her morning walk.

Julian Welch II was playing on the bungalow's terrace with Maurice and Amana.

"Come here, Jay," Christel said. He headed in her

direction and jumped. She picked him up and brought him back to his parents. "You're heavy. Yes, you are!"

Jay burst into delightful laughter.

He had a dark skin tone from Amana's side and Maurice's thin hair. Like the rest of his tribe, he'd adapted to the Welches' way of life as much as they had adapted to the tribe's. They were a resourceful and hardworking people. Coexisting with that white man's family made the tribe gradually lose their fear of the so-called civilized world.

They wanted to be educated in the white man's ways, eat some of their foods, and wear their clothes. Maurice found no resistance from his mother when he told her he wanted to help them. They'd been officially recognized by the Brazilian authorities, vaccinated against diseases they'd never heard of, had their legal documents issued, and were authorized to live permanently on the Welch property.

"I told you not to wait for lunch," Christel said to Maurice.

He took Jay from Christel's arms and handed him to Amana.

"Will you give us a moment?" he said.

Amana took Jay to a vegetable garden at the back of the lawn where the tribe spent most of their time working.

"Are you happy, Moe?" Christel said as Amana walked away with Jay.

"I've never dreamed of being so . . . connected." His eyes gleamed.

"I'm so happy for you."

"I know. I think you should go inside now. You have visitors."

"Here? Who?"

"C'mon."

Christel heard Denizard's voice inside the bungalow's main living room. As she headed further inside, she saw him seated, and then she saw two people sitting across from him whom Christel had wished she would never have to see again. Eleanor Delarge and Michael Bird, the TV host. She slowed down and glanced back at Maurice, who was walking up behind her and limping on one side. The jaguar attack still haunted him every time he ventured inside the woods.

Christel wanted to kill him. "Seriously?"

Accompanying the two journalists was a TV crew with heavy gear.

She was about to scream at them, but she noticed they were already recording. And they were not alone. Out of nowhere, twelve people—adults and children of Asian and unclear ethnicities—showed up from inside the dining room, guided by Kiara.

"Maurice?" Christel said.

He stood between her and the cameras. "People are entitled to give a proper thank-you, Mother," he whispered and got out of the way, leaving no chance for Christel to make a scene.

The adults circled Christel and applauded her.

The children came closer, immersing her in warm hugs. Christel glanced at Eleanor. She and Michael Bird were standing and applauding. Then Eleanor walked toward her old friend.

"Let Michael and I fix our poor judgment. If not for us, then for them," Eleanor said, indicating the people around them.

"How?"

"I know who you are, Chris. We owe you a chance to show the people who the woman behind the headlines really is."

Christel turned to glance at Maurice and Kiara. She was convinced they wouldn't let themselves be fooled by an opportunistic interview. Then she eyed Denizard. She was sure no one could fool him either. Maybe it was the hugging and warmth all around her that prompted Christel to let go of her defenses.

It's not such a bad idea, she thought.

There were things she wanted to say.

The truth was, all her worst nightmares had already materialized, and she'd come back from them stronger and wiser. She'd wanted a perfect husband, and found it in Everett. She'd feared losing him, and it had happened. Then life offered her another husband. She couldn't complain. Men had made her lose faith in humanity, but she'd found it again. She wanted a son, and now she had a grandson. There was a legacy at stake. How she would be remembered mattered. Like the trees of the Amazon rainforest, she'd been eaten by human insects, was deeply wounded, and had stood back up.

Christel took a deep breath and sat. If they wanted to talk to her, then she would offer a wholehearted interview. Being shocked or not was on them. She was who she was, and she hadn't done anything wrong. When she began sharing the first details of her life, many indeed shocked Maurice, Denizard, Kiara, and even Eleanor. Yet the more she revealed, the stronger she felt as a woman. As a force of nature.

She was addressing Michael's question and saying, "We're living in a world created in the image and likeness of men. Now, I've seen the worst and the best in them, and I think it's fair to ask: Who taught them to be such terrible leaders?"

"Now, you say you've dated many leaders. In what circumstances, if I may ask?" Michael Bird said.

"Before my career ended, and I can't say that being conditioned to serve men should be called a career, I met about one hundred different people every year."

"Can you give us names?"

"No, Michael. But I can paint a picture."

"Anything you want."

"Congressmen. Governors. And more than one president. I was young and psychologically conditioned at a young age. Now let me add some color to it. These are the very people who decide the future of our children, our health, and our education. People with no regard for women or children. They're highly articulated and proficient in the art of making people trust them. That's during daylight. When the lights are off, they abuse, rape, and hurt others in unthinkable ways. So, here we are. The people we trust and idolize. We scream and yell their names. Blindly."

"Maybe we're not as good as we think we are," Michael Bird said, himself a suspect of harassing young women.

"Frankly, men can be toxic, abusive, and unbearable. But I don't dream of a world dominated by women, no. The thirst for power is what drives narcissistic men to accomplish so little and mess up so much. No . . . it's not about that. It's about balance."

"You're saying male confidence doesn't translate to competence, am I correct?" Eleanor said.

Christel shrugged. "How would the environment look under a more feminine leadership? It's a question I ask myself. How would work relationships and businesses improve? I think we all know the answers."

"What makes women so different, you think?" Michael said.

"No one handles life-and-death issues better than women. Something in our nature impels us to give, unconditionally."

"Christel Welch, thank you," Michael Bird said, ending the interview.

Christel stood and saw Eleanor walking up to her. "You did great," Eleanor said.

"Now what—you want us to be friends again?" Christel said.

"I can't ask you to be my friend. I just want to be forgiven."

"We're talking, are we not?"

"Well, I ambushed you into talking."

"Yeah. You have a safe trip back."

Eleanor kissed her on the cheek and joined the TV crew as they began taking their gear outside. A boat waited at the dock. Kiara looked at them with keen eyes. Denizard and Maurice glanced at Christel and took in her admirable resilience. She welcomed their glances.

I did well.

Christel headed to the terrace.

She saw her family inside the bungalow, the tribe working in the garden, and Jay, the Welches' next generation. All around her were the fruits of good men like her father, Julian; her late husband, Everett; and her son, Maurice. Denizard's daughter, Aurora, still looked a little lost attempting to play with Jay and trying to find her place in that new family arrangement.

God bless them all.

Denizard approached her at the terrace.

"You don't look angry," he said.

"I should . . . I hate surprises. But I can't deny I feel good."

"What do you want to do now?" Denizard said.

"I feel like walking the talk. You know, to *give unconditionally?*"

"I like that, but we've already made our pledges to give. And you've done so much, Chris."

"I know. But pledges are such a male thing to do."

Denizard squinted. "Meaning?"

She held him around his waist. "Let's keep some to ourselves and give it all we have. Not just in this lifetime, Denis. Next week. Tomorrow. Every day for the rest of our lives."

"I'm madly in love with you."

She glanced away from him to capture Maurice, Amana, and Jay playing in the background where the tribe was.

"Let's do this. Save a little for our kids, and find people who need us."

"Sounds perfectly all right to me."

"You think Aurora will be OK with that?"

"She'll be in Switzerland studying arts."

"She'll be fine."

Little Jay spotted his grandmother at a distance and waved to draw her attention.

"Beautiful child," Denizard said.

"Colorful as a crimson topaz."

Christel took his hand and squeezed it.

CPSIA information can be obtained
at www.ICGtesting.com
Printed in the USA
FSHW020508140420
69137FS